THE WITCHER®

THE WITCHER: WITCH'S LAMENT #1 VARIANT COVER ART BY ANATO FINNSTARK

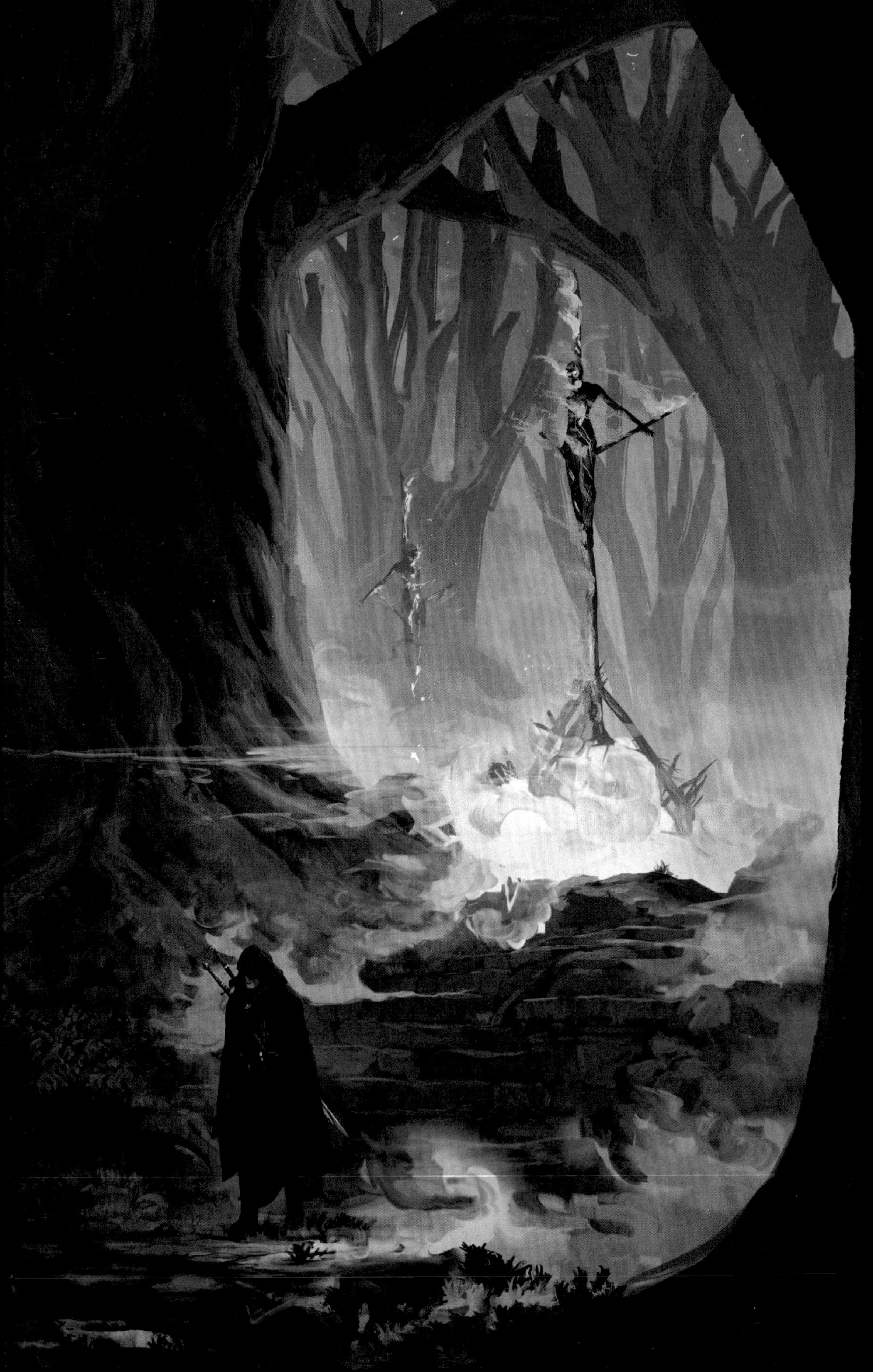

THE WITCHER®
WITCH'S LAMENT

STORY
Bartosz Sztybor

ART
Vanesa R. Del Rey

ART LAYOUT
John Starr

COLORS
Jordie Bellaire

LETTERS
Aditya Bidikar

COVER ART
Stefan Koidl

CHAPTER BREAK ART
Vanesa R. Del Rey

DARK HORSE BOOKS

President and Publisher	Mike Richardson
Editor	Judy Khuu
Assistant Editor	Rose Weitz
Designer	May Hijikuro
Digital Art Technician	Allyson Haller
CD Projekt Red Editorial	Bartosz Sztybor
CD Projekt Red English Dialogue Adaptation	Travis Currit

Special thanks to CD Projekt Red, including: Rafał Jaki, Business Development Director • Michał Nowakowski, SVP of Business Development • Adam Badowski, Head of Studio • Marcin Blacha, Story Director

The Witcher *game is based on a novel of Andrzej Sapkowski.*

THE WITCHER VOLUME 6: WITCH'S LAMENT

This volume collects issues #1 through #4 of the Dark Horse Comics series *The Witcher: Witch's Lament*.

Published by
Dark Horse Books
A division of
Dark Horse Comics LLC
10956 SE Main Street, Milwaukie, OR 97222

DarkHorse.com
TheWitcher.com
Facebook.com/DarkHorseComics
Twitter.com/DarkHorseComics
Comic Shop Locator Service: comicshoplocator.com

First edition: December 2021
Ebook ISBN 978-1-50672-224-5
Trade Paperback ISBN 978-1-50672-223-8

10 9 8 7 6 5 4 3 2 1
Printed in China

Library of Congress Cataloging-in-Publication Data

Names: Sztybor, Bartosz, writer. | Del Rey, Vanesa R., artist. | Bellaire, Jordie, colourist | Bidikar, Aditya, letterer. | Sapkowski, Andrzej. Wiedźmin.
Title: Witch's lament / writer, Bartosz Sztybor ; artist, Vanesa del Rey ; colors, Jordie Bellaire ; letters, Aditya Bidikar.
Description: Milwaukie, OR : Dark Horse Books, 2021. | Series: The Witcher ; volume 6 | "The Witcher game is based on the prose of Andrzej Sapkowski"
Identifiers: LCCN 2021023082 (print) | LCCN 2021023083 (ebook) | ISBN 9781506722238 (trade paperback) | ISBN 9781506722245 (ebook)
Subjects: LCSH: Comic books, strips, etc. | LCGFT: Fantasy comics. | Comics (Graphic works)
Classification: LCC PN6728.W5887 S99 2021 (print) | LCC PN6728.W5887 (ebook) | DDC 741.5/973--dc23
LC record available at https://lccn.loc.gov/2021023082
LC ebook record available at https://lccn.loc.gov/2021023083

CD PROJEKT RED®

CHAPTER ONE

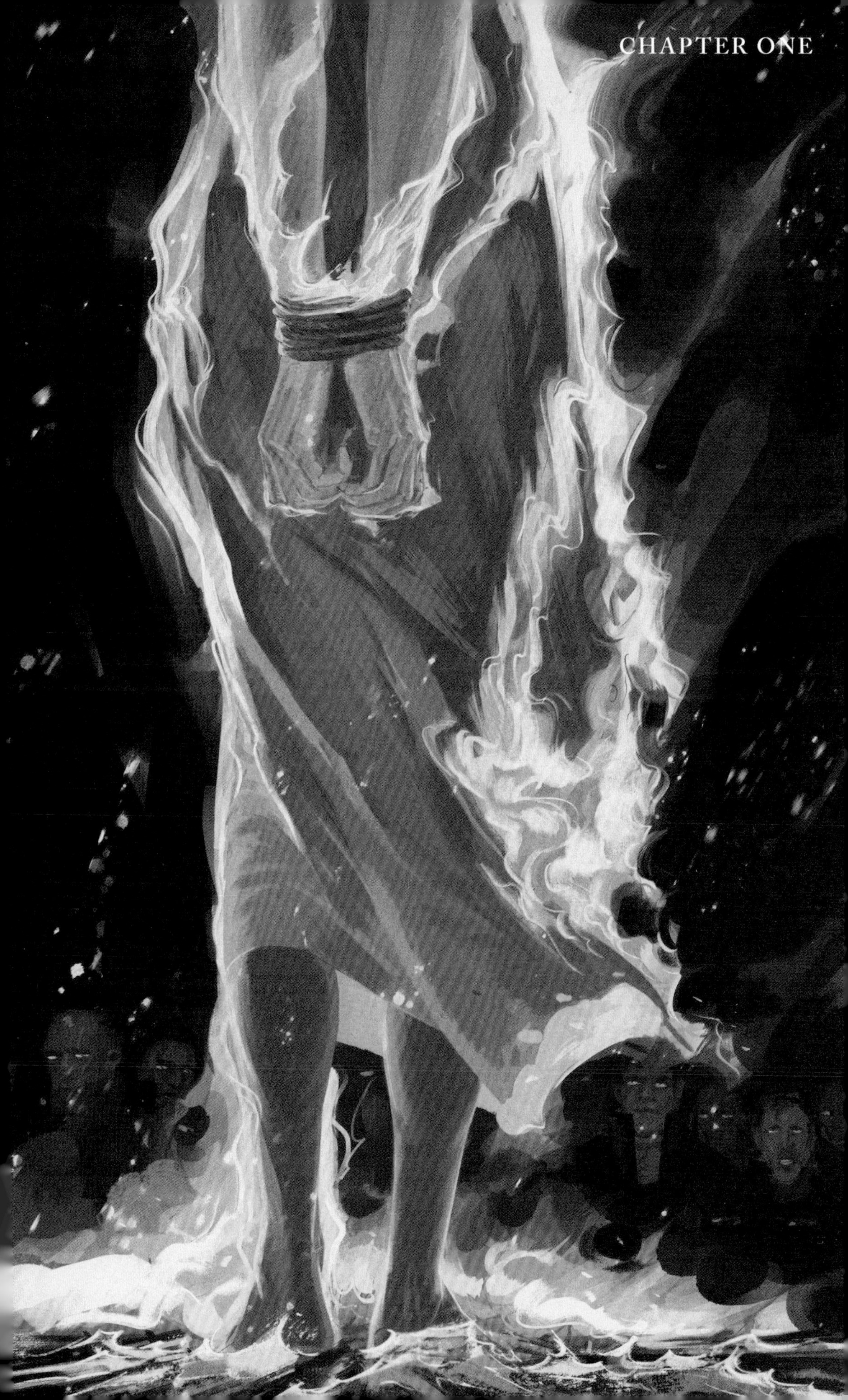

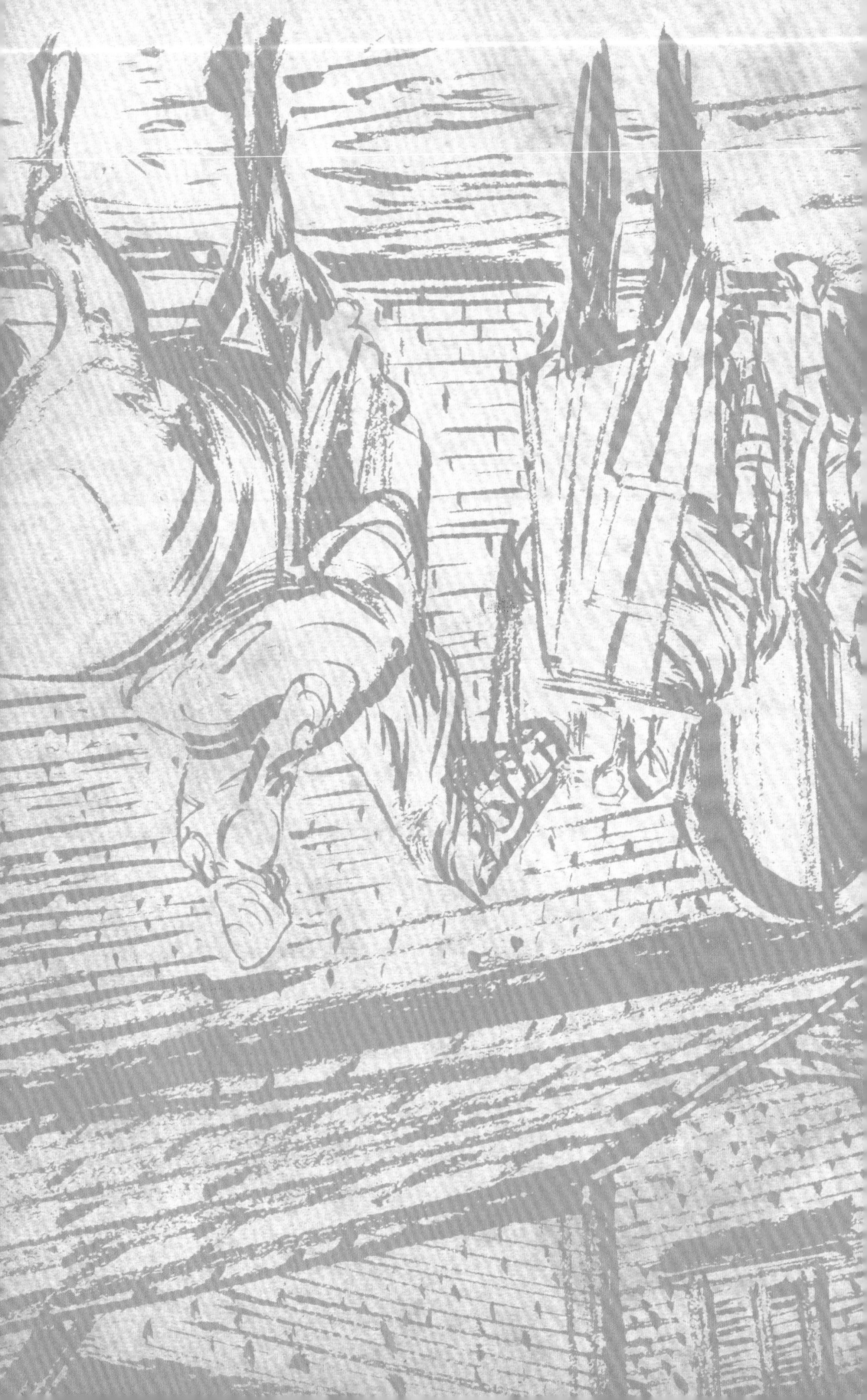

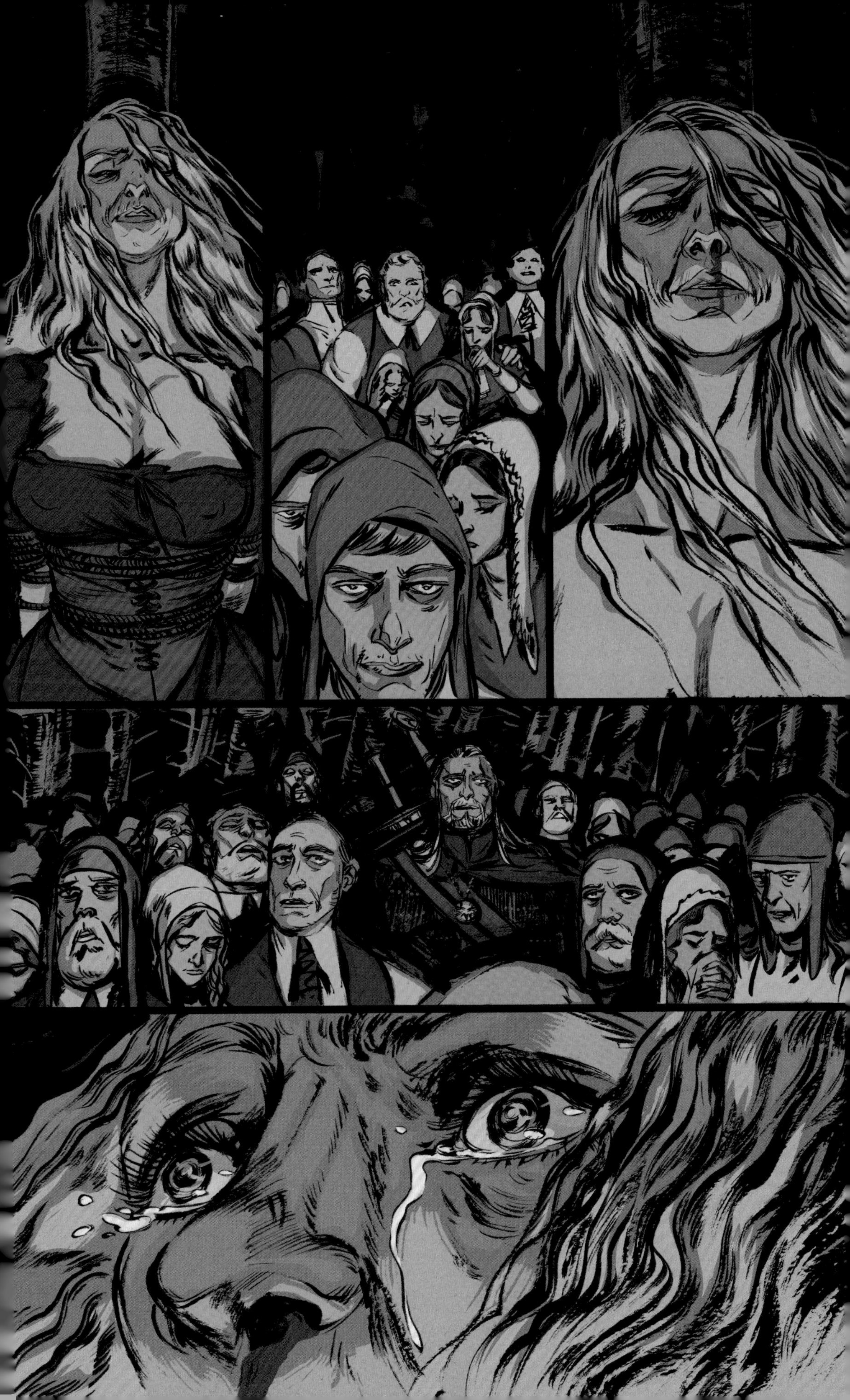

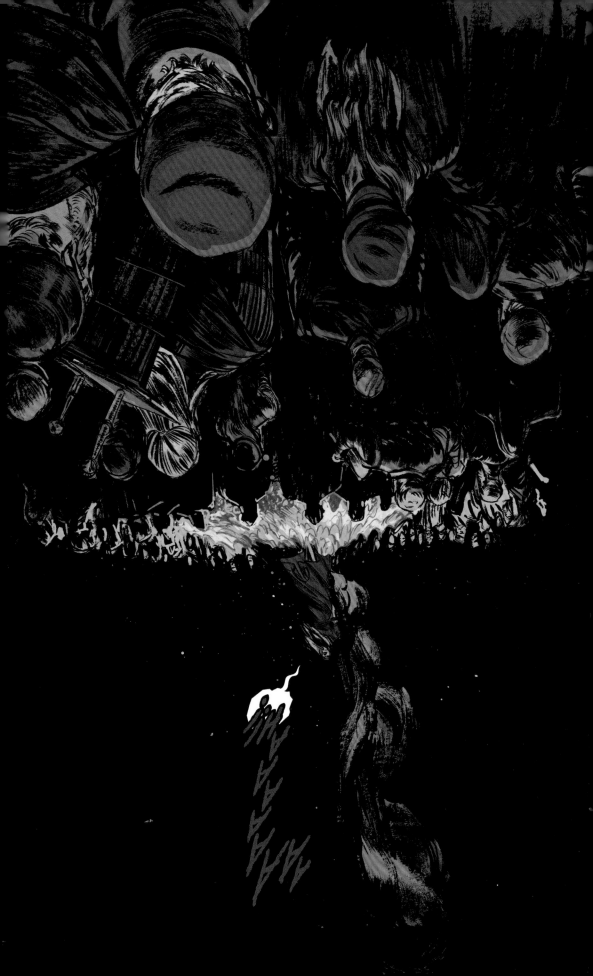

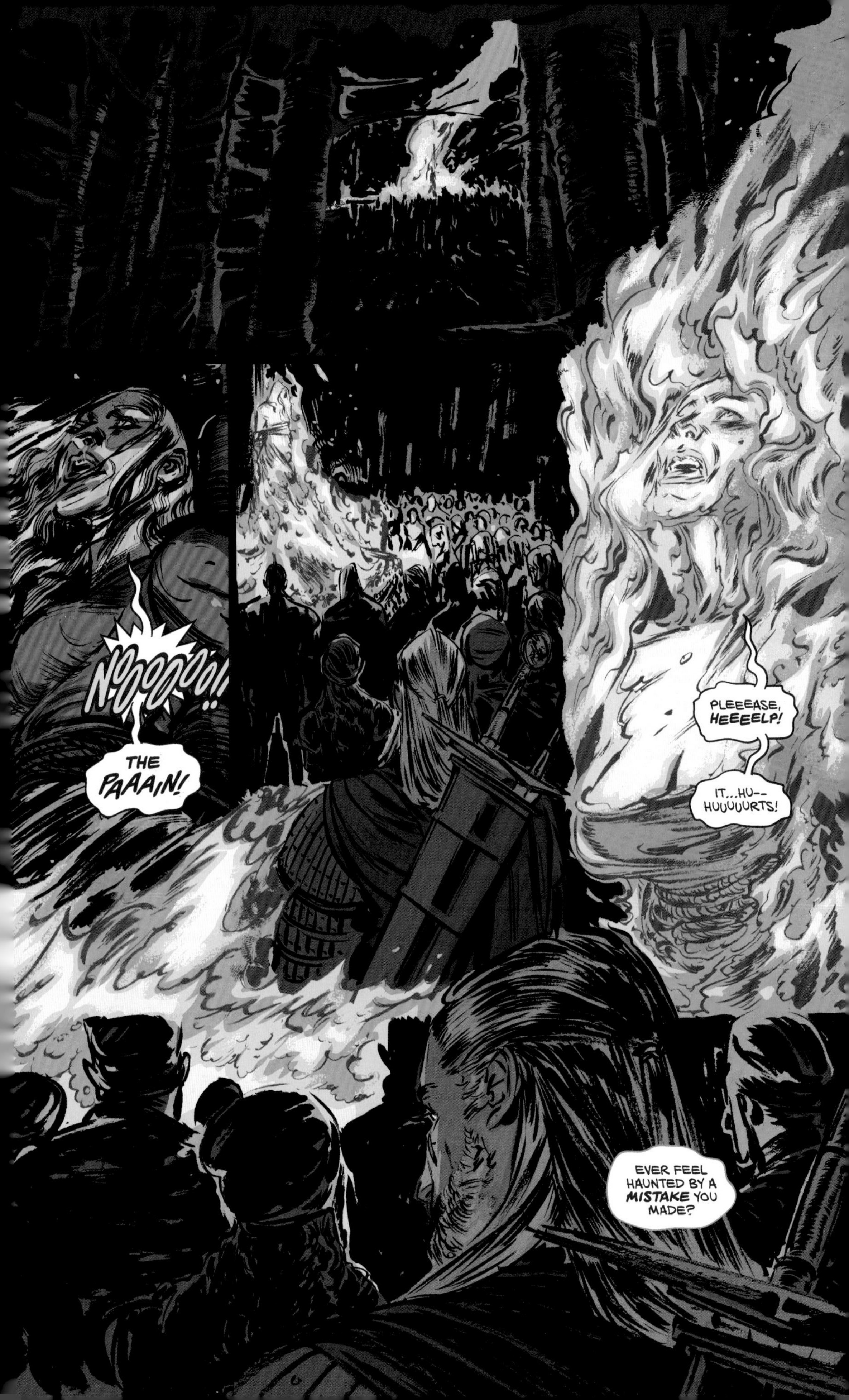
NOOOOOO!!
THE PAAAIN!
PLEEEASE, HEEEELP!
IT... HU-- HUUUUURTS!
EVER FEEL HAUNTED BY A MISTAKE YOU MADE?

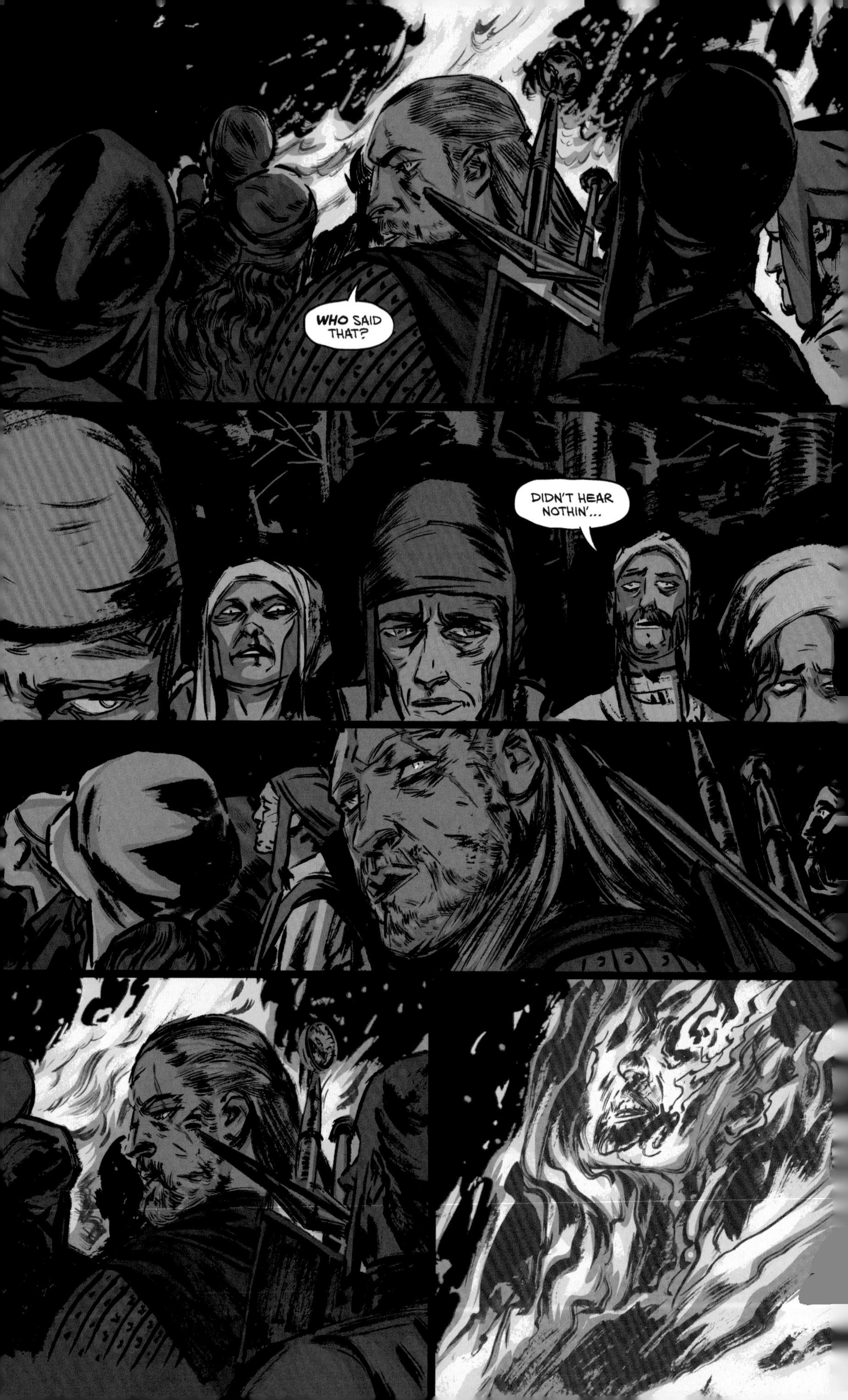
WHO SAID THAT?
DIDN'T HEAR NOTHIN'...

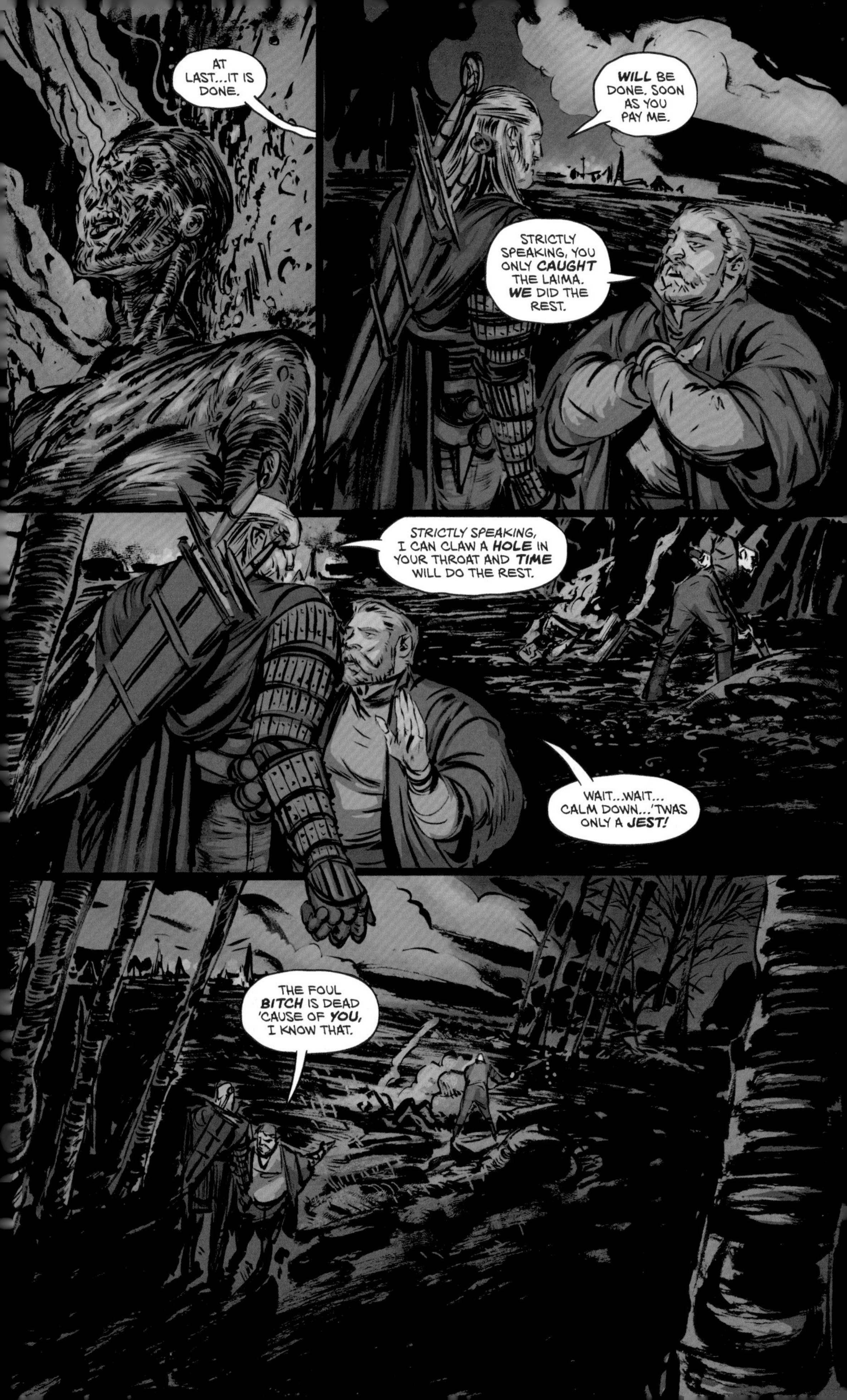
AT LAST...IT IS DONE.
WILL BE DONE. SOON AS YOU PAY ME.
STRICTLY SPEAKING, YOU ONLY CAUGHT THE LAIMA. WE DID THE REST.
STRICTLY SPEAKING, I CAN CLAW A HOLE IN YOUR THROAT AND TIME WILL DO THE REST.
WAIT...WAIT... CALM DOWN...'TWAS ONLY A JEST!
THE FOUL BITCH IS DEAD 'CAUSE OF YOU, I KNOW THAT.

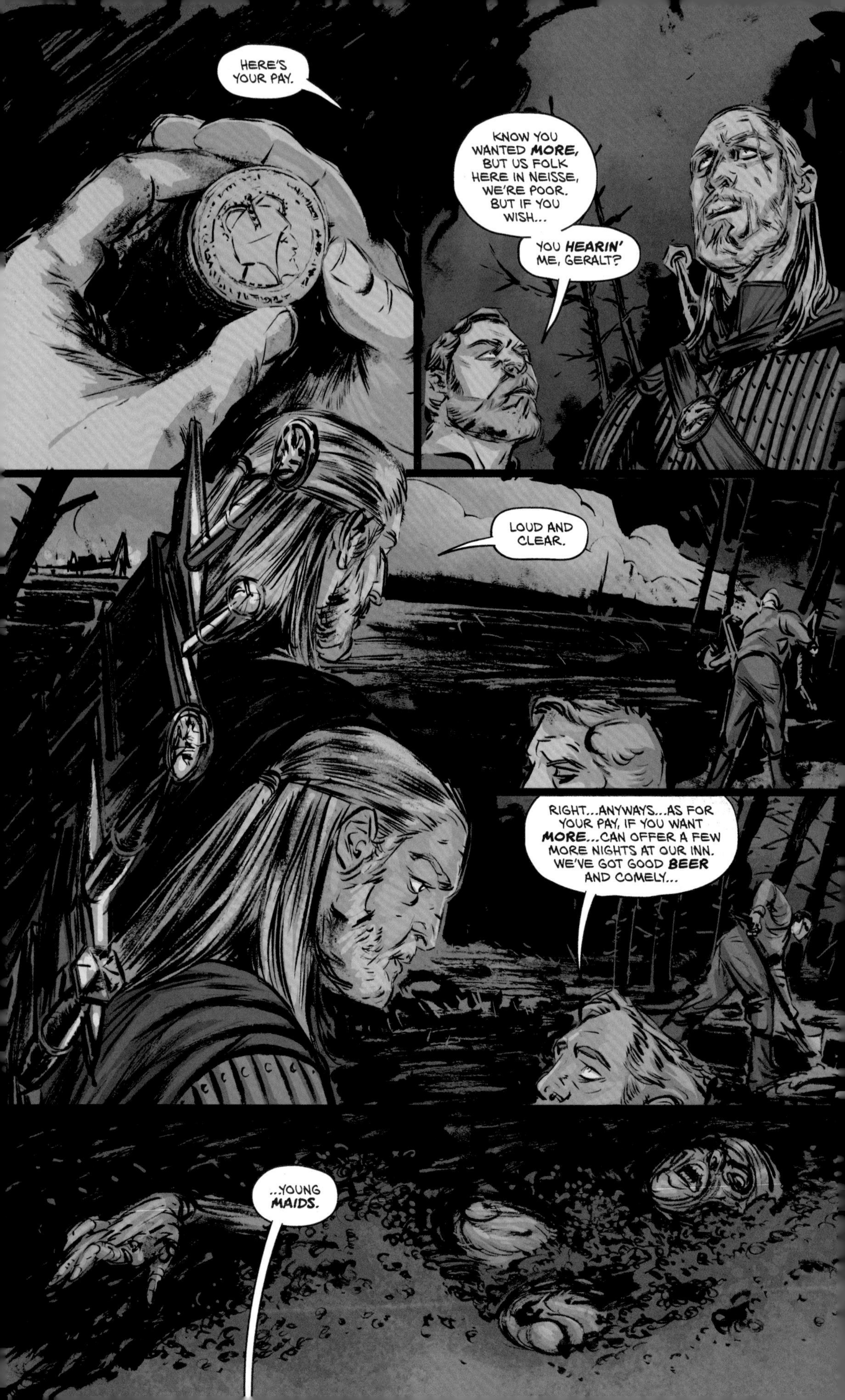
HERE'S YOUR PAY.
KNOW YOU WANTED **MORE,** BUT US FOLK HERE IN NEISSE, WE'RE POOR. BUT IF YOU WISH...
YOU **HEARIN'** ME, GERALT?
LOUD AND CLEAR.
RIGHT...ANYWAYS...AS FOR YOUR PAY, IF YOU WANT **MORE**...CAN OFFER A FEW MORE NIGHTS AT OUR INN. WE'VE GOT GOOD **BEER** AND COMELY...
...YOUNG **MAIDS.**

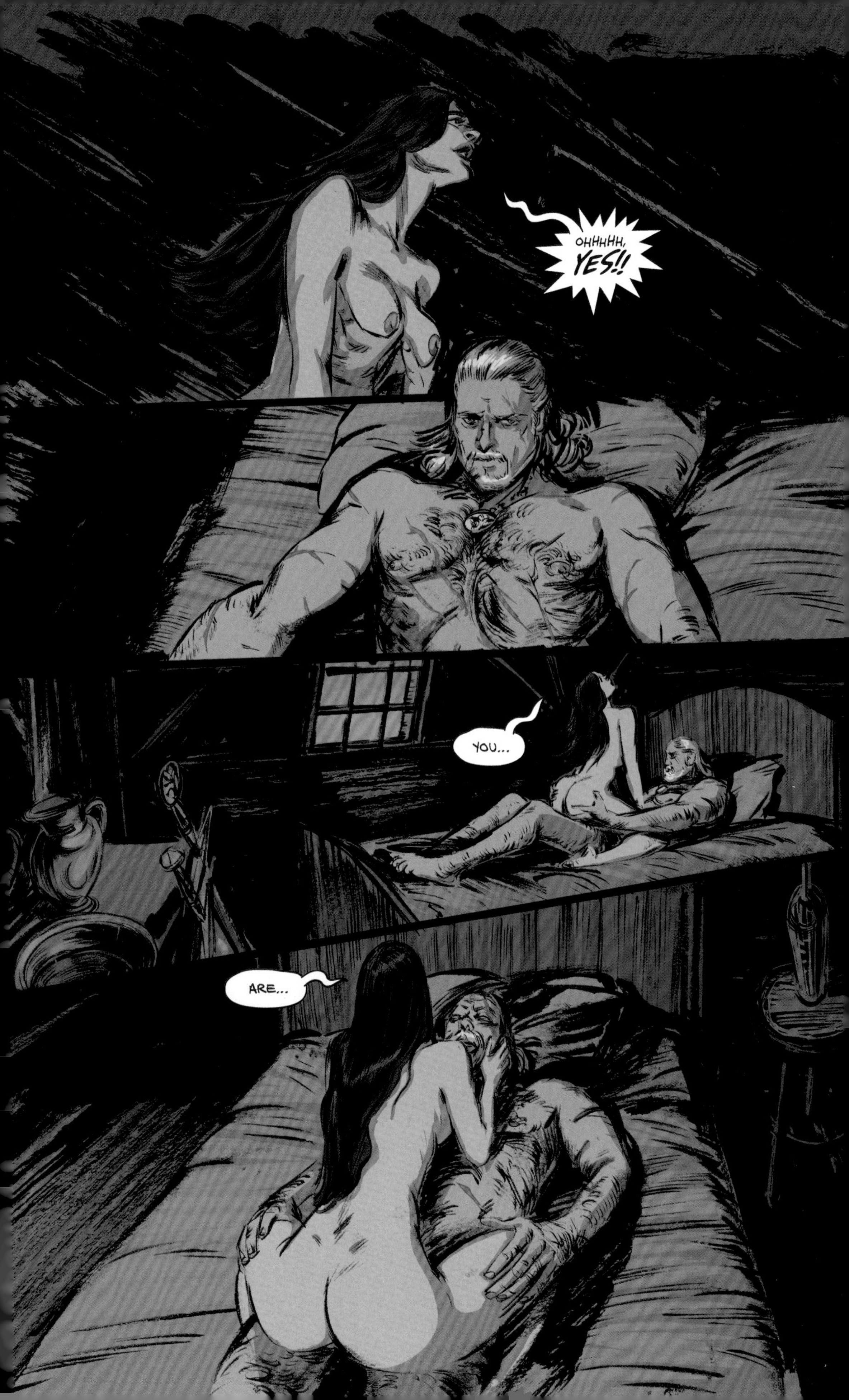
OHHHHH,
YES!!
YOU...
ARE...

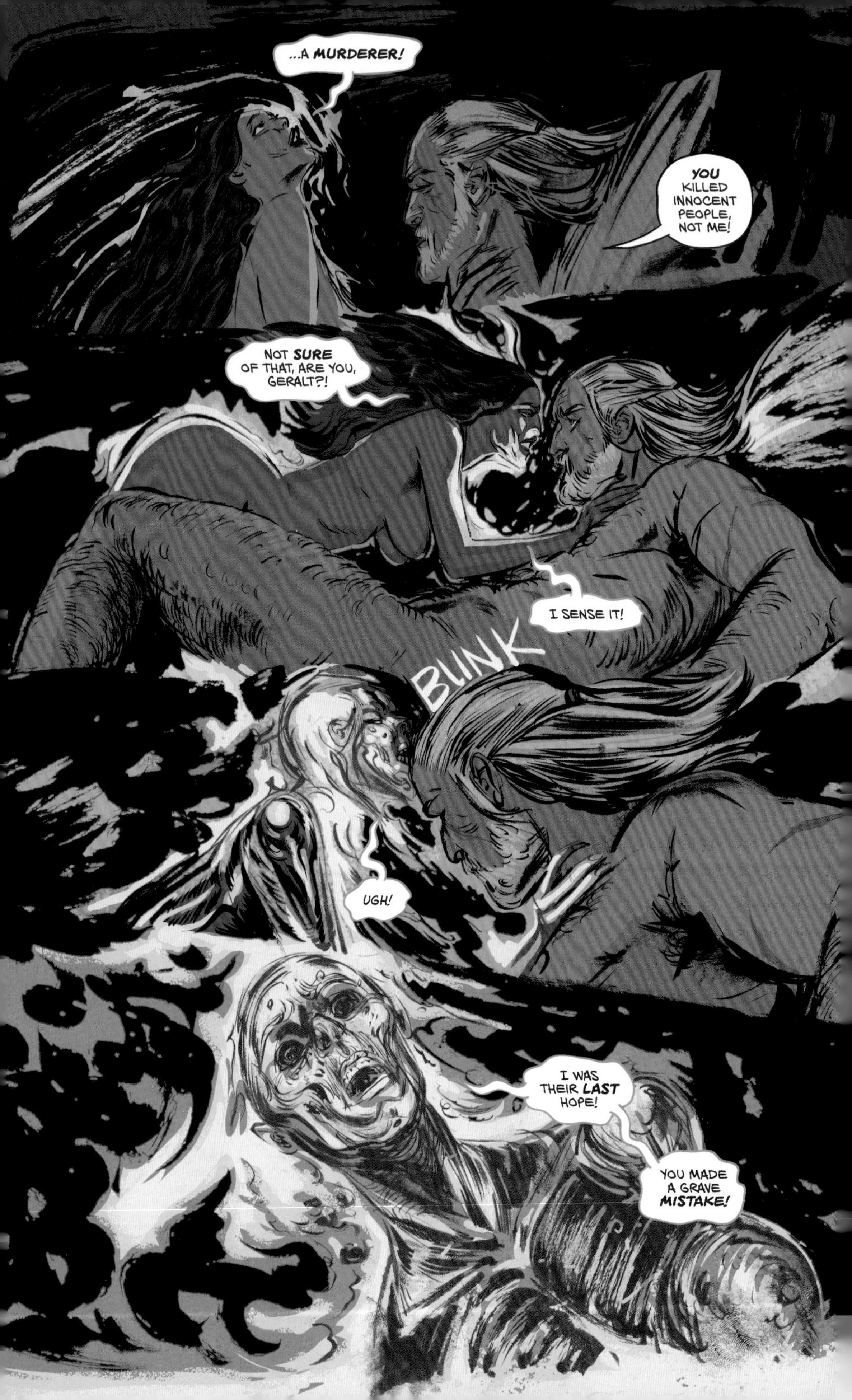
...A **MURDERER!**
YOU KILLED INNOCENT PEOPLE, NOT ME!
NOT **SURE** OF THAT, ARE YOU, GERALT?!
I SENSE IT!
BLINK
UGH!
I WAS THEIR **LAST** HOPE!
YOU MADE A GRAVE **MISTAKE!**

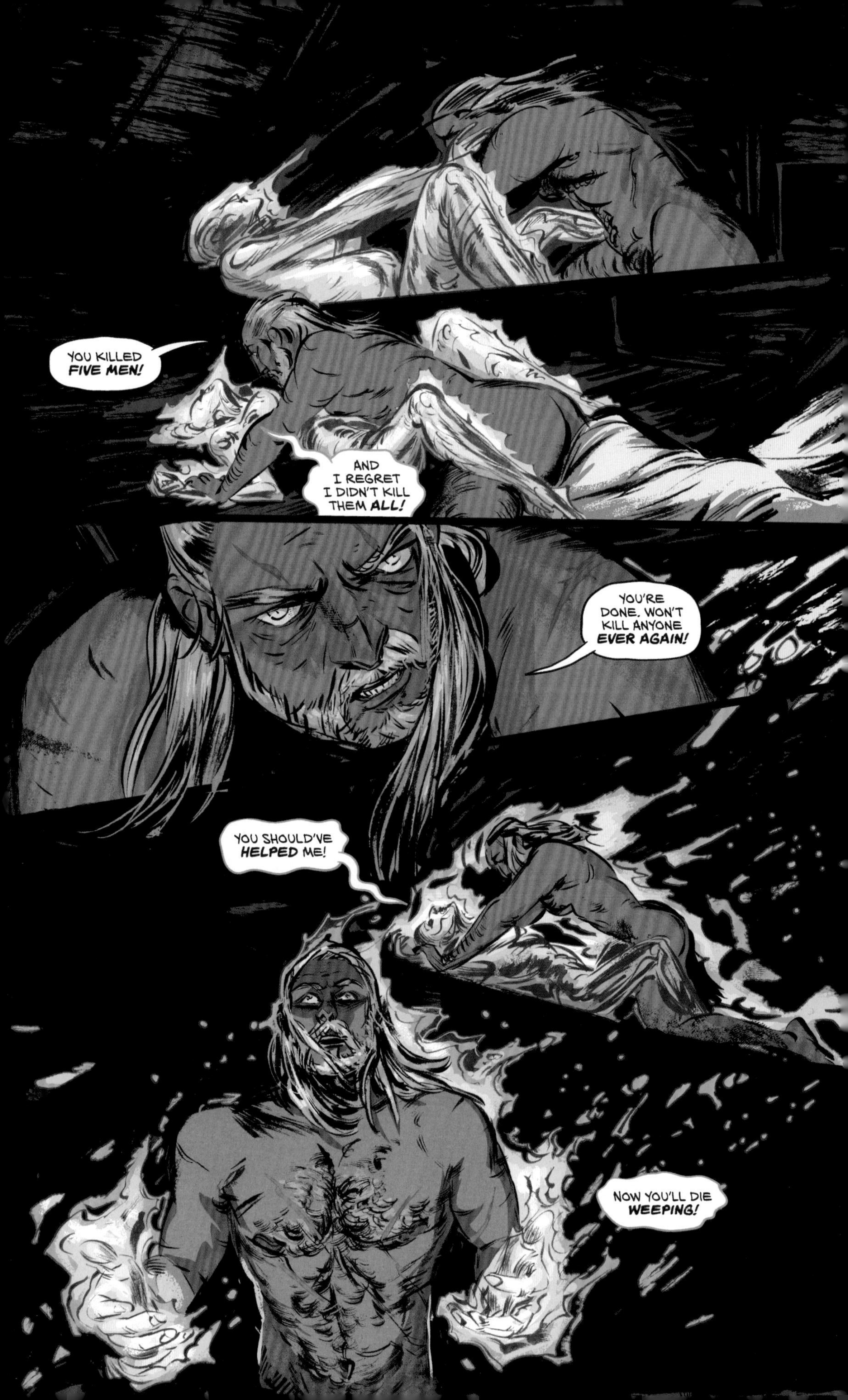
YOU KILLED FIVE MEN!
AND I REGRET I DIDN'T KILL THEM ALL!
YOU'RE DONE. WON'T KILL ANYONE EVER AGAIN!
YOU SHOULD'VE HELPED ME!
NOW YOU'LL DIE WEEPING!

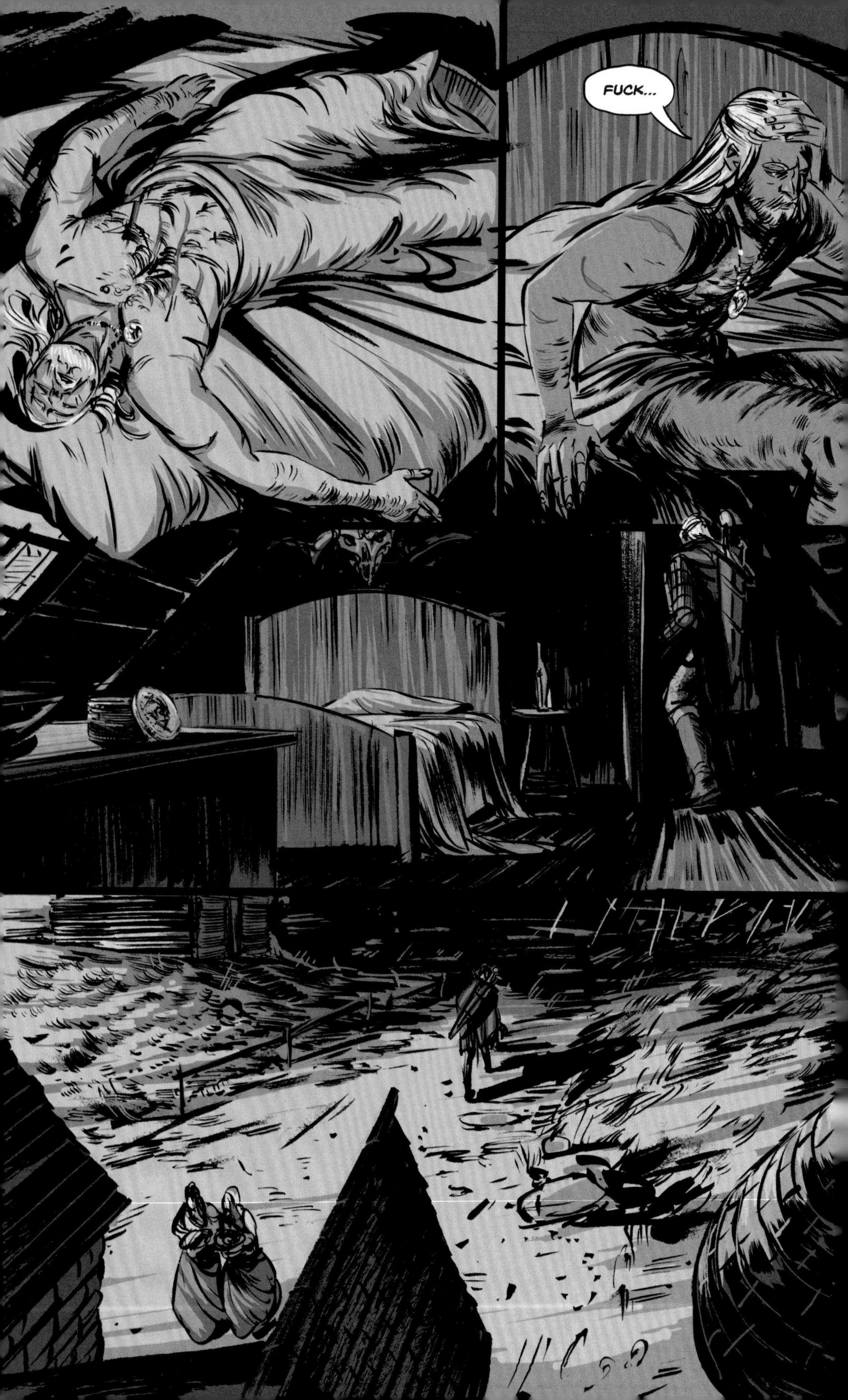
FUCK...

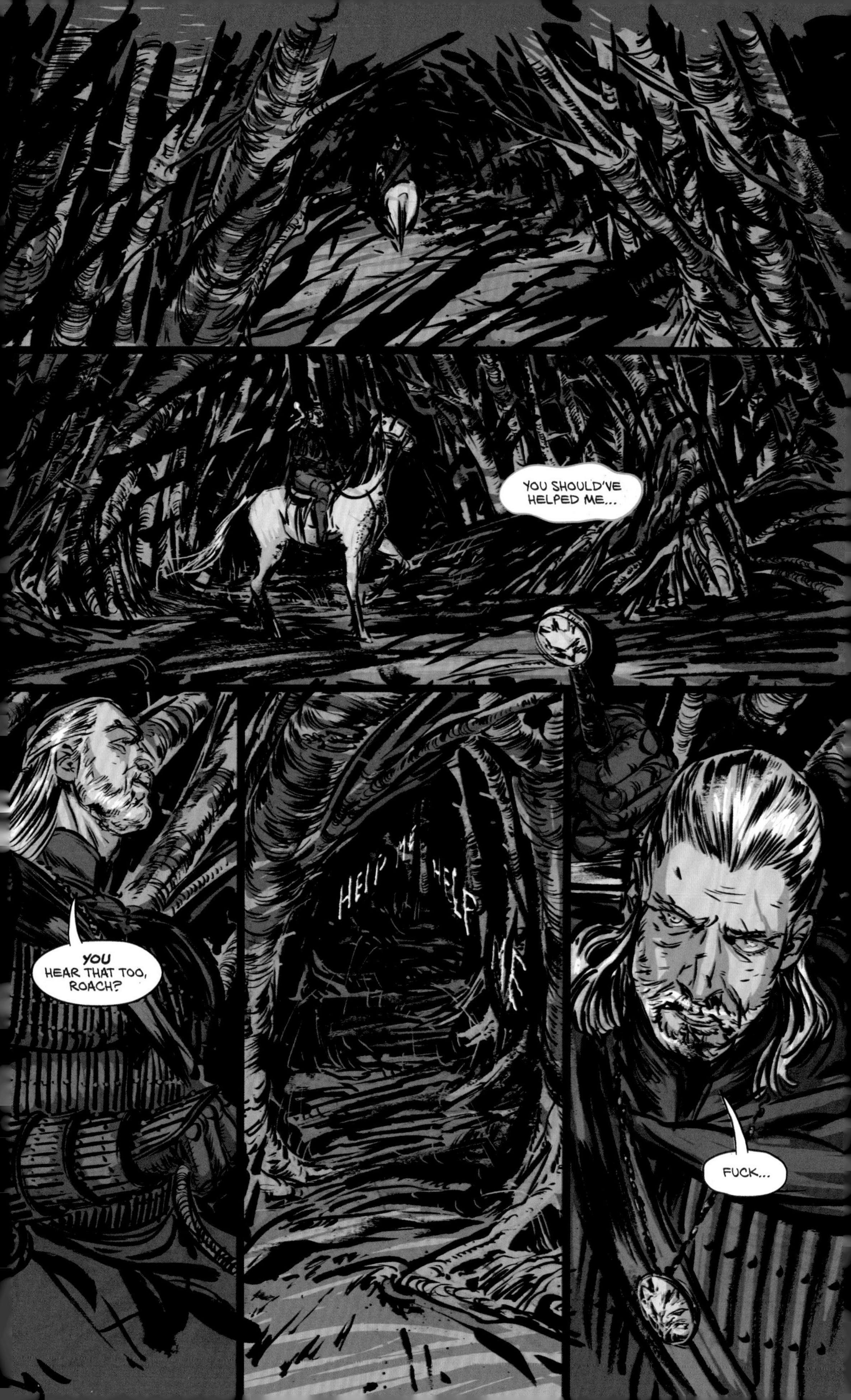
YOU SHOULD'VE HELPED ME...
YOU HEAR THAT TOO, ROACH?
HELP ME
HELP ME
FUCK...

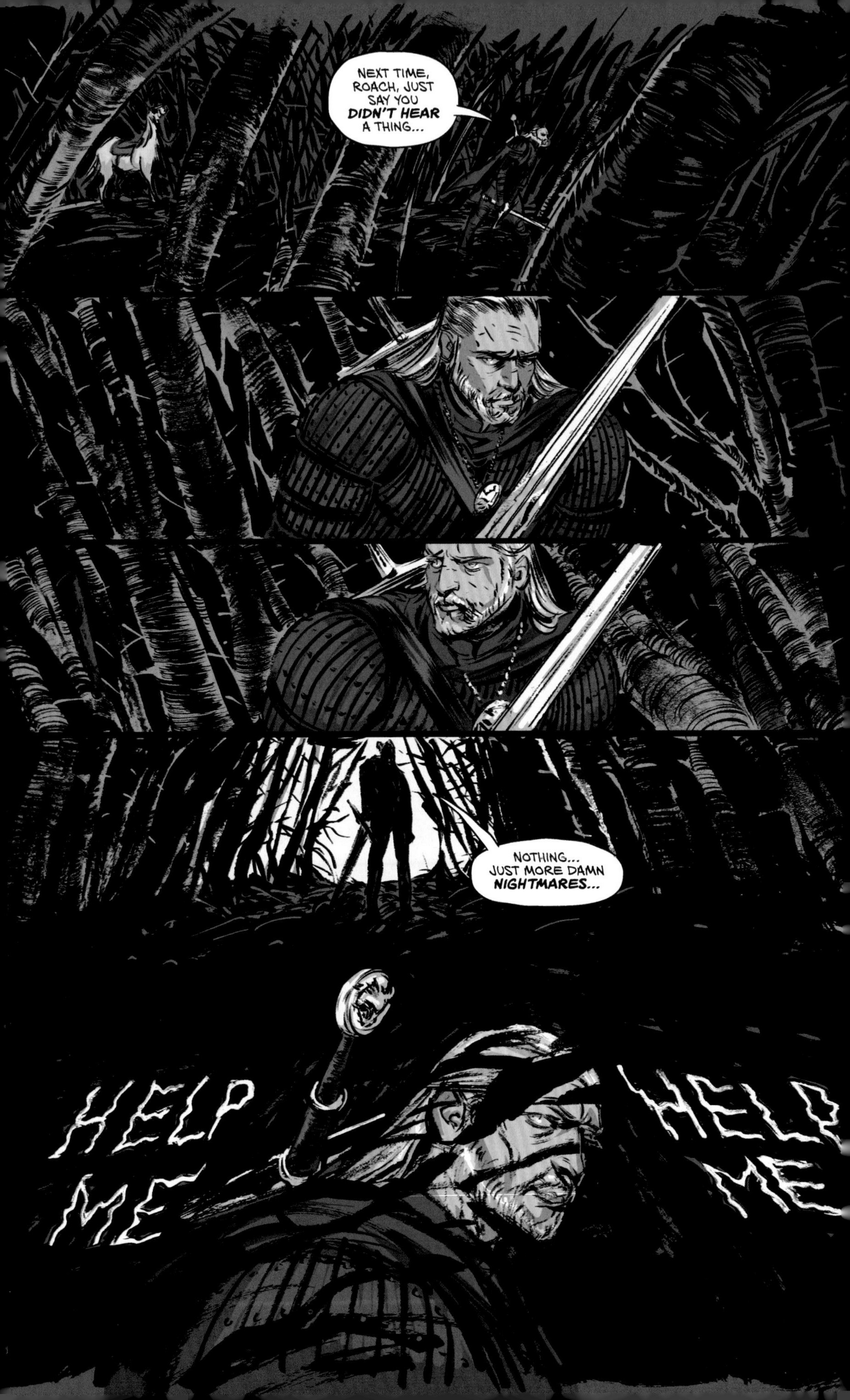
NEXT TIME, ROACH, JUST SAY YOU **DIDN'T HEAR** A THING...
NOTHING... JUST MORE DAMN **NIGHTMARES...**
HELP ME
HELP ME

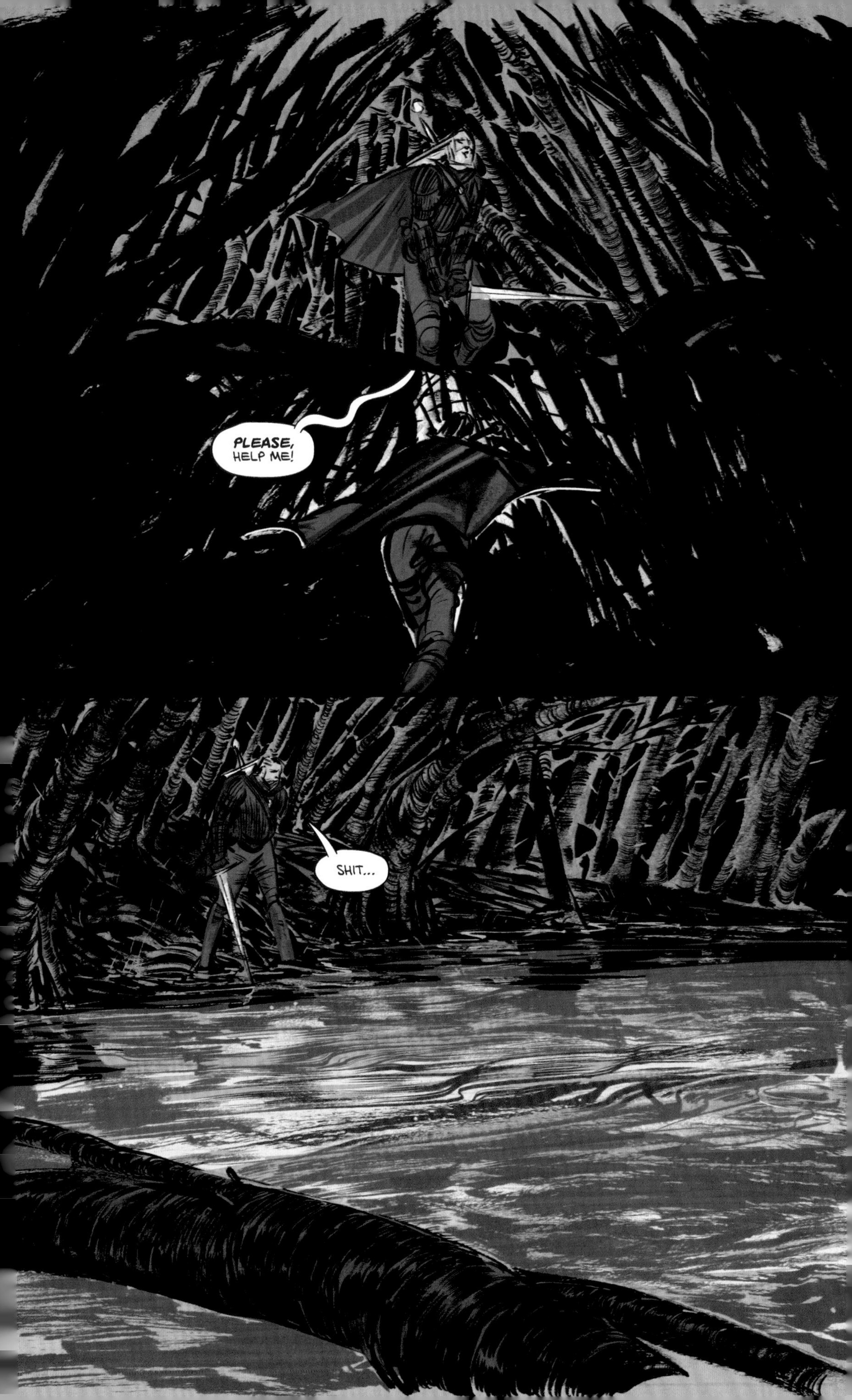
PLEASE, HELP ME!
SHIT...

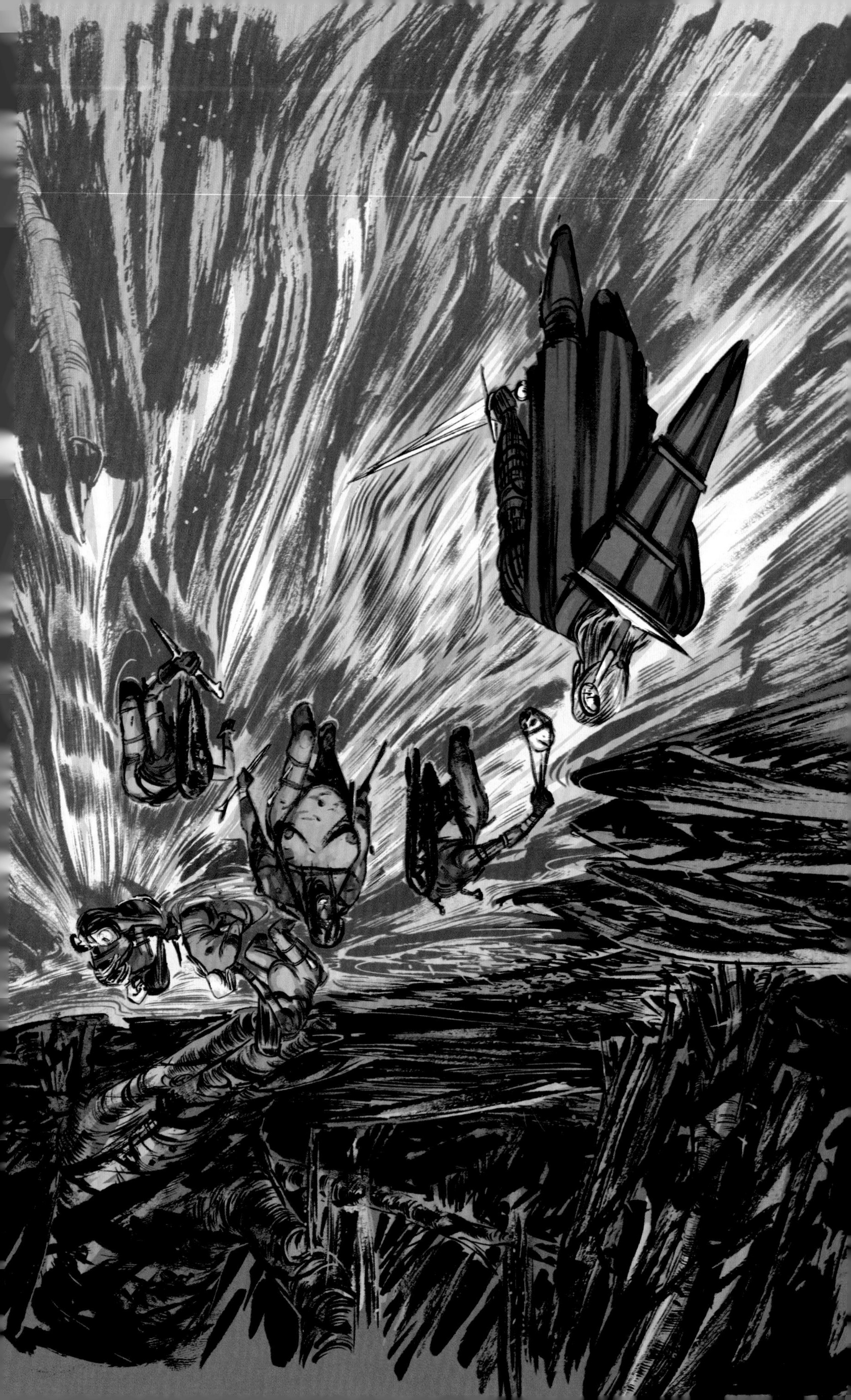

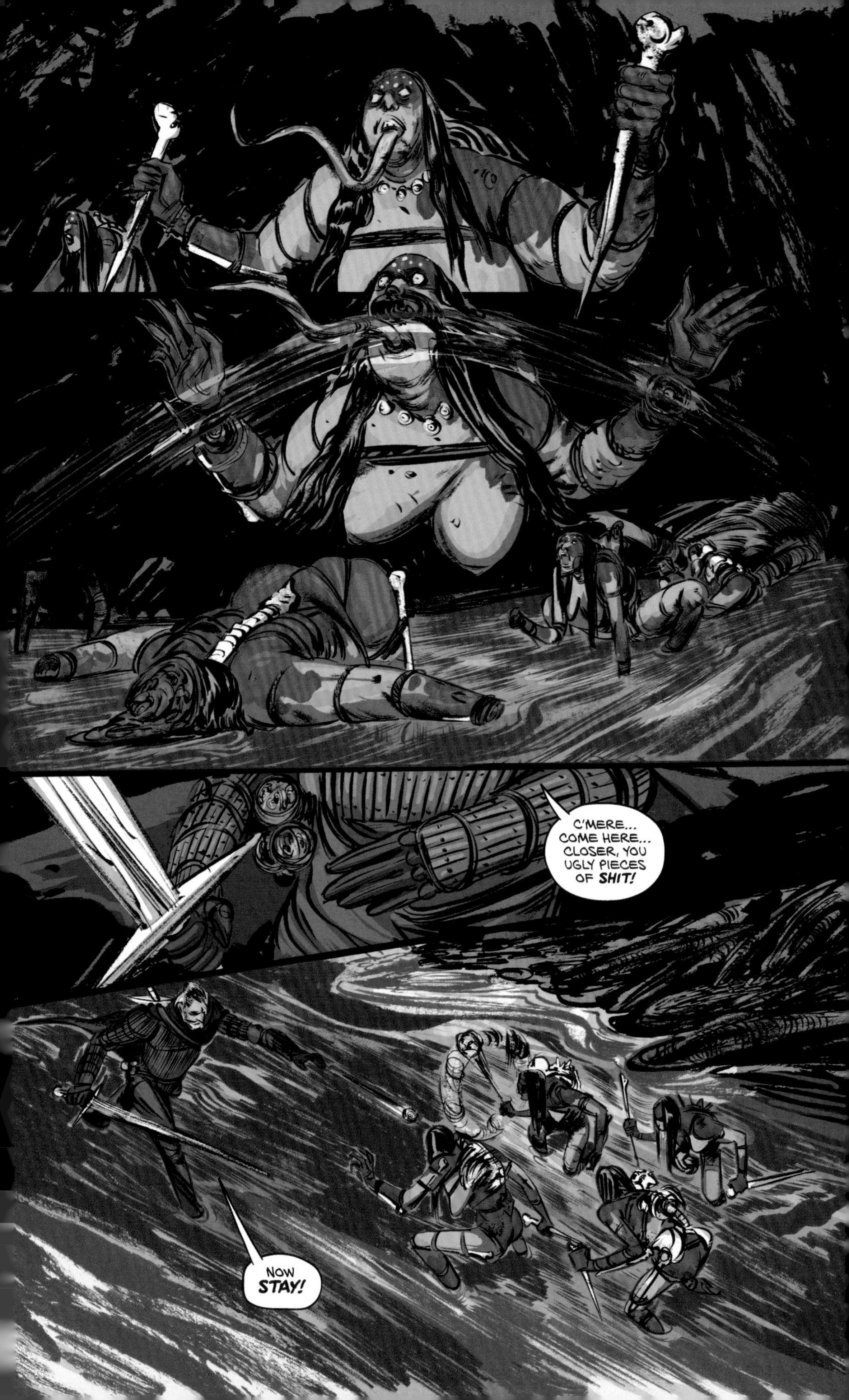
C'MERE... COME HERE... CLOSER, YOU UGLY PIECES OF SHIT!
NOW STAY!

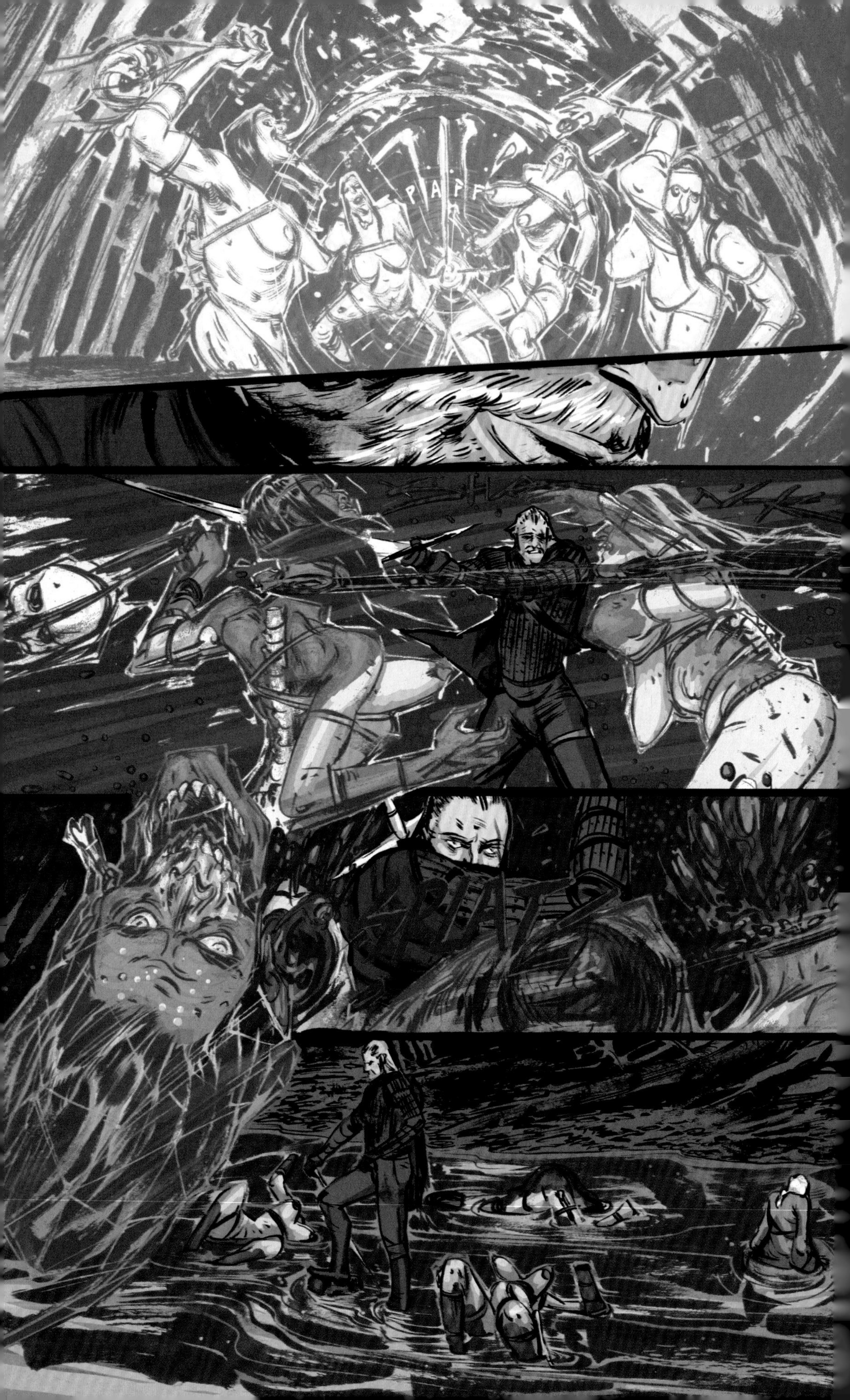
PAFF

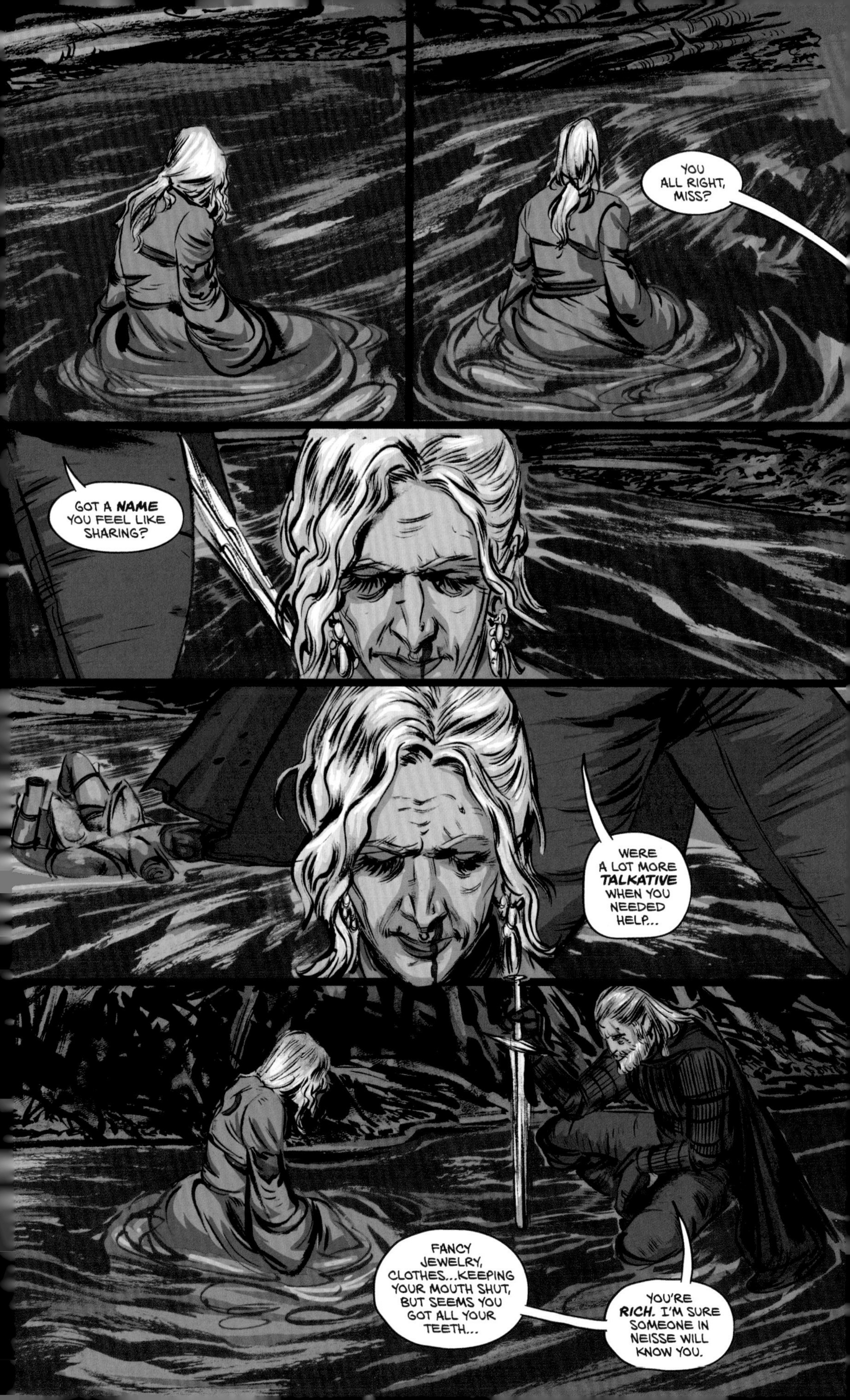
YOU ALL RIGHT, MISS?
GOT A **NAME** YOU FEEL LIKE SHARING?
WERE A LOT MORE **TALKATIVE** WHEN YOU NEEDED HELP...
FANCY JEWELRY, CLOTHES...KEEPING YOUR MOUTH SHUT, BUT SEEMS YOU GOT ALL YOUR TEETH...
YOU'RE **RICH.** I'M SURE SOMEONE IN NEISSE WILL KNOW YOU.

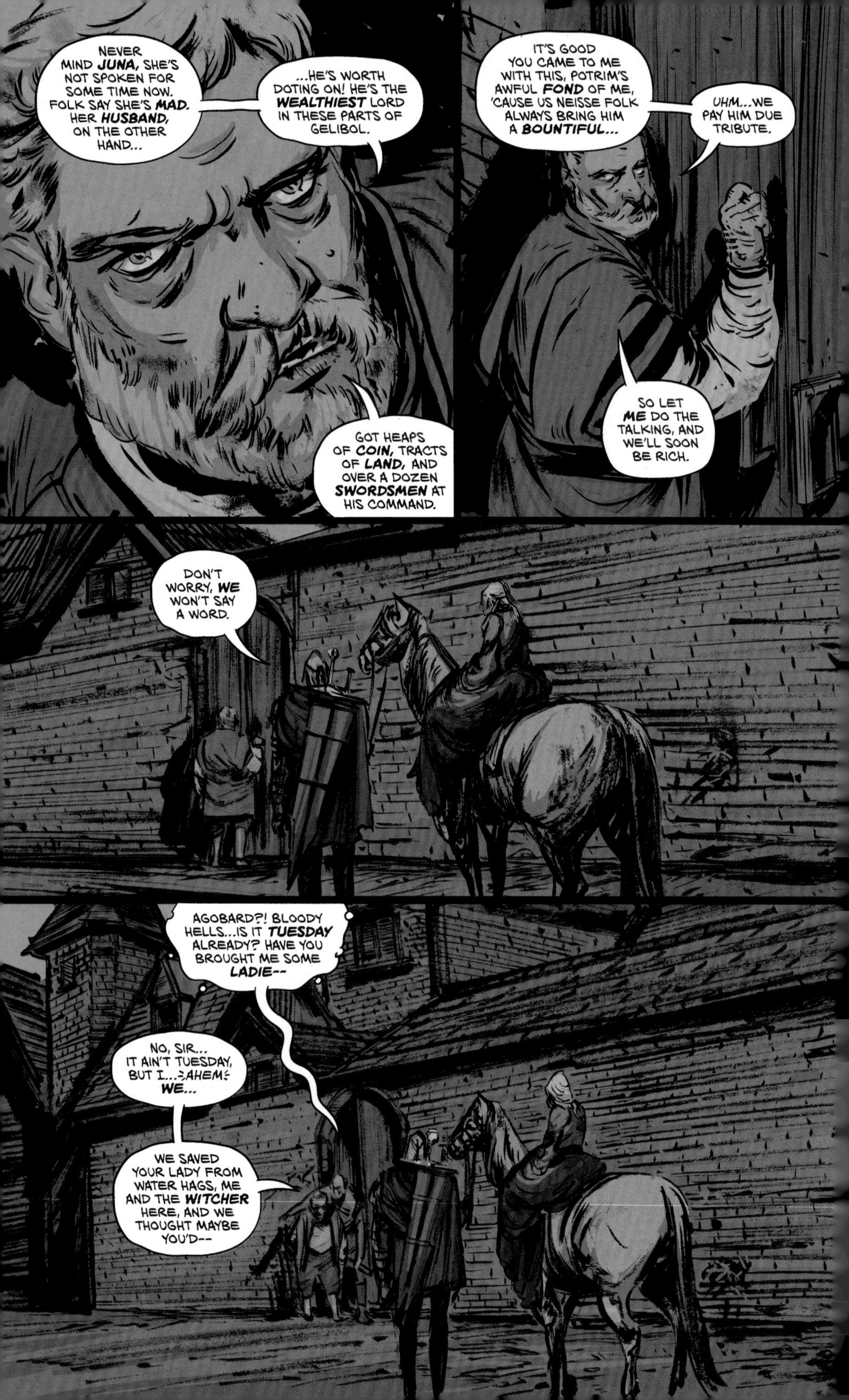
NEVER MIND **JUNA,** SHE'S NOT SPOKEN FOR SOME TIME NOW. FOLK SAY SHE'S **MAD.** HER **HUSBAND,** ON THE OTHER HAND...
...HE'S WORTH DOTING ON! HE'S THE **WEALTHIEST** LORD IN THESE PARTS OF GELIBOL.
GOT HEAPS OF **COIN,** TRACTS OF **LAND,** AND OVER A DOZEN **SWORDSMEN** AT HIS COMMAND.
IT'S GOOD YOU CAME TO ME WITH THIS, POTRIM'S AWFUL **FOND** OF ME, 'CAUSE US NEISSE FOLK ALWAYS BRING HIM A **BOUNTIFUL...**
UHM...WE PAY HIM DUE TRIBUTE.
SO LET **ME** DO THE TALKING, AND WE'LL SOON BE RICH.
DON'T WORRY, **WE** WON'T SAY A WORD.
AGOBARD?! BLOODY HELLS...IS IT **TUESDAY** ALREADY? HAVE YOU BROUGHT ME SOME **LADIE--**
NO, SIR... IT AIN'T TUESDAY, BUT I... AHEM **WE...**
WE SAVED YOUR LADY FROM WATER HAGS, ME AND THE **WITCHER** HERE, AND WE THOUGHT MAYBE YOU'D--

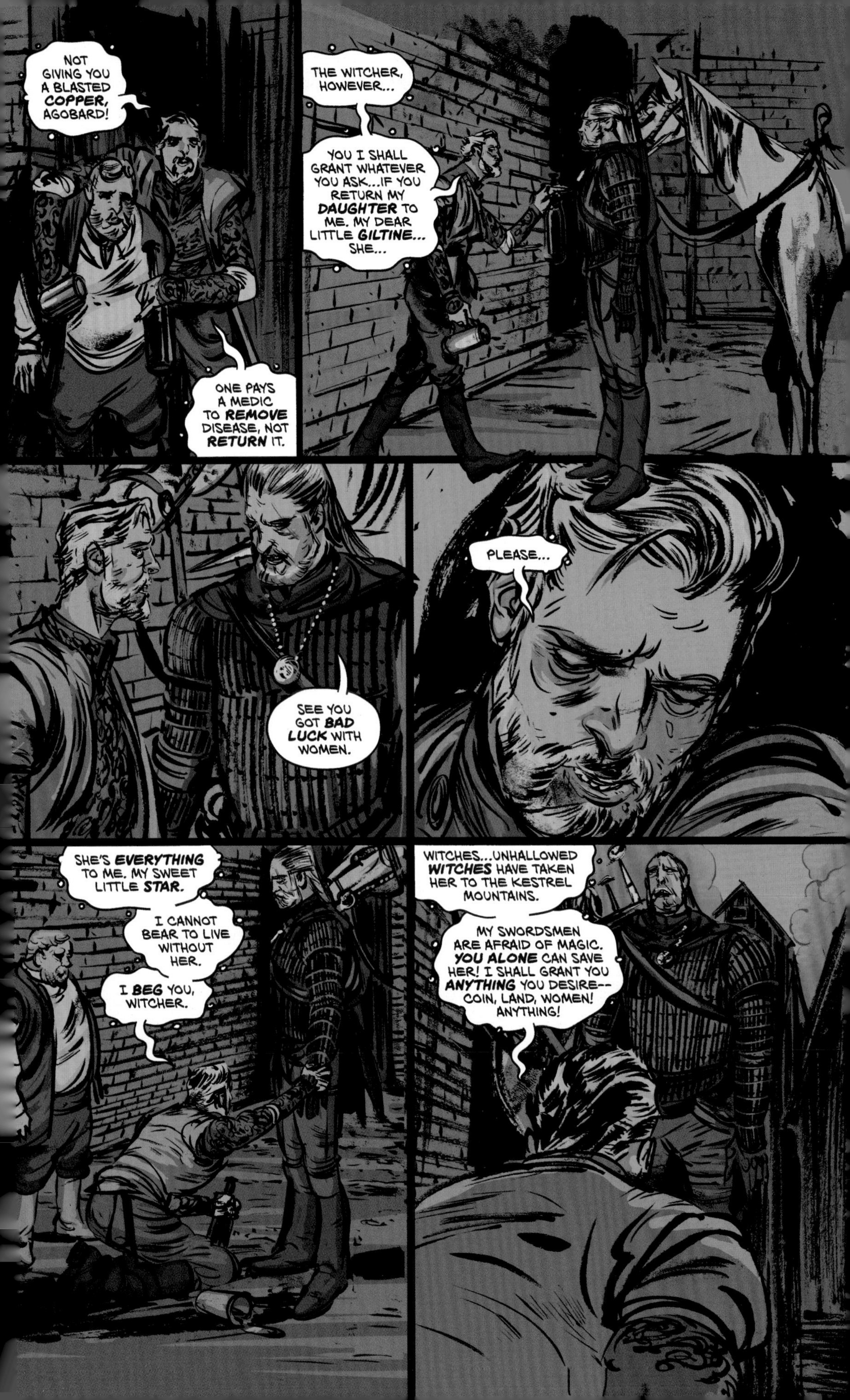
NOT GIVING YOU A BLASTED COPPER, AGOBARD!
ONE PAYS A MEDIC TO REMOVE DISEASE, NOT RETURN IT.
THE WITCHER, HOWEVER...
YOU I SHALL GRANT WHATEVER YOU ASK...IF YOU RETURN MY DAUGHTER TO ME. MY DEAR LITTLE GILTINE... SHE...
SEE YOU GOT BAD LUCK WITH WOMEN.
PLEASE...
SHE'S EVERYTHING TO ME. MY SWEET LITTLE STAR.
I CANNOT BEAR TO LIVE WITHOUT HER.
I BEG YOU, WITCHER.
WITCHES...UNHALLOWED WITCHES HAVE TAKEN HER TO THE KESTREL MOUNTAINS.
MY SWORDSMEN ARE AFRAID OF MAGIC. YOU ALONE CAN SAVE HER! I SHALL GRANT YOU ANYTHING YOU DESIRE--COIN, LAND, WOMEN! ANYTHING!

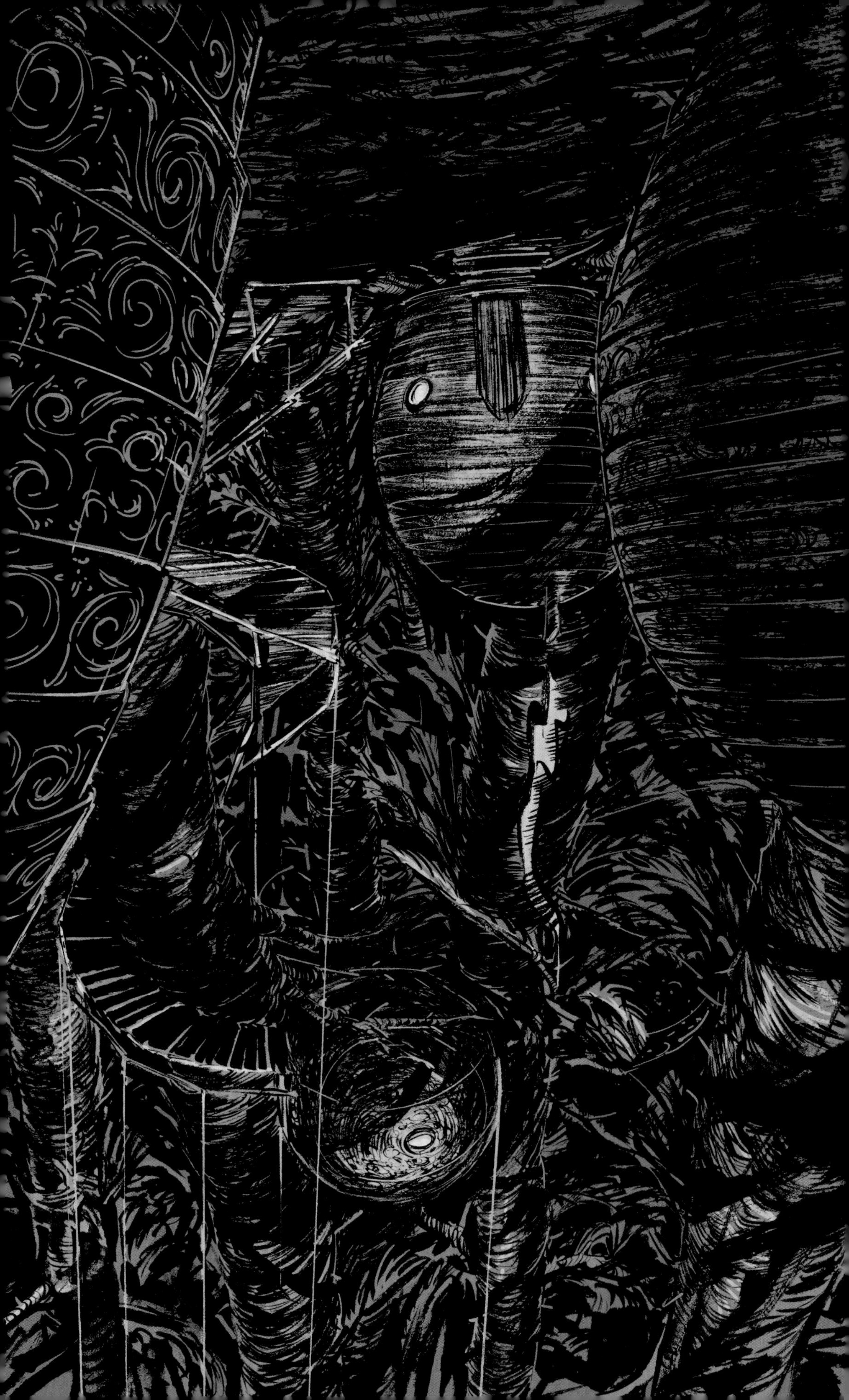

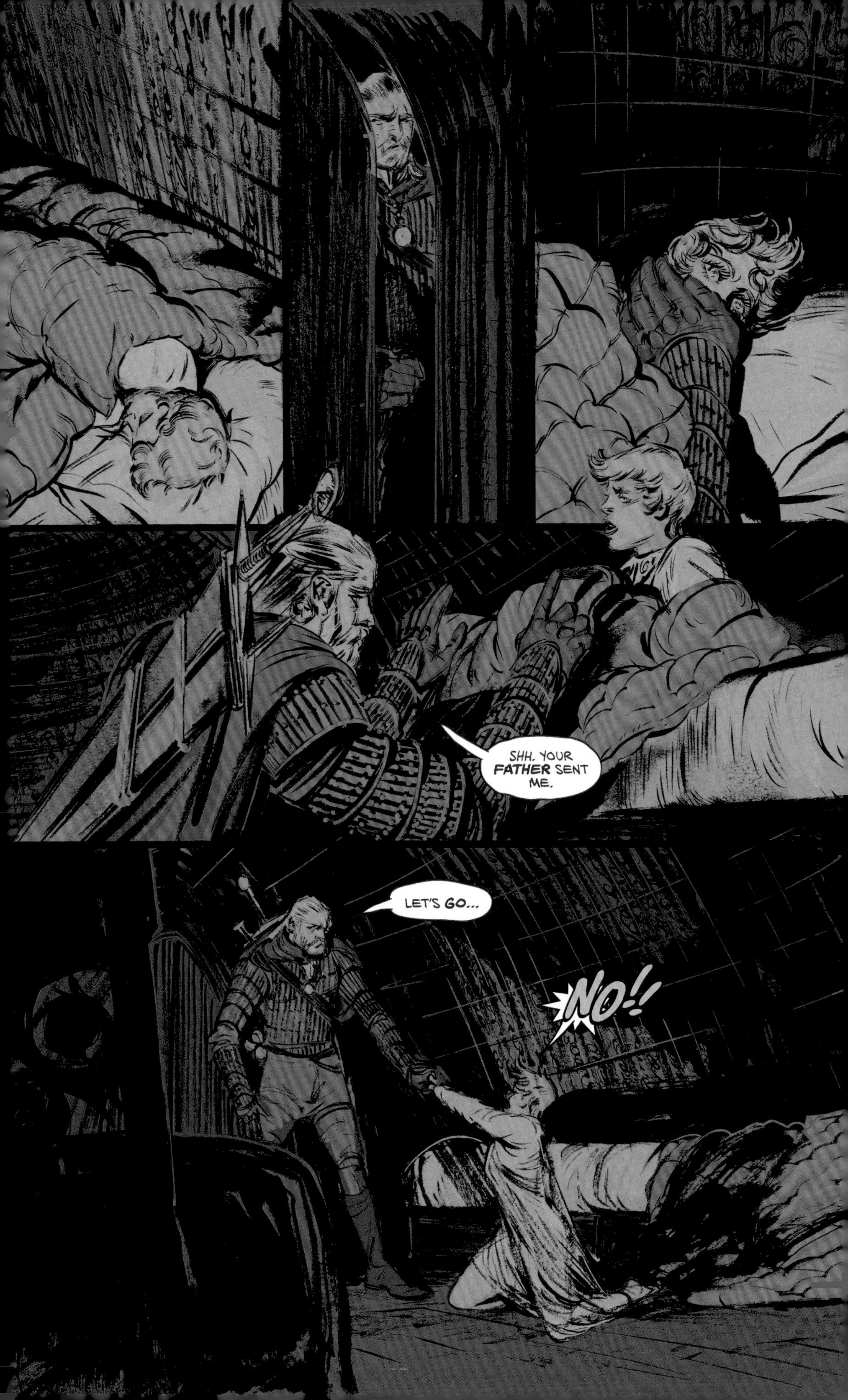
SHH. YOUR FATHER SENT ME.
LET'S GO...
NO!!

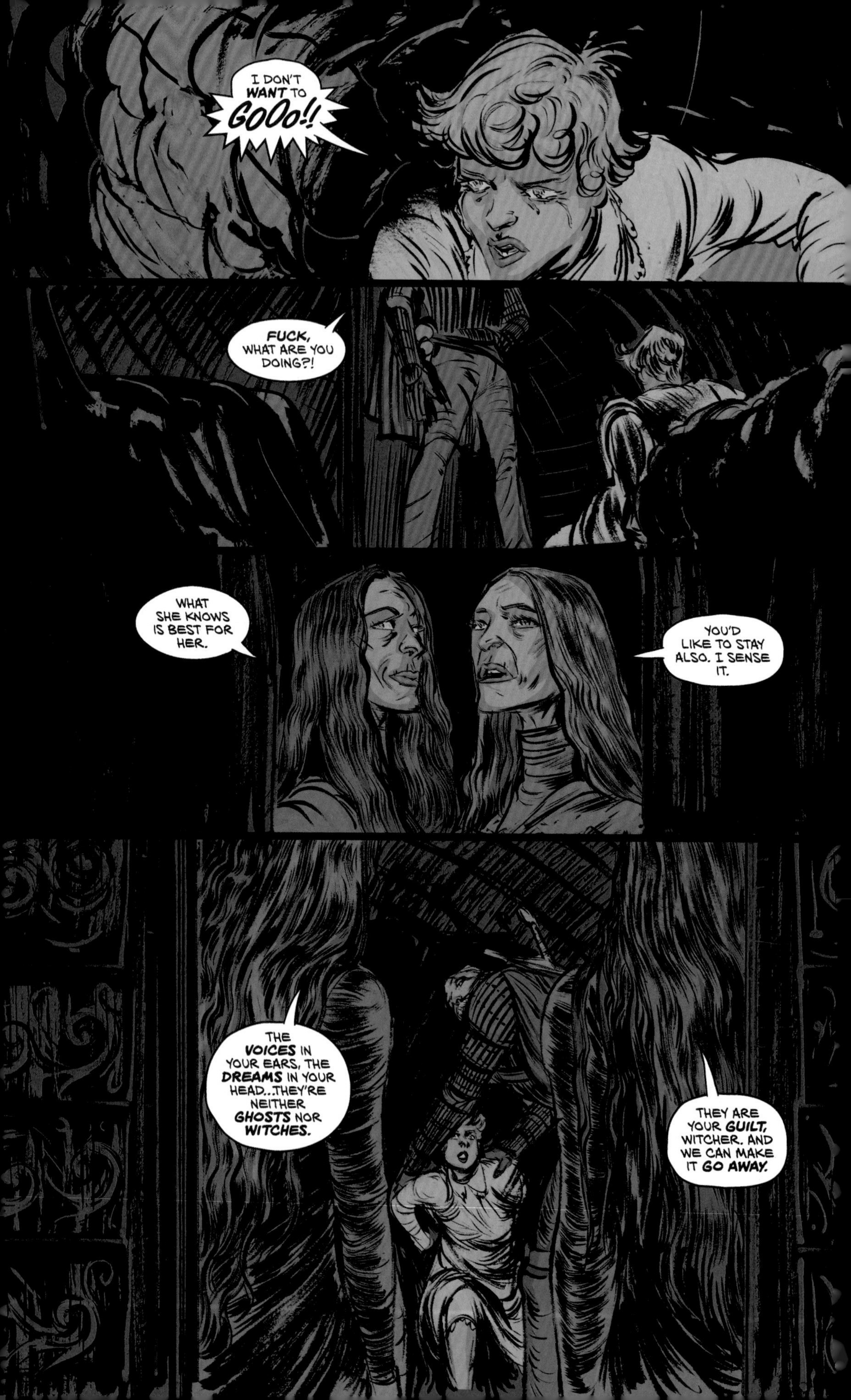
I DON'T WANT TO GOOo!!
FUCK, WHAT ARE YOU DOING?!
WHAT SHE KNOWS IS BEST FOR HER.
YOU'D LIKE TO STAY ALSO. I SENSE IT.
THE VOICES IN YOUR EARS, THE DREAMS IN YOUR HEAD..THEY'RE NEITHER GHOSTS NOR WITCHES.
THEY ARE YOUR GUILT, WITCHER. AND WE CAN MAKE IT GO AWAY.

CHAPTER TWO

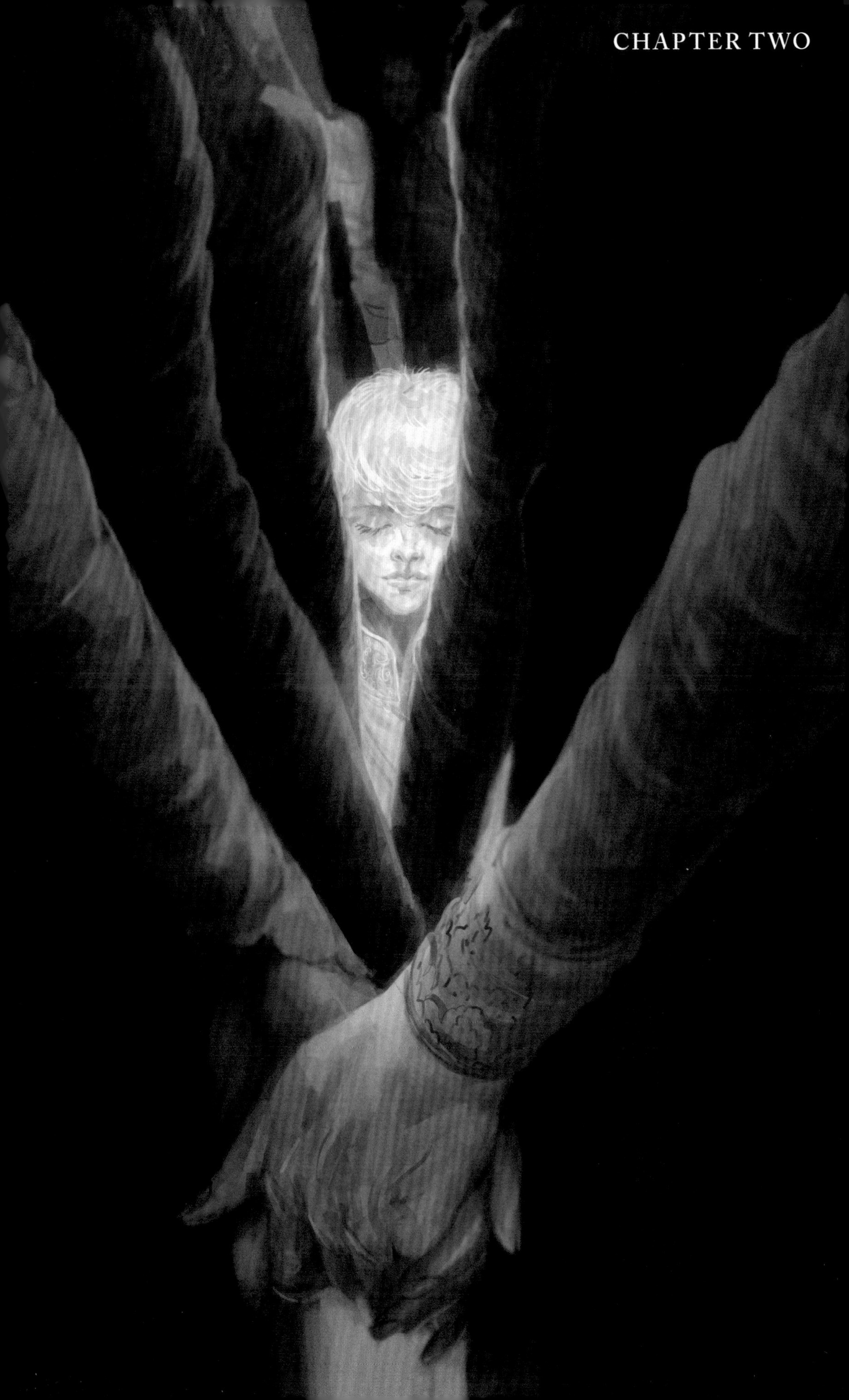

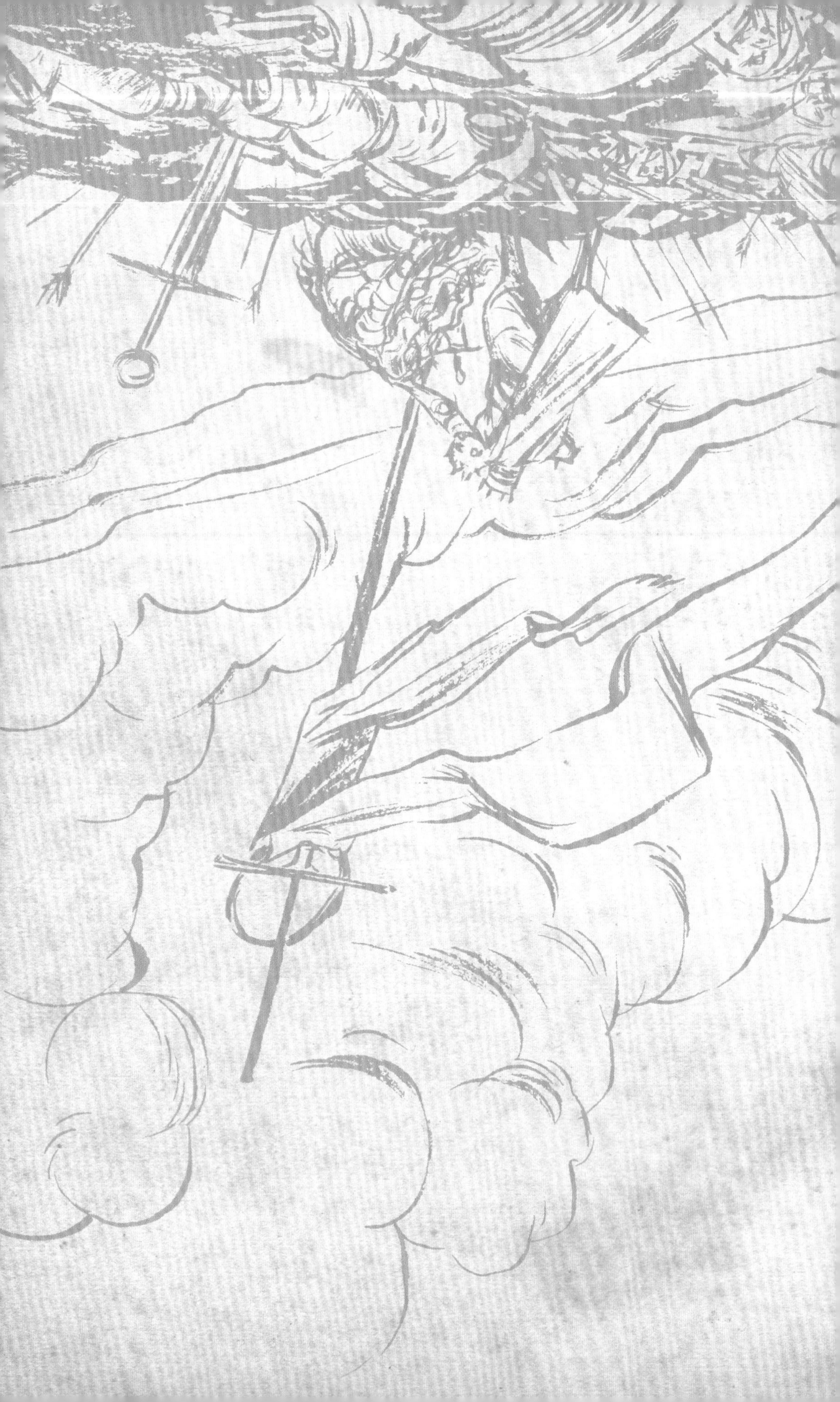

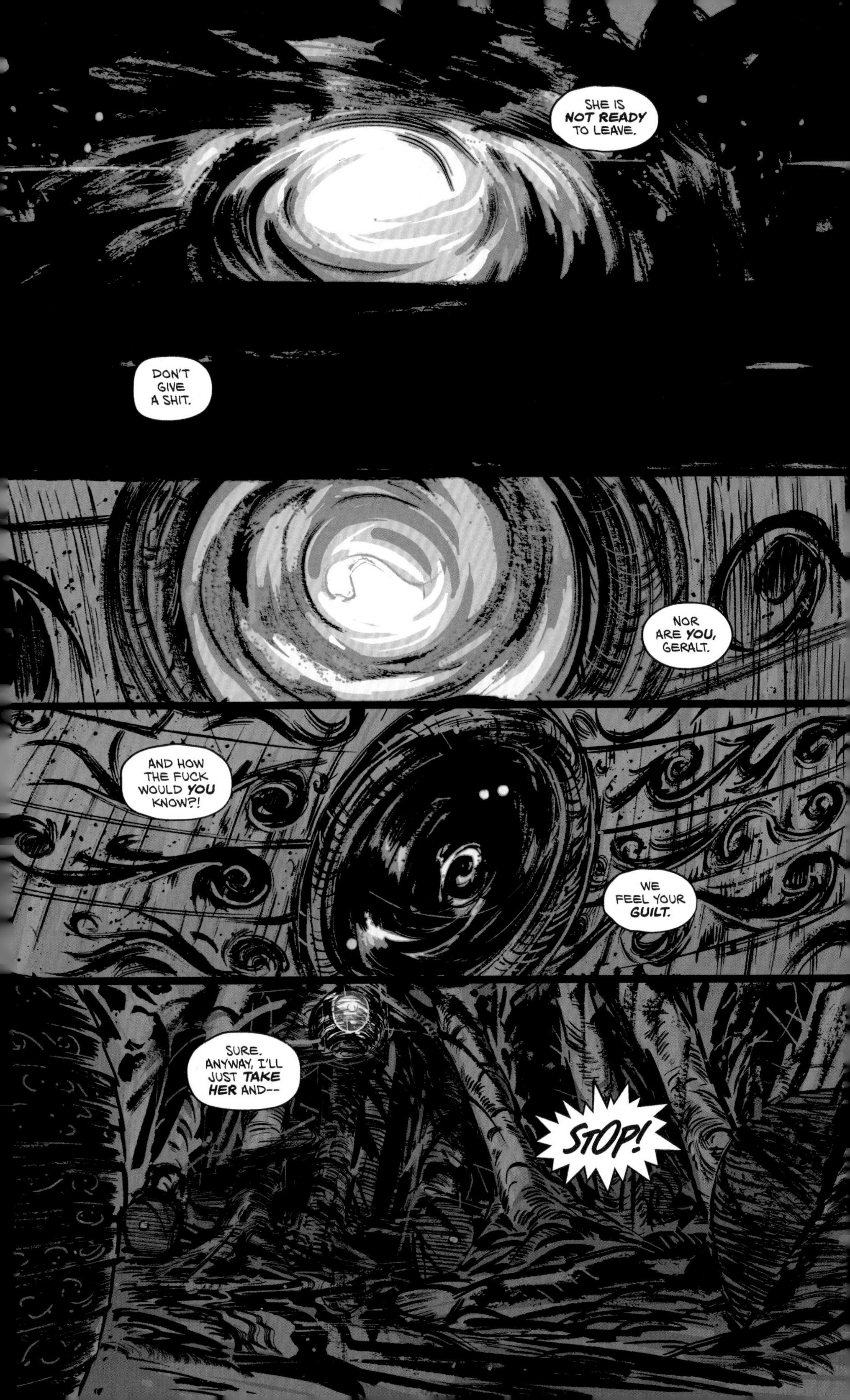
SHE IS NOT READY TO LEAVE.
DON'T GIVE A SHIT.
NOR ARE YOU, GERALT.
AND HOW THE FUCK WOULD YOU KNOW?!
WE FEEL YOUR GUILT.
SURE. ANYWAY, I'LL JUST TAKE HER AND--
STOP!

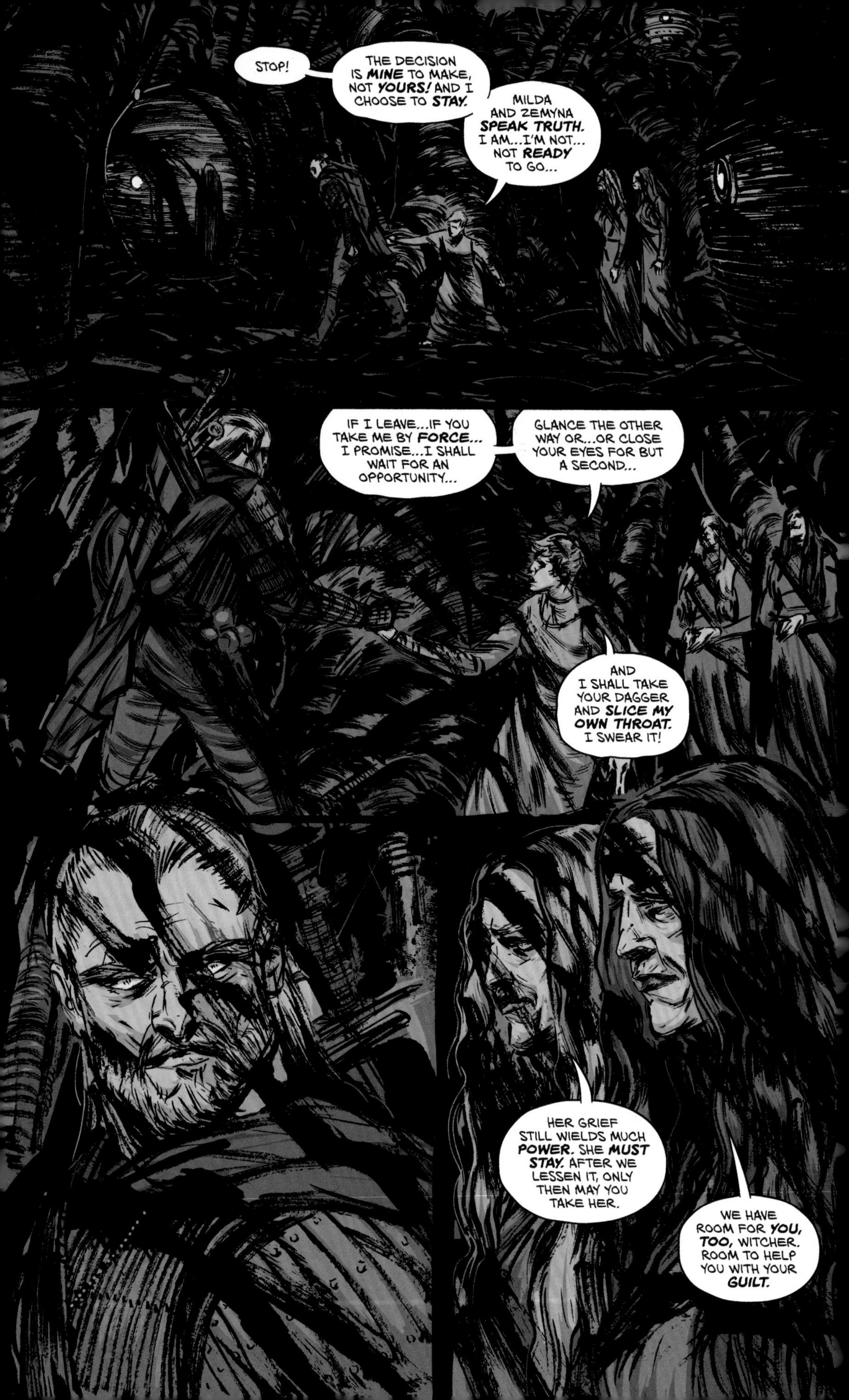
STOP!
THE DECISION IS **MINE** TO MAKE, NOT **YOURS!** AND I CHOOSE TO **STAY.**
MILDA AND ZEMYNA **SPEAK TRUTH.** I AM...I'M NOT... NOT **READY** TO GO...
IF I LEAVE...IF YOU TAKE ME BY **FORCE...** I PROMISE...I SHALL WAIT FOR AN OPPORTUNITY...
GLANCE THE OTHER WAY OR...OR CLOSE YOUR EYES FOR BUT A SECOND...
AND I SHALL TAKE YOUR DAGGER AND **SLICE MY OWN THROAT.** I SWEAR IT!
HER GRIEF STILL WIELDS MUCH **POWER.** SHE **MUST STAY.** AFTER WE LESSEN IT, ONLY THEN MAY YOU TAKE HER.
WE HAVE ROOM FOR **YOU, TOO,** WITCHER. ROOM TO HELP YOU WITH YOUR **GUILT.**

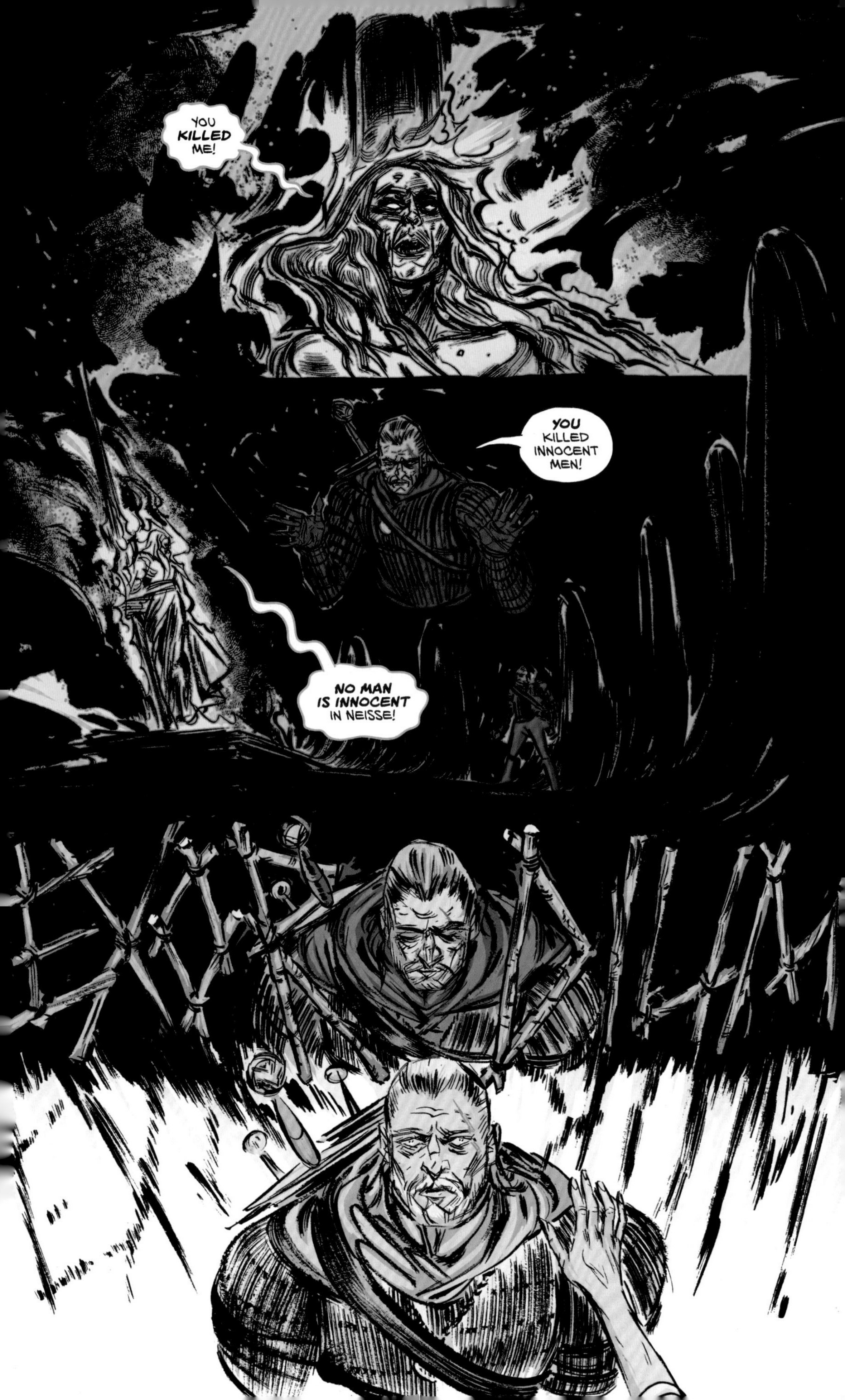
YOU KILLED ME!
YOU KILLED INNOCENT MEN!
NO MAN IS INNOCENT IN NEISSE!

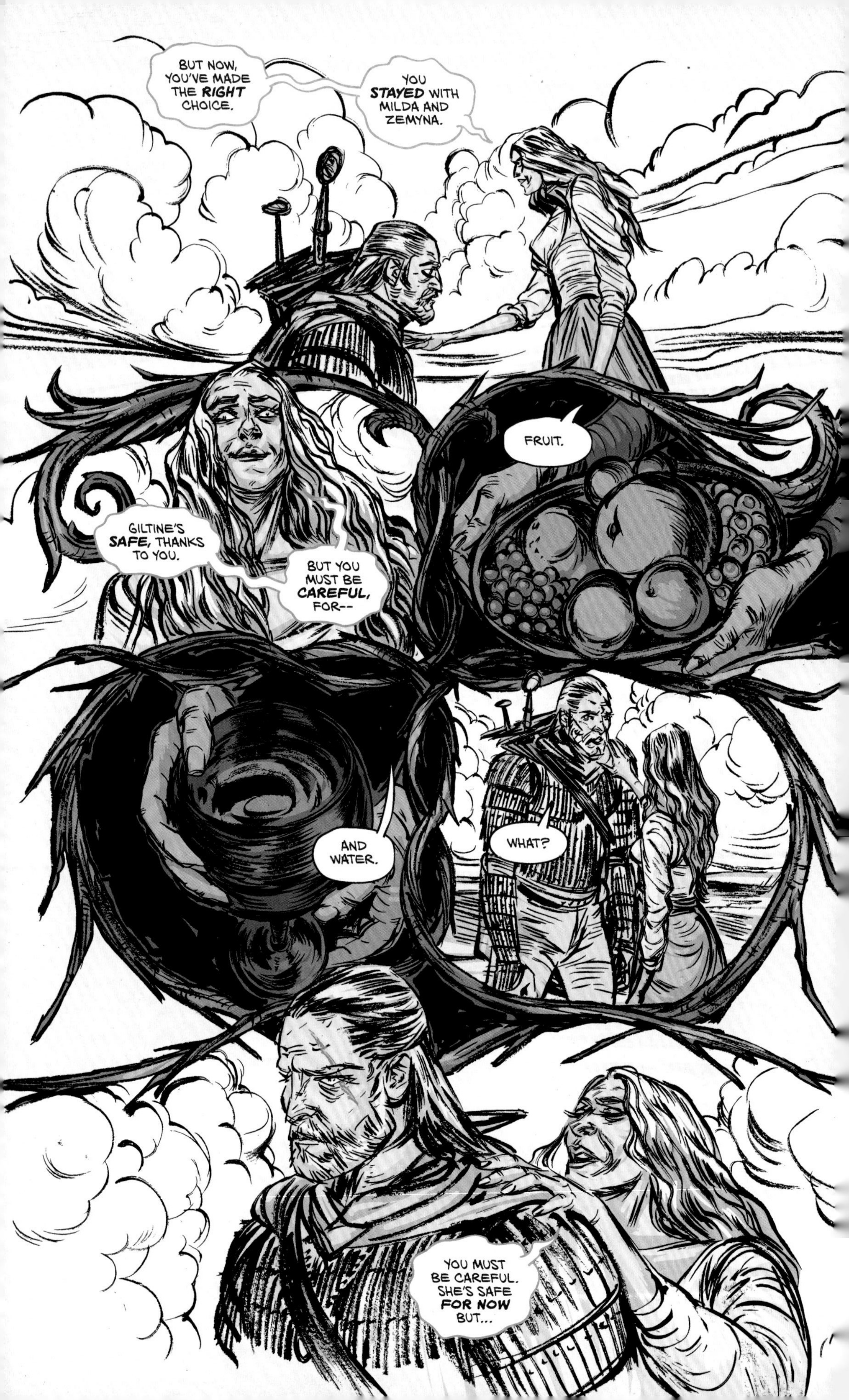
BUT NOW, YOU'VE MADE THE **RIGHT** CHOICE.
YOU **STAYED** WITH MILDA AND ZEMYNA.
FRUIT.
GILTINE'S **SAFE,** THANKS TO YOU.
BUT YOU MUST BE **CAREFUL,** FOR--
AND WATER.
WHAT?
YOU MUST BE CAREFUL. SHE'S SAFE **FOR NOW** BUT...

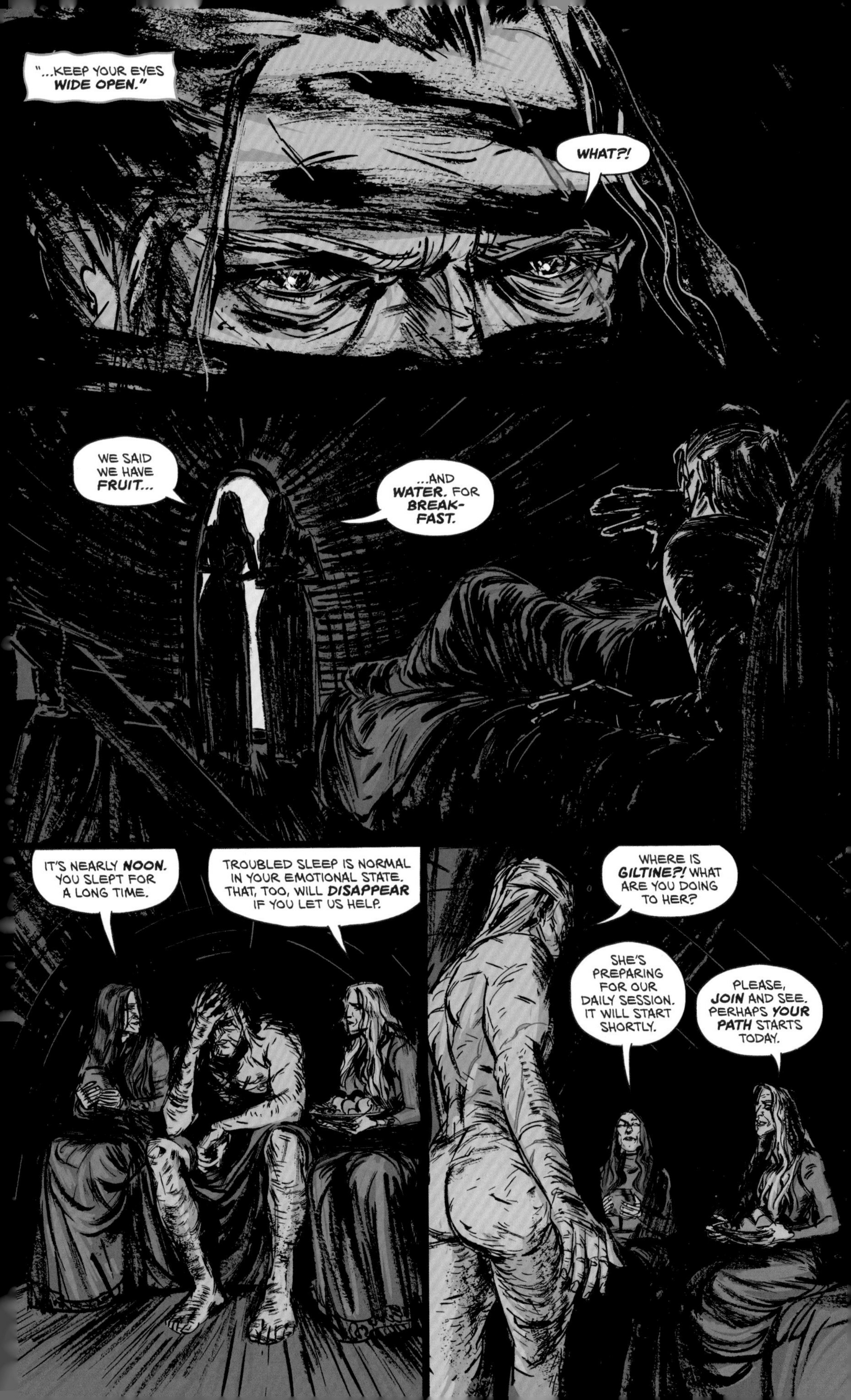
"...KEEP YOUR EYES WIDE OPEN."
WHAT?!
WE SAID WE HAVE FRUIT...
...AND WATER. FOR BREAK-FAST.
IT'S NEARLY NOON. YOU SLEPT FOR A LONG TIME.
TROUBLED SLEEP IS NORMAL IN YOUR EMOTIONAL STATE. THAT, TOO, WILL DISAPPEAR IF YOU LET US HELP.
WHERE IS GILTINE?! WHAT ARE YOU DOING TO HER?
SHE'S PREPARING FOR OUR DAILY SESSION. IT WILL START SHORTLY.
PLEASE, JOIN AND SEE. PERHAPS YOUR PATH STARTS TODAY.

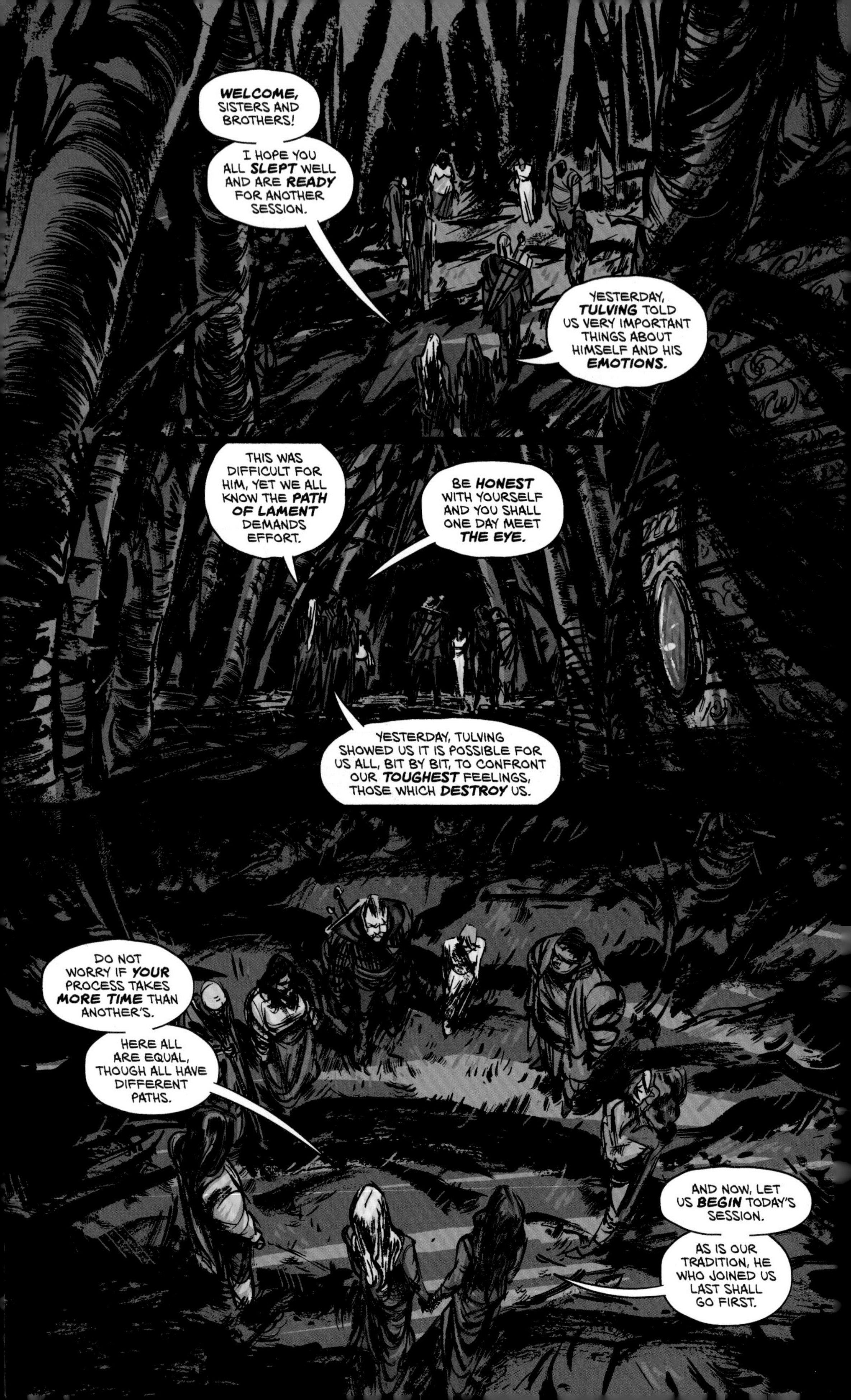

WELCOME, SISTERS AND BROTHERS!
I HOPE YOU ALL SLEPT WELL AND ARE READY FOR ANOTHER SESSION.
YESTERDAY, TULVING TOLD US VERY IMPORTANT THINGS ABOUT HIMSELF AND HIS EMOTIONS.
THIS WAS DIFFICULT FOR HIM, YET WE ALL KNOW THE PATH OF LAMENT DEMANDS EFFORT.
BE HONEST WITH YOURSELF AND YOU SHALL ONE DAY MEET THE EYE.
YESTERDAY, TULVING SHOWED US IT IS POSSIBLE FOR US ALL, BIT BY BIT, TO CONFRONT OUR TOUGHEST FEELINGS, THOSE WHICH DESTROY US.
DO NOT WORRY IF YOUR PROCESS TAKES MORE TIME THAN ANOTHER'S.
HERE ALL ARE EQUAL, THOUGH ALL HAVE DIFFERENT PATHS.
AND NOW, LET US BEGIN TODAY'S SESSION.
AS IS OUR TRADITION, HE WHO JOINED US LAST SHALL GO FIRST.

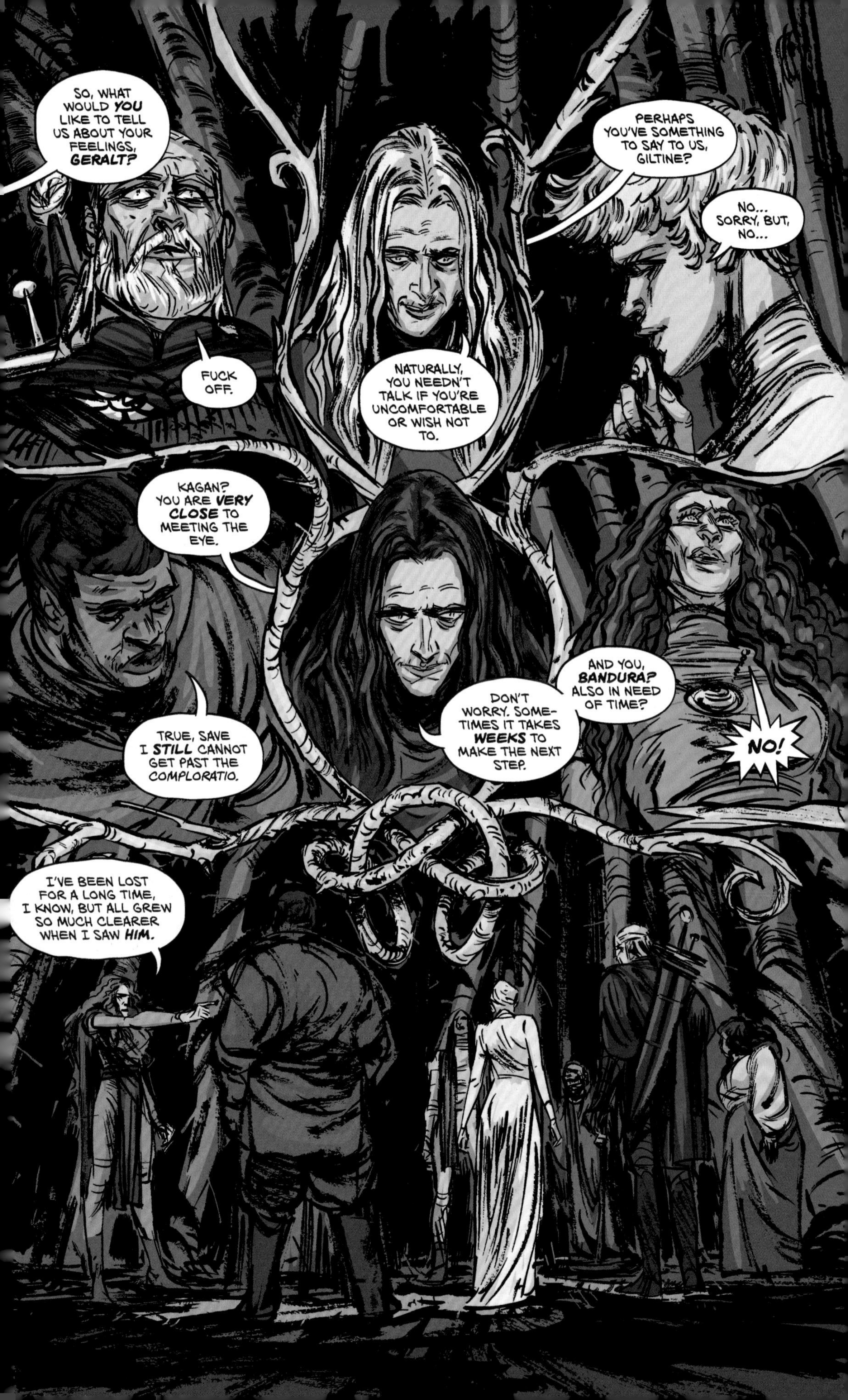
SO, WHAT WOULD YOU LIKE TO TELL US ABOUT YOUR FEELINGS, GERALT?
FUCK OFF.
NATURALLY, YOU NEEDN'T TALK IF YOU'RE UNCOMFORTABLE OR WISH NOT TO.
PERHAPS YOU'VE SOMETHING TO SAY TO US, GILTINE?
NO... SORRY, BUT, NO...
KAGAN? YOU ARE VERY CLOSE TO MEETING THE EYE.
TRUE, SAVE I STILL CANNOT GET PAST THE COMPLORATIO.
DON'T WORRY. SOME-TIMES IT TAKES WEEKS TO MAKE THE NEXT STEP.
AND YOU, BANDURA? ALSO IN NEED OF TIME?
NO!
I'VE BEEN LOST FOR A LONG TIME, I KNOW, BUT ALL GREW SO MUCH CLEARER WHEN I SAW HIM.

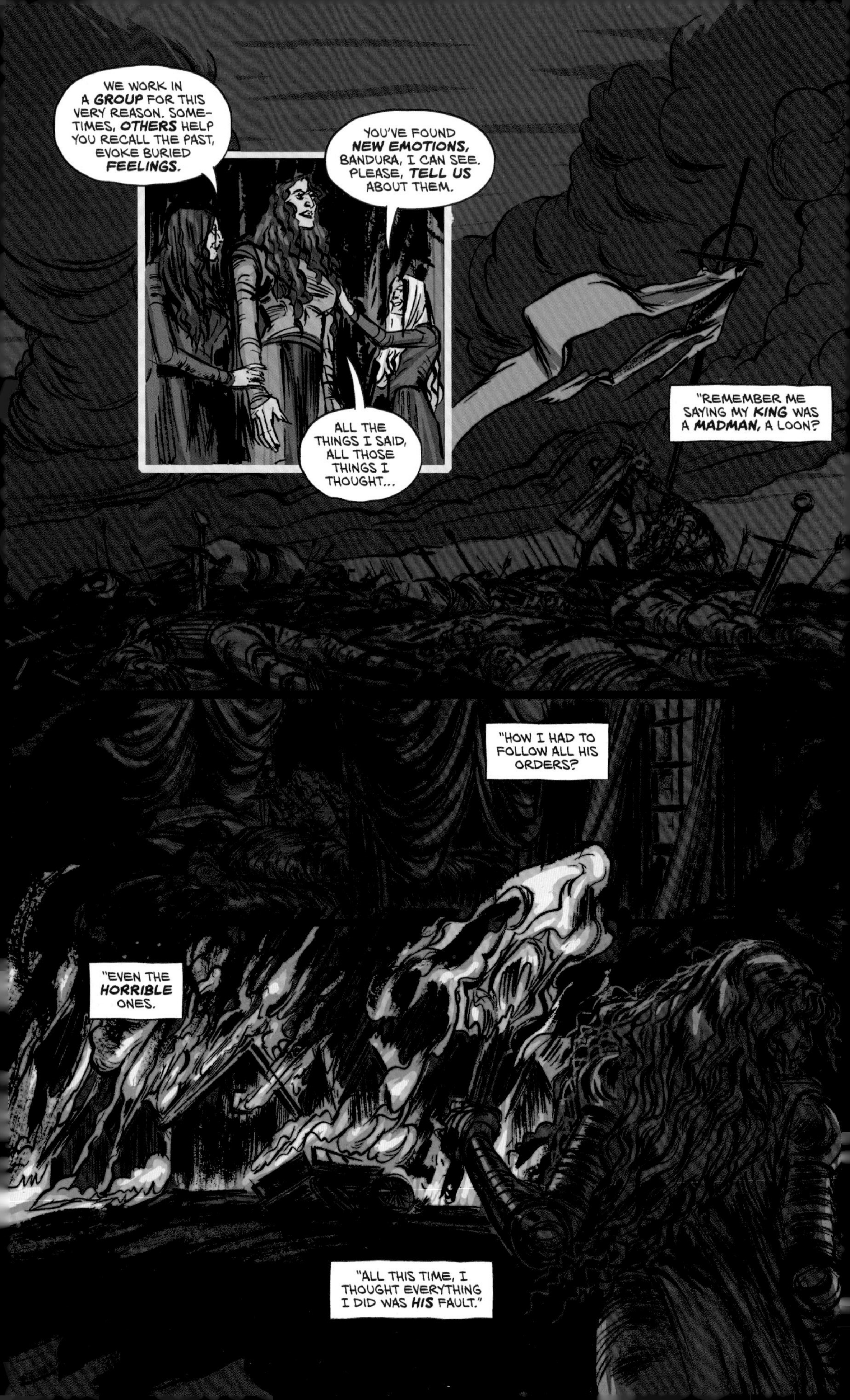
WE WORK IN A **GROUP** FOR THIS VERY REASON. SOME-TIMES, **OTHERS** HELP YOU RECALL THE PAST, EVOKE BURIED **FEELINGS.**
YOU'VE FOUND **NEW EMOTIONS,** BANDURA, I CAN SEE. PLEASE, **TELL US** ABOUT THEM.
ALL THE THINGS I SAID, ALL THOSE THINGS I THOUGHT...
"REMEMBER ME SAYING MY **KING** WAS A **MADMAN,** A LOON?
"HOW I HAD TO FOLLOW ALL HIS ORDERS?
"EVEN THE **HORRIBLE** ONES.
"ALL THIS TIME, I THOUGHT EVERYTHING I DID WAS **HIS** FAULT."

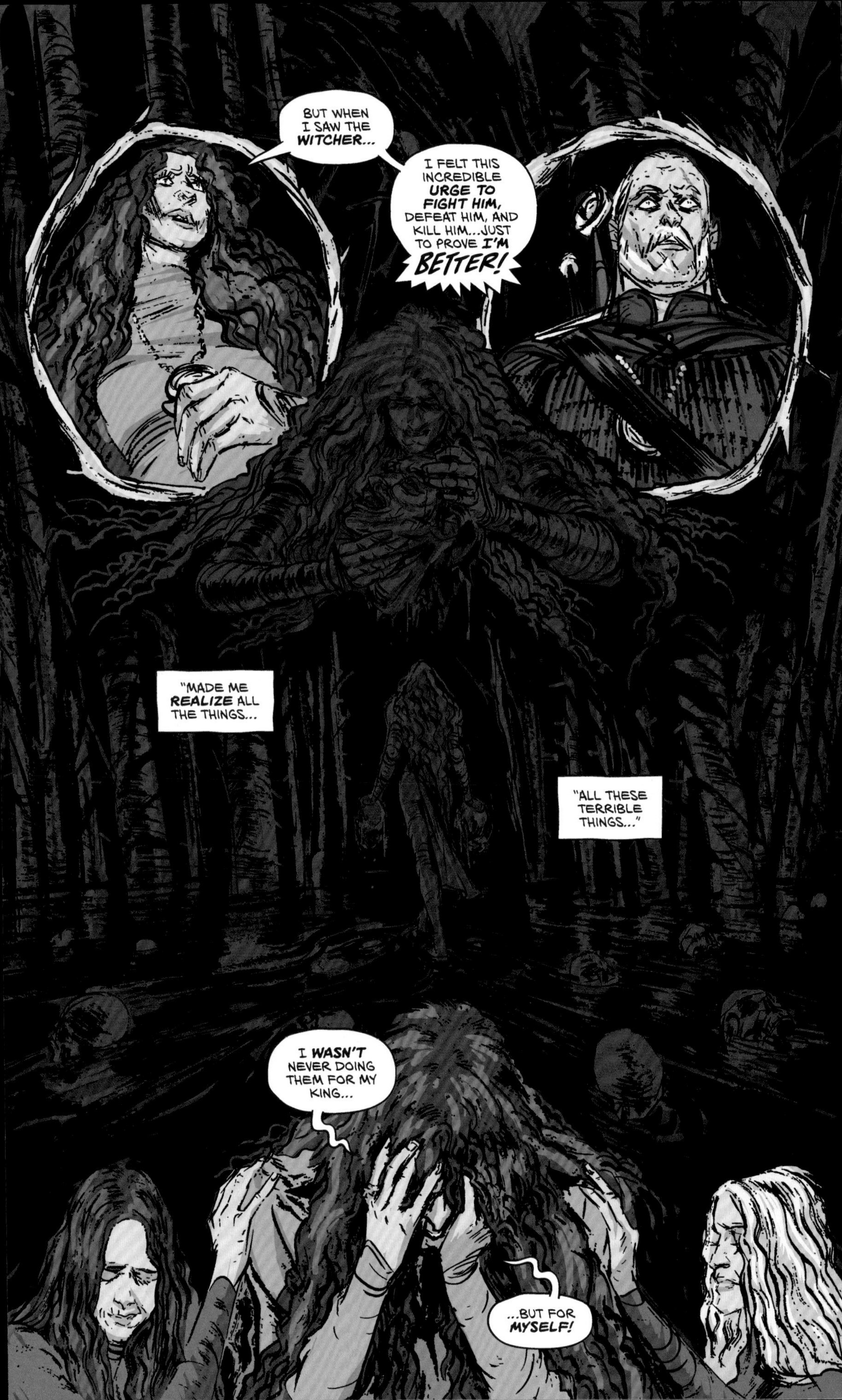
BUT WHEN I SAW THE WITCHER...
I FELT THIS INCREDIBLE URGE TO FIGHT HIM, DEFEAT HIM, AND KILL HIM...JUST TO PROVE I'M BETTER!
"MADE ME REALIZE ALL THE THINGS...
"ALL THESE TERRIBLE THINGS..."
I WASN'T NEVER DOING THEM FOR MY KING...
...BUT FOR MYSELF!

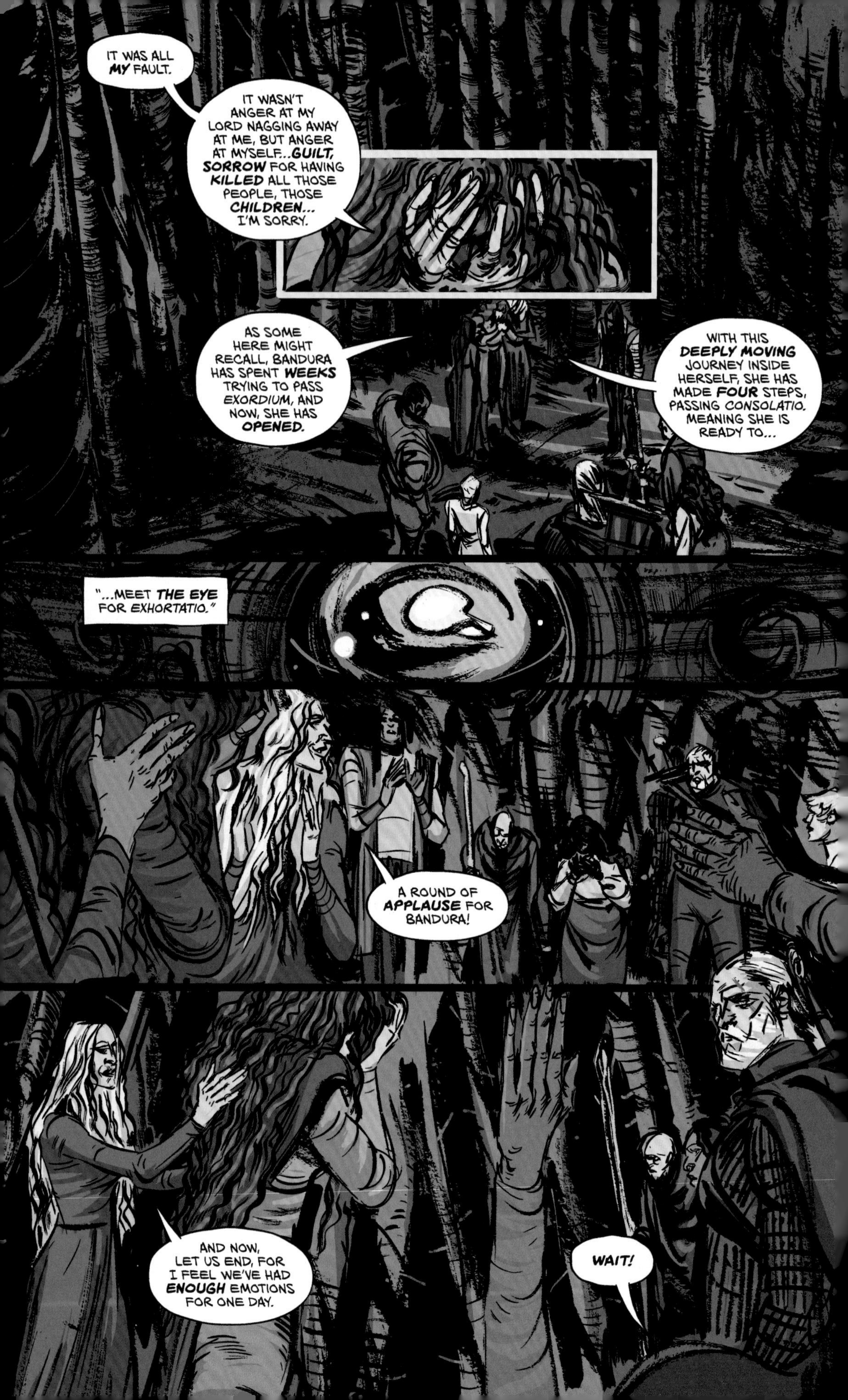
IT WAS ALL **MY** FAULT.
IT WASN'T ANGER AT MY LORD NAGGING AWAY AT ME, BUT ANGER AT MYSELF... **GUILT, SORROW** FOR HAVING **KILLED** ALL THOSE PEOPLE, THOSE **CHILDREN...** I'M SORRY.
AS SOME HERE MIGHT RECALL, BANDURA HAS SPENT **WEEKS** TRYING TO PASS EXORDIUM, AND NOW, SHE HAS **OPENED.**
WITH THIS **DEEPLY MOVING** JOURNEY INSIDE HERSELF, SHE HAS MADE **FOUR** STEPS, PASSING CONSOLATIO. MEANING SHE IS READY TO...
"...MEET **THE EYE** FOR EXHORTATIO."
A ROUND OF **APPLAUSE** FOR BANDURA!
AND NOW, LET US END, FOR I FEEL WE'VE HAD **ENOUGH** EMOTIONS FOR ONE DAY.
WAIT!

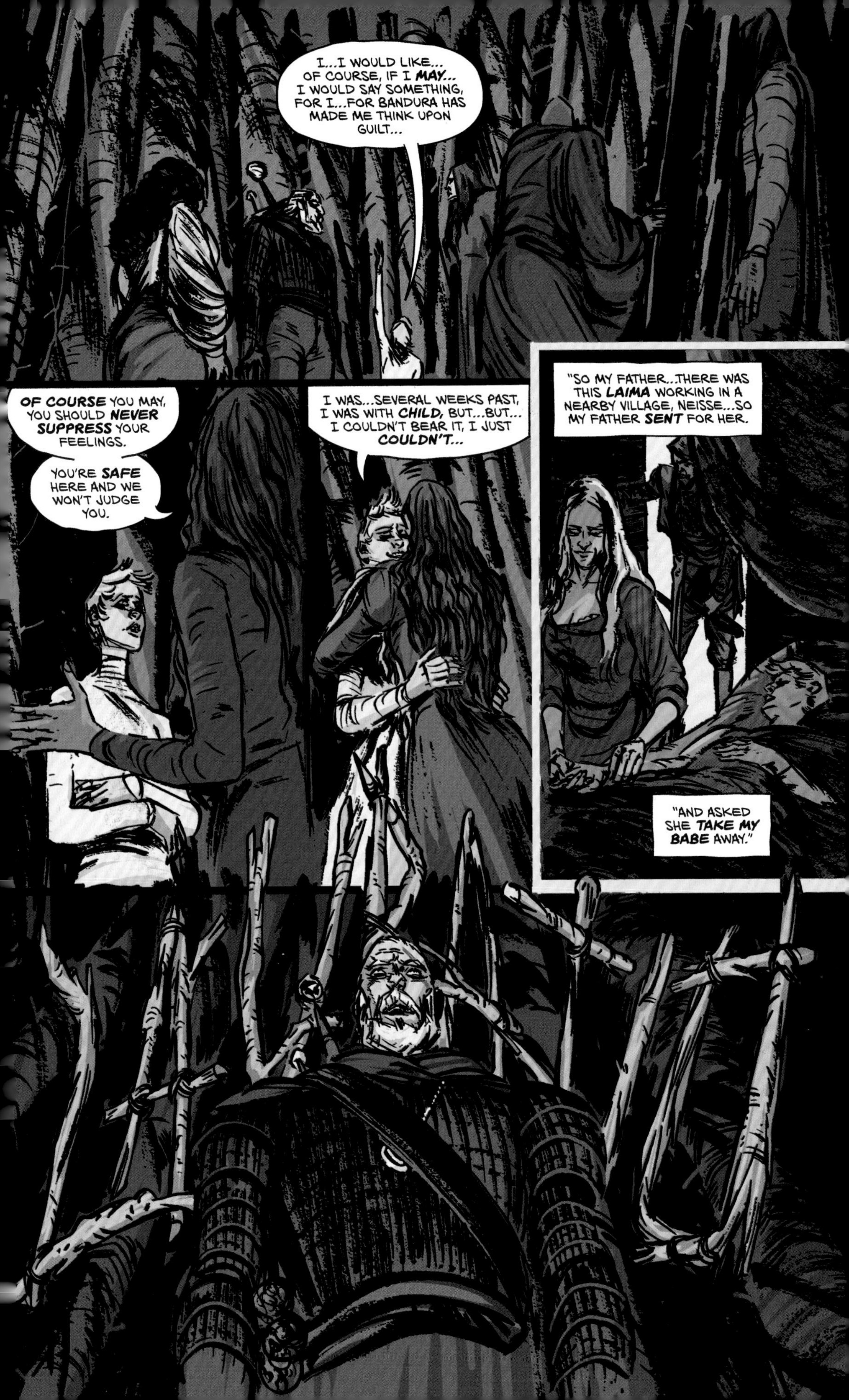
I...I WOULD LIKE... OF COURSE, IF I MAY... I WOULD SAY SOMETHING, FOR I...FOR BANDURA HAS MADE ME THINK UPON GUILT...
OF COURSE YOU MAY, YOU SHOULD NEVER SUPPRESS YOUR FEELINGS.
YOU'RE SAFE HERE AND WE WON'T JUDGE YOU.
I WAS...SEVERAL WEEKS PAST, I WAS WITH CHILD, BUT...BUT... I COULDN'T BEAR IT, I JUST COULDN'T...
"SO MY FATHER...THERE WAS THIS LAIMA WORKING IN A NEARBY VILLAGE, NEISSE...SO MY FATHER SENT FOR HER.
"AND ASKED SHE TAKE MY BABE AWAY."

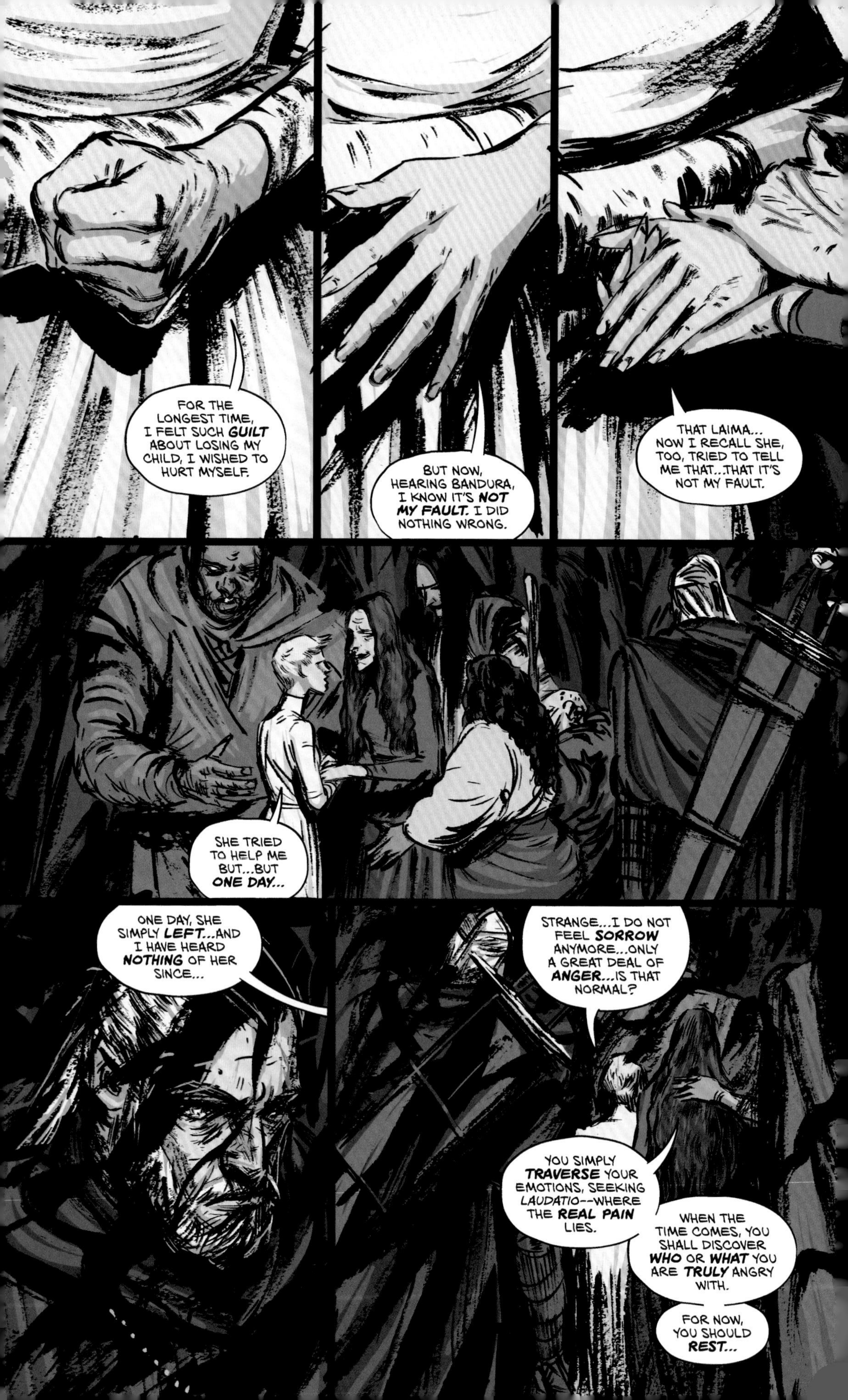
FOR THE LONGEST TIME, I FELT SUCH **GUILT** ABOUT LOSING MY CHILD, I WISHED TO HURT MYSELF.
BUT NOW, HEARING BANDURA, I KNOW IT'S ***NOT MY FAULT.*** I DID NOTHING WRONG.
THAT LAIMA... NOW I RECALL SHE, TOO, TRIED TO TELL ME THAT...THAT IT'S NOT MY FAULT.
SHE TRIED TO HELP ME BUT...BUT ***ONE DAY...***
ONE DAY, SHE SIMPLY ***LEFT...***AND I HAVE HEARD ***NOTHING*** OF HER SINCE...
STRANGE...I DO NOT FEEL ***SORROW*** ANYMORE...ONLY A GREAT DEAL OF ***ANGER...***IS THAT NORMAL?
YOU SIMPLY ***TRAVERSE*** YOUR EMOTIONS, SEEKING *LAUDATIO*--WHERE THE ***REAL PAIN*** LIES.
WHEN THE TIME COMES, YOU SHALL DISCOVER ***WHO*** OR ***WHAT*** YOU ARE ***TRULY*** ANGRY WITH.
FOR NOW, YOU SHOULD ***REST...***

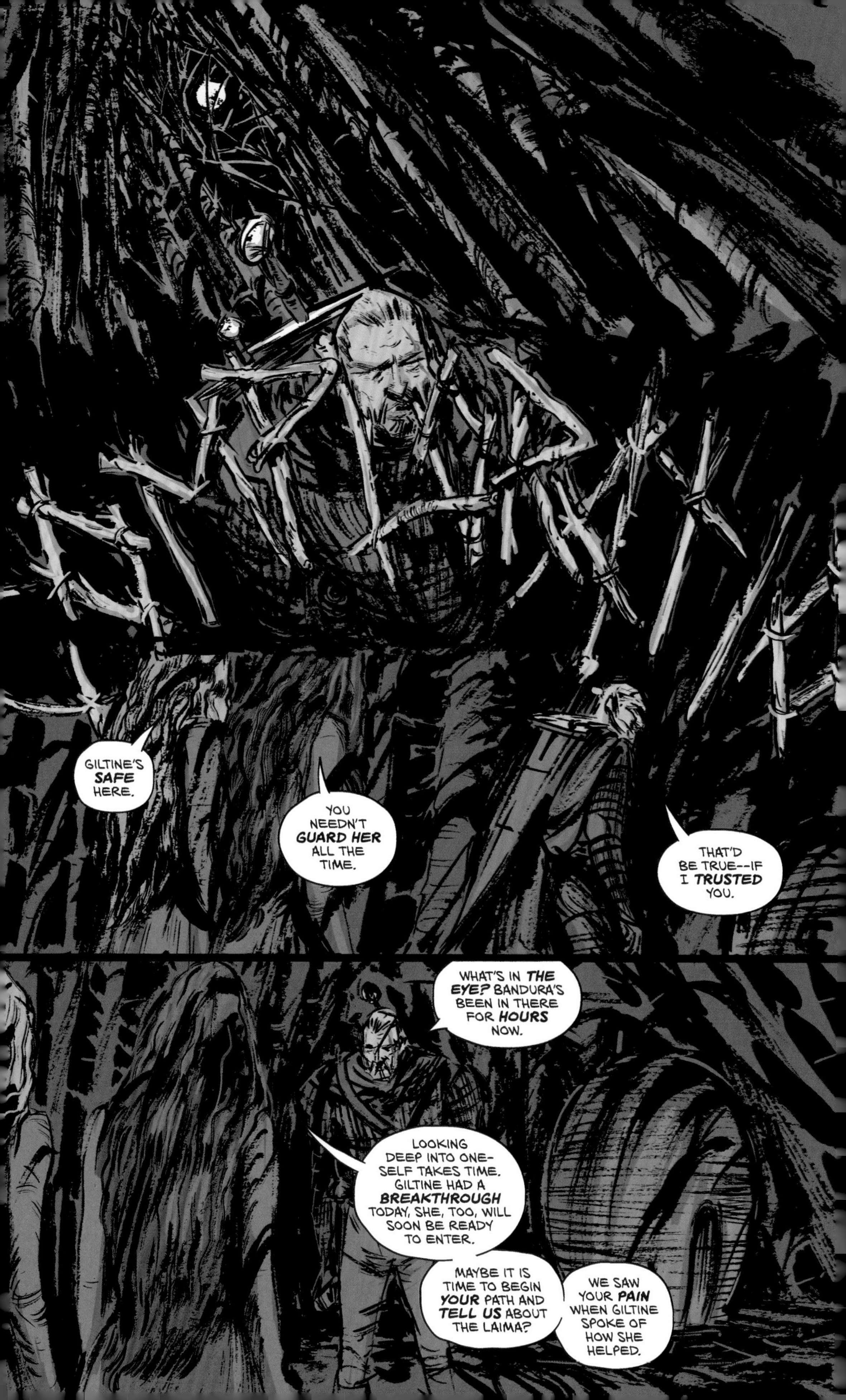
GILTINE'S SAFE HERE.
YOU NEEDN'T GUARD HER ALL THE TIME.
THAT'D BE TRUE--IF I TRUSTED YOU.
WHAT'S IN THE EYE? BANDURA'S BEEN IN THERE FOR HOURS NOW.
LOOKING DEEP INTO ONE-SELF TAKES TIME. GILTINE HAD A BREAKTHROUGH TODAY. SHE, TOO, WILL SOON BE READY TO ENTER.
MAYBE IT IS TIME TO BEGIN YOUR PATH AND TELL US ABOUT THE LAIMA?
WE SAW YOUR PAIN WHEN GILTINE SPOKE OF HOW SHE HELPED.

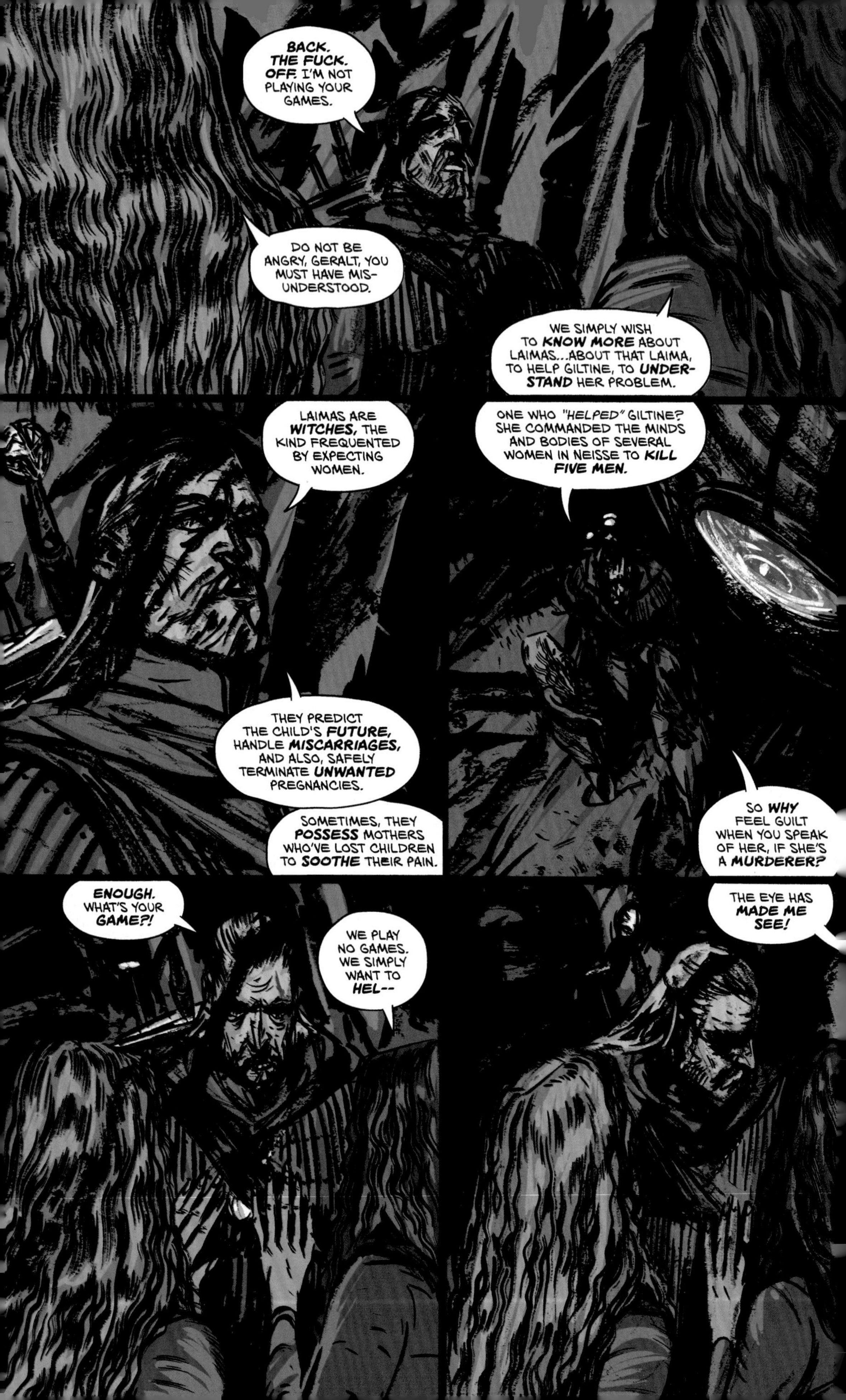
BACK. THE FUCK. OFF. I'M NOT PLAYING YOUR GAMES.
DO NOT BE ANGRY, GERALT, YOU MUST HAVE MIS-UNDERSTOOD.
WE SIMPLY WISH TO **KNOW MORE** ABOUT LAIMAS...ABOUT THAT LAIMA, TO HELP GILTINE, TO **UNDER-STAND** HER PROBLEM.
LAIMAS ARE **WITCHES,** THE KIND FREQUENTED BY EXPECTING WOMEN.
THEY PREDICT THE CHILD'S **FUTURE,** HANDLE **MISCARRIAGES,** AND ALSO, SAFELY TERMINATE **UNWANTED** PREGNANCIES.
SOMETIMES, THEY **POSSESS** MOTHERS WHO'VE LOST CHILDREN TO **SOOTHE** THEIR PAIN.
ONE WHO *"HELPED"* GILTINE? SHE COMMANDED THE MINDS AND BODIES OF SEVERAL WOMEN IN NEISSE TO **KILL FIVE MEN.**
SO **WHY** FEEL GUILT WHEN YOU SPEAK OF HER, IF SHE'S A **MURDERER?**
ENOUGH. WHAT'S YOUR **GAME?!**
WE PLAY NO GAMES. WE SIMPLY WANT TO **HEL--**
THE EYE HAS **MADE ME SEE!**

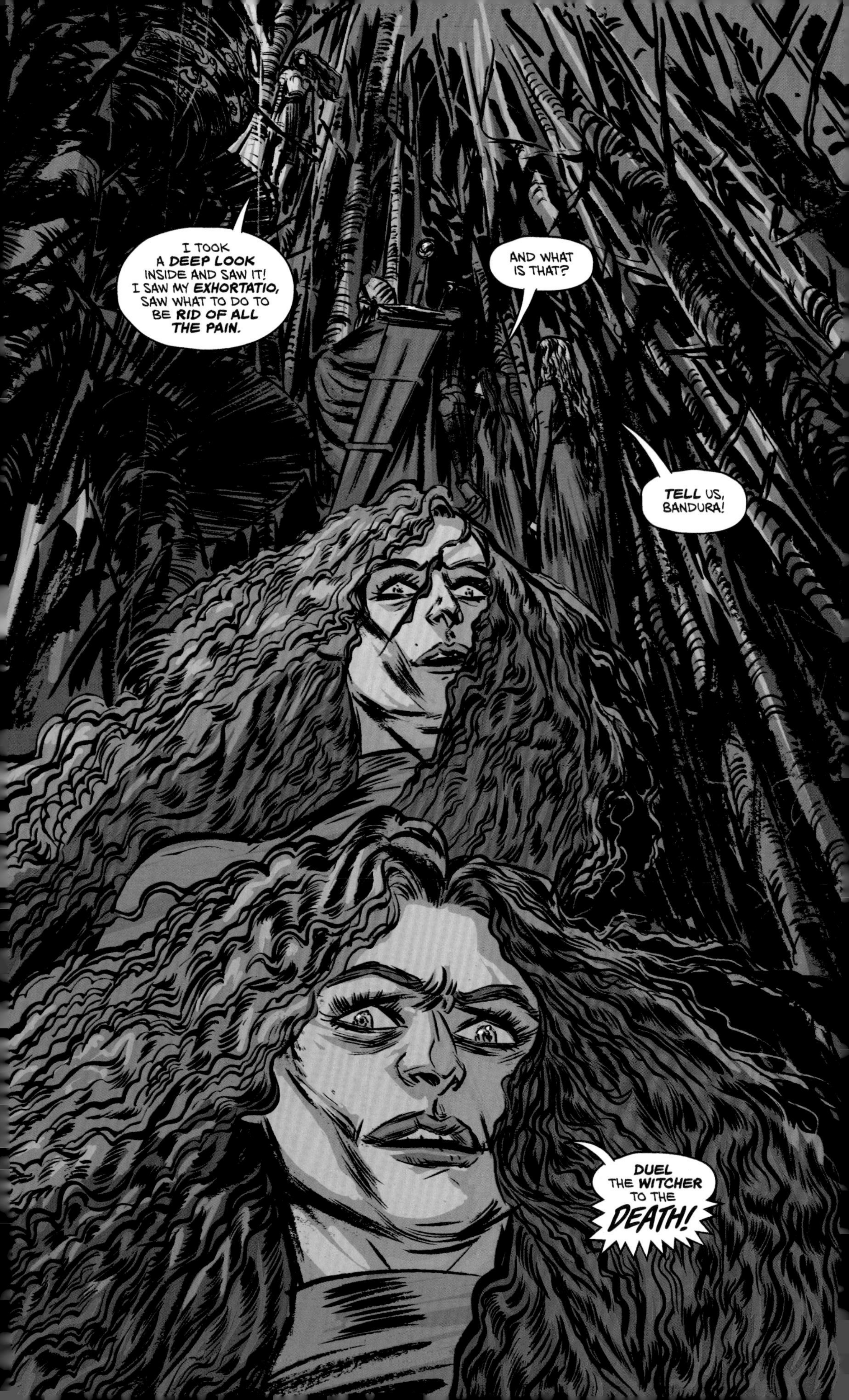
I TOOK A DEEP LOOK INSIDE AND SAW IT! I SAW MY EXHORTATIO, SAW WHAT TO DO TO BE RID OF ALL THE PAIN.
AND WHAT IS THAT?
TELL US, BANDURA!
DUEL THE WITCHER TO THE DEATH!

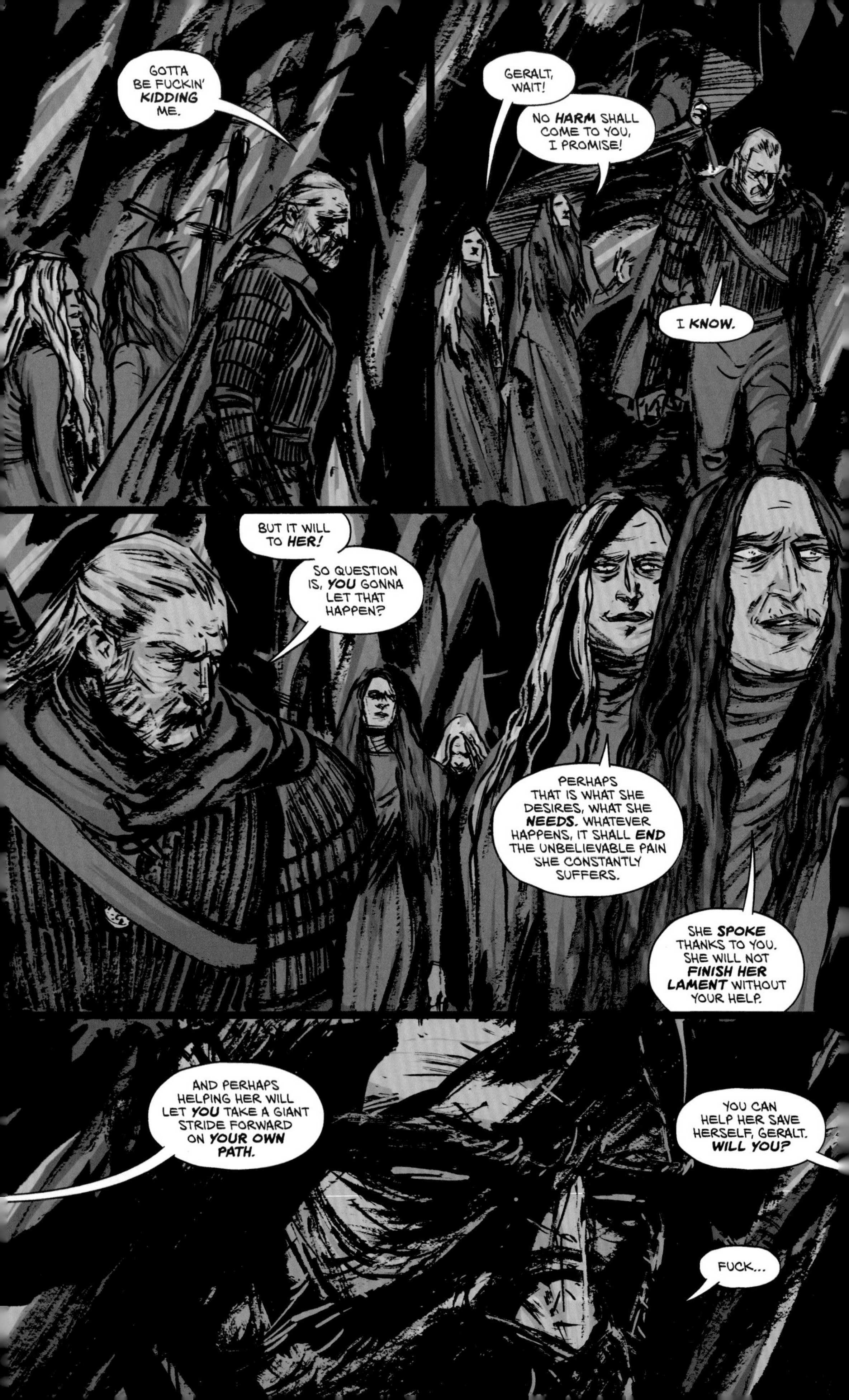
GOTTA BE FUCKIN' **KIDDING** ME.
GERALT, WAIT!
NO **HARM** SHALL COME TO YOU, I PROMISE!
I **KNOW.**
BUT IT WILL TO **HER!**
SO QUESTION IS, **YOU** GONNA LET THAT HAPPEN?
PERHAPS THAT IS WHAT SHE DESIRES, WHAT SHE **NEEDS.** WHATEVER HAPPENS, IT SHALL **END** THE UNBELIEVABLE PAIN SHE CONSTANTLY SUFFERS.
SHE **SPOKE** THANKS TO YOU. SHE WILL NOT **FINISH HER LAMENT** WITHOUT YOUR HELP.
AND PERHAPS HELPING HER WILL LET **YOU** TAKE A GIANT STRIDE FORWARD ON **YOUR OWN PATH.**
YOU CAN HELP HER SAVE HERSELF, GERALT. **WILL YOU?**
FUCK...

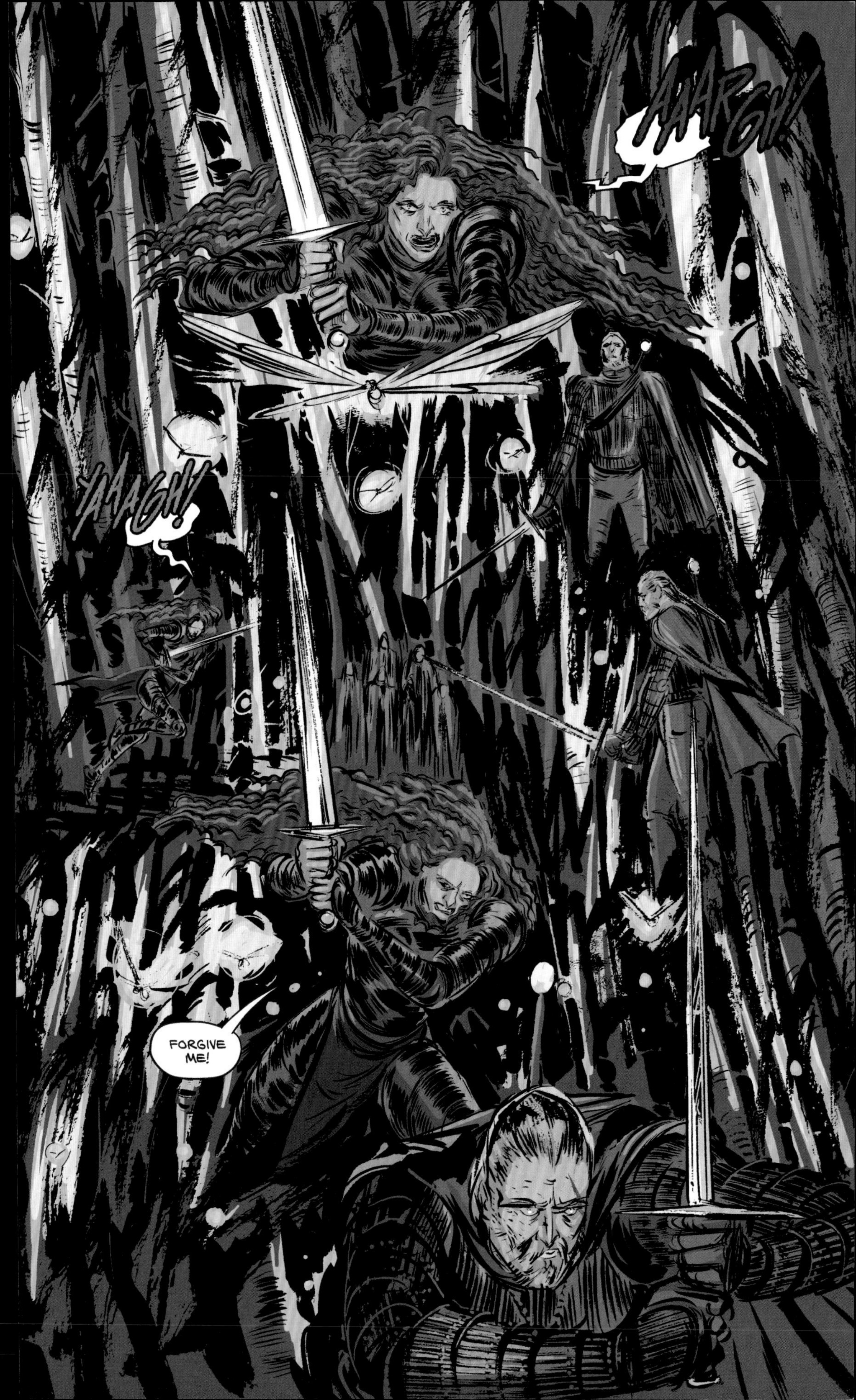
AARGH!
YAAGH!
FORGIVE ME!

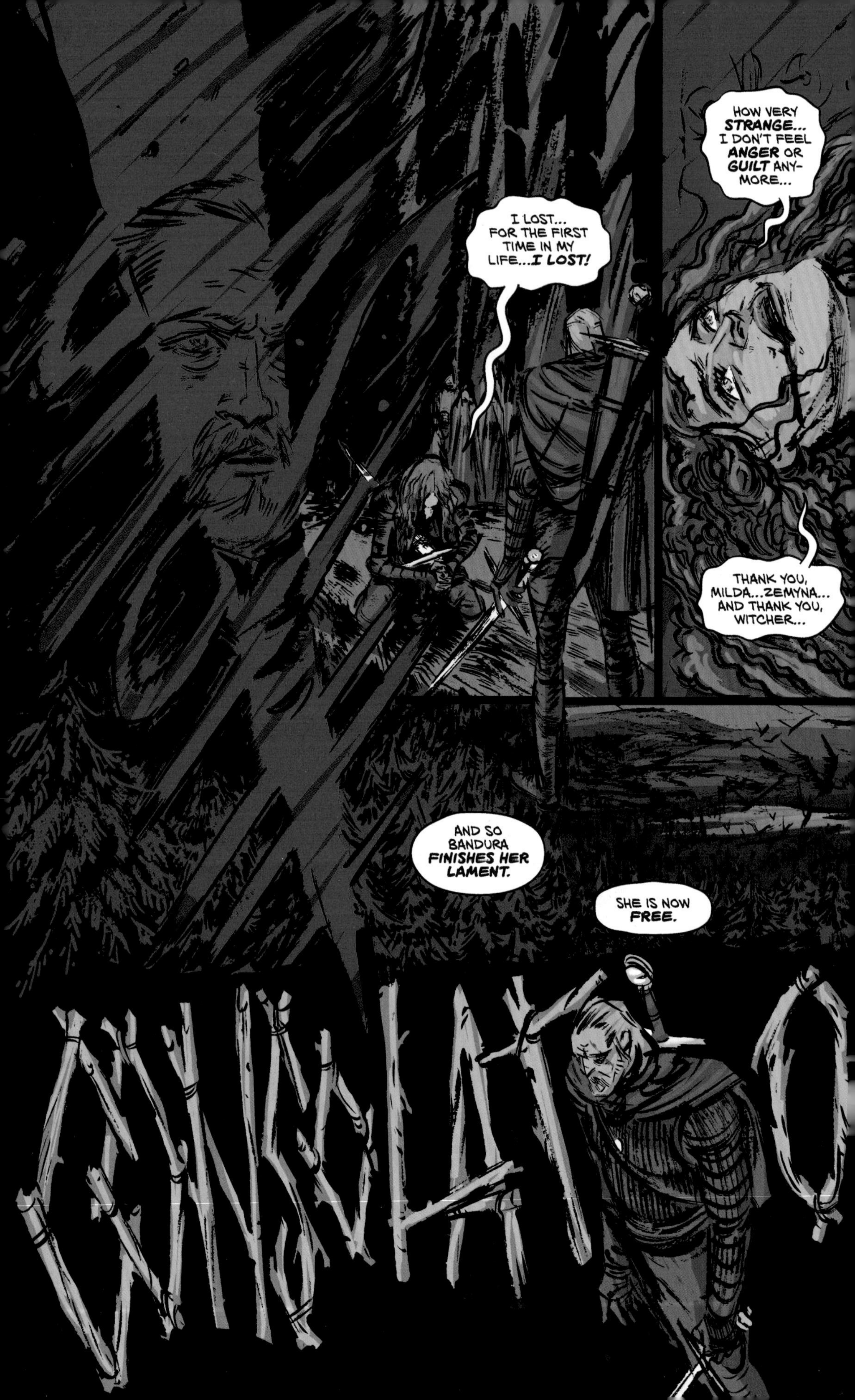
I LOST... FOR THE FIRST TIME IN MY LIFE...I LOST!
HOW VERY STRANGE... I DON'T FEEL ANGER OR GUILT ANY-MORE...
THANK YOU, MILDA...ZEMYNA... AND THANK YOU, WITCHER...
AND SO BANDURA FINISHES HER LAMENT.
SHE IS NOW FREE.

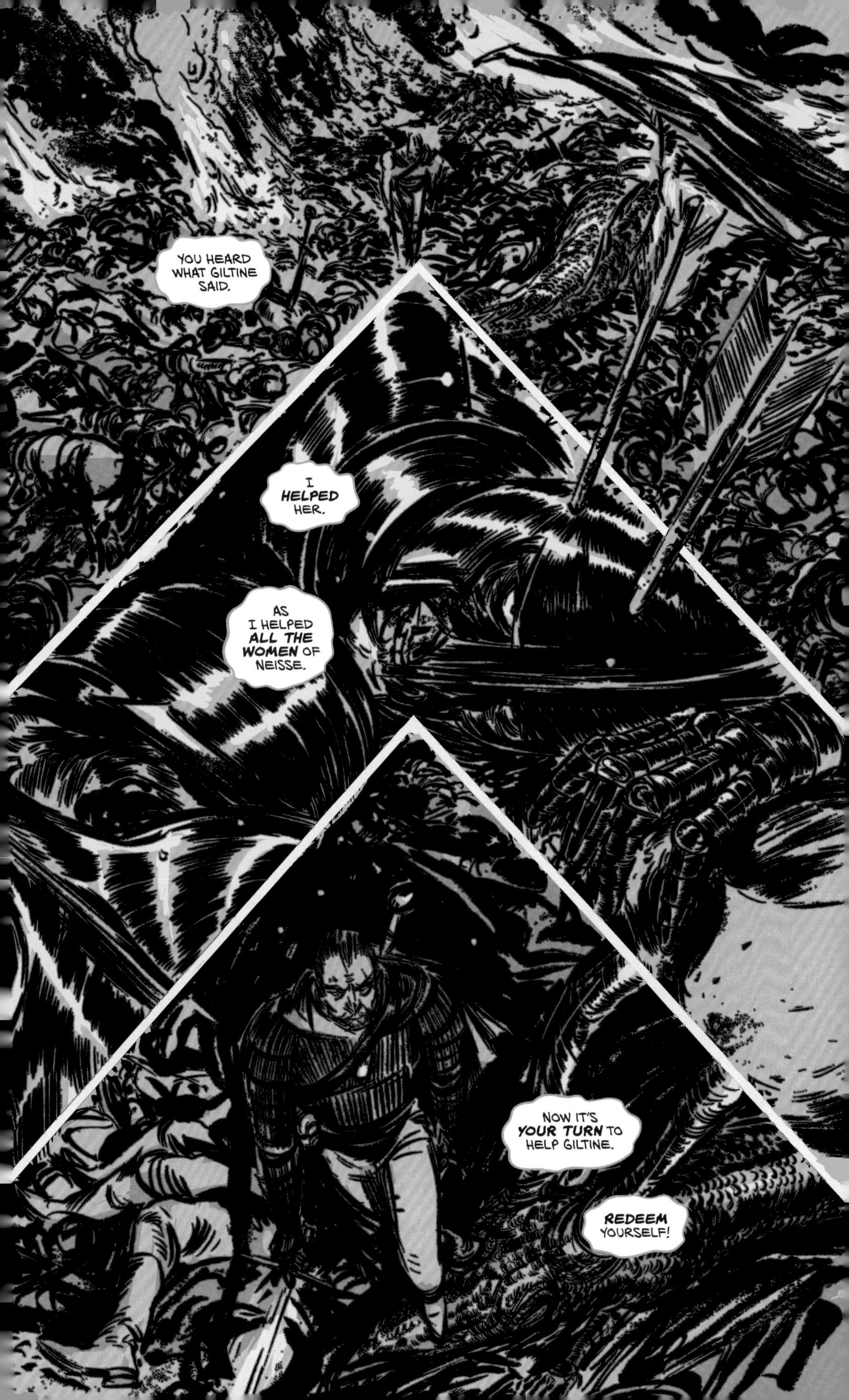
YOU HEARD WHAT GILTINE SAID.
I **HELPED** HER.
AS I HELPED ***ALL THE WOMEN*** OF NEISSE.
NOW IT'S ***YOUR TURN*** TO HELP GILTINE.
REDEEM YOURSELF!

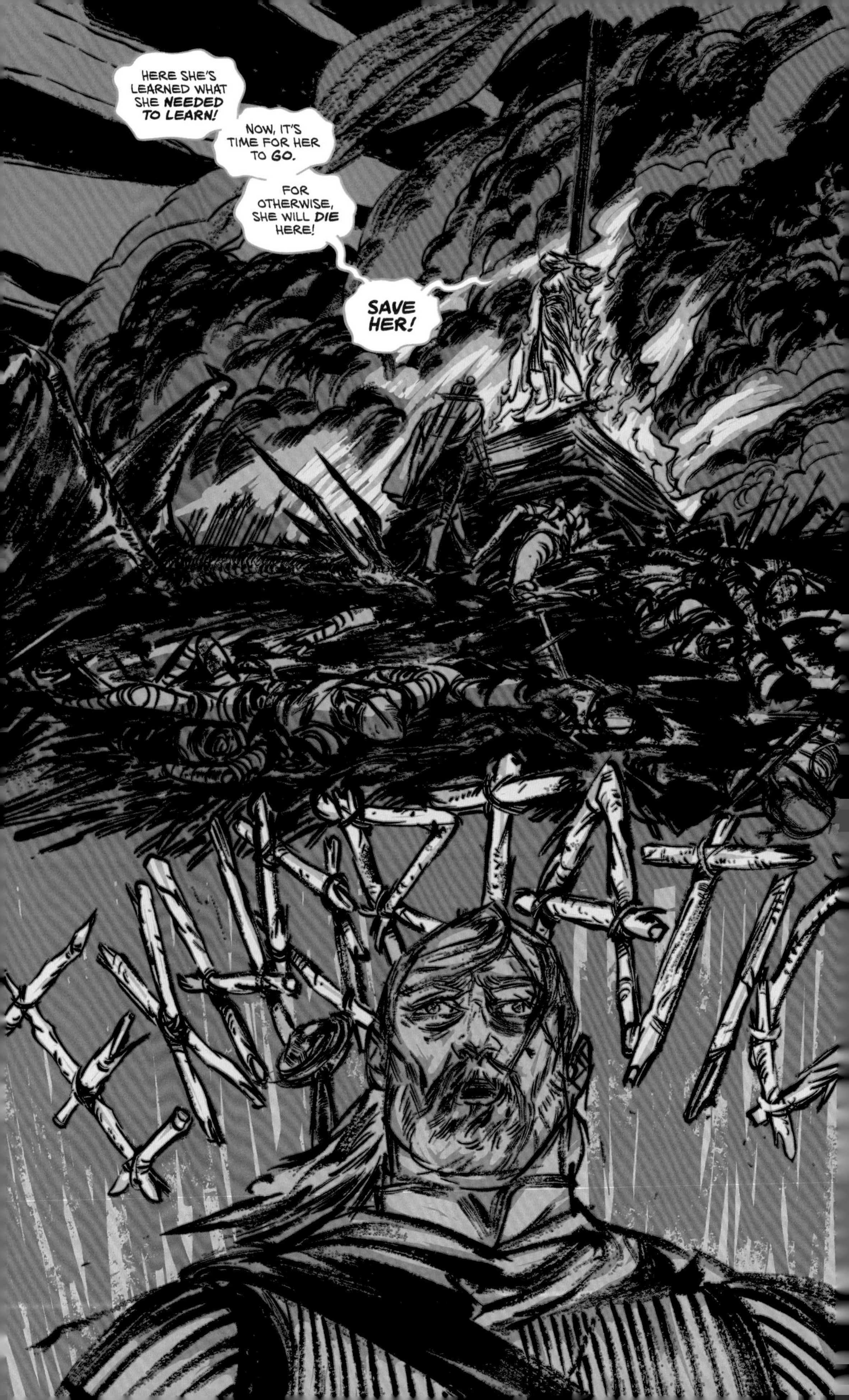
HERE SHE'S LEARNED WHAT SHE **NEEDED TO LEARN!**
NOW, IT'S TIME FOR HER TO **GO.**
FOR OTHERWISE, SHE WILL **DIE** HERE!
SAVE HER!

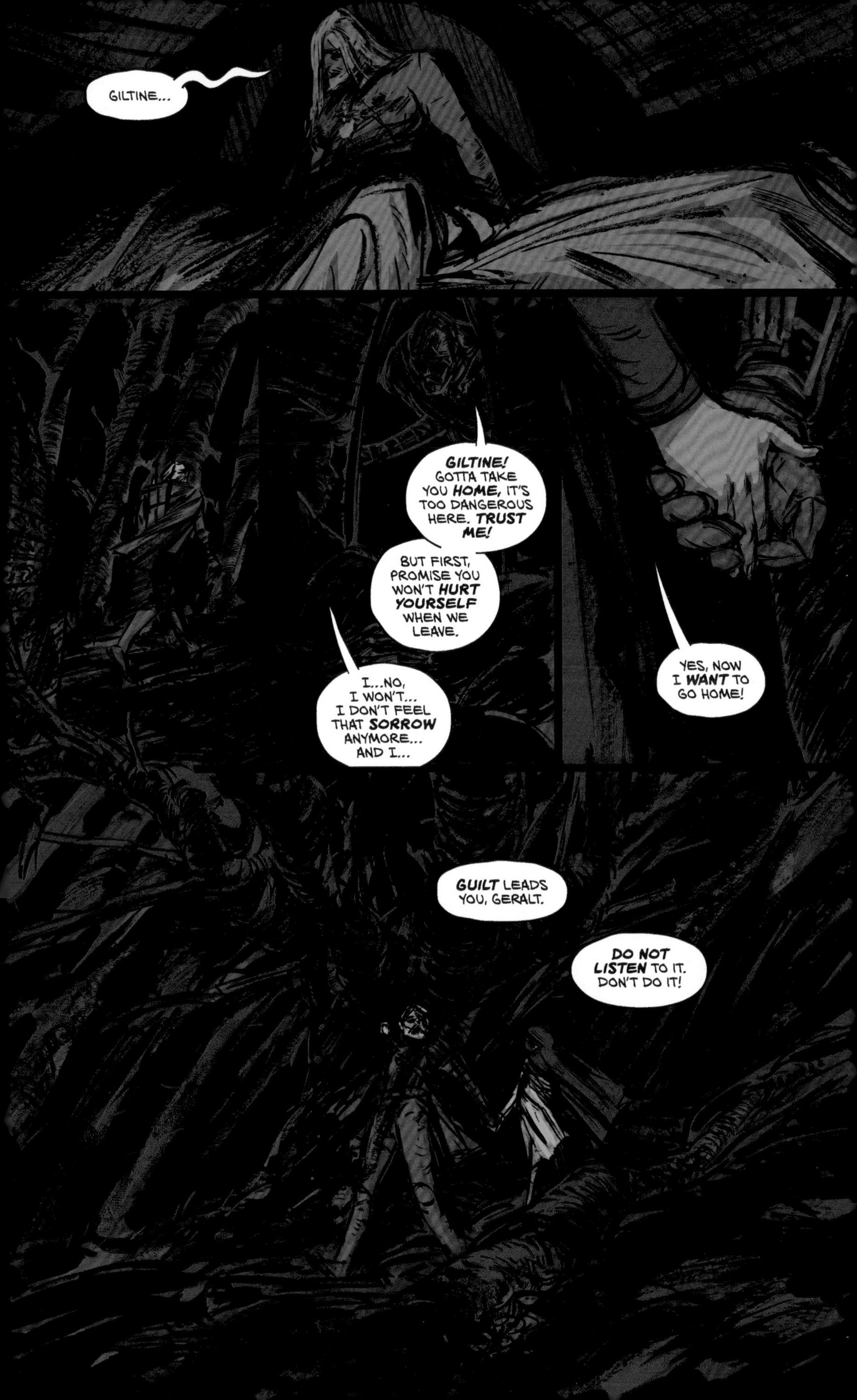
GILTINE...
GILTINE! GOTTA TAKE YOU HOME, IT'S TOO DANGEROUS HERE. TRUST ME!
BUT FIRST, PROMISE YOU WON'T HURT YOURSELF WHEN WE LEAVE.
I...NO, I WON'T... I DON'T FEEL THAT SORROW ANYMORE... AND I...
YES, NOW I WANT TO GO HOME!
GUILT LEADS YOU, GERALT.
DO NOT LISTEN TO IT. DON'T DO IT!

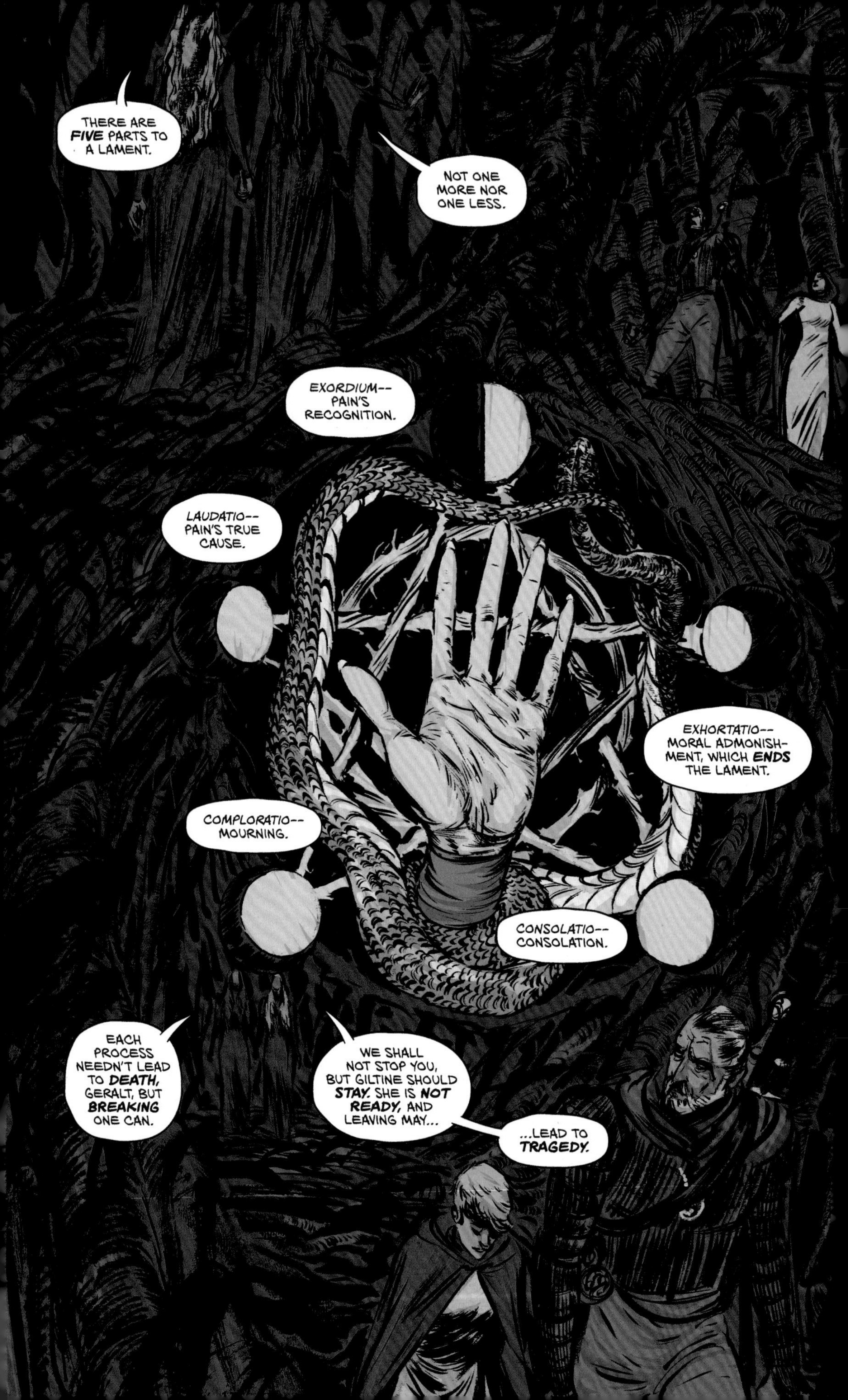
THERE ARE **FIVE** PARTS TO A LAMENT.
NOT ONE MORE NOR ONE LESS.
EXORDIUM-- PAIN'S RECOGNITION.
LAUDATIO-- PAIN'S TRUE CAUSE.
EXHORTATIO-- MORAL ADMONISHMENT, WHICH **ENDS** THE LAMENT.
COMPLORATIO-- MOURNING.
CONSOLATIO-- CONSOLATION.
EACH PROCESS NEEDN'T LEAD TO **DEATH,** GERALT, BUT **BREAKING** ONE CAN.
WE SHALL NOT STOP YOU, BUT GILTINE SHOULD **STAY.** SHE IS **NOT READY,** AND LEAVING MAY...
...LEAD TO **TRAGEDY.**

CHAPTER THREE

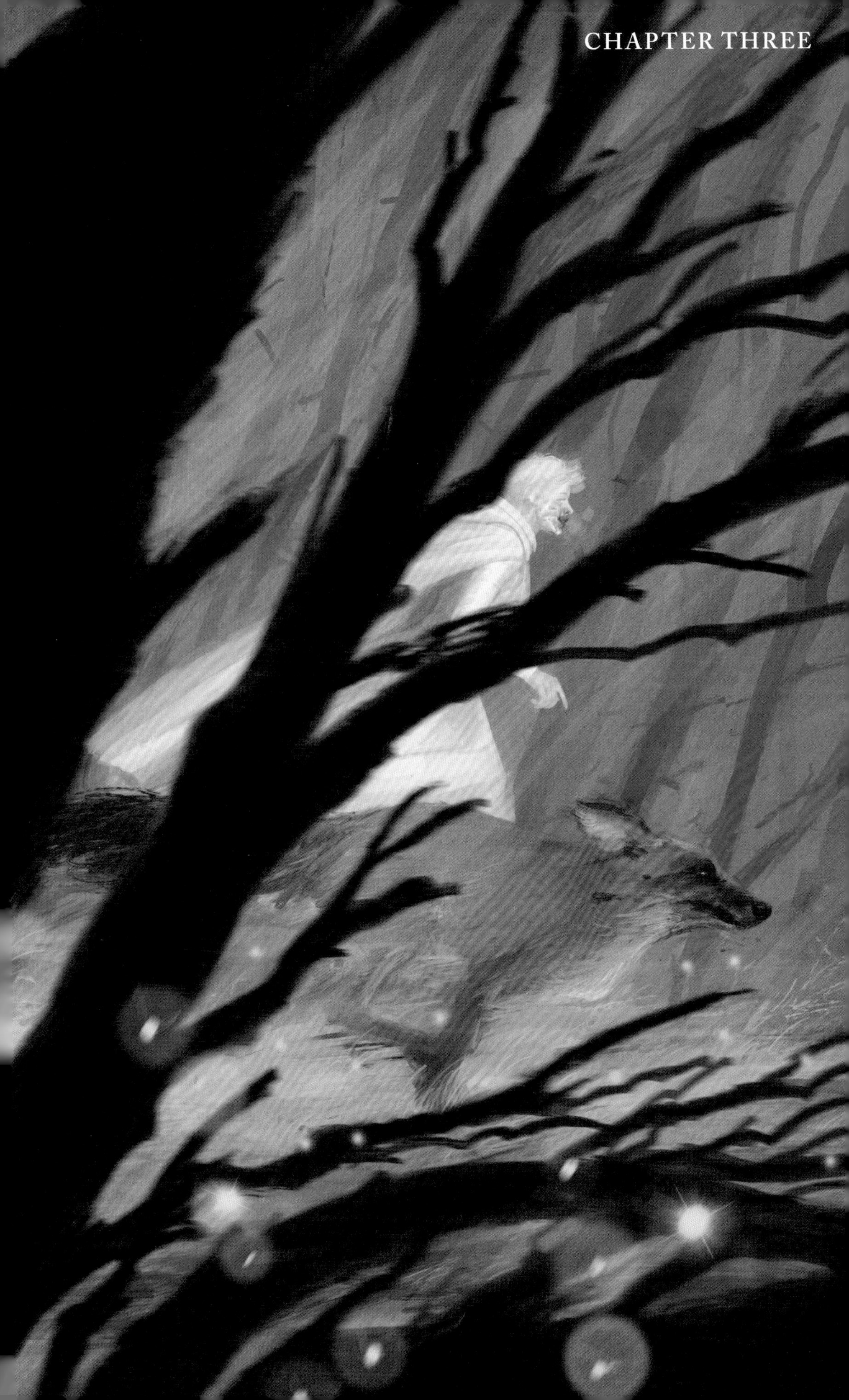

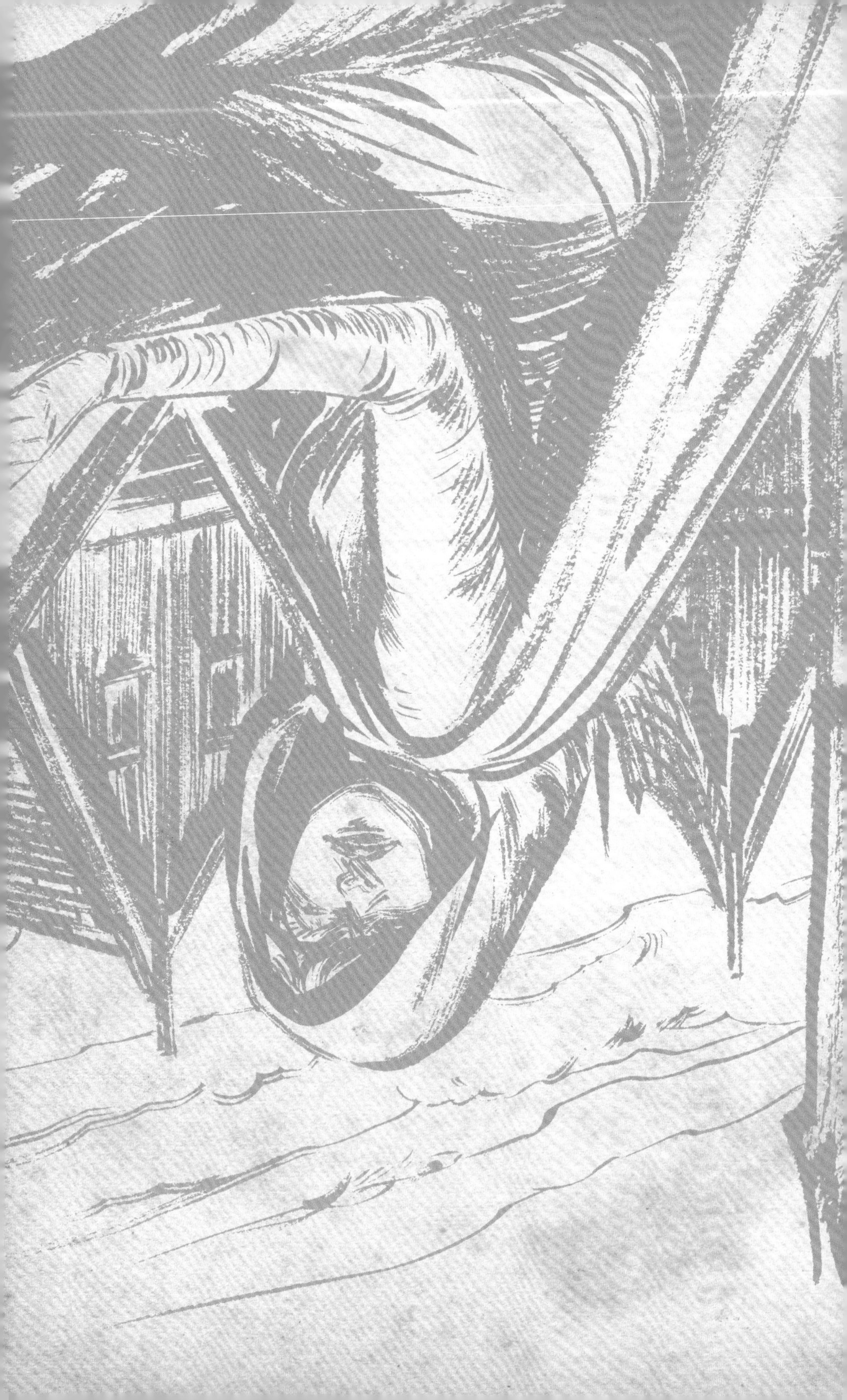

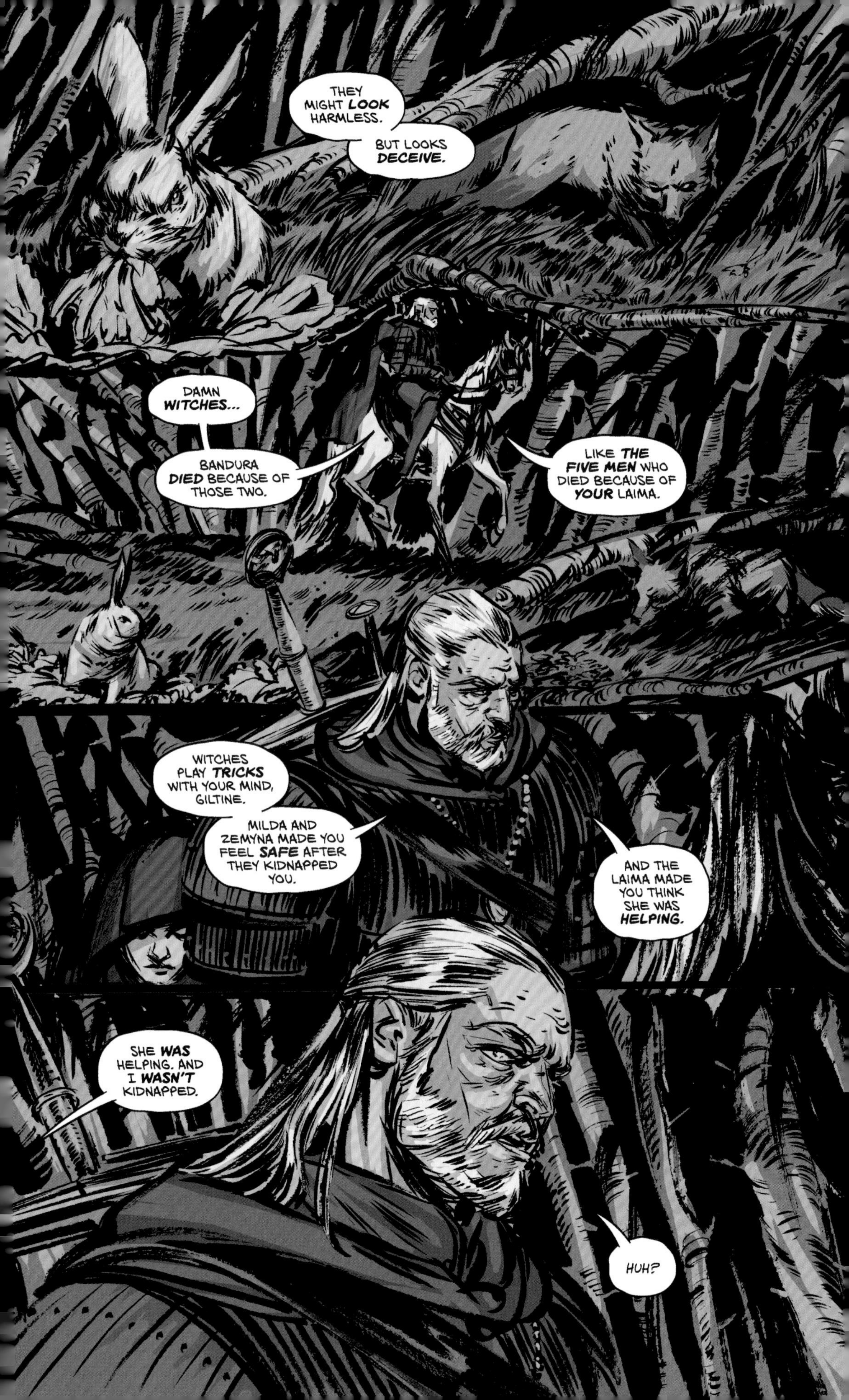
THEY MIGHT LOOK HARMLESS.
BUT LOOKS DECEIVE.
DAMN WITCHES...
BANDURA DIED BECAUSE OF THOSE TWO.
LIKE THE FIVE MEN WHO DIED BECAUSE OF YOUR LAIMA.
WITCHES PLAY TRICKS WITH YOUR MIND, GILTINE.
MILDA AND ZEMYNA MADE YOU FEEL SAFE AFTER THEY KIDNAPPED YOU.
AND THE LAIMA MADE YOU THINK SHE WAS HELPING.
SHE WAS HELPING. AND I WASN'T KIDNAPPED.
HUH?

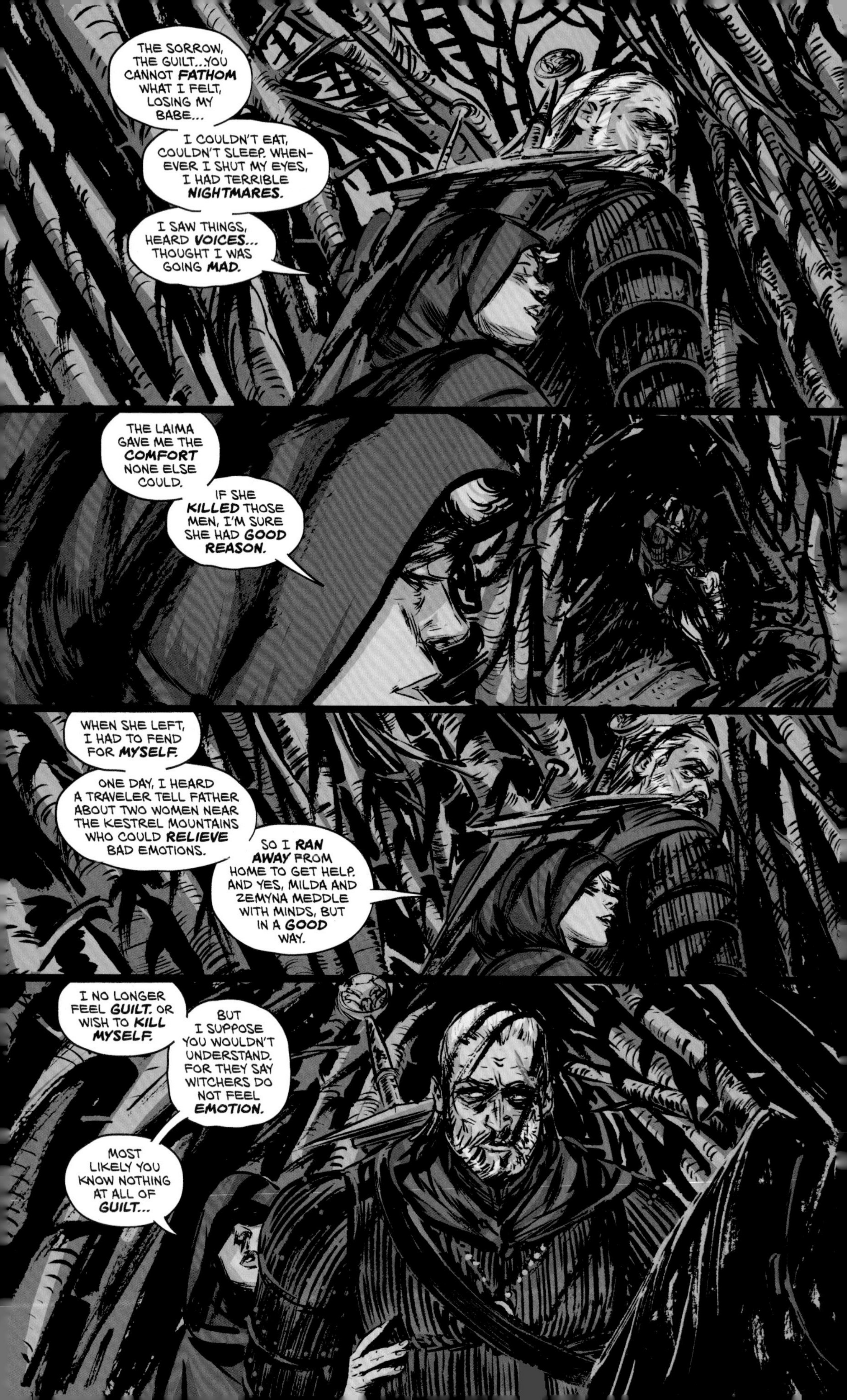

THE SORROW, THE GUILT...YOU CANNOT **FATHOM** WHAT I FELT, LOSING MY BABE...
I COULDN'T EAT, COULDN'T SLEEP. WHENEVER I SHUT MY EYES, I HAD TERRIBLE **NIGHTMARES.**
I SAW THINGS, HEARD **VOICES...** THOUGHT I WAS GOING **MAD.**
THE LAIMA GAVE ME THE **COMFORT** NONE ELSE COULD.
IF SHE **KILLED** THOSE MEN, I'M SURE SHE HAD **GOOD REASON.**
WHEN SHE LEFT, I HAD TO FEND FOR **MYSELF.**
ONE DAY, I HEARD A TRAVELER TELL FATHER ABOUT TWO WOMEN NEAR THE KESTREL MOUNTAINS WHO COULD **RELIEVE** BAD EMOTIONS.
SO I **RAN AWAY** FROM HOME TO GET HELP. AND YES, MILDA AND ZEMYNA MEDDLE WITH MINDS, BUT IN A **GOOD** WAY.
I NO LONGER FEEL **GUILT.** OR WISH TO **KILL MYSELF.**
BUT I SUPPOSE YOU WOULDN'T UNDERSTAND, FOR THEY SAY WITCHERS DO NOT FEEL **EMOTION.**
MOST LIKELY YOU KNOW NOTHING AT ALL OF **GUILT...**

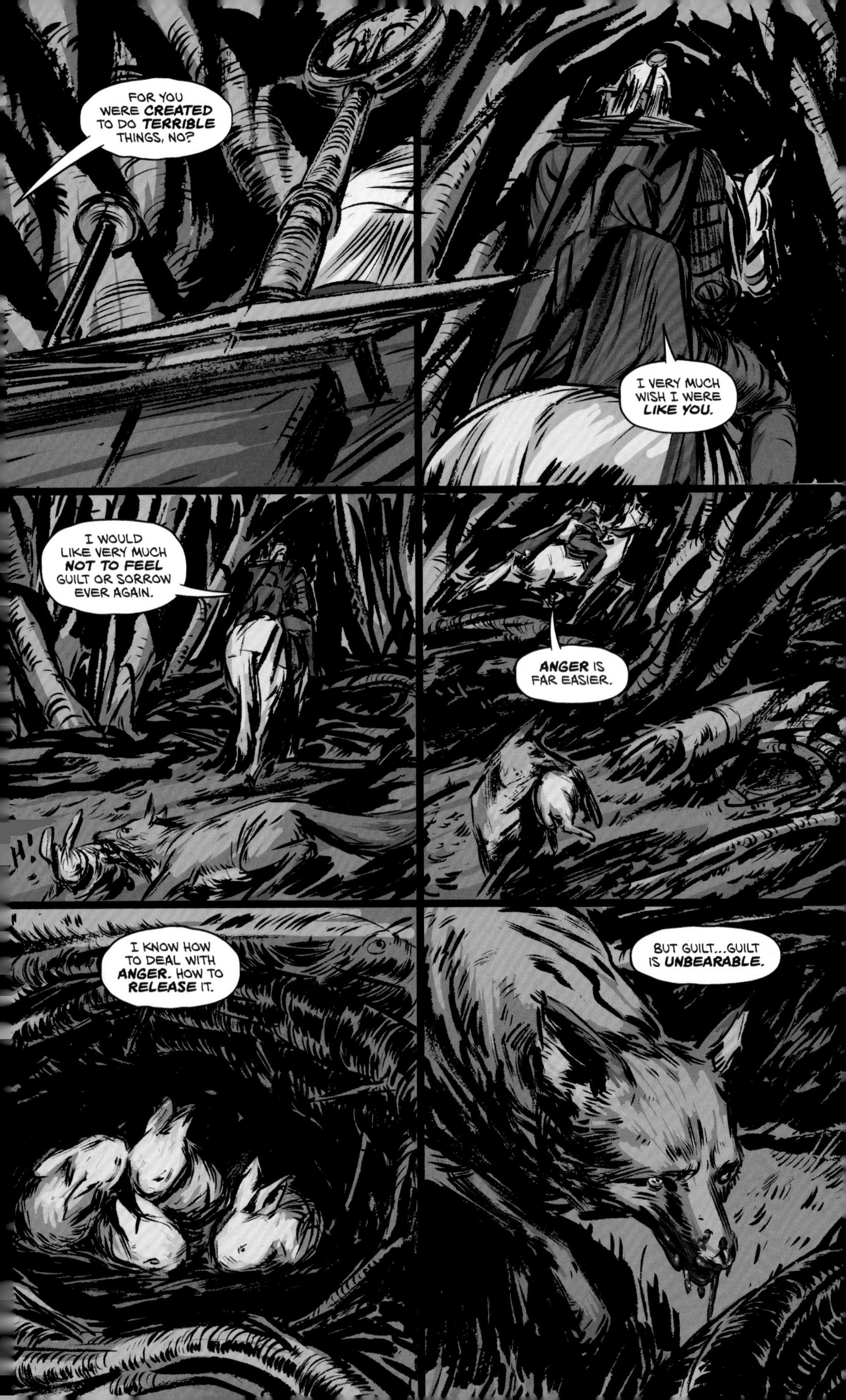
FOR YOU WERE CREATED TO DO TERRIBLE THINGS, NO?
I VERY MUCH WISH I WERE LIKE YOU.
I WOULD LIKE VERY MUCH NOT TO FEEL GUILT OR SORROW EVER AGAIN.
ANGER IS FAR EASIER.
I KNOW HOW TO DEAL WITH ANGER. HOW TO RELEASE IT.
BUT GUILT...GUILT IS UNBEARABLE.

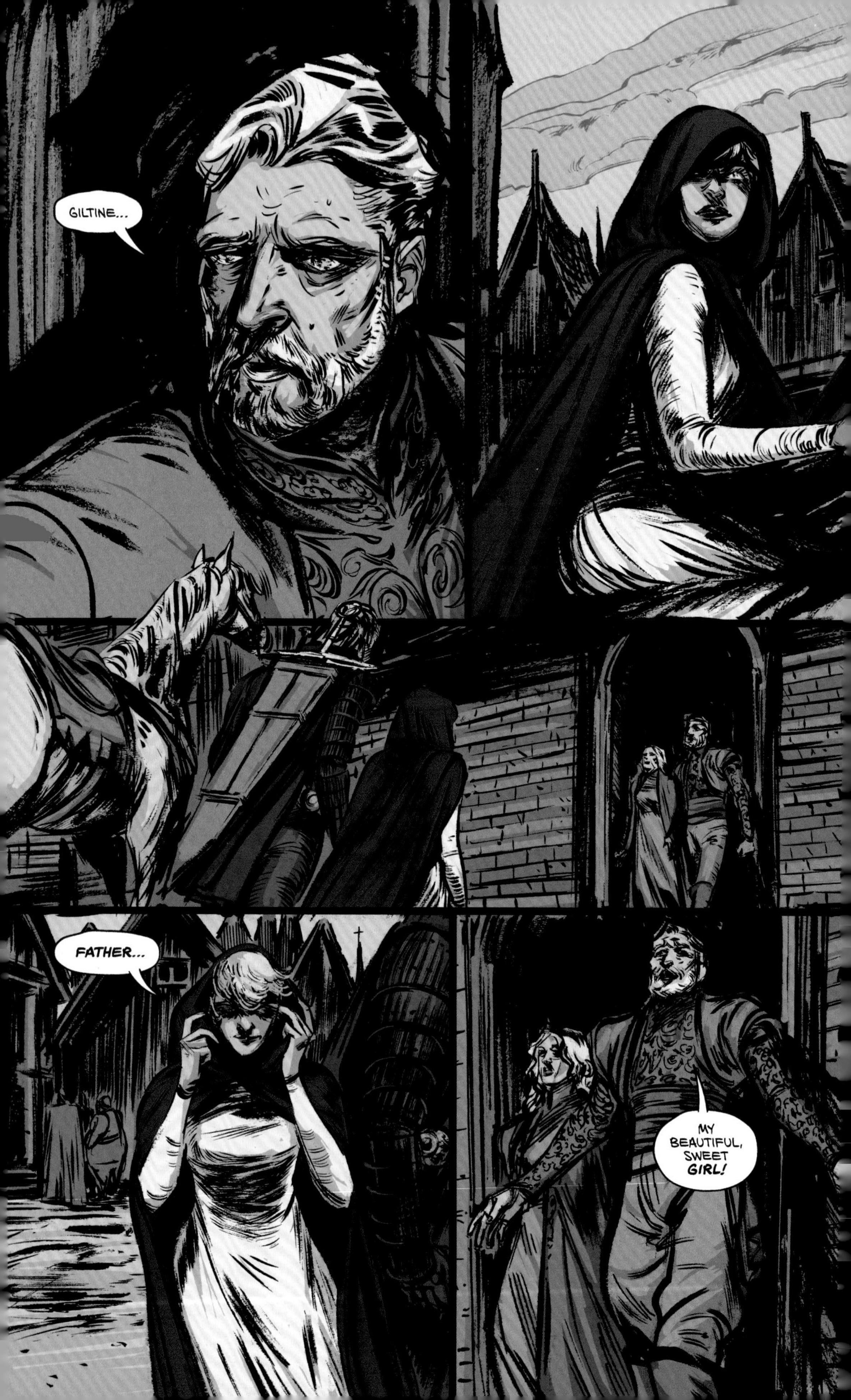
GILTINE...
FATHER...
MY BEAUTIFUL, SWEET GIRL!

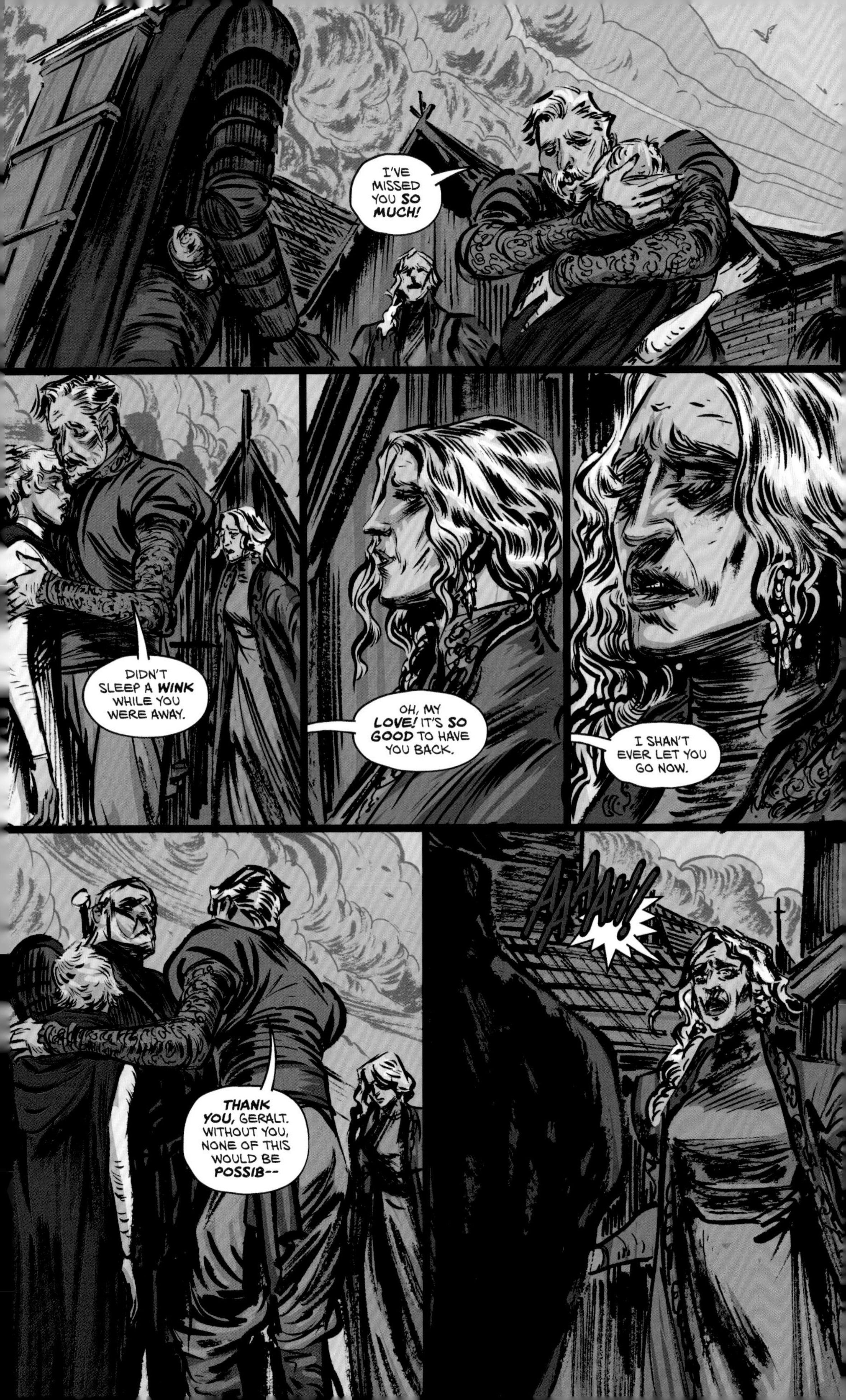
I'VE MISSED YOU **SO MUCH!**
DIDN'T SLEEP A **WINK** WHILE YOU WERE AWAY.
OH, MY **LOVE!** IT'S **SO GOOD** TO HAVE YOU BACK.
I SHAN'T EVER LET YOU GO NOW.
THANK YOU, GERALT. WITHOUT YOU, NONE OF THIS WOULD BE **POSSIB--**
AAAAH!!

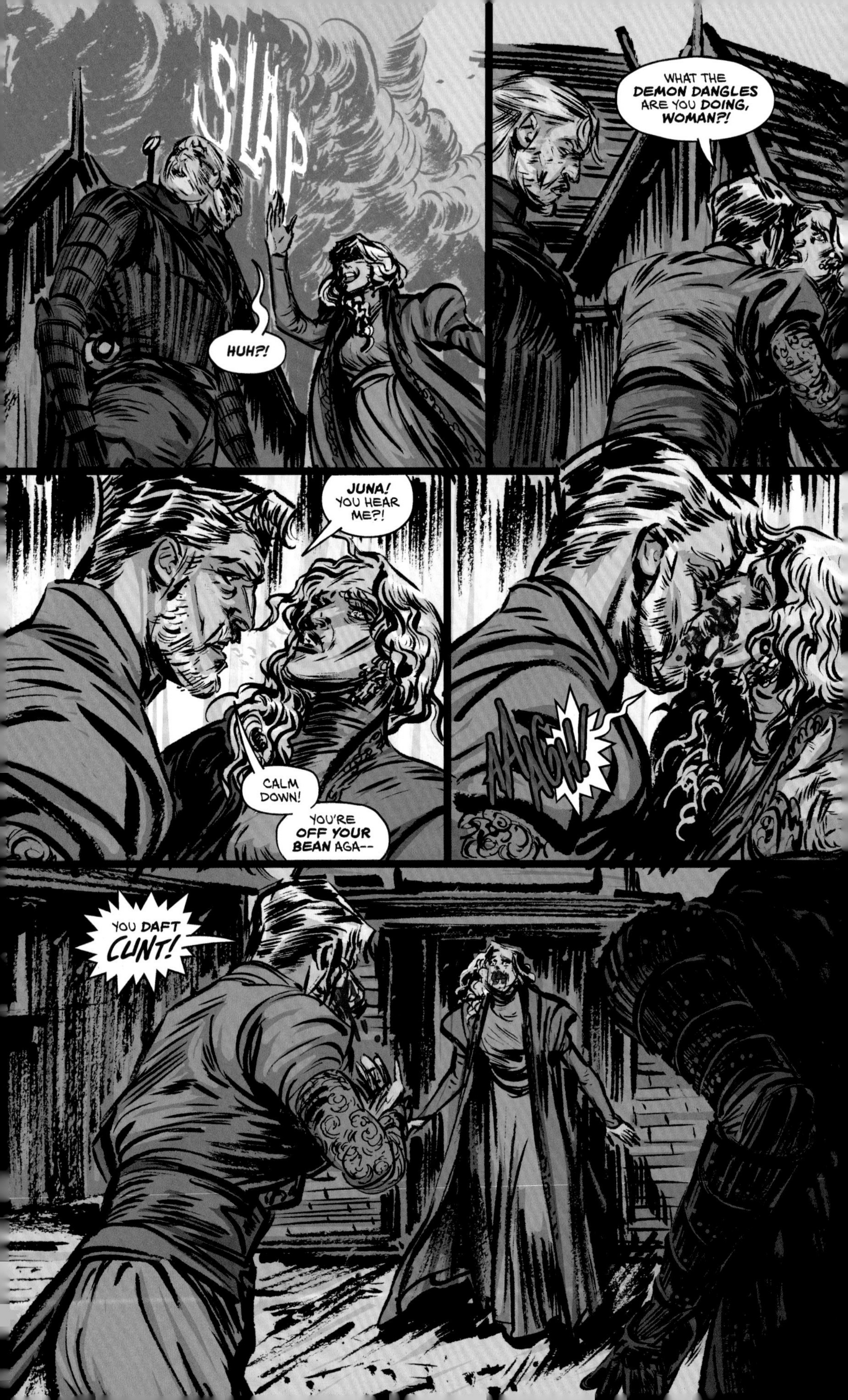
SLAP
HUH?!
WHAT THE DEMON DANGLES ARE YOU DOING, WOMAN?!
JUNA! YOU HEAR ME?!
CALM DOWN!
YOU'RE OFF YOUR BEAN AGA--
AAAGH!
YOU DAFT CUNT!

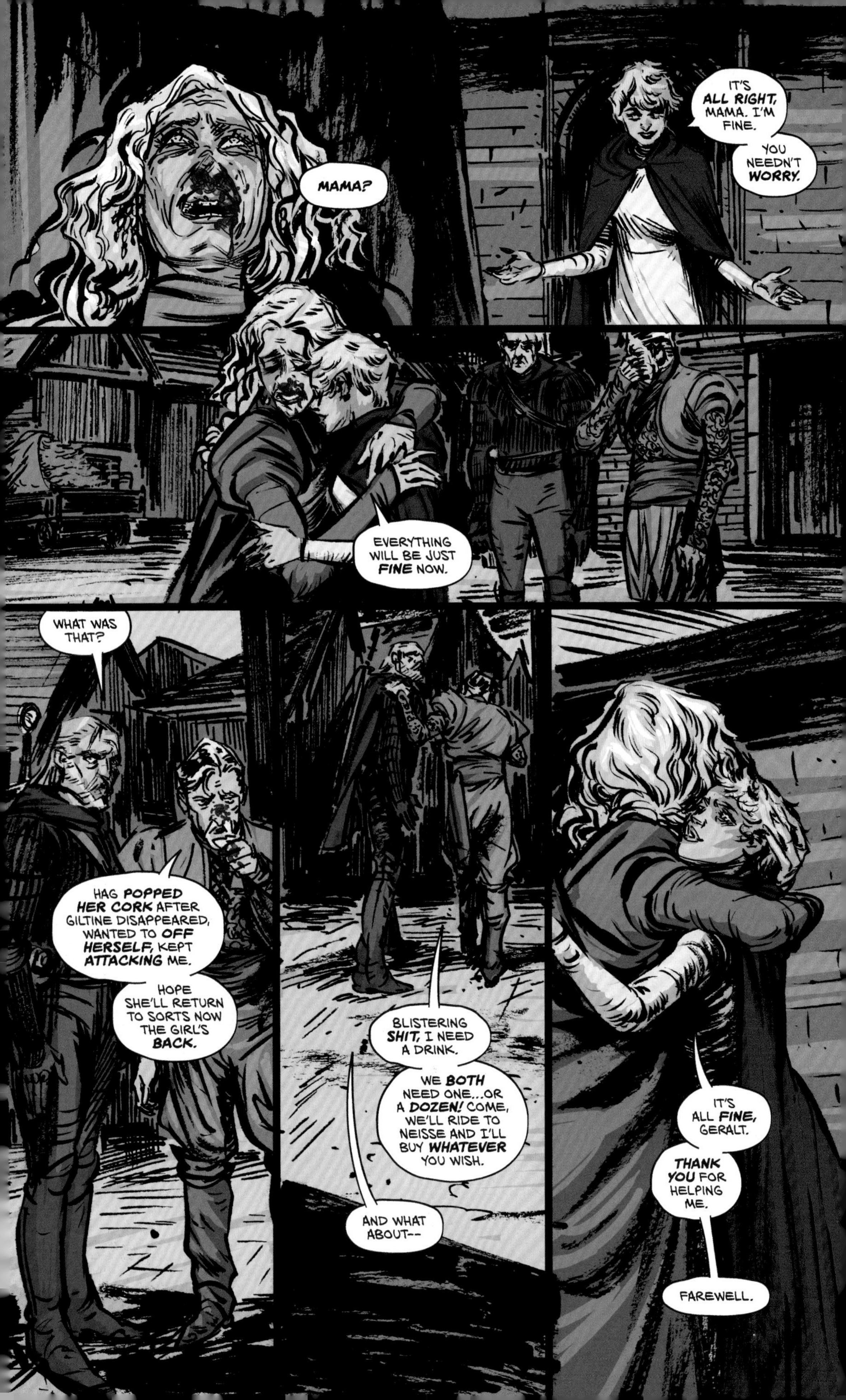
MAMA?
IT'S ALL RIGHT, MAMA. I'M FINE.
YOU NEEDN'T WORRY.
EVERYTHING WILL BE JUST FINE NOW.
WHAT WAS THAT?
HAG POPPED HER CORK AFTER GILTINE DISAPPEARED, WANTED TO OFF HERSELF, KEPT ATTACKING ME.
HOPE SHE'LL RETURN TO SORTS NOW THE GIRL'S BACK.
BLISTERING SHIT, I NEED A DRINK.
WE BOTH NEED ONE...OR A DOZEN! COME, WE'LL RIDE TO NEISSE AND I'LL BUY WHATEVER YOU WISH.
AND WHAT ABOUT--
IT'S ALL FINE, GERALT.
THANK YOU FOR HELPING ME.
FAREWELL.

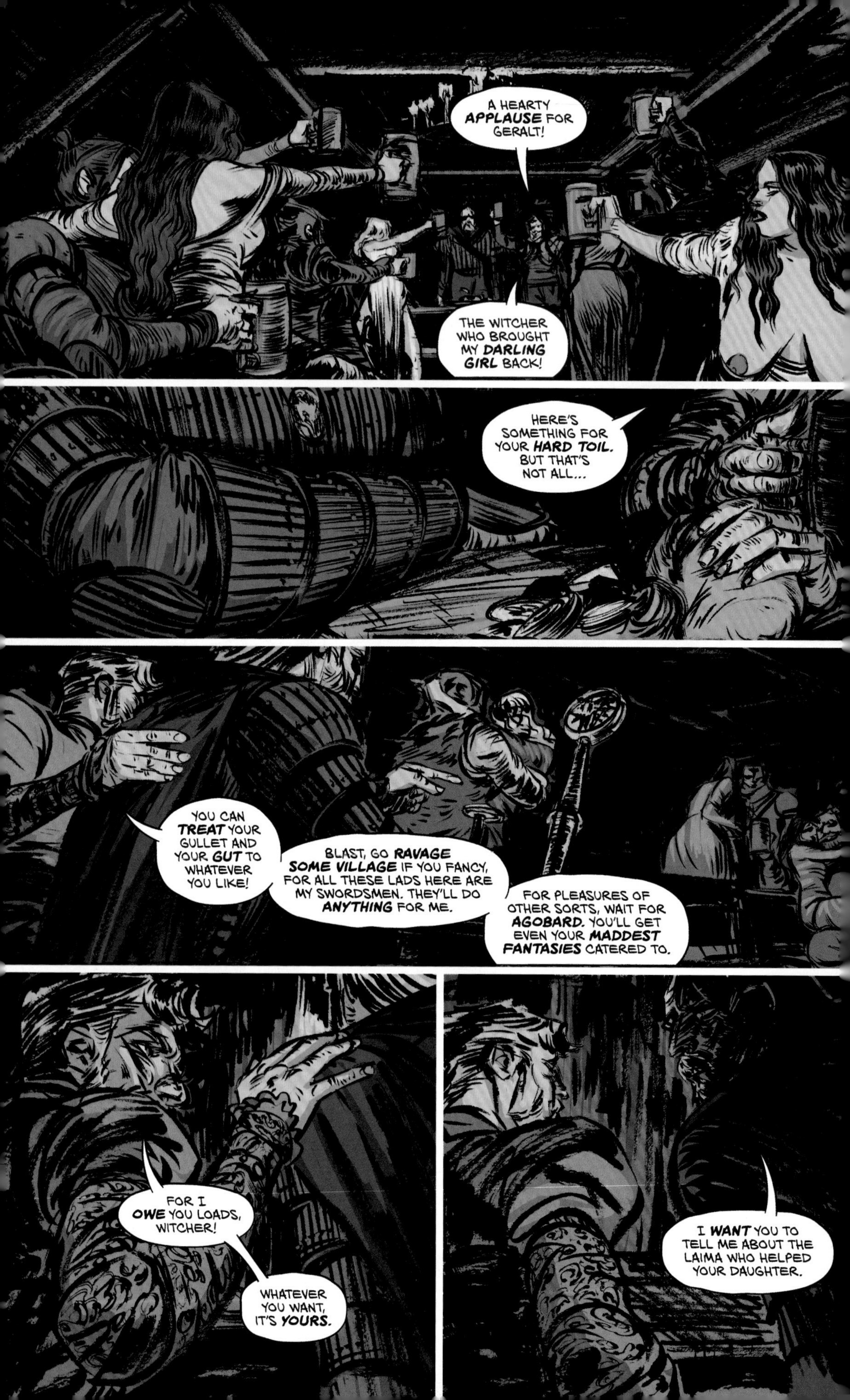
A HEARTY **APPLAUSE** FOR GERALT!
THE WITCHER WHO BROUGHT MY **DARLING GIRL** BACK!
HERE'S SOMETHING FOR YOUR **HARD TOIL.** BUT THAT'S NOT ALL...
YOU CAN **TREAT** YOUR GULLET AND YOUR **GUT** TO WHATEVER YOU LIKE!
BLAST, GO **RAVAGE SOME VILLAGE** IF YOU FANCY, FOR ALL THESE LADS HERE ARE MY SWORDSMEN. THEY'LL DO **ANYTHING** FOR ME.
FOR PLEASURES OF OTHER SORTS, WAIT FOR **AGOBARD.** YOU'LL GET EVEN YOUR **MADDEST FANTASIES** CATERED TO.
FOR I **OWE** YOU LOADS, WITCHER!
WHATEVER YOU WANT, IT'S **YOURS.**
I **WANT** YOU TO TELL ME ABOUT THE LAIMA WHO HELPED YOUR DAUGHTER.

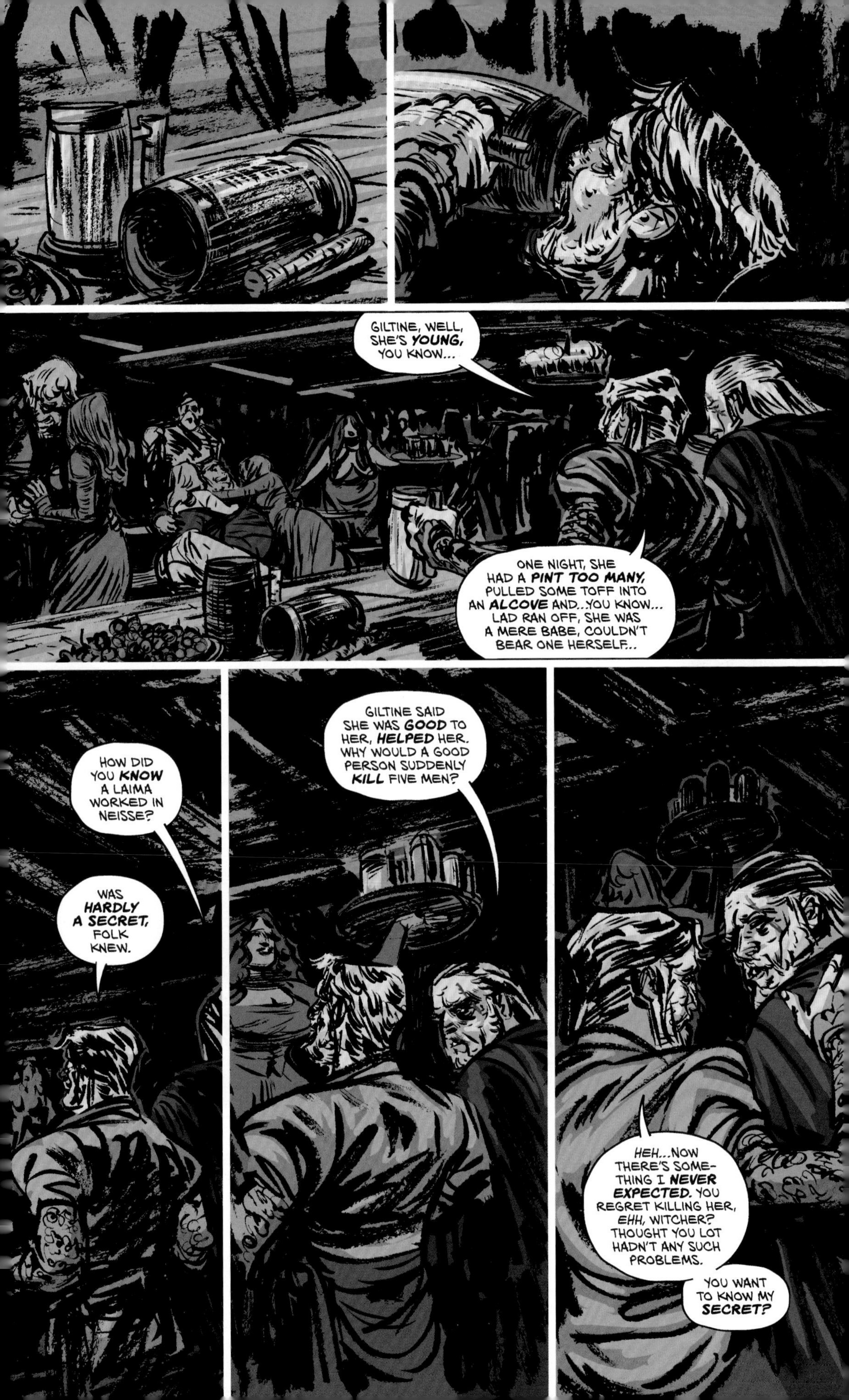
GILTINE, WELL, SHE'S **YOUNG,** YOU KNOW...
ONE NIGHT, SHE HAD A **PINT TOO MANY,** PULLED SOME TOFF INTO AN **ALCOVE** AND...YOU KNOW... LAD RAN OFF, SHE WAS A MERE BABE, COULDN'T BEAR ONE HERSELF...
HOW DID YOU **KNOW** A LAIMA WORKED IN NEISSE?
WAS **HARDLY A SECRET,** FOLK KNEW.
GILTINE SAID SHE WAS **GOOD** TO HER, **HELPED** HER. WHY WOULD A GOOD PERSON SUDDENLY **KILL** FIVE MEN?
*HEH...*NOW THERE'S SOME-THING I **NEVER EXPECTED.** YOU REGRET KILLING HER, *EHH,* WITCHER? THOUGHT YOU LOT HADN'T ANY SUCH PROBLEMS.
YOU WANT TO KNOW MY **SECRET?**

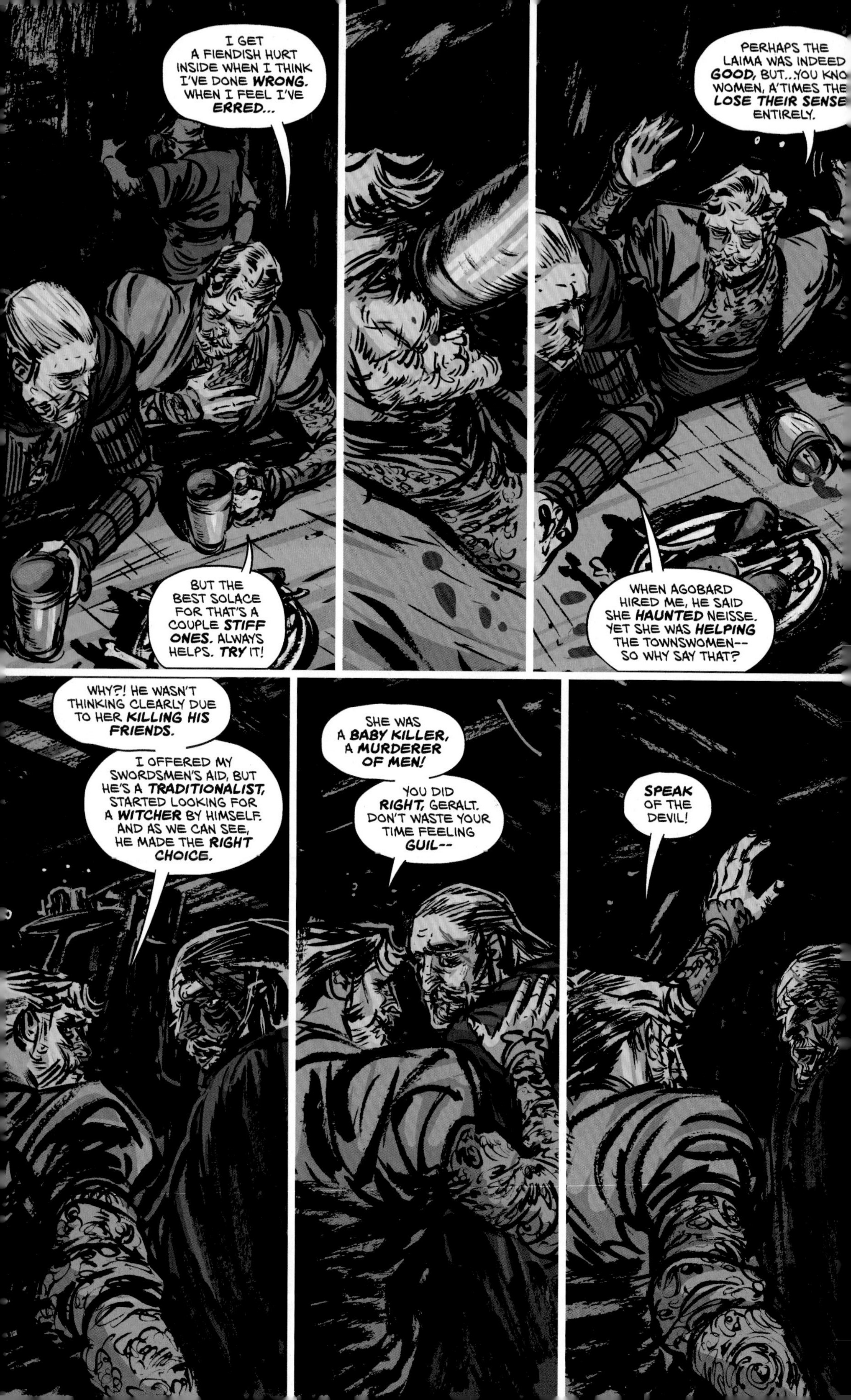
I GET A FIENDISH HURT INSIDE WHEN I THINK I'VE DONE **WRONG.** WHEN I FEEL I'VE **ERRED...**
BUT THE BEST SOLACE FOR THAT'S A COUPLE **STIFF ONES.** ALWAYS HELPS. **TRY** IT!
PERHAPS THE LAIMA WAS INDEED **GOOD,** BUT...YOU KNO WOMEN, A'TIMES THE **LOSE THEIR SENSE** ENTIRELY.
WHEN AGOBARD HIRED ME, HE SAID SHE **HAUNTED** NEISSE. YET SHE WAS **HELPING** THE TOWNSWOMEN-- SO WHY SAY THAT?
WHY?! HE WASN'T THINKING CLEARLY DUE TO HER **KILLING HIS FRIENDS.**
I OFFERED MY SWORDSMEN'S AID, BUT HE'S A **TRADITIONALIST,** STARTED LOOKING FOR A **WITCHER** BY HIMSELF. AND AS WE CAN SEE, HE MADE THE **RIGHT CHOICE.**
SHE WAS A **BABY KILLER,** A **MURDERER OF MEN!**
YOU DID **RIGHT,** GERALT. DON'T WASTE YOUR TIME FEELING **GUIL--**
SPEAK OF THE DEVIL!

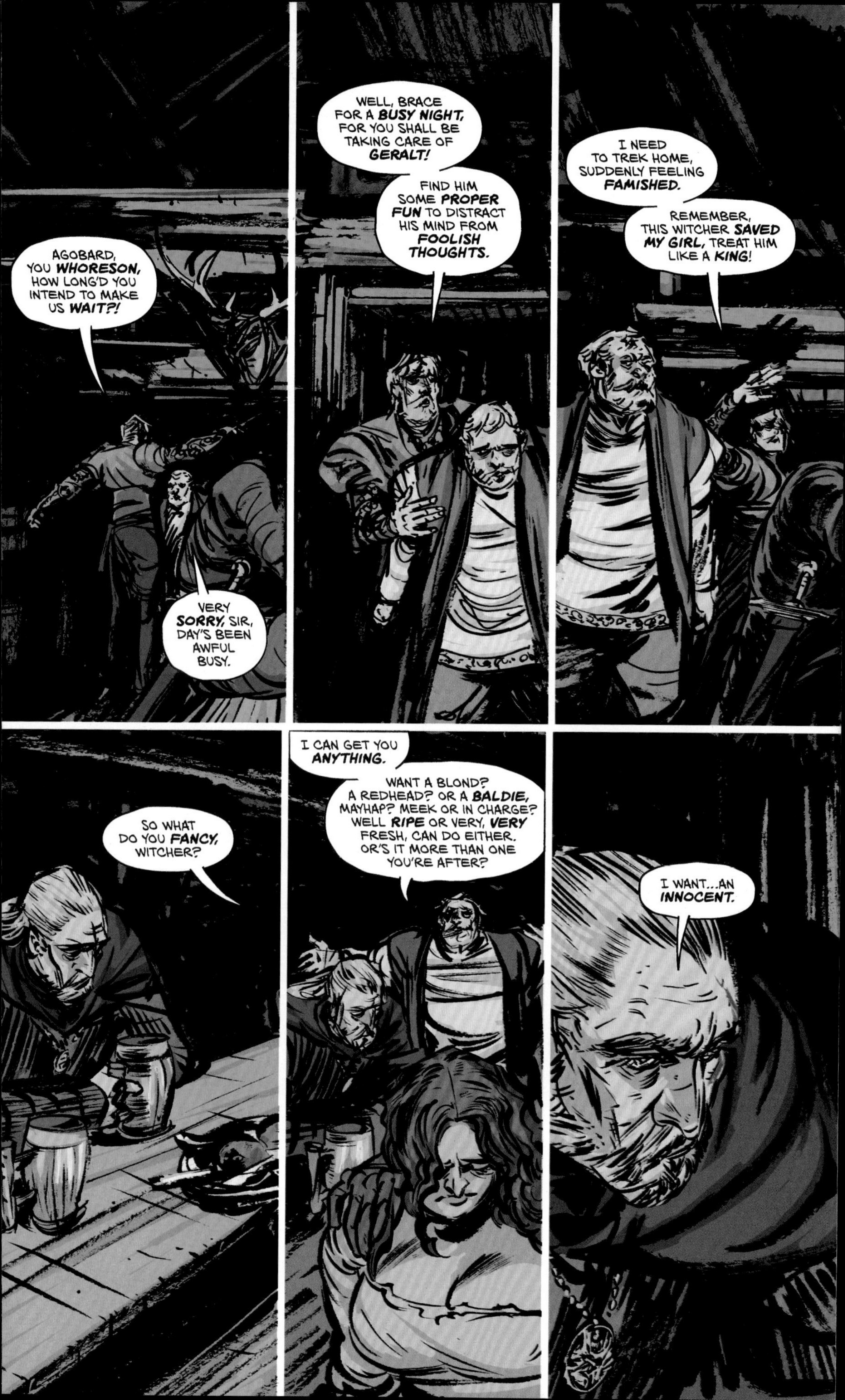
AGOBARD, YOU WHORESON, HOW LONG'D YOU INTEND TO MAKE US WAIT?!
VERY SORRY, SIR, DAY'S BEEN AWFUL BUSY.
WELL, BRACE FOR A BUSY NIGHT, FOR YOU SHALL BE TAKING CARE OF GERALT!
FIND HIM SOME PROPER FUN TO DISTRACT HIS MIND FROM FOOLISH THOUGHTS.
I NEED TO TREK HOME, SUDDENLY FEELING FAMISHED.
REMEMBER, THIS WITCHER SAVED MY GIRL, TREAT HIM LIKE A KING!
SO WHAT DO YOU FANCY, WITCHER?
I CAN GET YOU ANYTHING.
WANT A BLOND? A REDHEAD? OR A BALDIE, MAYHAP? MEEK OR IN CHARGE? WELL RIPE OR VERY, VERY FRESH, CAN DO EITHER. OR'S IT MORE THAN ONE YOU'RE AFTER?
I WANT...AN INNOCENT.

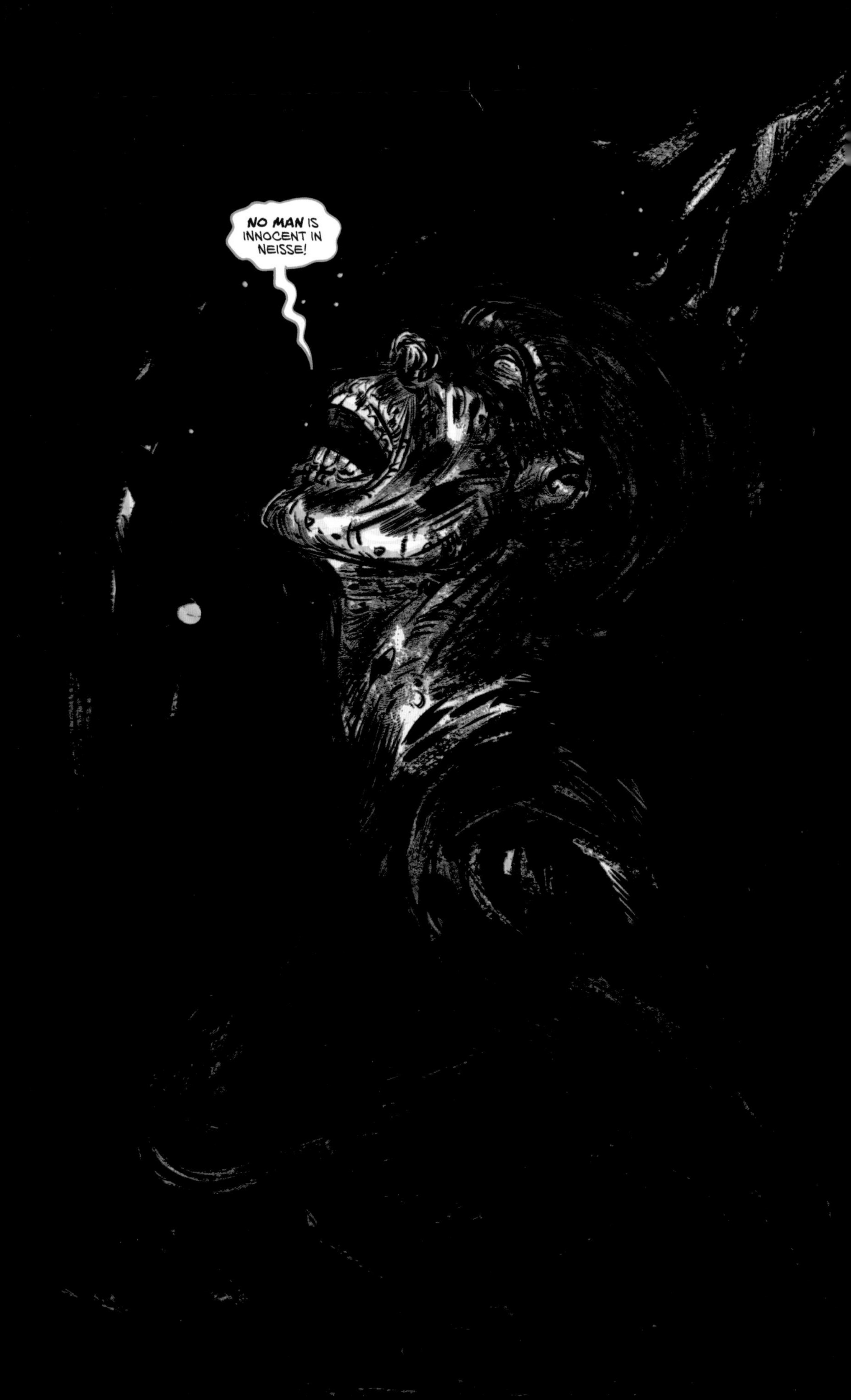
NO MAN IS INNOCENT IN NEISSE!

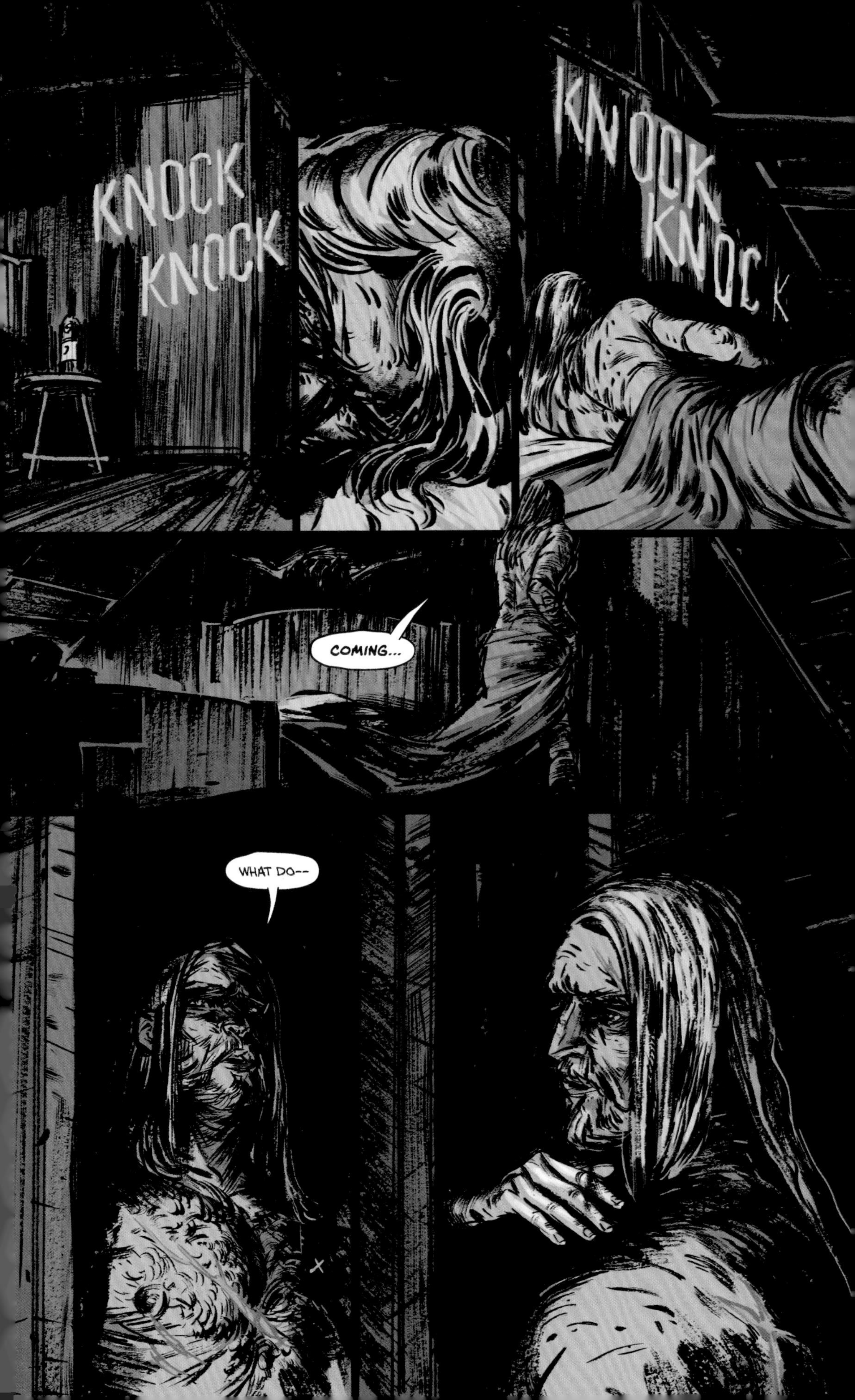
KNOCK
KNOCK
KNOCK
KNOCK
COMING...
WHAT DO--

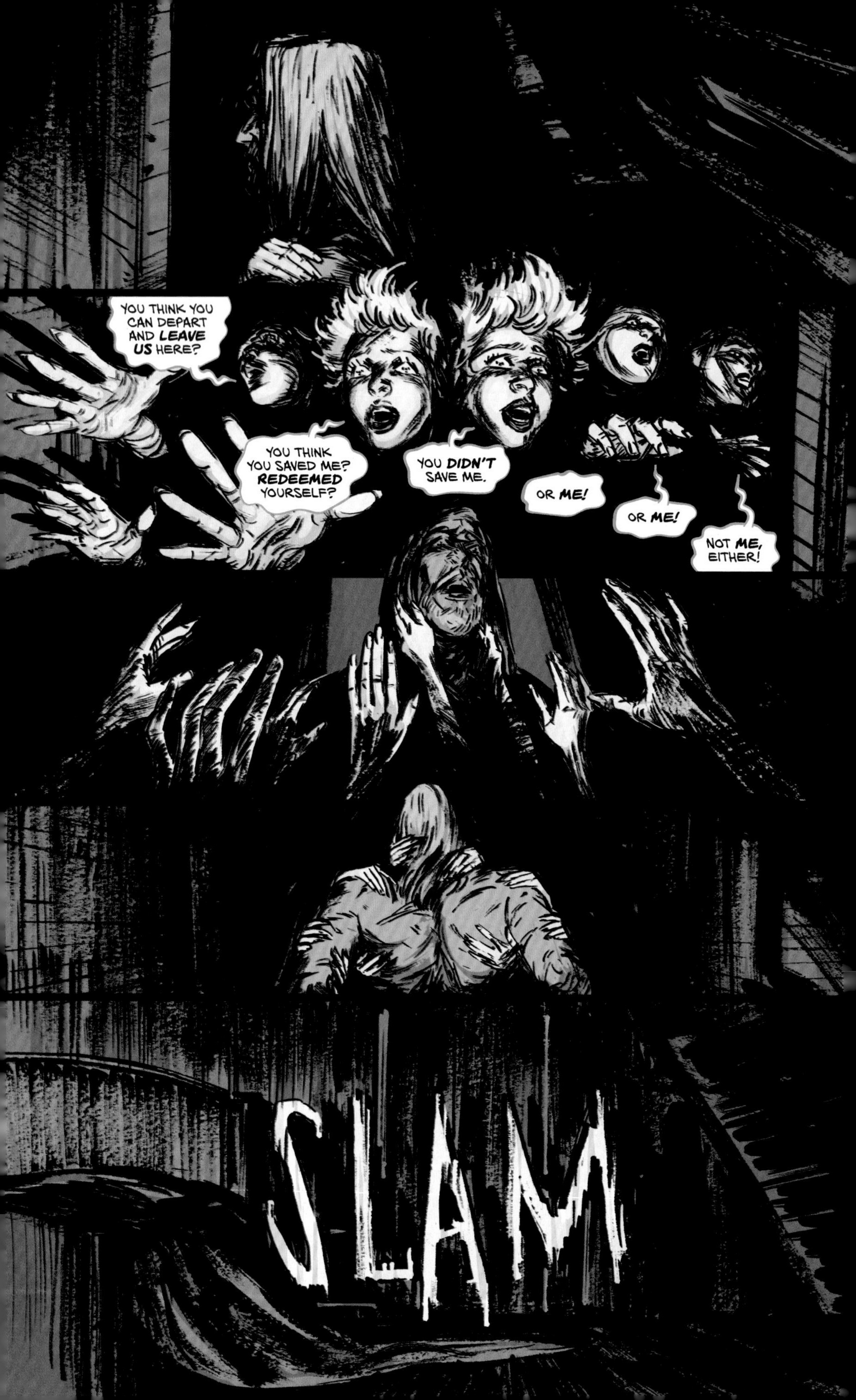
YOU THINK YOU CAN DEPART AND **LEAVE US** HERE?
YOU THINK YOU SAVED ME? **REDEEMED** YOURSELF?
YOU **DIDN'T** SAVE ME.
OR **ME!**
OR **ME!**
NOT **ME,** EITHER!
SLAM

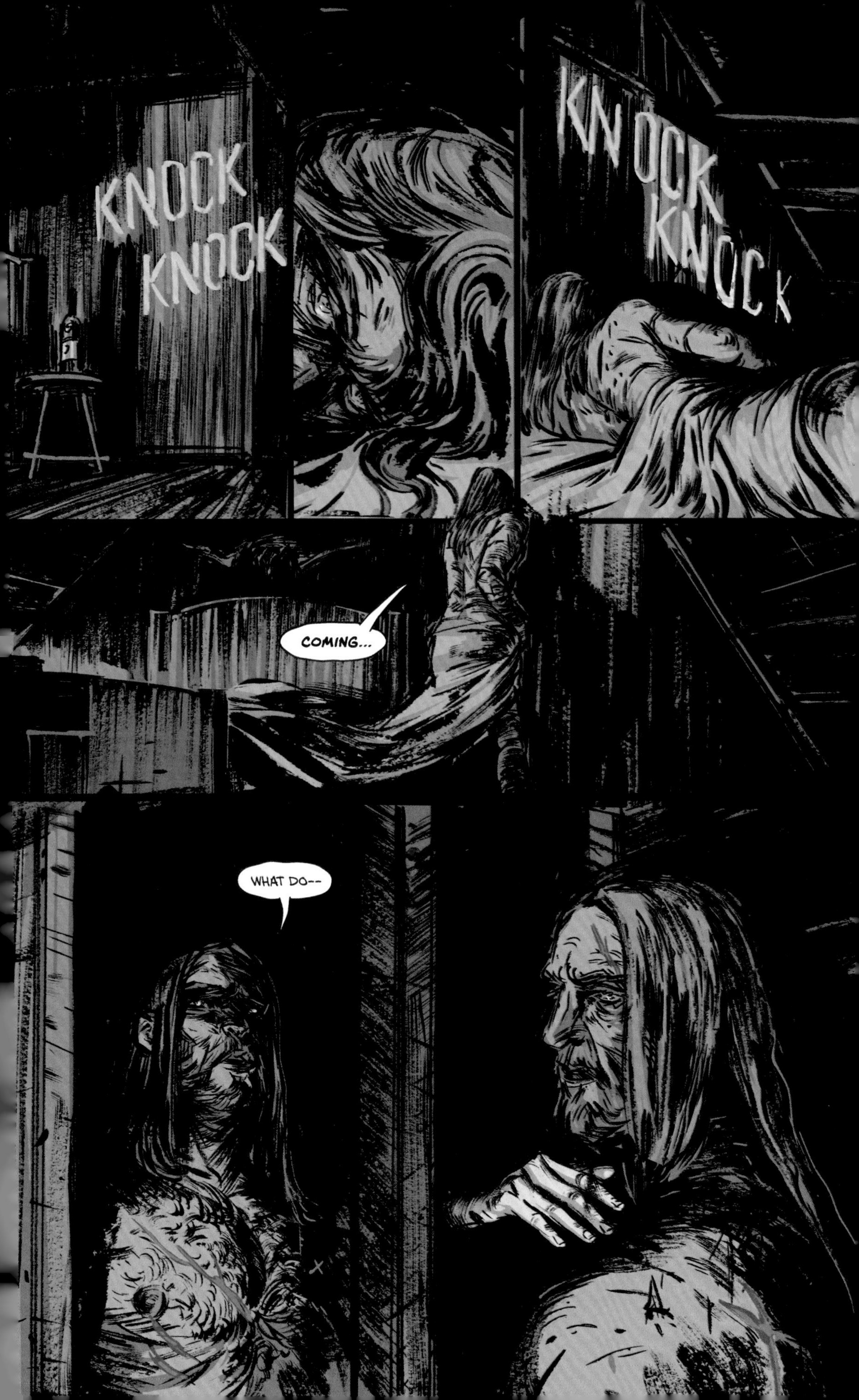
KNOCK KNOCK
KNOCK KNOCK
COMING...
WHAT DO--

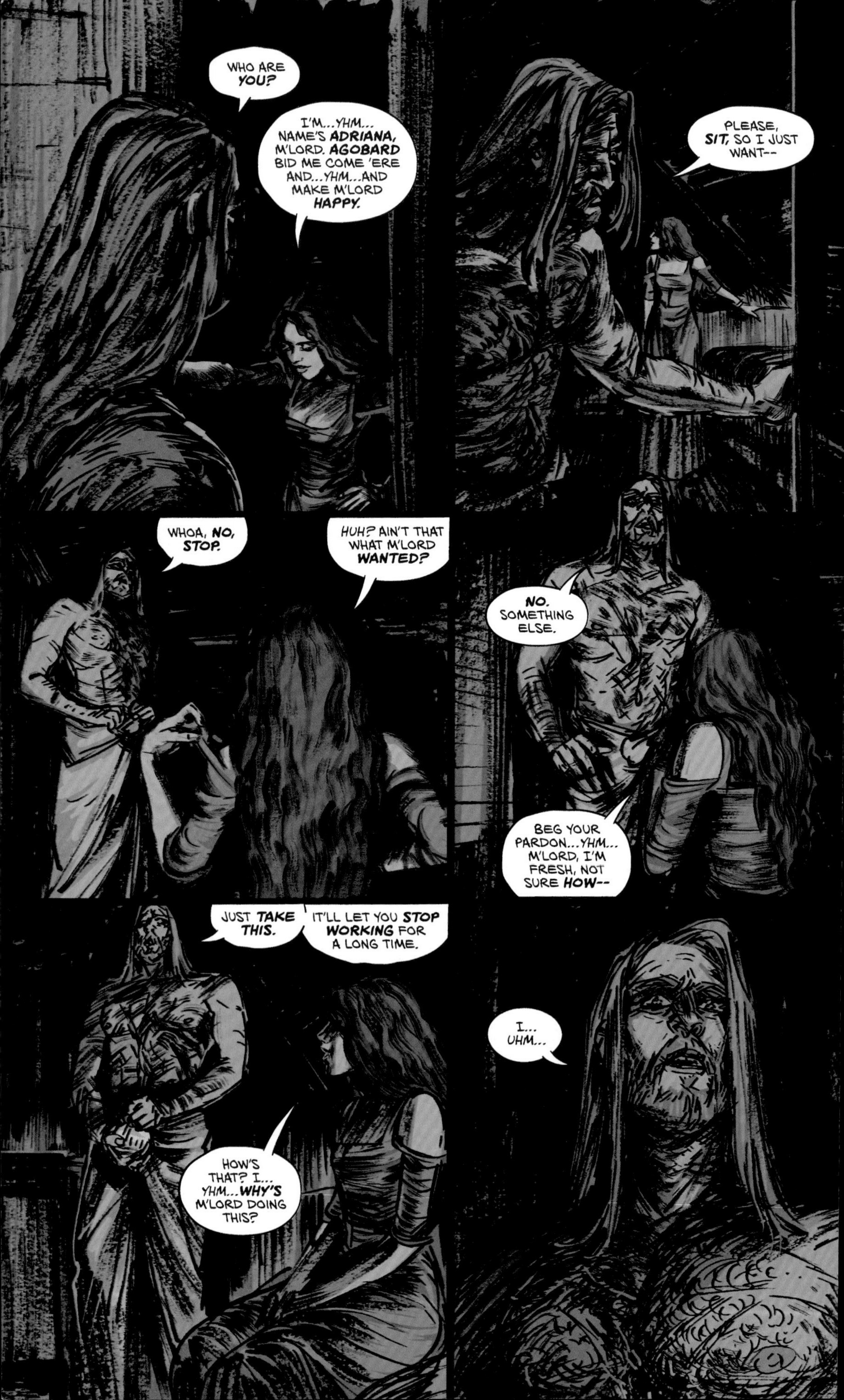
WHO ARE YOU?
I'M...YHM... NAME'S ADRIANA, M'LORD. AGOBARD BID ME COME 'ERE AND...YHM...AND MAKE M'LORD HAPPY.
PLEASE, SIT, SO I JUST WANT--
WHOA, NO, STOP.
HUH? AIN'T THAT WHAT M'LORD WANTED?
NO. SOMETHING ELSE.
BEG YOUR PARDON...YHM... M'LORD, I'M FRESH, NOT SURE HOW--
JUST TAKE THIS.
IT'LL LET YOU STOP WORKING FOR A LONG TIME.
HOW'S THAT? I... YHM...WHY'S M'LORD DOING THIS?
I... UHM...

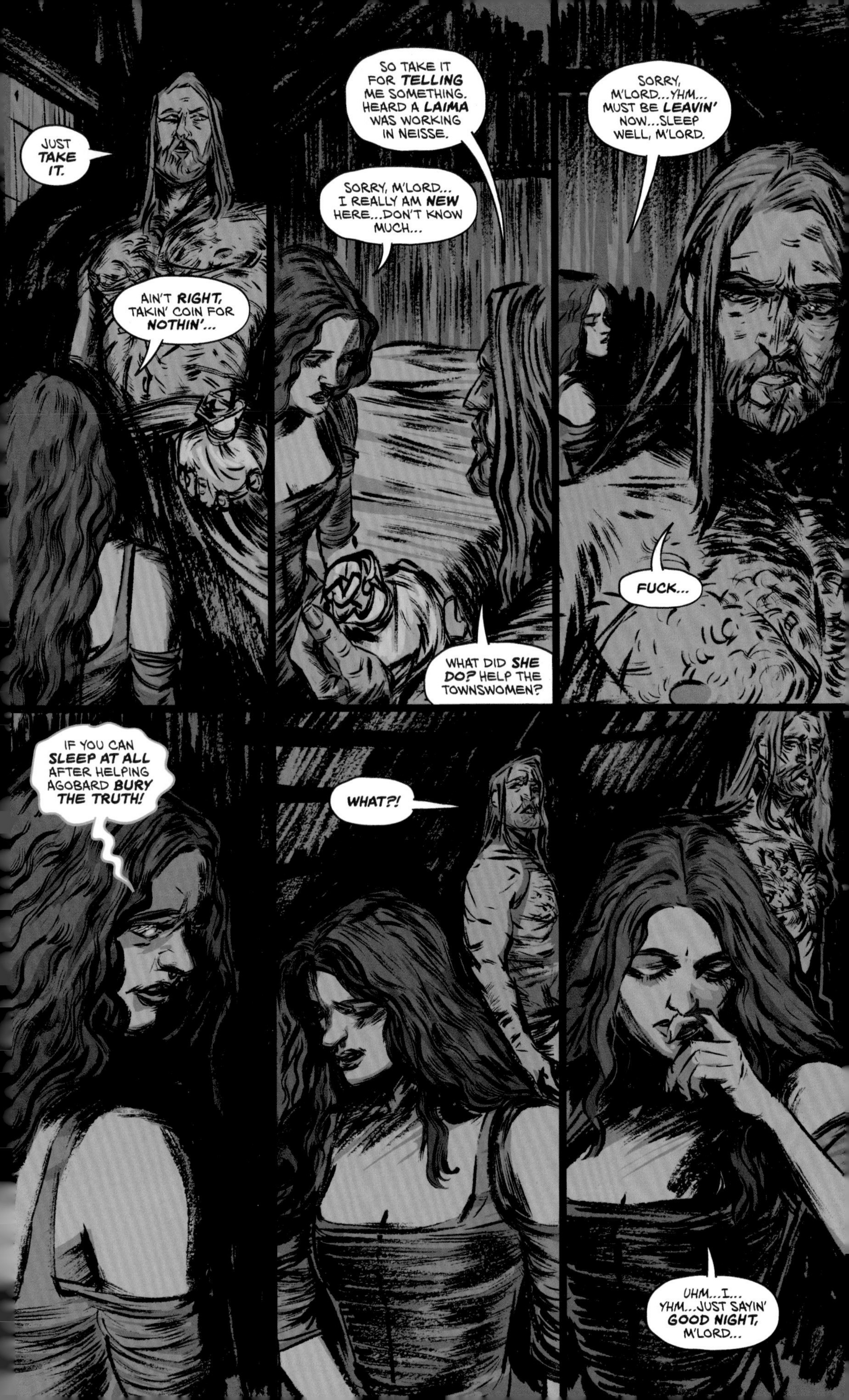
JUST TAKE IT.
AIN'T RIGHT, TAKIN' COIN FOR NOTHIN'...
SO TAKE IT FOR TELLING ME SOMETHING. HEARD A LAIMA WAS WORKING IN NEISSE.
SORRY, M'LORD... I REALLY AM NEW HERE...DON'T KNOW MUCH...
WHAT DID SHE DO? HELP THE TOWNSWOMEN?
SORRY, M'LORD...YHM... MUST BE LEAVIN' NOW...SLEEP WELL, M'LORD.
FUCK...
IF YOU CAN SLEEP AT ALL AFTER HELPING AGOBARD BURY THE TRUTH!
WHAT?!
UHM...I... YHM...JUST SAYIN' GOOD NIGHT, M'LORD...

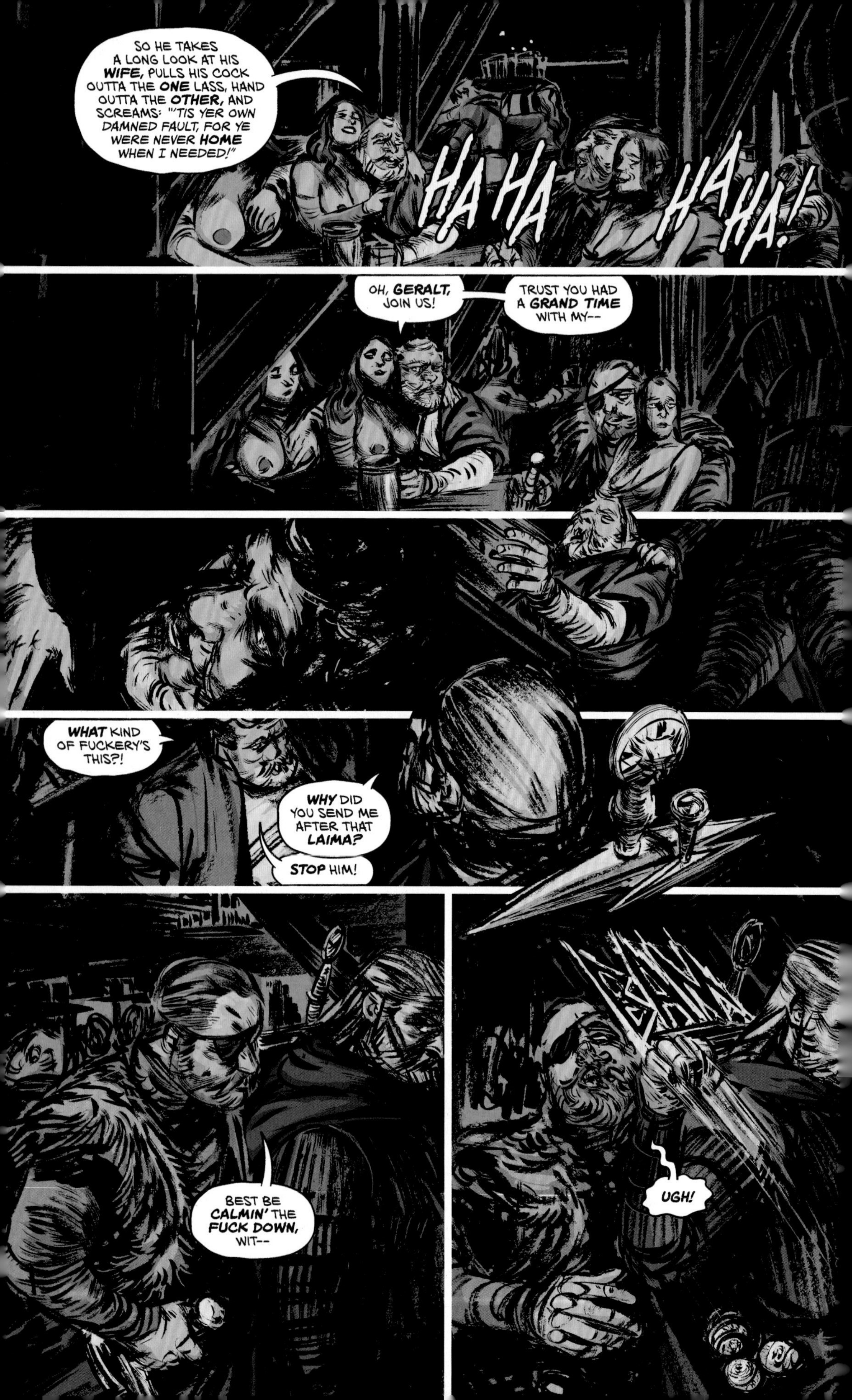
SO HE TAKES A LONG LOOK AT HIS **WIFE,** PULLS HIS COCK OUTTA THE **ONE** LASS, HAND OUTTA THE **OTHER,** AND SCREAMS: "'TIS YER OWN DAMNED FAULT, FOR YE WERE NEVER **HOME** WHEN I NEEDED!"
HA HA
HA HA!
OH, **GERALT,** JOIN US!
TRUST YOU HAD A **GRAND TIME** WITH MY--
WHAT KIND OF FUCKERY'S THIS?!
WHY DID YOU SEND ME AFTER THAT **LAIMA?**
STOP HIM!
BEST BE **CALMIN'** THE **FUCK DOWN,** WIT--
UGH!

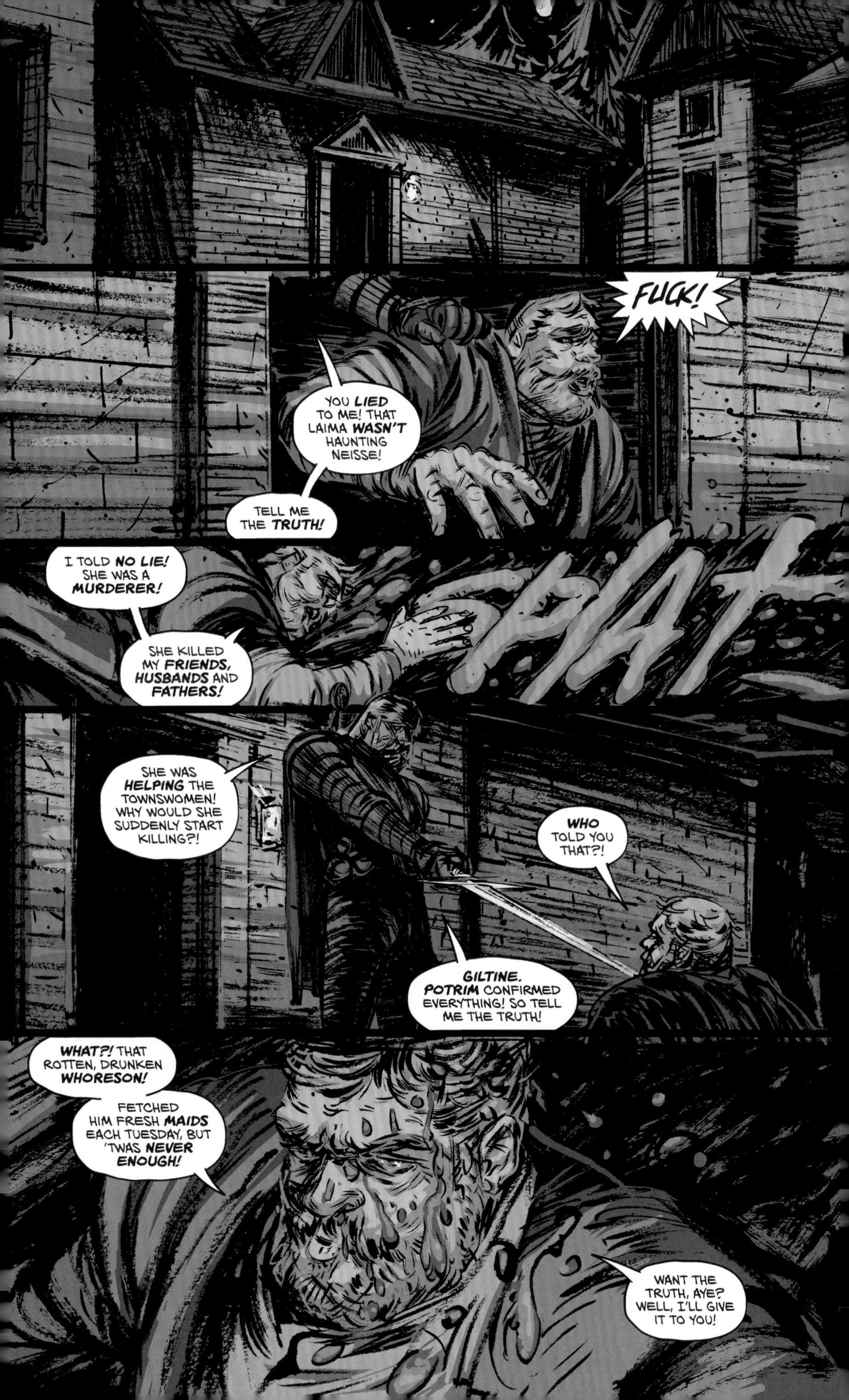

FUCK!
YOU LIED TO ME! THAT LAIMA WASN'T HAUNTING NEISSE!
TELL ME THE TRUTH!
I TOLD NO LIE! SHE WAS A MURDERER!
SHE KILLED MY FRIENDS, HUSBANDS AND FATHERS!
SHE WAS HELPING THE TOWNSWOMEN! WHY WOULD SHE SUDDENLY START KILLING?!
WHO TOLD YOU THAT?!
GILTINE. POTRIM CONFIRMED EVERYTHING! SO TELL ME THE TRUTH!
WHAT?! THAT ROTTEN, DRUNKEN WHORESON!
FETCHED HIM FRESH MAIDS EACH TUESDAY, BUT 'TWAS NEVER ENOUGH!
WANT THE TRUTH, AYE? WELL, I'LL GIVE IT TO YOU!

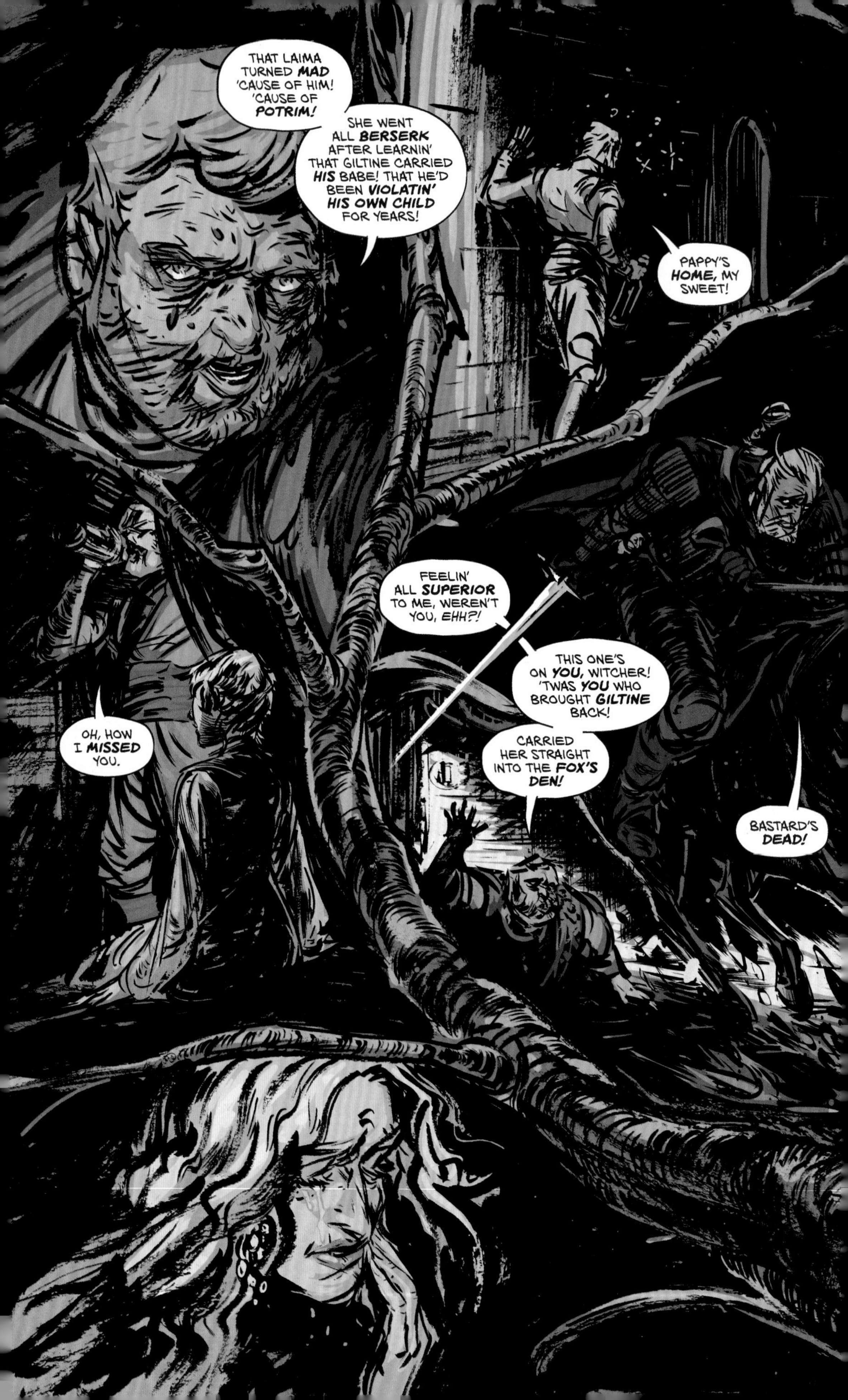
THAT LAIMA TURNED MAD 'CAUSE OF HIM! 'CAUSE OF POTRIM!
SHE WENT ALL BERSERK AFTER LEARNIN' THAT GILTINE CARRIED HIS BABE! THAT HE'D BEEN VIOLATIN' HIS OWN CHILD FOR YEARS!
PAPPY'S HOME, MY SWEET!
OH, HOW I MISSED YOU.
FEELIN' ALL SUPERIOR TO ME, WEREN'T YOU, EHH?!
THIS ONE'S ON YOU, WITCHER! 'TWAS YOU WHO BROUGHT GILTINE BACK!
CARRIED HER STRAIGHT INTO THE FOX'S DEN!
BASTARD'S DEAD!

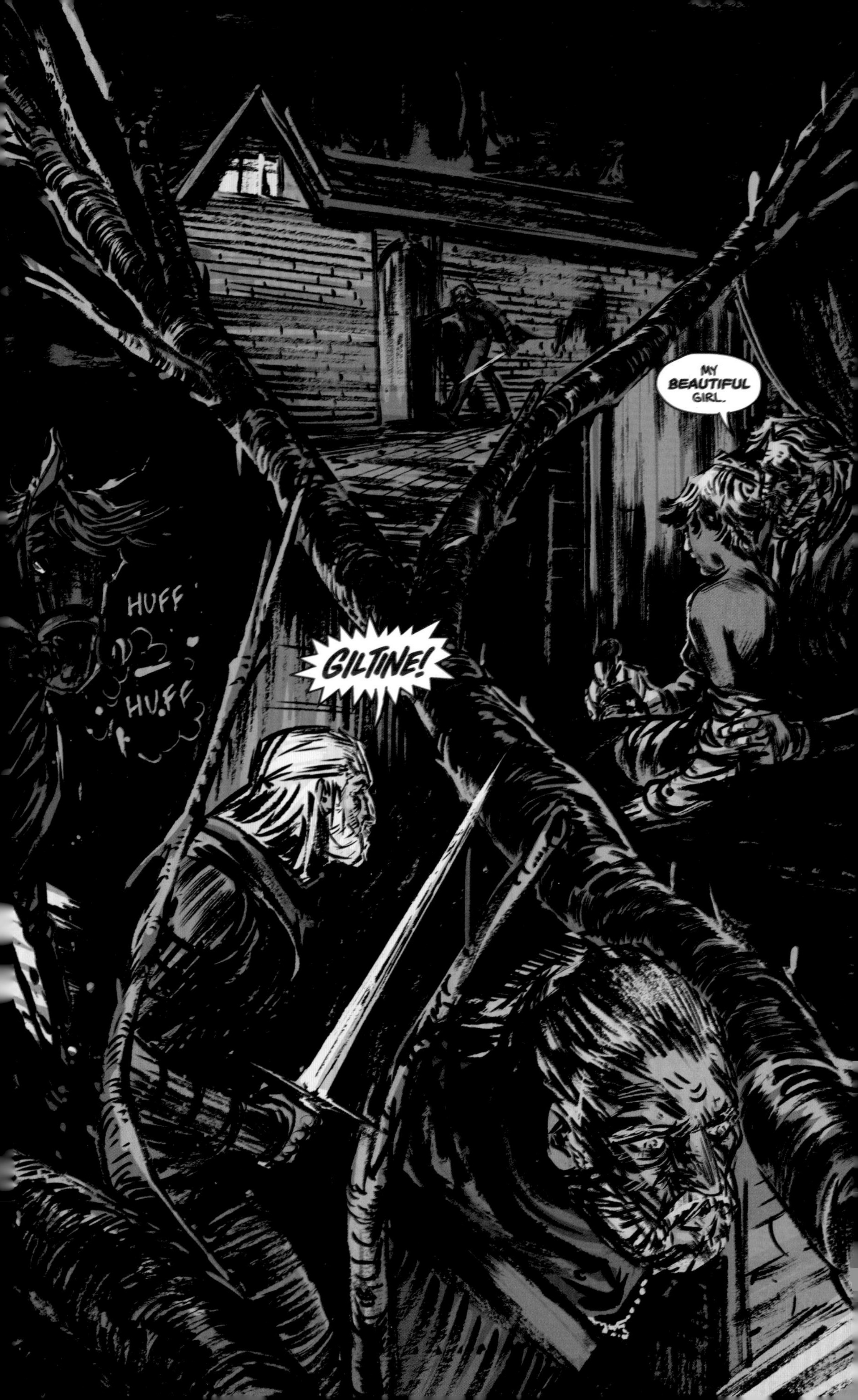
MY BEAUTIFUL GIRL.
HUFF
HUFF
GILTINE!

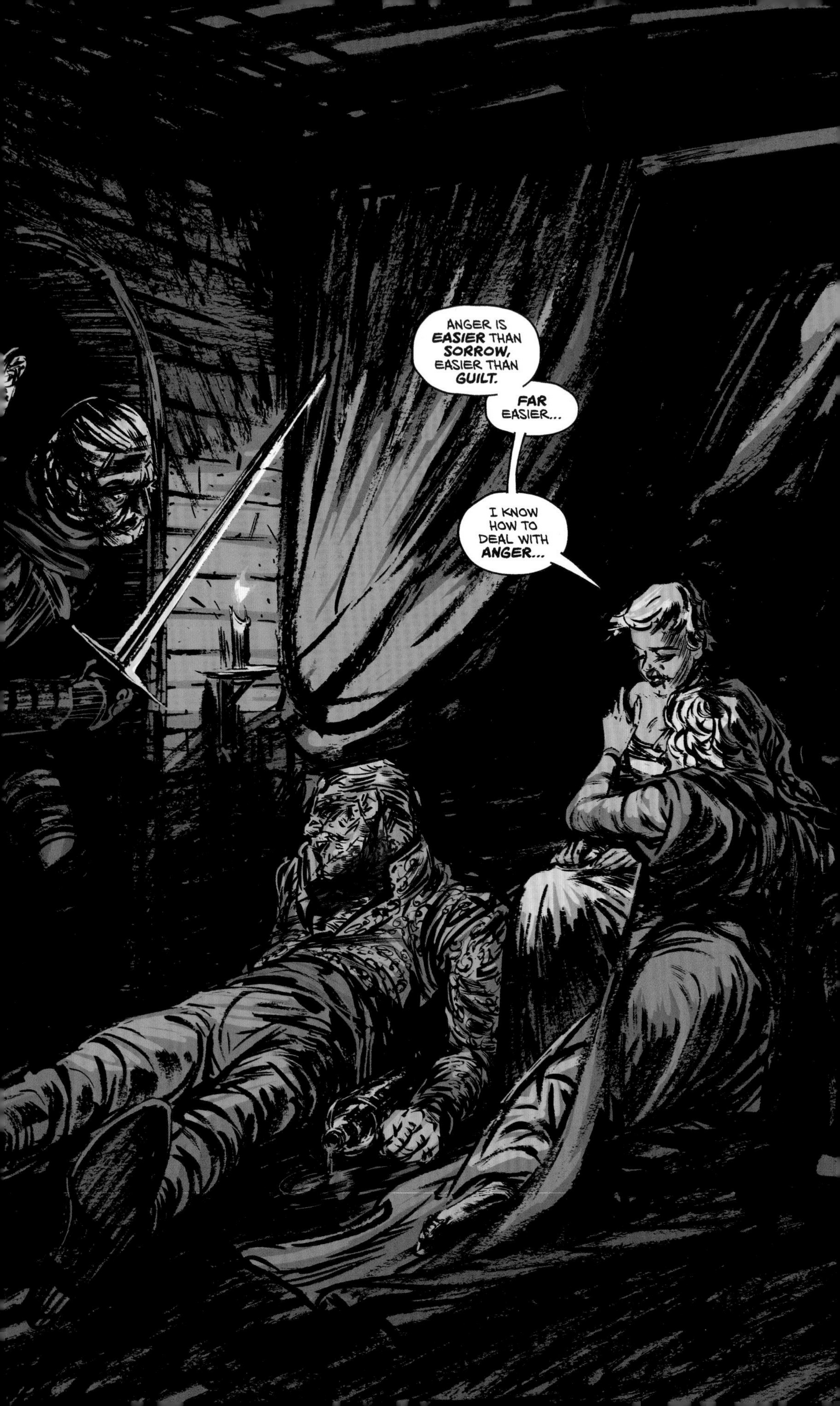
ANGER IS **EASIER** THAN **SORROW,** EASIER THAN **GUILT.**
FAR EASIER...
I KNOW HOW TO DEAL WITH **ANGER...**

CHAPTER FOUR

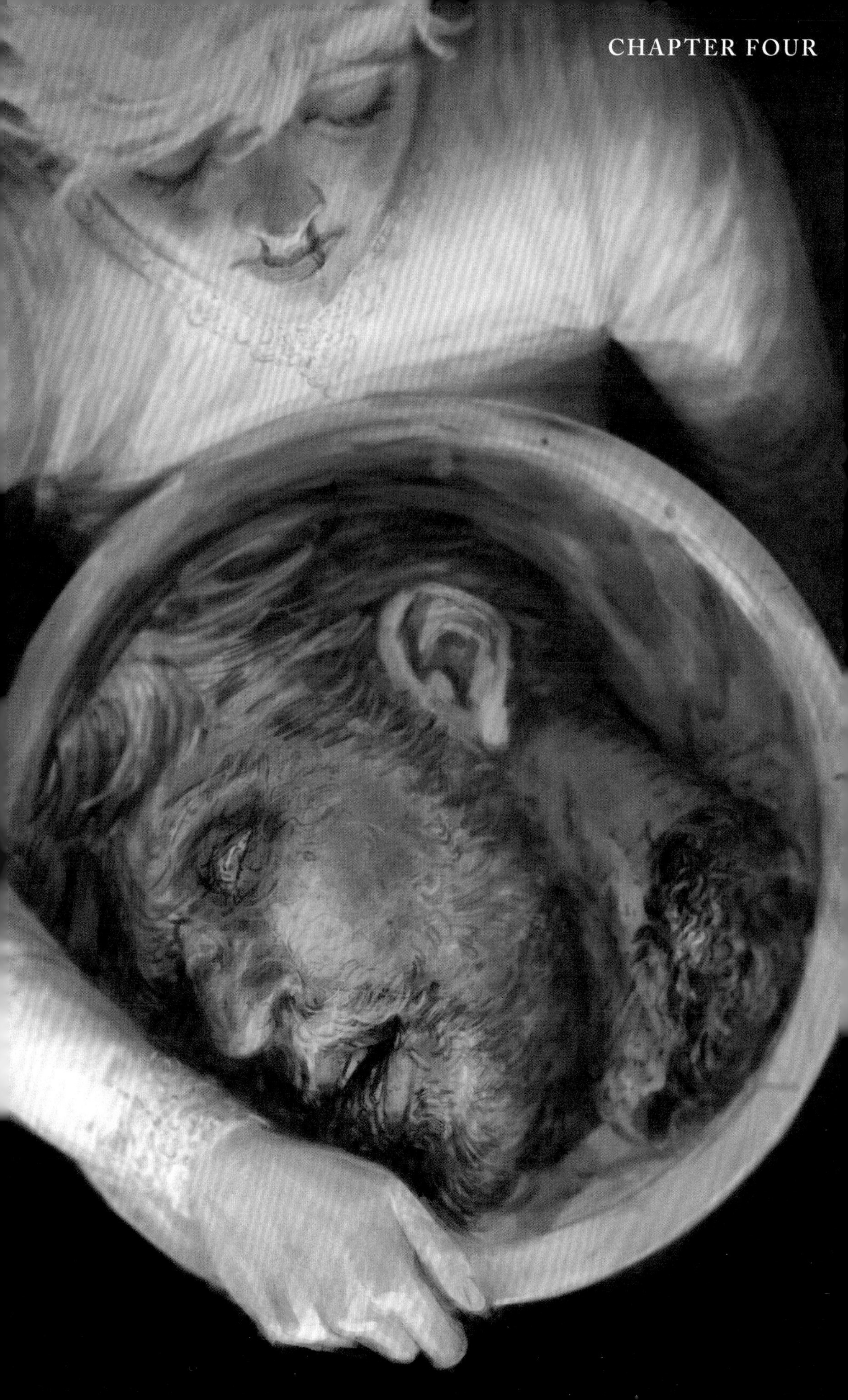

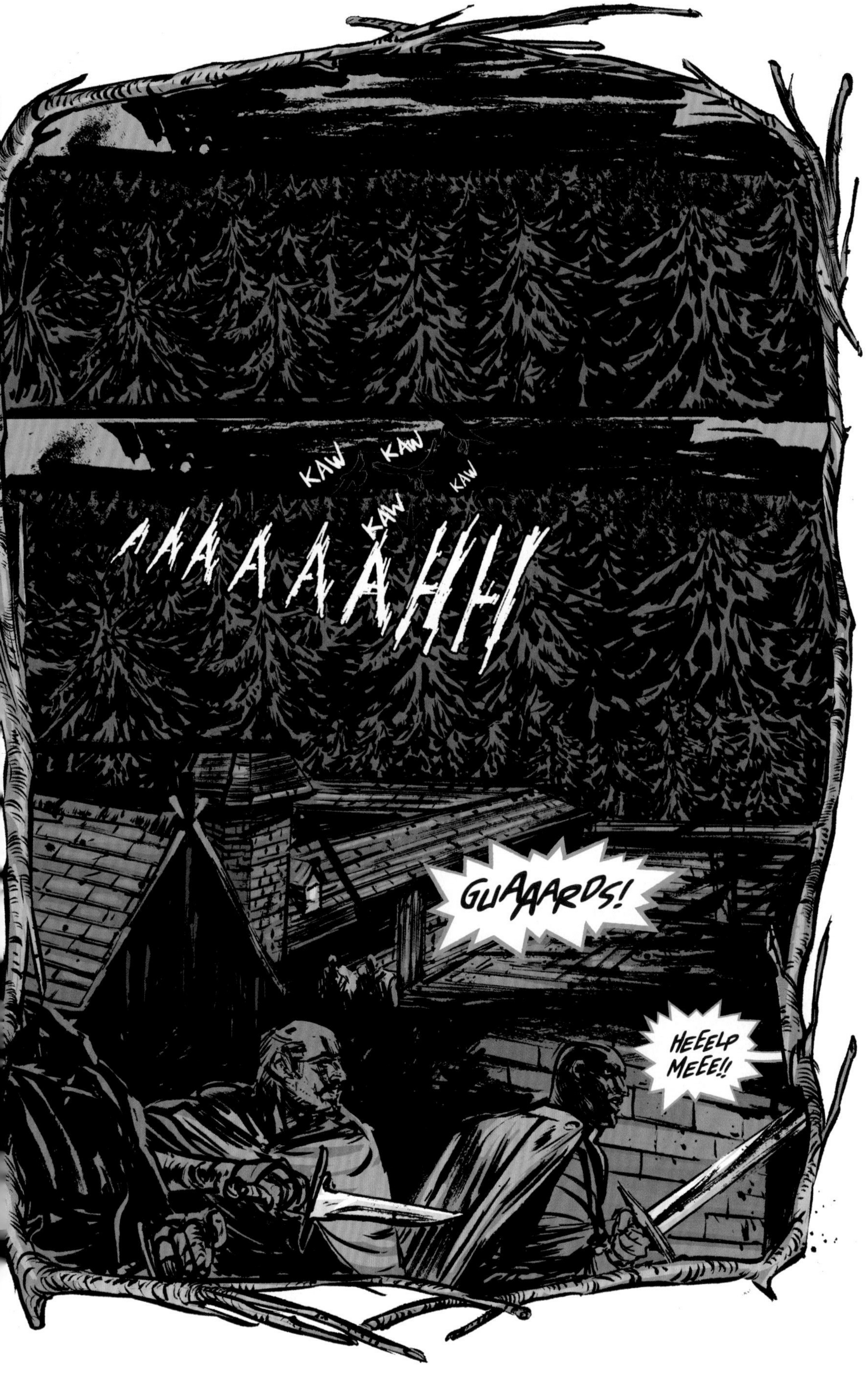
KAW
KAW
KAW
KAW
AAAAAAAHH
GUAAARDS!
HEEELP MEEE!!

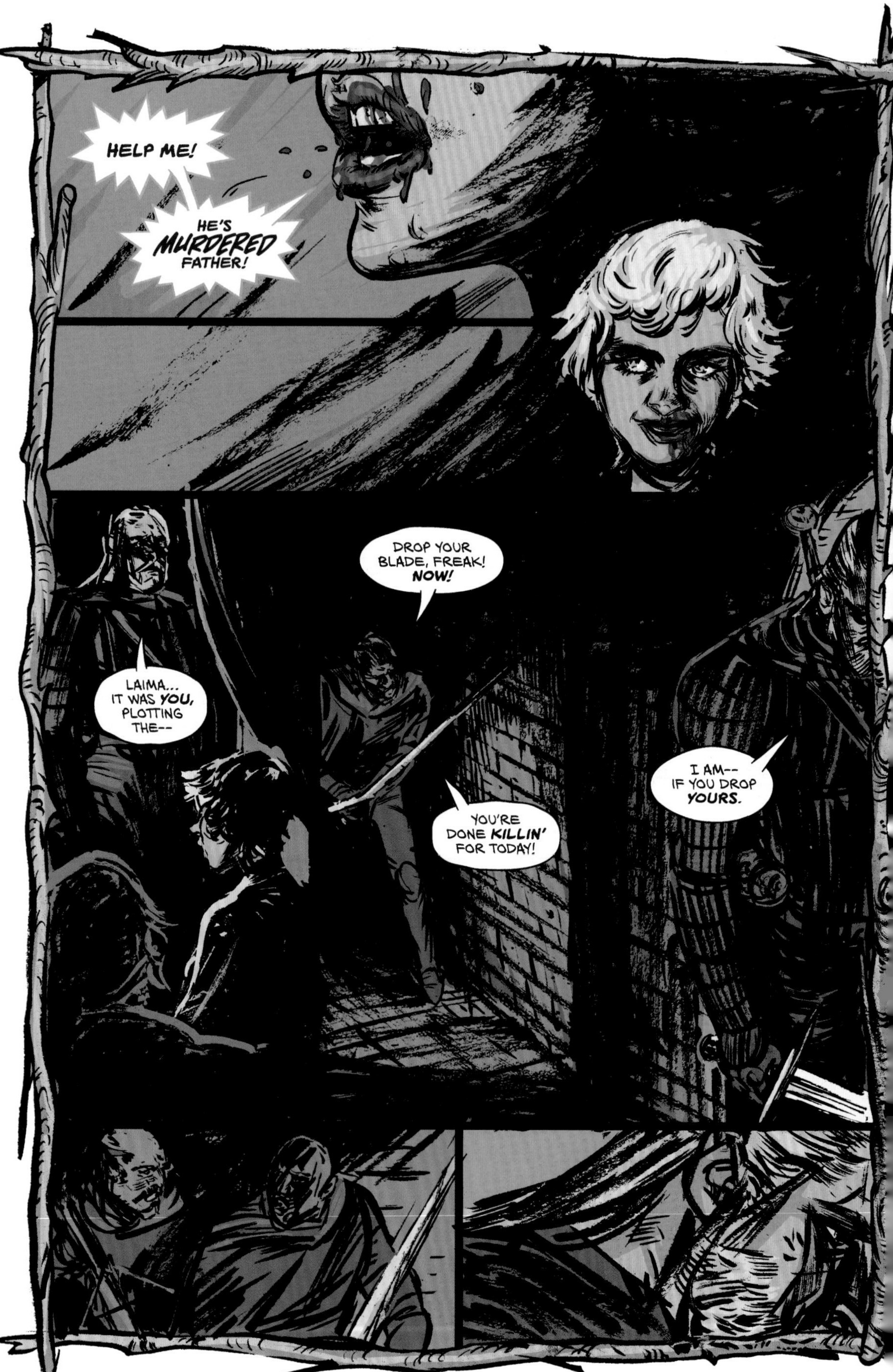

HELP ME!
HE'S MURDERED FATHER!
LAIMA... IT WAS YOU, PLOTTING THE--
DROP YOUR BLADE, FREAK! NOW!
YOU'RE DONE KILLIN' FOR TODAY!
I AM-- IF YOU DROP YOURS.

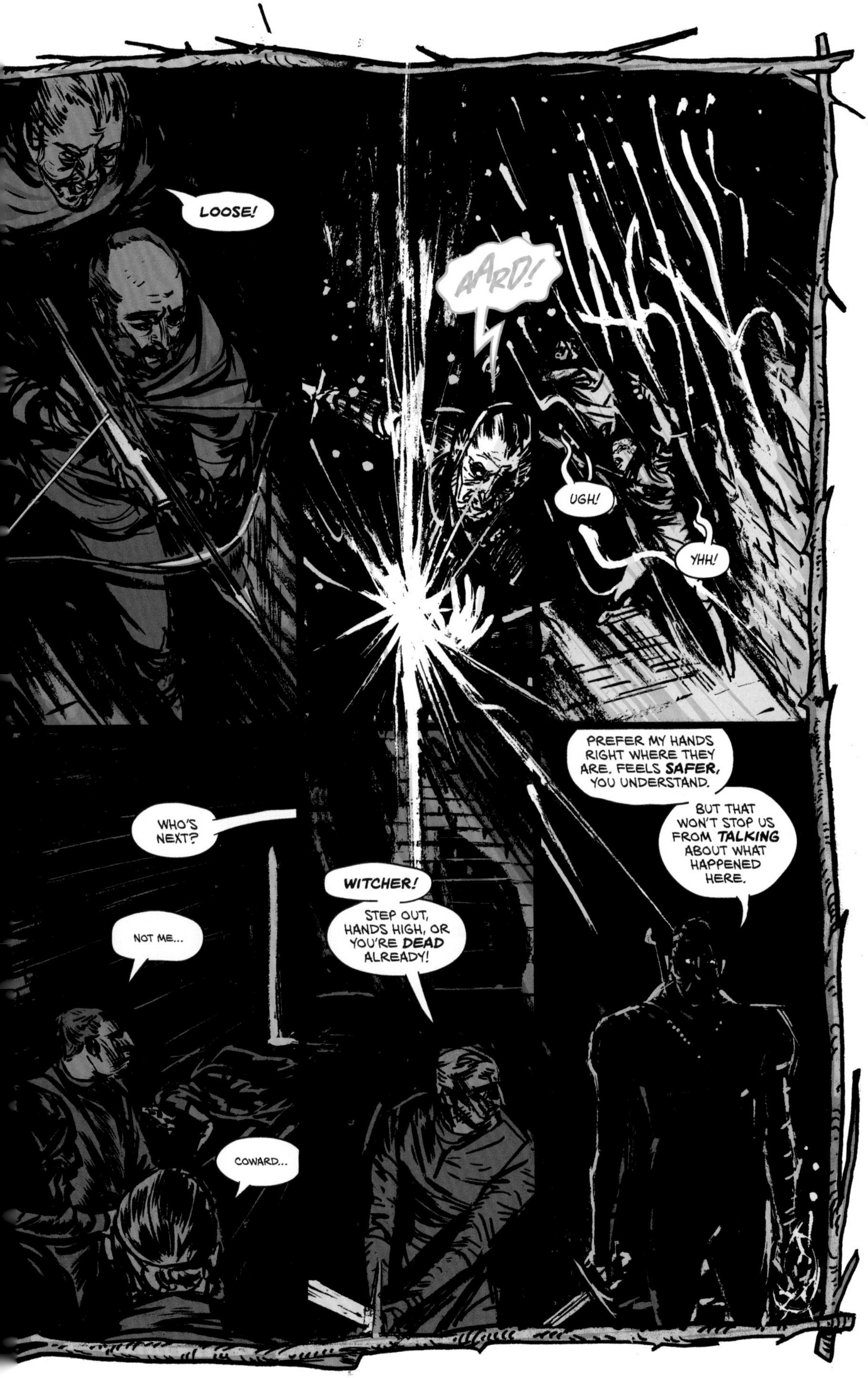
LOOSE!
AARD!
UGH!
YHH!
WHO'S NEXT?
NOT ME...
COWARD...
WITCHER!
STEP OUT, HANDS HIGH, OR YOU'RE DEAD ALREADY!
PREFER MY HANDS RIGHT WHERE THEY ARE. FEELS SAFER, YOU UNDERSTAND.
BUT THAT WON'T STOP US FROM TALKING ABOUT WHAT HAPPENED HERE.

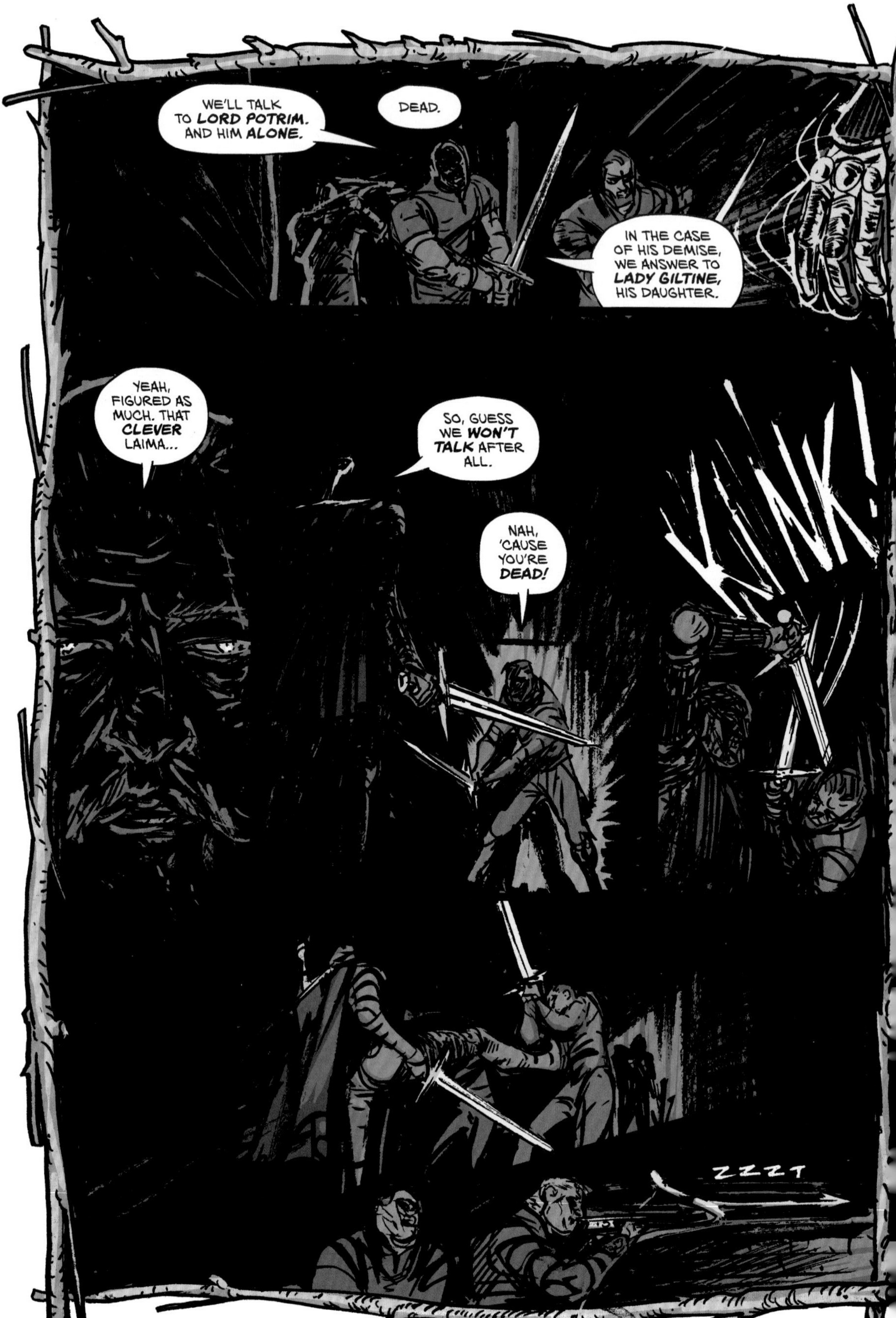
WE'LL TALK TO LORD POTRIM. AND HIM ALONE.
DEAD.
IN THE CASE OF HIS DEMISE, WE ANSWER TO LADY GILTINE, HIS DAUGHTER.
YEAH, FIGURED AS MUCH. THAT CLEVER LAIMA...
SO, GUESS WE WON'T TALK AFTER ALL.
NAH, 'CAUSE YOU'RE DEAD!
KLINK!
ZZZT

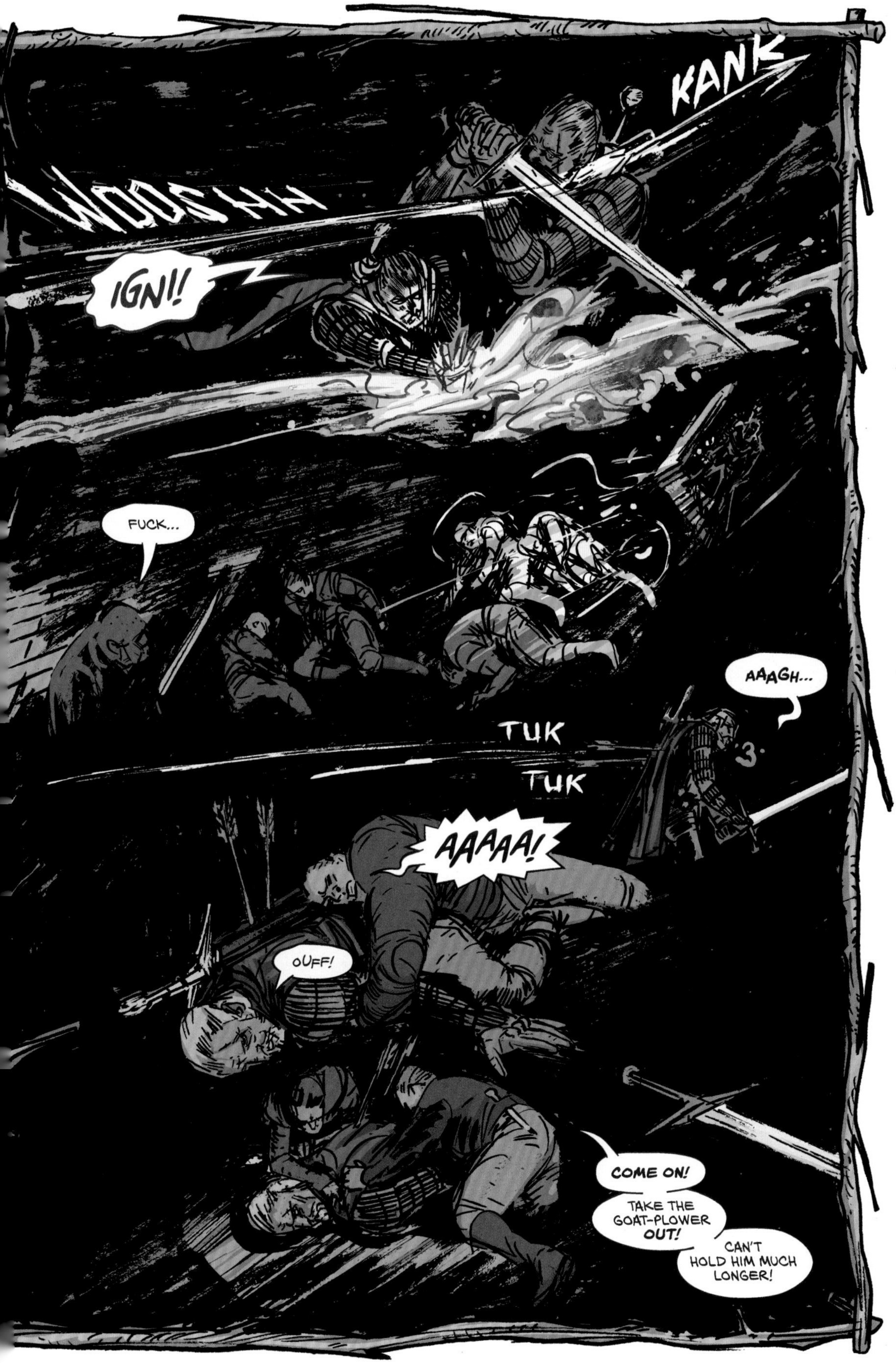
KANK
WOOSHH
IGNI!
FUCK...
AAAGH...
TUK
TUK
AAAAA!
OUFF!
COME ON!
TAKE THE GOAT-PLOWER OUT!
CAN'T HOLD HIM MUCH LONGER!

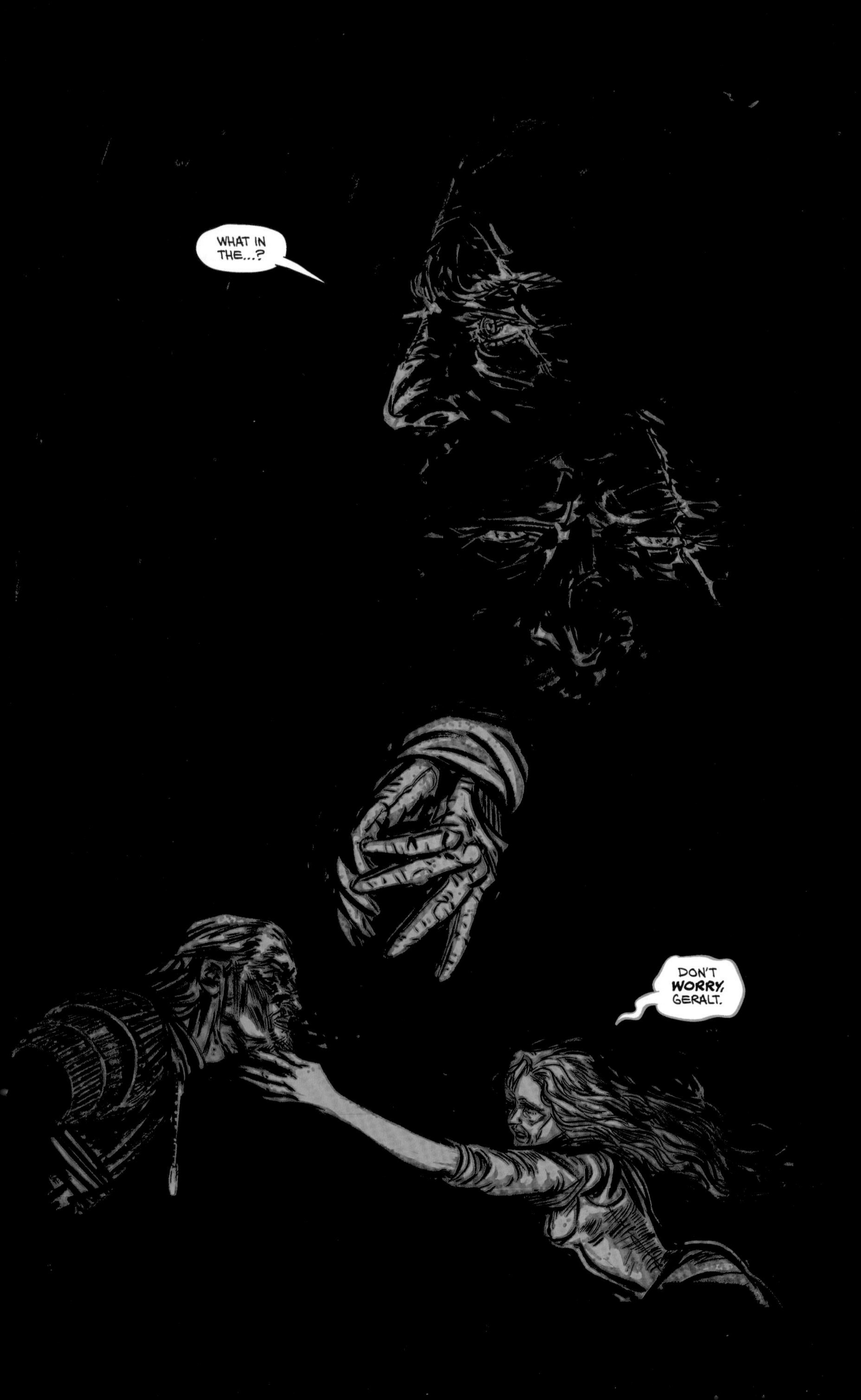
WHAT IN THE...?
DON'T **WORRY,** GERALT.

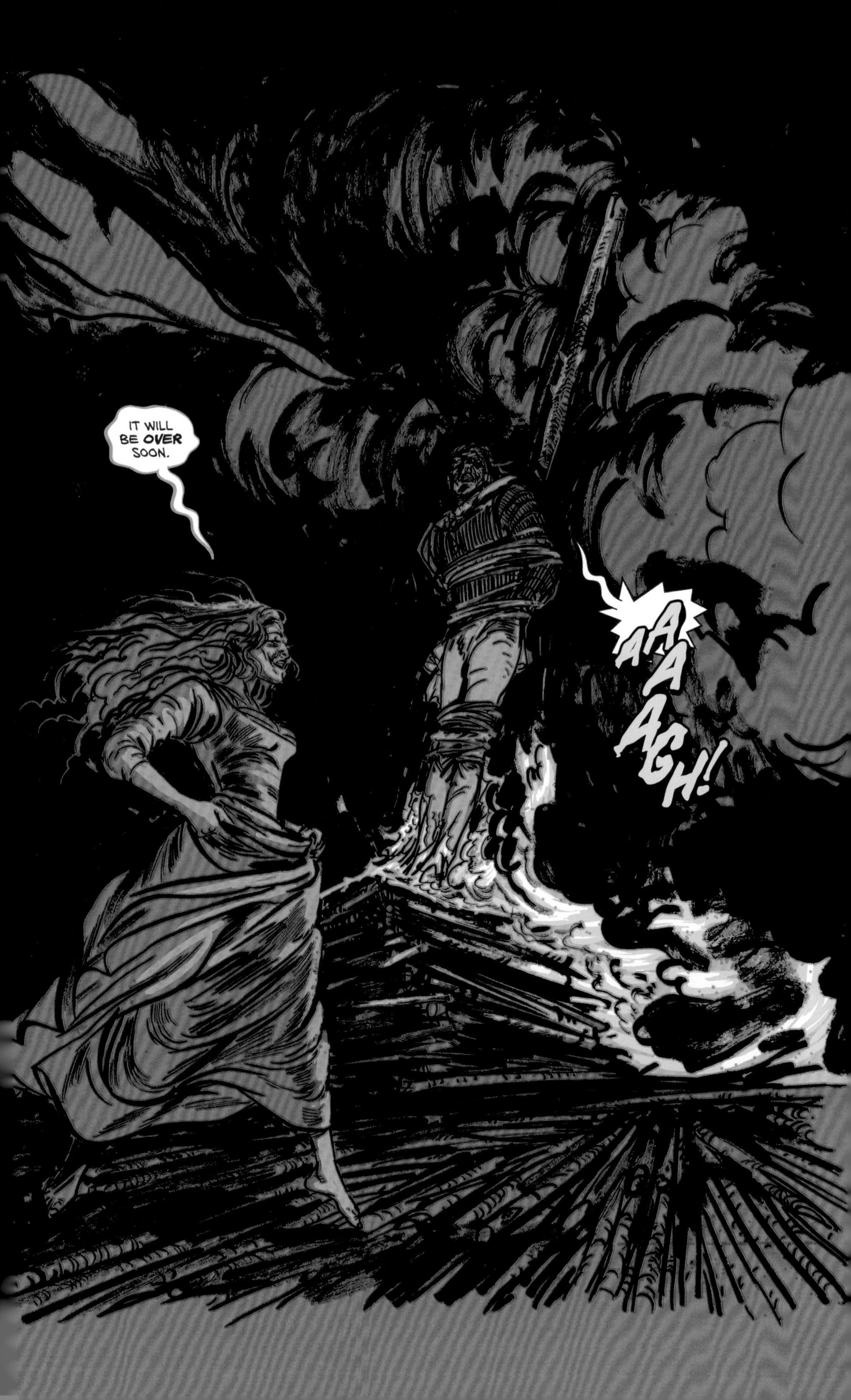
IT WILL BE OVER SOON.
AAAAAGH!

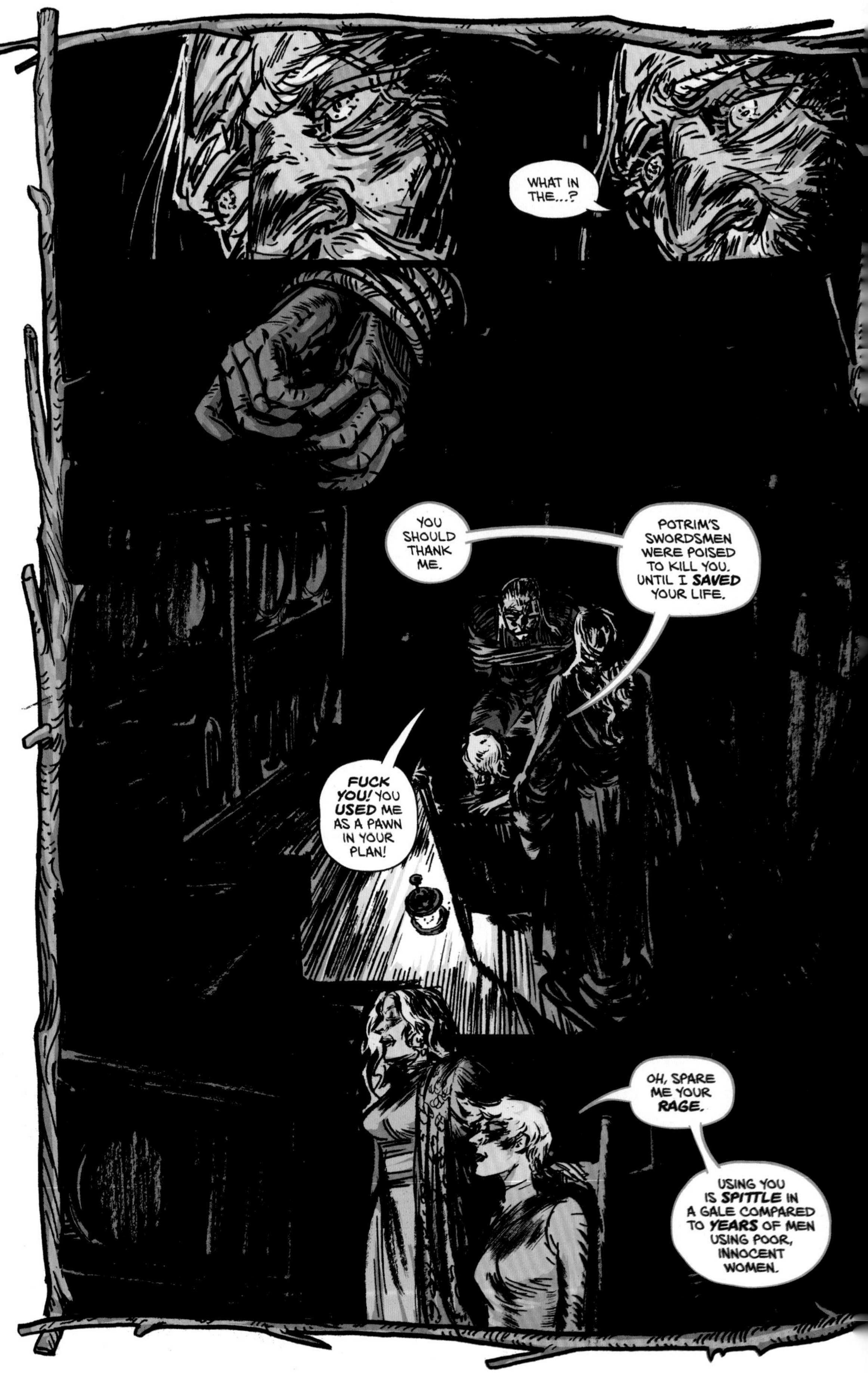
WHAT IN THE...?
YOU SHOULD THANK ME.
POTRIM'S SWORDSMEN WERE POISED TO KILL YOU. UNTIL I **SAVED** YOUR LIFE.
FUCK YOU! YOU **USED** ME AS A PAWN IN YOUR PLAN!
OH, SPARE ME YOUR **RAGE.**
USING YOU IS **SPITTLE** IN A GALE COMPARED TO **YEARS** OF MEN USING POOR, INNOCENT WOMEN.

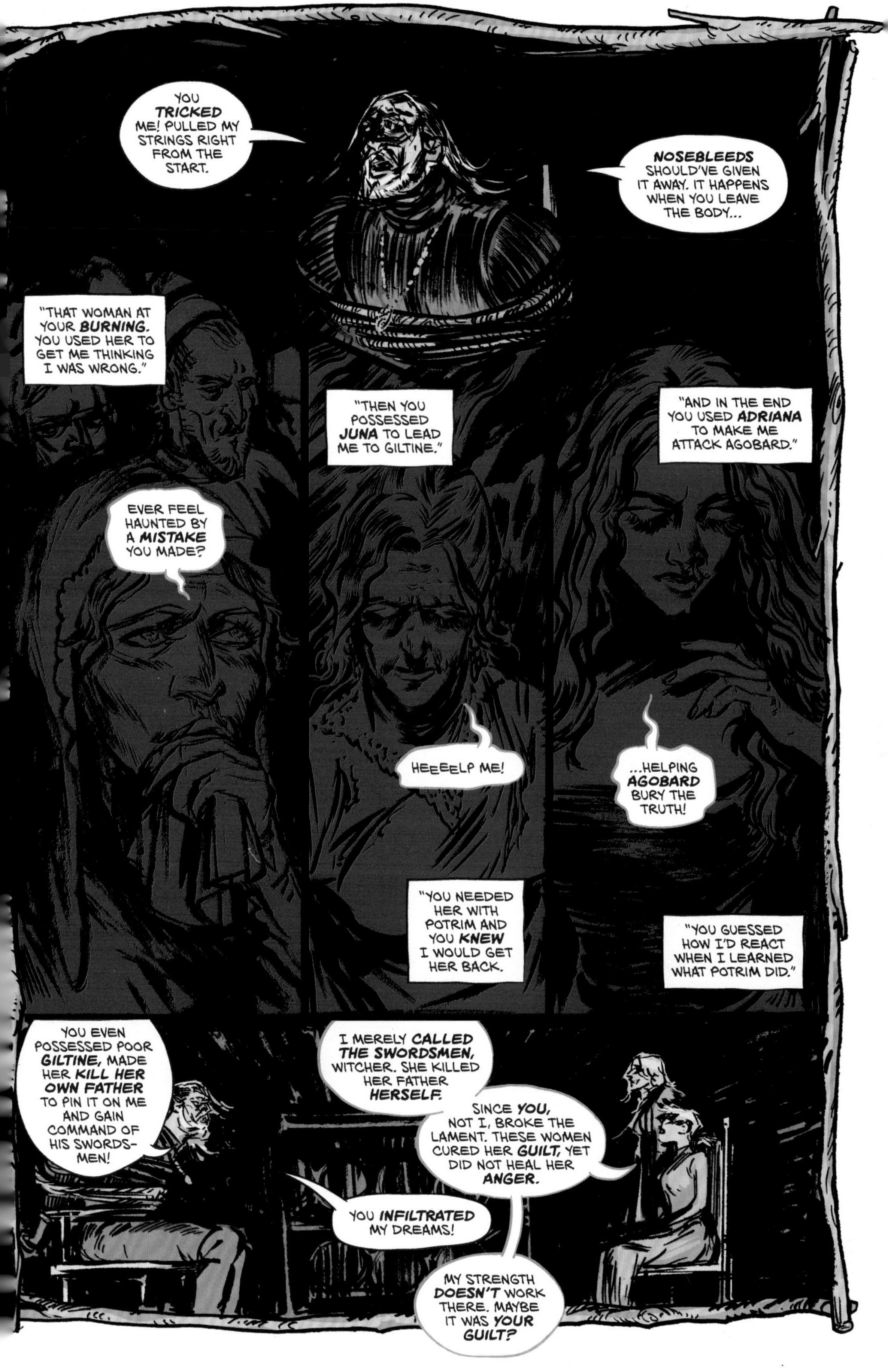
YOU **TRICKED** ME! PULLED MY STRINGS RIGHT FROM THE START.
NOSEBLEEDS SHOULD'VE GIVEN IT AWAY. IT HAPPENS WHEN YOU LEAVE THE BODY...
"THAT WOMAN AT YOUR **BURNING**. YOU USED HER TO GET ME THINKING I WAS WRONG."
EVER FEEL HAUNTED BY A **MISTAKE** YOU MADE?
"THEN YOU POSSESSED **JUNA** TO LEAD ME TO GILTINE."
HEEEELP ME!
"YOU NEEDED HER WITH POTRIM AND YOU **KNEW** I WOULD GET HER BACK.
"AND IN THE END YOU USED **ADRIANA** TO MAKE ME ATTACK AGOBARD."
...HELPING **AGOBARD** BURY THE TRUTH!
"YOU GUESSED HOW I'D REACT WHEN I LEARNED WHAT POTRIM DID."
YOU EVEN POSSESSED POOR **GILTINE,** MADE HER **KILL HER OWN FATHER** TO PIN IT ON ME AND GAIN COMMAND OF HIS SWORDSMEN!
I MERELY **CALLED THE SWORDSMEN,** WITCHER. SHE KILLED HER FATHER **HERSELF.**
SINCE **YOU,** NOT I, BROKE THE LAMENT. THESE WOMEN CURED HER **GUILT,** YET DID NOT HEAL HER **ANGER.**
YOU **INFILTRATED** MY DREAMS!
MY STRENGTH **DOESN'T** WORK THERE. MAYBE IT WAS **YOUR GUILT?**

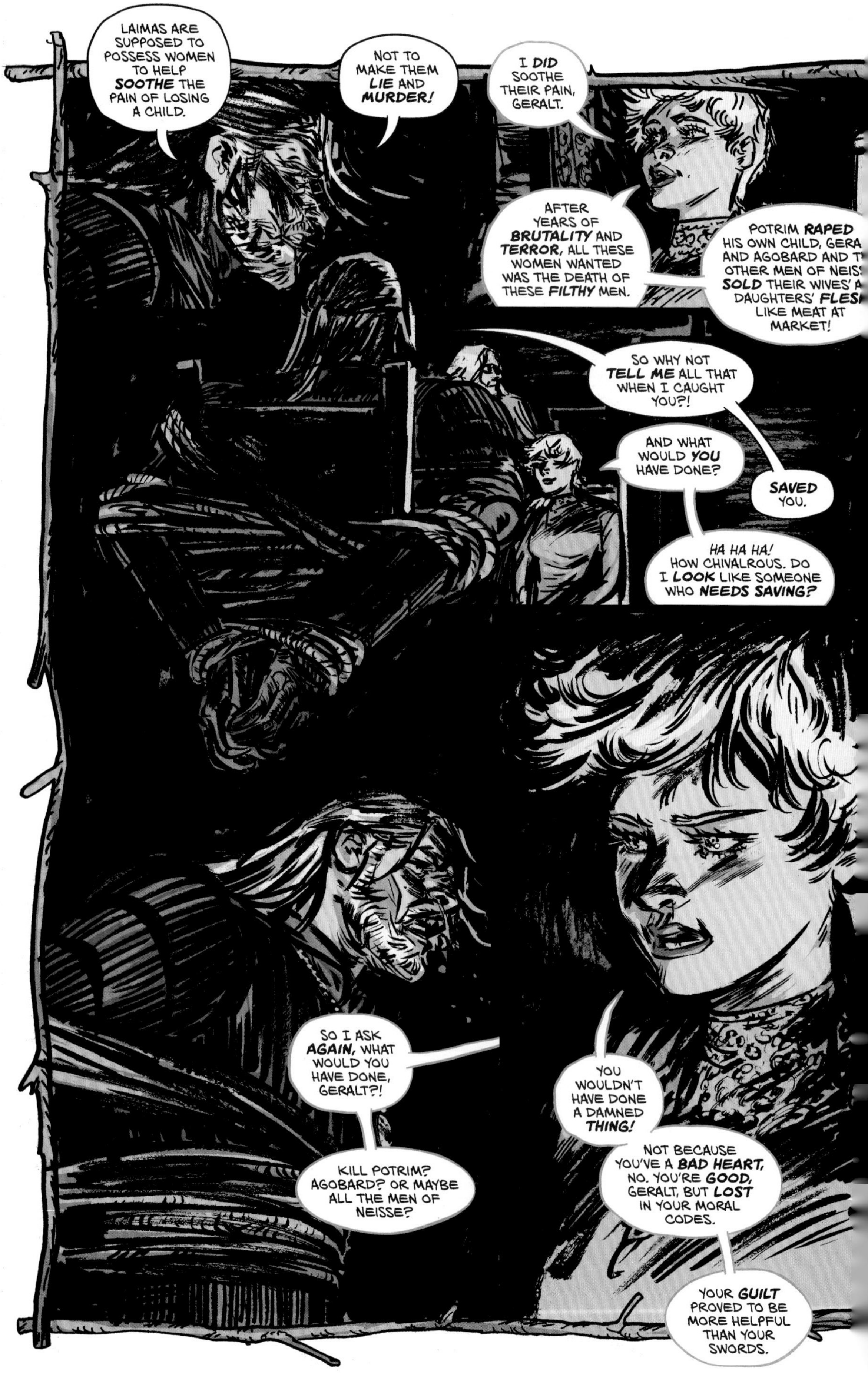

LAIMAS ARE SUPPOSED TO POSSESS WOMEN TO HELP **SOOTHE** THE PAIN OF LOSING A CHILD.
NOT TO MAKE THEM ***LIE*** AND ***MURDER!***
I ***DID*** SOOTHE THEIR PAIN, GERALT.
AFTER YEARS OF ***BRUTALITY*** AND ***TERROR,*** ALL THESE WOMEN WANTED WAS THE DEATH OF THESE ***FILTHY*** MEN.
POTRIM ***RAPED*** HIS OWN CHILD, GERA AND AGOBARD AND T OTHER MEN OF NEIS ***SOLD*** THEIR WIVES' A DAUGHTERS' ***FLES*** LIKE MEAT AT MARKET!
SO WHY NOT **TELL ME** ALL THAT WHEN I CAUGHT YOU?!
AND WHAT WOULD ***YOU*** HAVE DONE?
SAVED YOU.
HA HA HA! HOW CHIVALROUS. DO I **LOOK** LIKE SOMEONE WHO ***NEEDS SAVING?***
SO I ASK ***AGAIN,*** WHAT WOULD YOU HAVE DONE, GERALT?!
KILL POTRIM? AGOBARD? OR MAYBE ALL THE MEN OF NEISSE?
YOU WOULDN'T HAVE DONE A DAMNED ***THING!***
NOT BECAUSE YOU'VE A ***BAD HEART,*** NO. YOU'RE ***GOOD,*** GERALT, BUT ***LOST*** IN YOUR MORAL CODES.
YOUR ***GUILT*** PROVED TO BE MORE HELPFUL THAN YOUR SWORDS.

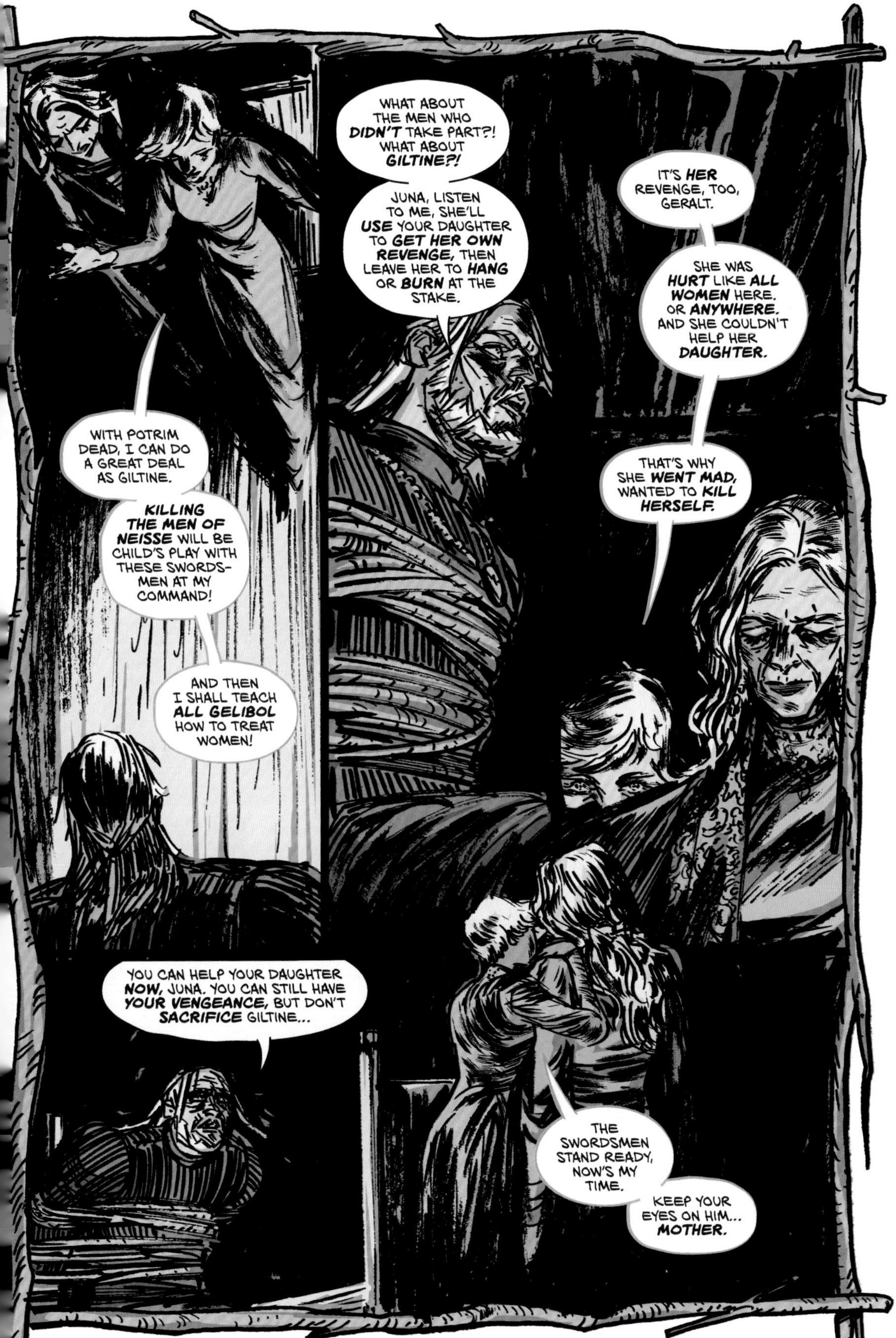
WITH POTRIM DEAD, I CAN DO A GREAT DEAL AS GILTINE.
KILLING THE MEN OF NEISSE WILL BE CHILD'S PLAY WITH THESE SWORDS-MEN AT MY COMMAND!
AND THEN I SHALL TEACH ALL GELIBOL HOW TO TREAT WOMEN!
WHAT ABOUT THE MEN WHO DIDN'T TAKE PART?! WHAT ABOUT GILTINE?!
JUNA, LISTEN TO ME, SHE'LL USE YOUR DAUGHTER TO GET HER OWN REVENGE, THEN LEAVE HER TO HANG OR BURN AT THE STAKE.
IT'S HER REVENGE, TOO, GERALT.
SHE WAS HURT LIKE ALL WOMEN HERE. OR ANYWHERE. AND SHE COULDN'T HELP HER DAUGHTER.
THAT'S WHY SHE WENT MAD, WANTED TO KILL HERSELF.
YOU CAN HELP YOUR DAUGHTER NOW, JUNA. YOU CAN STILL HAVE YOUR VENGEANCE, BUT DON'T SACRIFICE GILTINE...
THE SWORDSMEN STAND READY, NOW'S MY TIME.
KEEP YOUR EYES ON HIM... MOTHER.

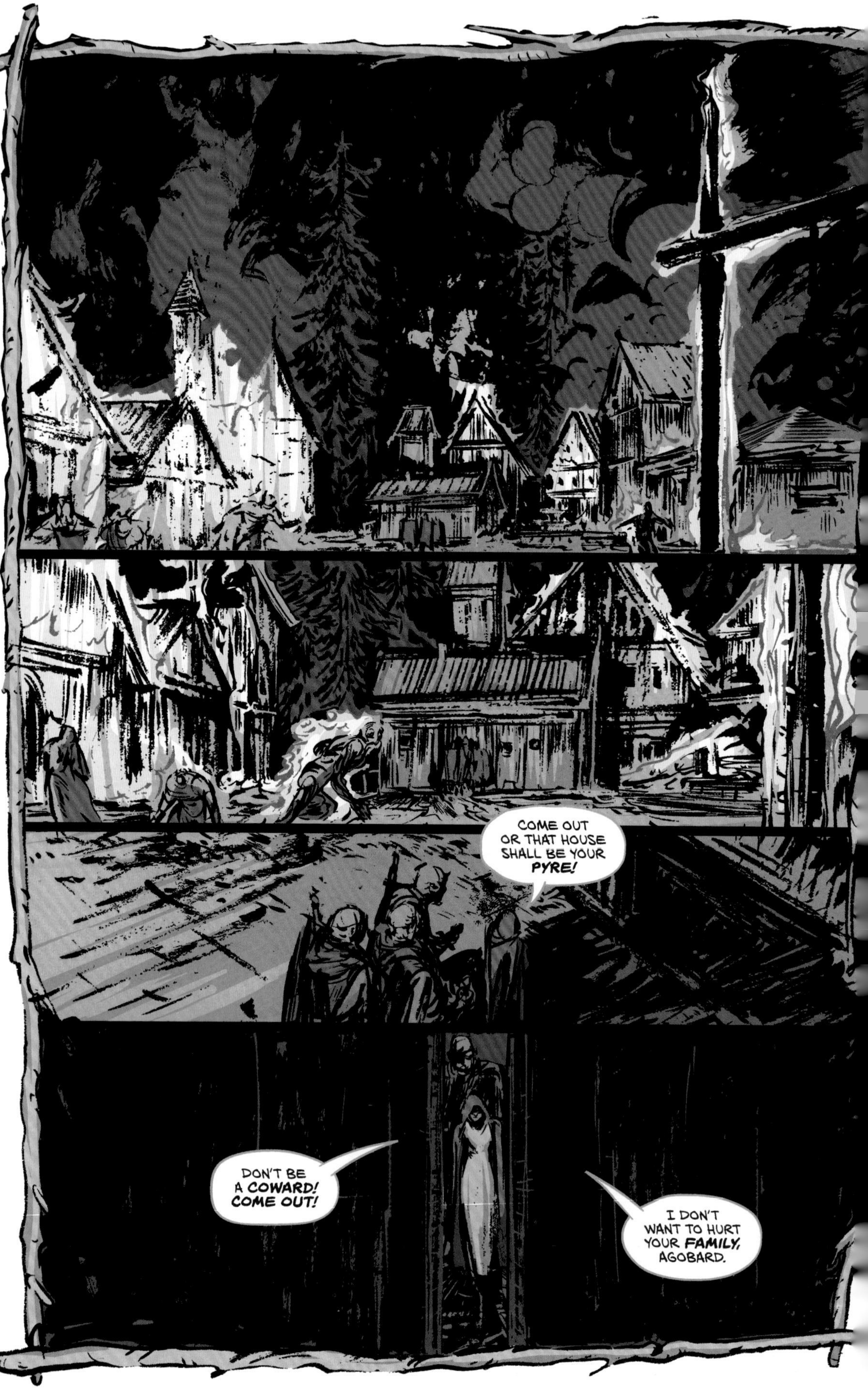
COME OUT OR THAT HOUSE SHALL BE YOUR **PYRE!**
DON'T BE A **COWARD! COME OUT!**
I DON'T WANT TO HURT YOUR **FAMILY,** AGOBARD.

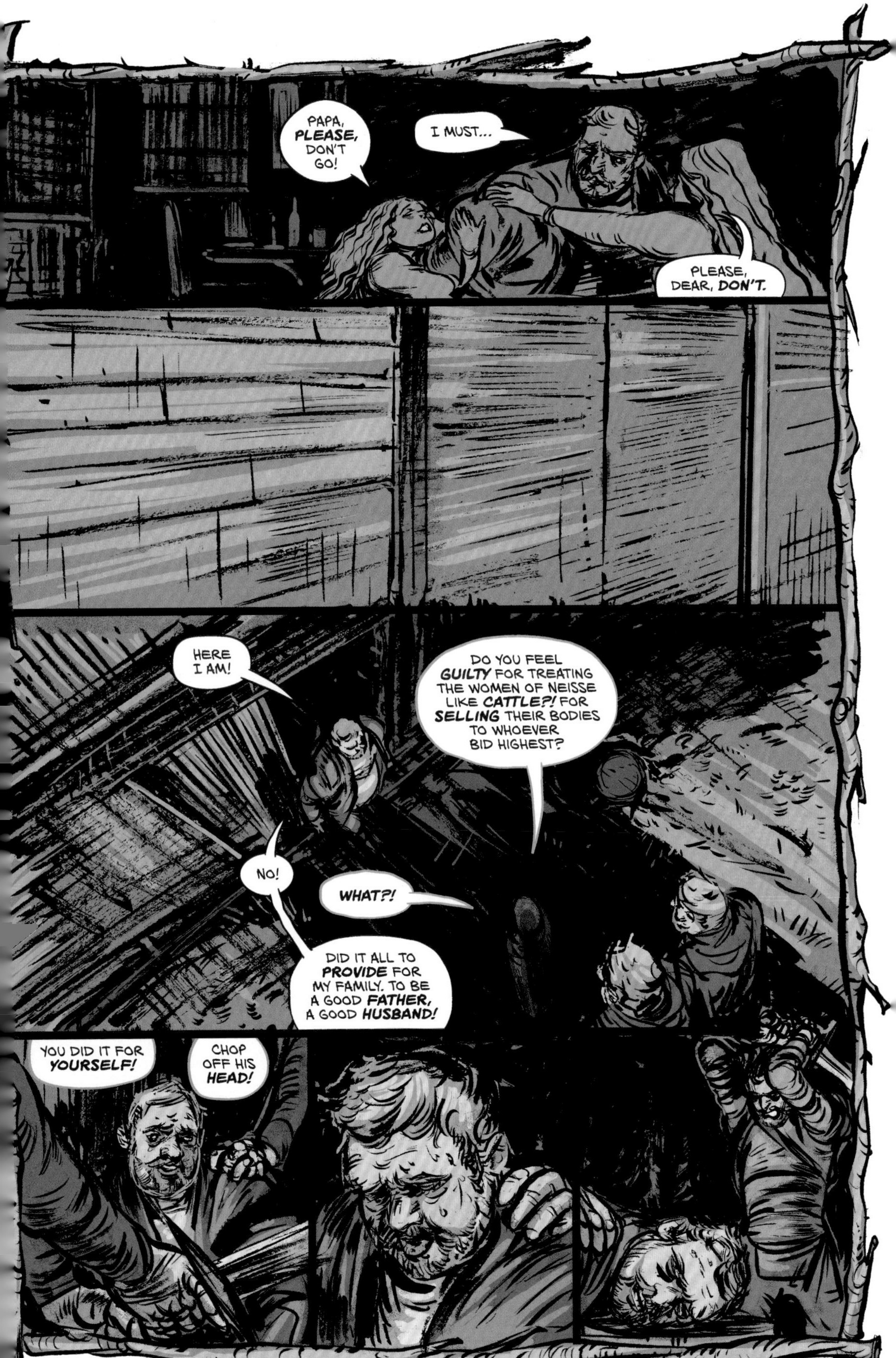
PAPA, PLEASE, DON'T GO!
I MUST...
PLEASE, DEAR, DON'T.
HERE I AM!
DO YOU FEEL GUILTY FOR TREATING THE WOMEN OF NEISSE LIKE CATTLE?! FOR SELLING THEIR BODIES TO WHOEVER BID HIGHEST?
NO!
WHAT?!
DID IT ALL TO PROVIDE FOR MY FAMILY. TO BE A GOOD FATHER, A GOOD HUSBAND!
YOU DID IT FOR YOURSELF!
CHOP OFF HIS HEAD!

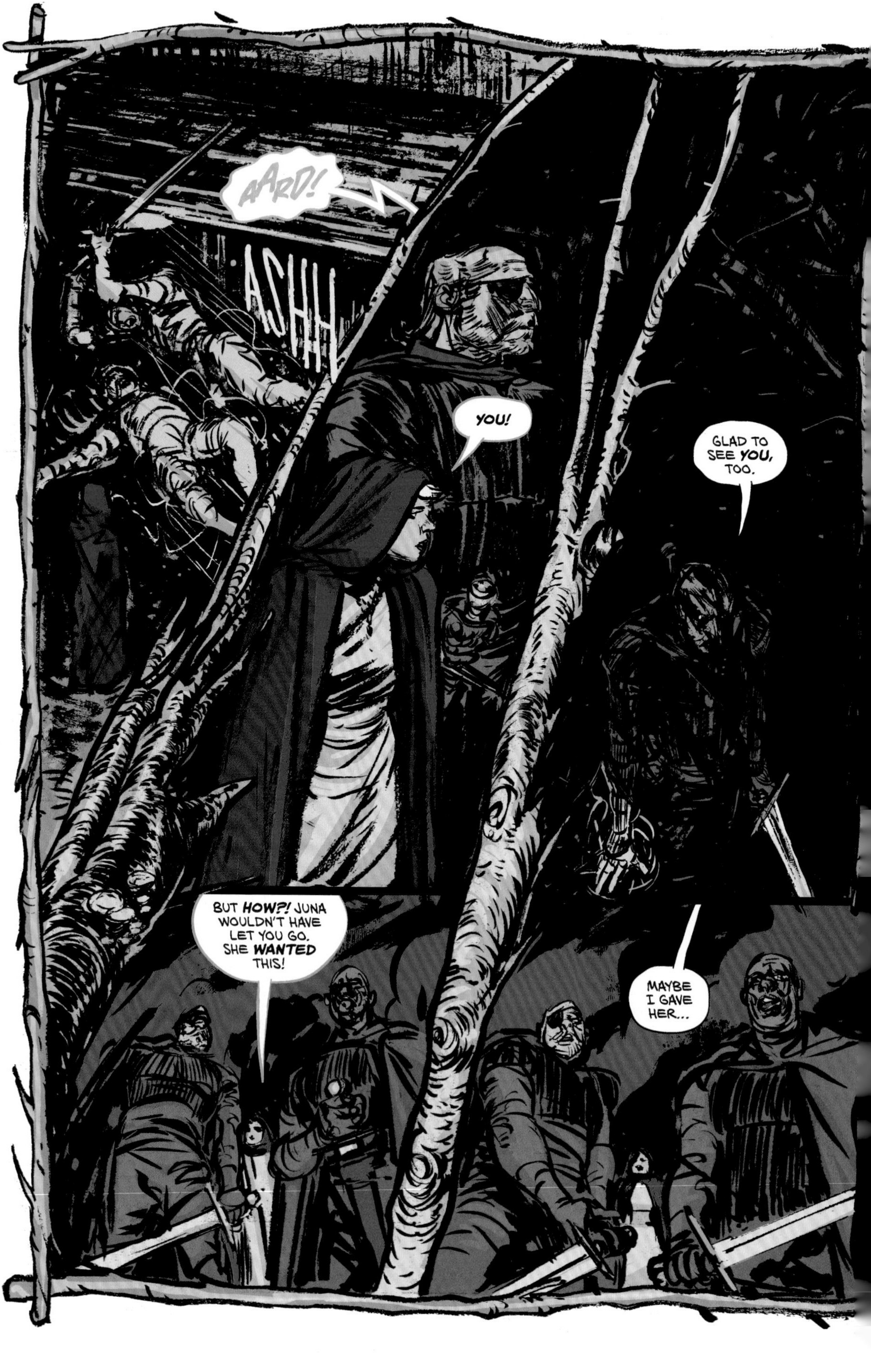
AARD!
ASHH
YOU!
GLAD TO SEE YOU, TOO.
BUT HOW?! JUNA WOULDN'T HAVE LET YOU GO. SHE WANTED THIS!
MAYBE I GAVE HER...

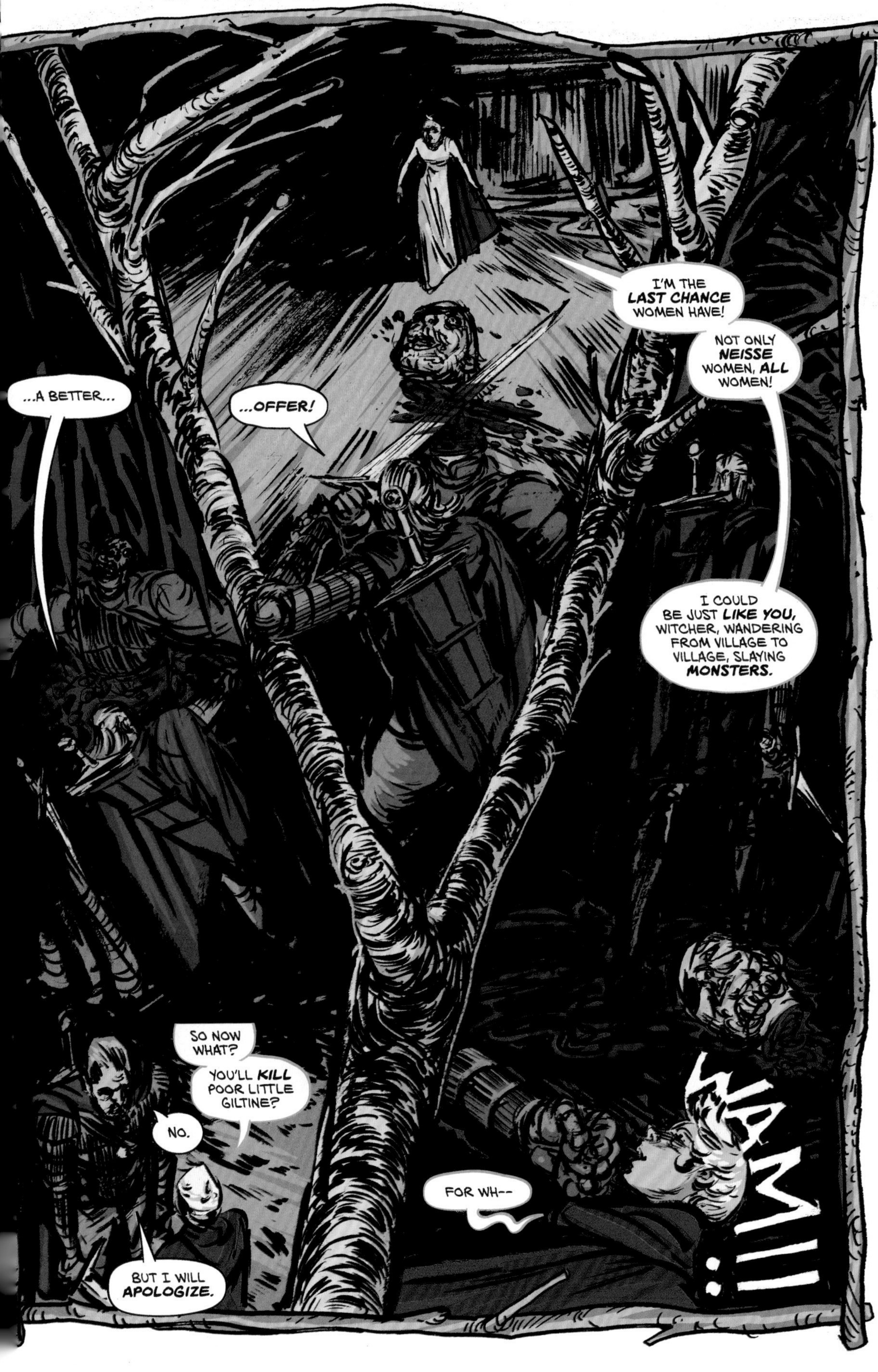
I'M THE LAST CHANCE WOMEN HAVE!
NOT ONLY NEISSE WOMEN, ALL WOMEN!
I COULD BE JUST LIKE YOU, WITCHER, WANDERING FROM VILLAGE TO VILLAGE, SLAYING MONSTERS.
...A BETTER...
...OFFER!
SO NOW WHAT?
YOU'LL KILL POOR LITTLE GILTINE?
NO.
BUT I WILL APOLOGIZE.
FOR WH--
WHAM!!

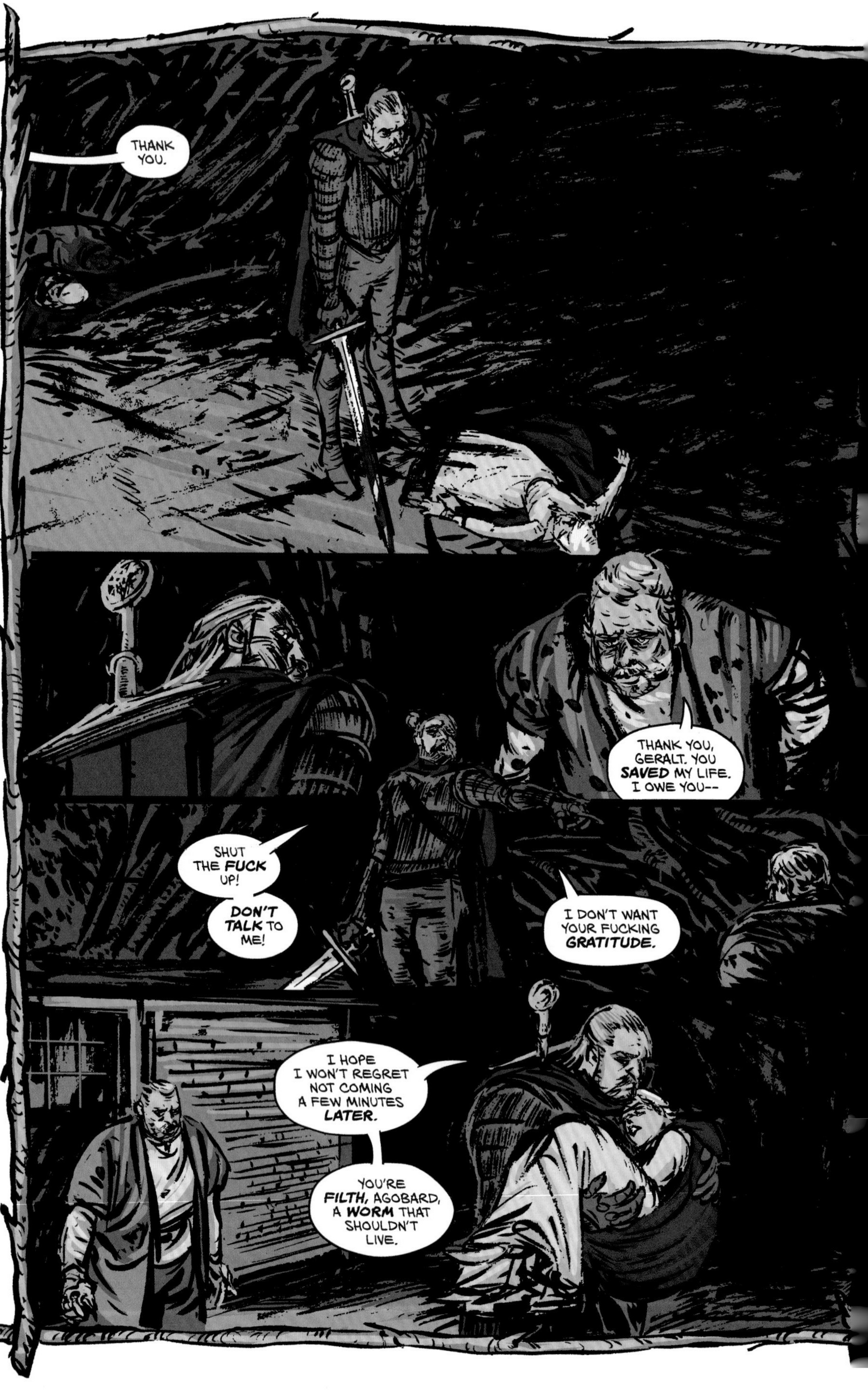
THANK YOU.
THANK YOU, GERALT. YOU **SAVED** MY LIFE. I OWE YOU--
SHUT THE **FUCK** UP!
DON'T TALK TO ME!
I DON'T WANT YOUR FUCKING ***GRATITUDE.***
I HOPE I WON'T REGRET NOT COMING A FEW MINUTES ***LATER.***
YOU'RE ***FILTH,*** AGOBARD, A ***WORM*** THAT SHOULDN'T LIVE.

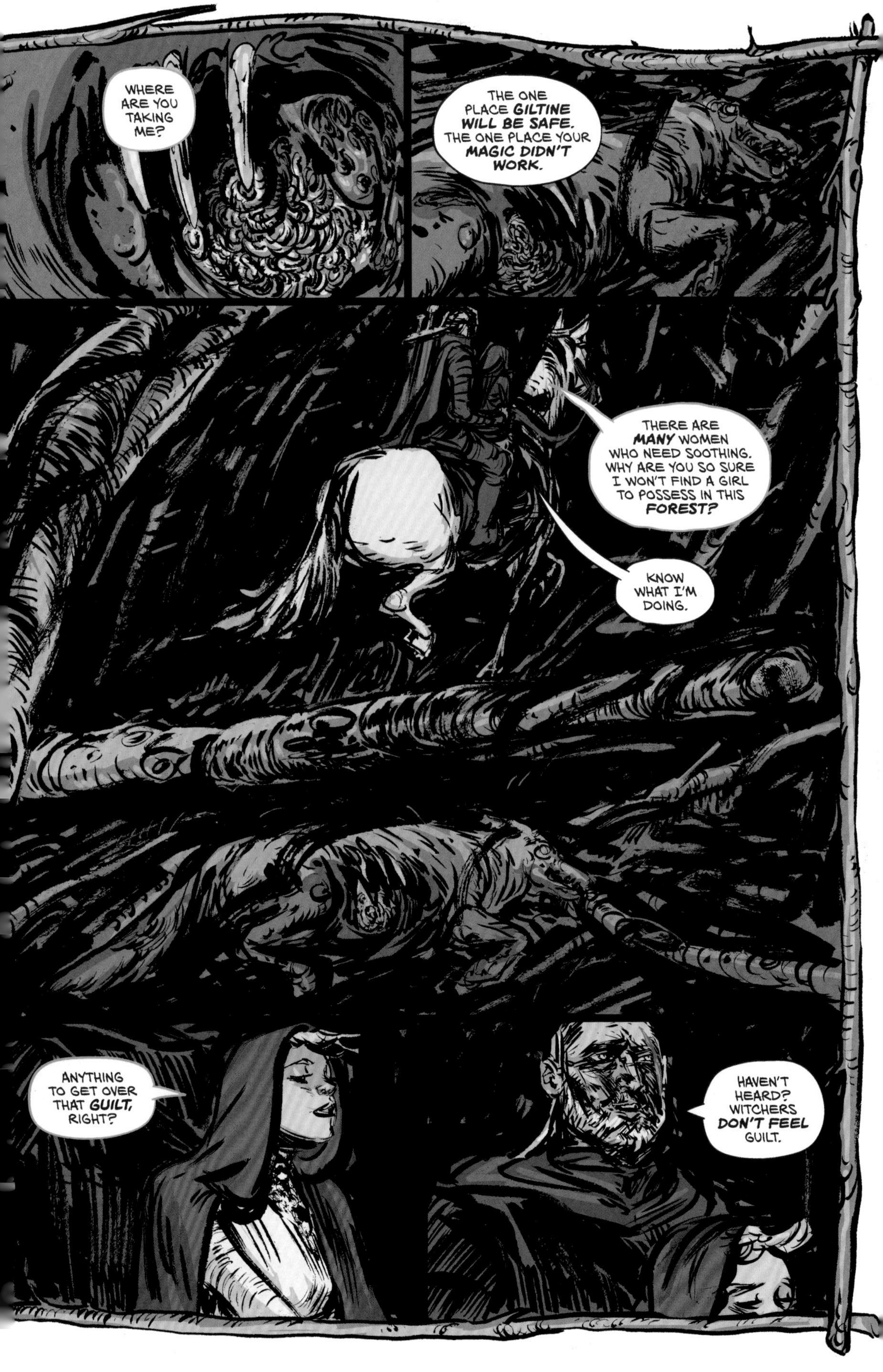
WHERE ARE YOU TAKING ME?
THE ONE PLACE GILTINE WILL BE SAFE. THE ONE PLACE YOUR MAGIC DIDN'T WORK.
THERE ARE MANY WOMEN WHO NEED SOOTHING. WHY ARE YOU SO SURE I WON'T FIND A GIRL TO POSSESS IN THIS FOREST?
KNOW WHAT I'M DOING.
ANYTHING TO GET OVER THAT GUILT, RIGHT?
HAVEN'T HEARD? WITCHERS DON'T FEEL GUILT.

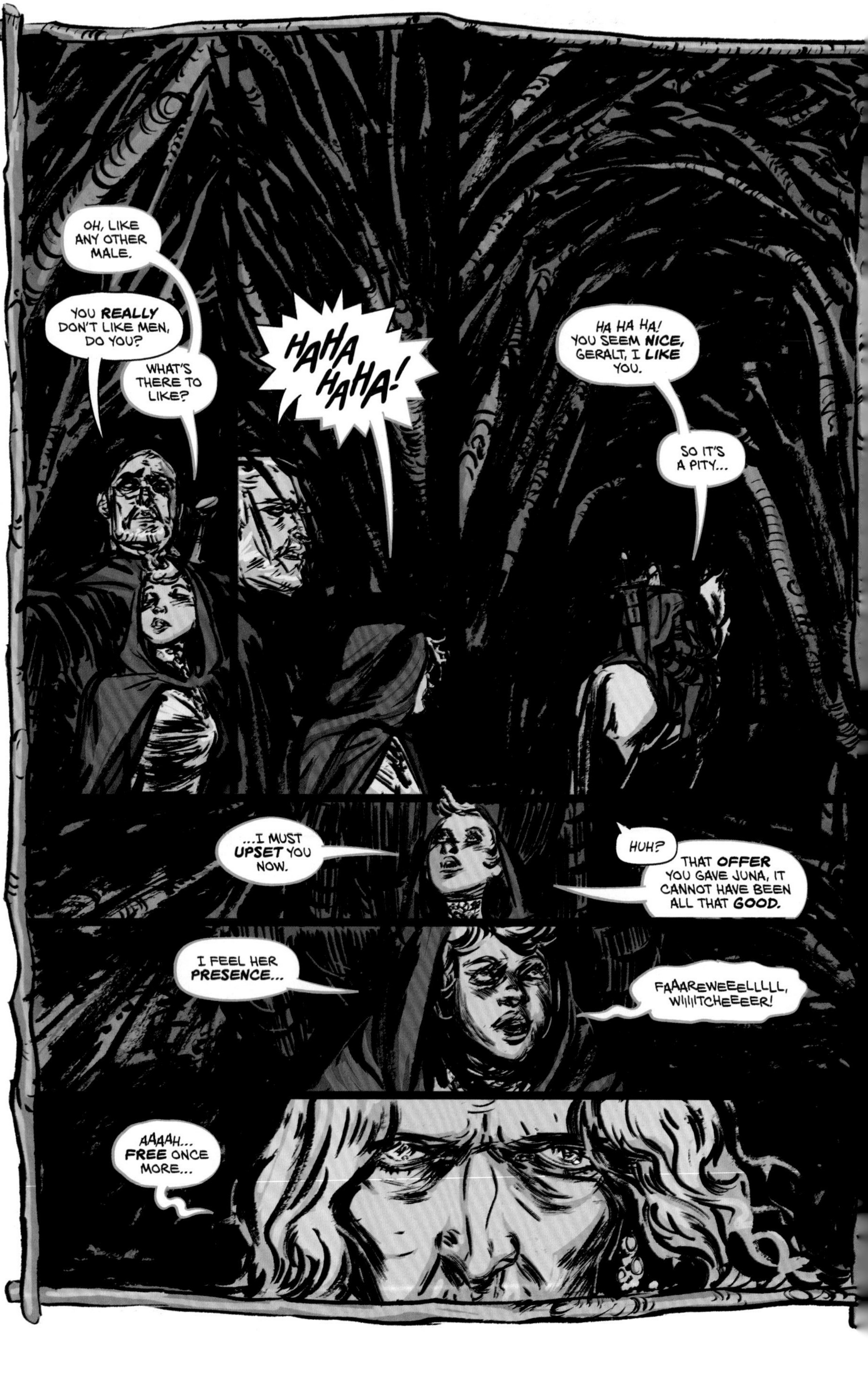
YOU REALLY DON'T LIKE MEN, DO YOU?
OH, LIKE ANY OTHER MALE.
WHAT'S THERE TO LIKE?
HAHA HAHA!
HA HA HA! YOU SEEM NICE, GERALT, I LIKE YOU.
SO IT'S A PITY...
...I MUST UPSET YOU NOW.
HUH?
THAT OFFER YOU GAVE JUNA, IT CANNOT HAVE BEEN ALL THAT GOOD.
I FEEL HER PRESENCE...
FAAAREWEEELLLLL, WIIIIITCHEEEER!
AAAAH... FREE ONCE MORE...

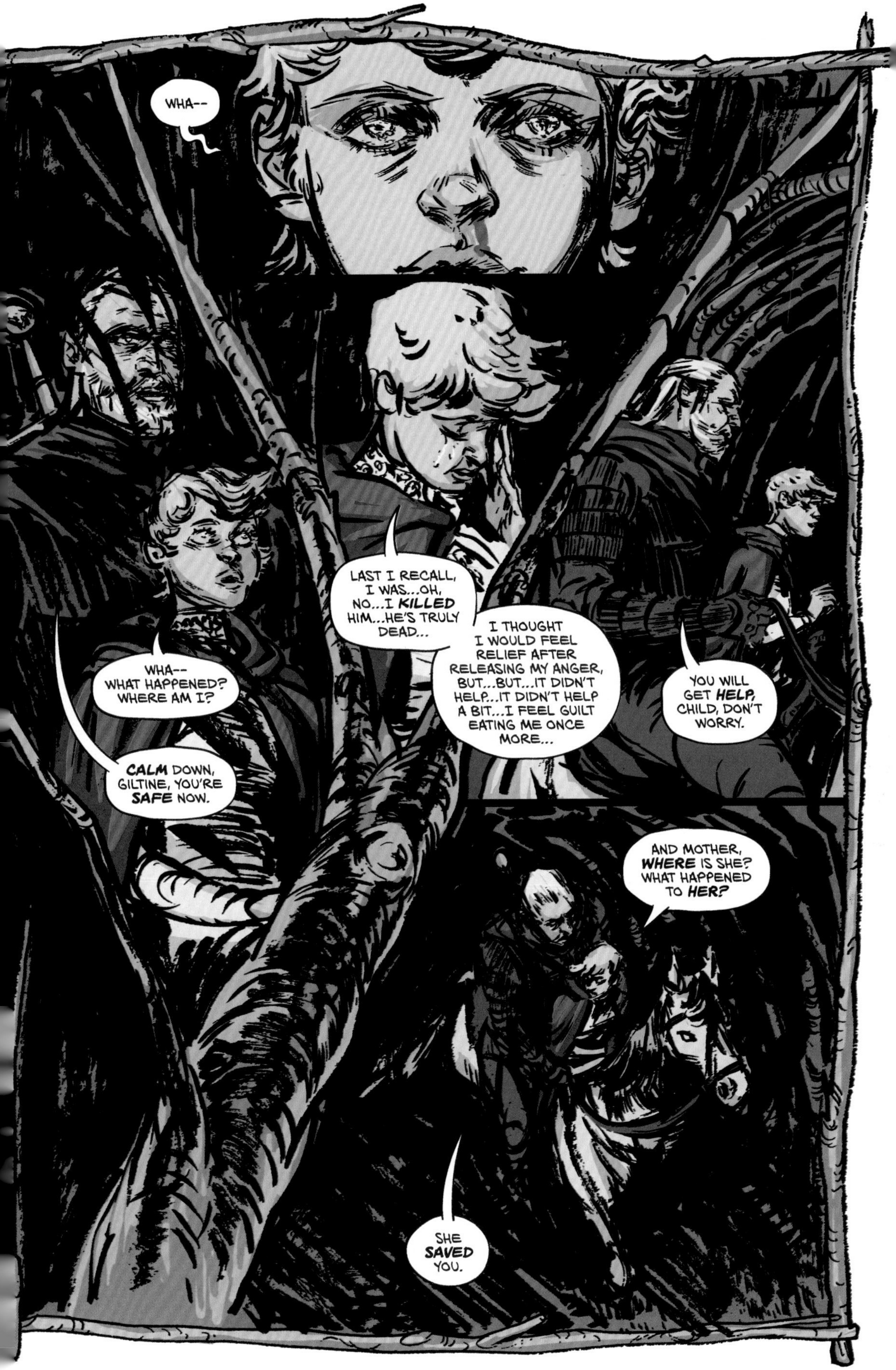
WHA--
WHA-- WHAT HAPPENED? WHERE AM I?
CALM DOWN, GILTINE, YOU'RE SAFE NOW.
LAST I RECALL, I WAS...OH, NO...I KILLED HIM...HE'S TRULY DEAD...
I THOUGHT I WOULD FEEL RELIEF AFTER RELEASING MY ANGER, BUT...BUT...IT DIDN'T HELP...IT DIDN'T HELP A BIT...I FEEL GUILT EATING ME ONCE MORE...
YOU WILL GET HELP, CHILD, DON'T WORRY.
AND MOTHER, WHERE IS SHE? WHAT HAPPENED TO HER?
SHE SAVED YOU.

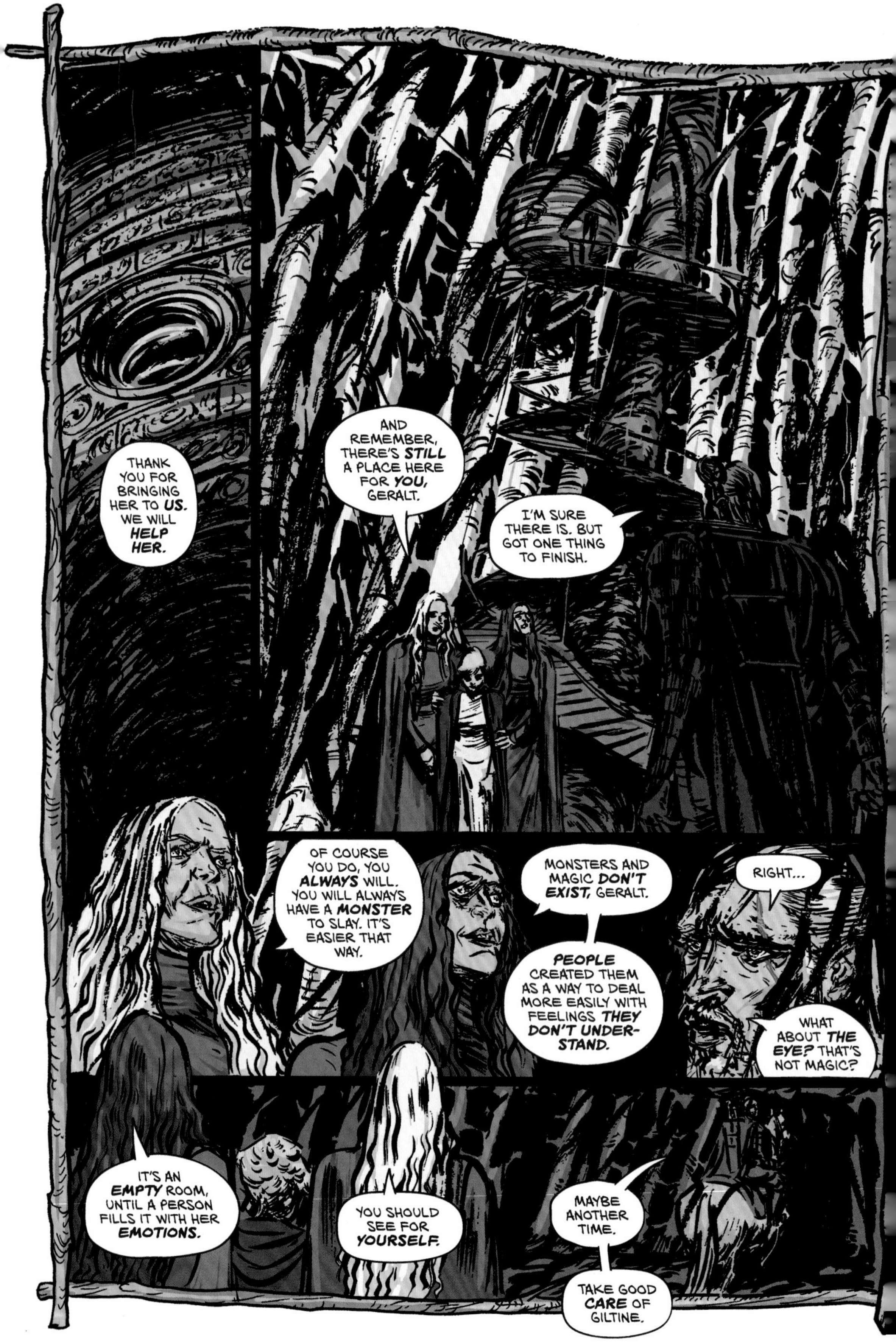
THANK YOU FOR BRINGING HER TO **US.** WE WILL ***HELP HER.***
AND REMEMBER, THERE'S ***STILL*** A PLACE HERE FOR ***YOU,*** GERALT.
I'M SURE THERE IS. BUT GOT ONE THING TO FINISH.
OF COURSE YOU DO, YOU **ALWAYS** WILL. YOU WILL ALWAYS HAVE A ***MONSTER*** TO SLAY. IT'S EASIER THAT WAY.
MONSTERS AND MAGIC ***DON'T EXIST,*** GERALT.
PEOPLE CREATED THEM AS A WAY TO DEAL MORE EASILY WITH FEELINGS ***THEY DON'T UNDER-STAND.***
RIGHT...
WHAT ABOUT ***THE EYE?*** THAT'S NOT MAGIC?
IT'S AN ***EMPTY*** ROOM, UNTIL A PERSON FILLS IT WITH HER ***EMOTIONS.***
YOU SHOULD SEE FOR ***YOURSELF.***
MAYBE ANOTHER TIME.
TAKE GOOD ***CARE*** OF GILTINE.

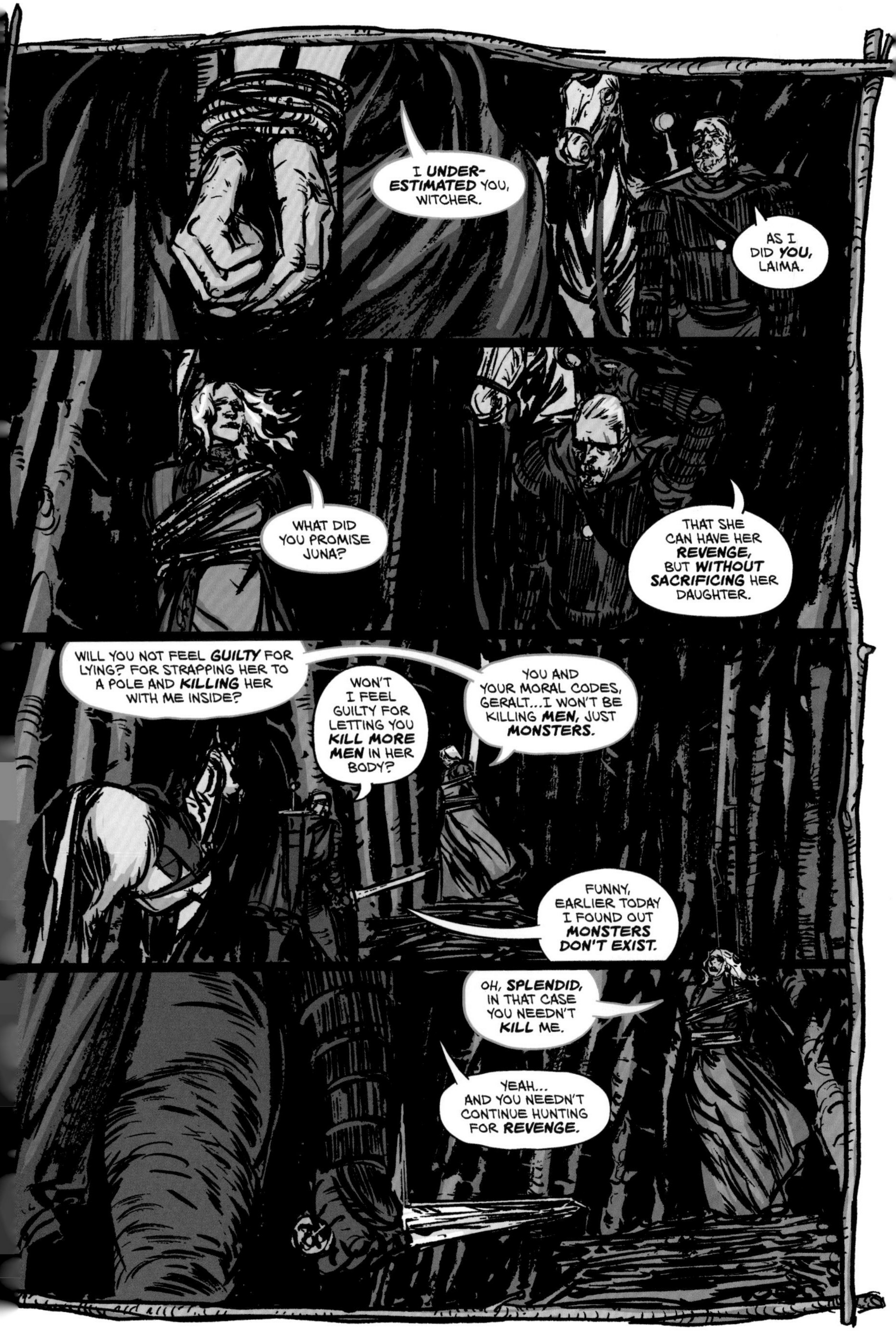
I UNDER-ESTIMATED YOU, WITCHER.
AS I DID YOU, LAIMA.
WHAT DID YOU PROMISE JUNA?
THAT SHE CAN HAVE HER REVENGE, BUT WITHOUT SACRIFICING HER DAUGHTER.
WILL YOU NOT FEEL GUILTY FOR LYING? FOR STRAPPING HER TO A POLE AND KILLING HER WITH ME INSIDE?
WON'T I FEEL GUILTY FOR LETTING YOU KILL MORE MEN IN HER BODY?
YOU AND YOUR MORAL CODES, GERALT...I WON'T BE KILLING MEN, JUST MONSTERS.
FUNNY, EARLIER TODAY I FOUND OUT MONSTERS DON'T EXIST.
OH, SPLENDID, IN THAT CASE YOU NEEDN'T KILL ME.
YEAH... AND YOU NEEDN'T CONTINUE HUNTING FOR REVENGE.

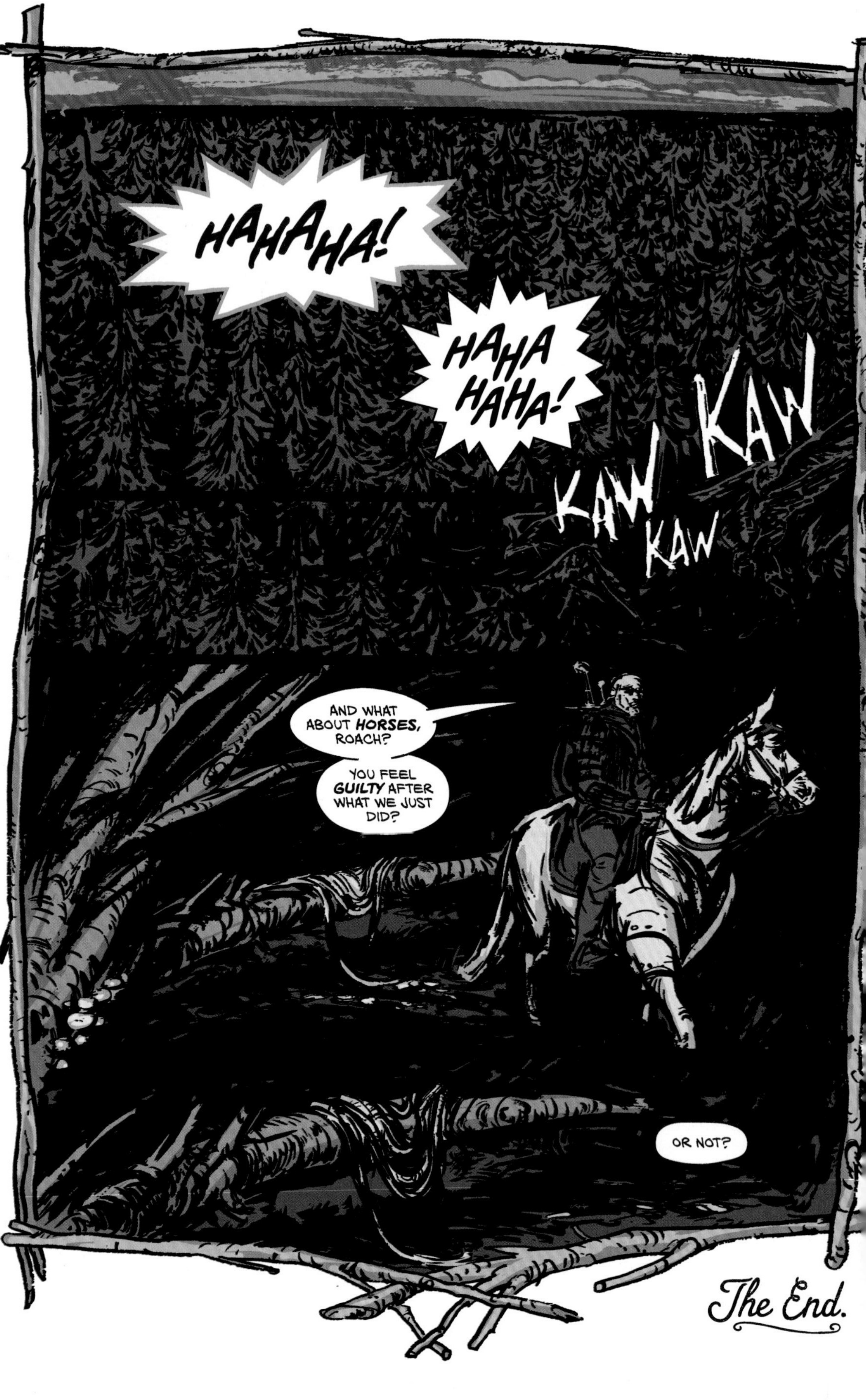
HAHAHA!
HAHA HAHA!
KAW KAW KAW
AND WHAT ABOUT **HORSES,** ROACH?
YOU FEEL **GUILTY** AFTER WHAT WE JUST DID?
OR NOT?

The End.

THE WITCHER: WITCH'S LAMENT #1 DARK HORSE DIRECT VARIANT COVER ART BY ANATO FINNSTARK

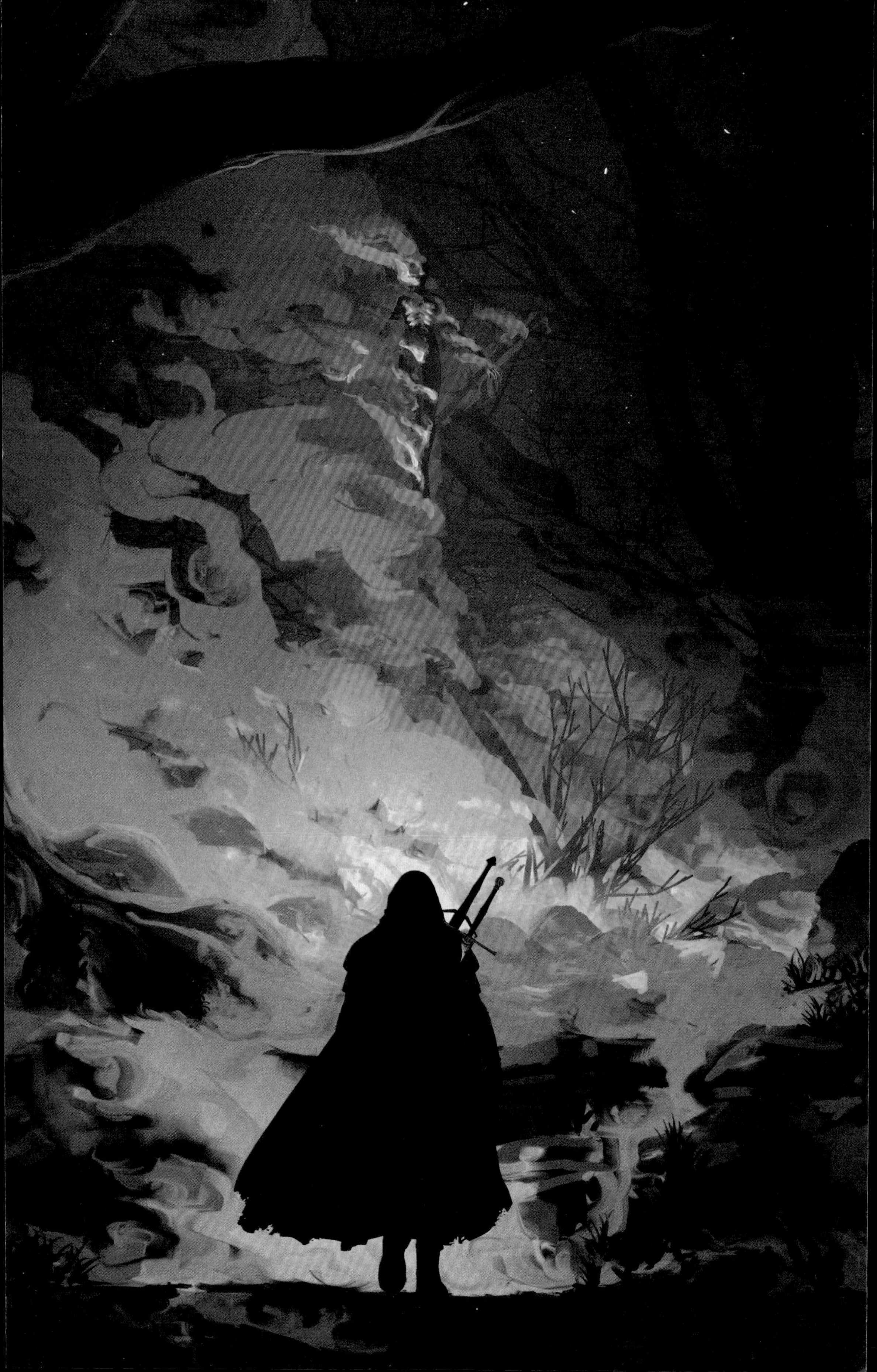

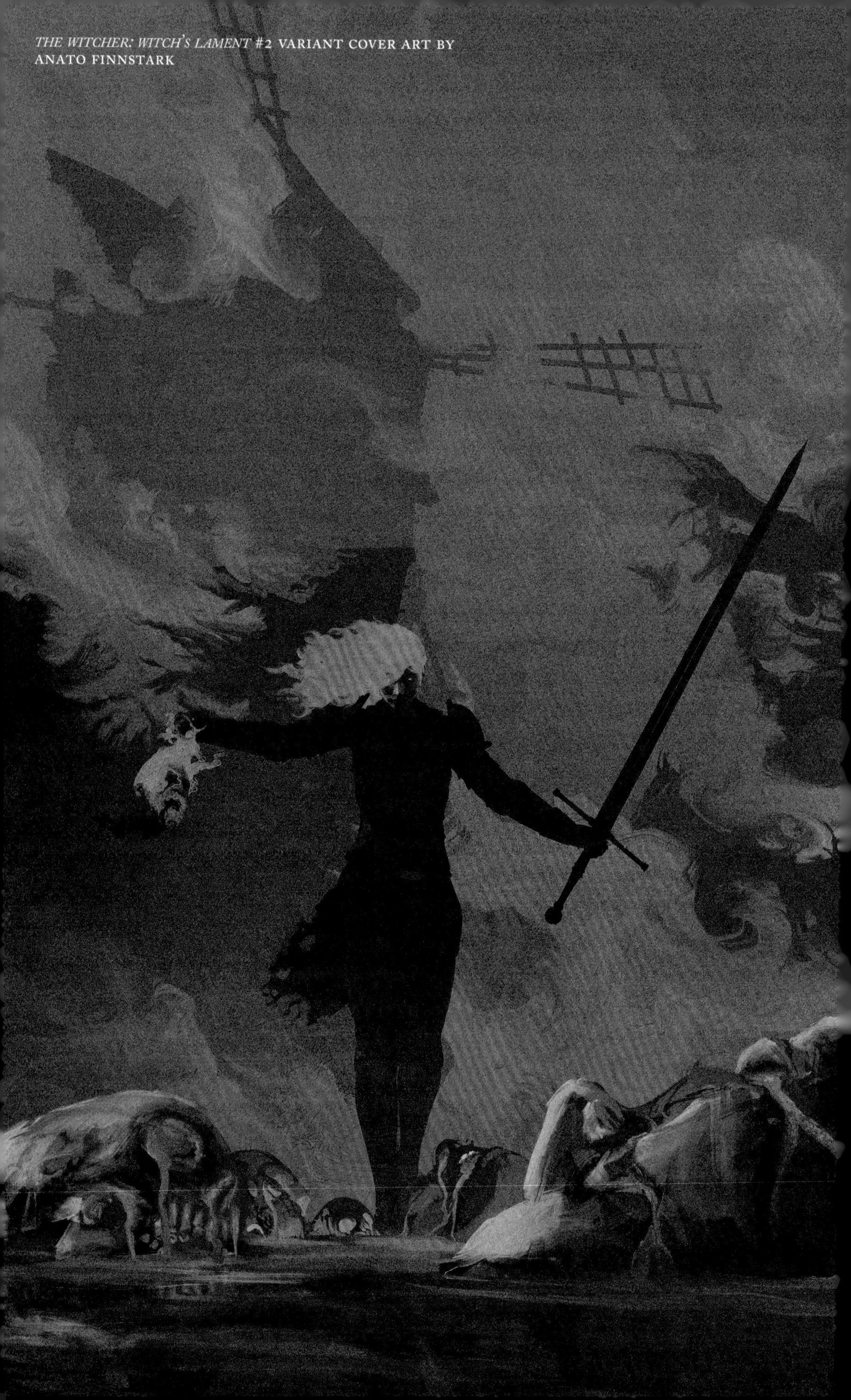

THE WITCHER: WITCH'S LAMENT #2 VARIANT COVER ART BY
ANATO FINNSTARK

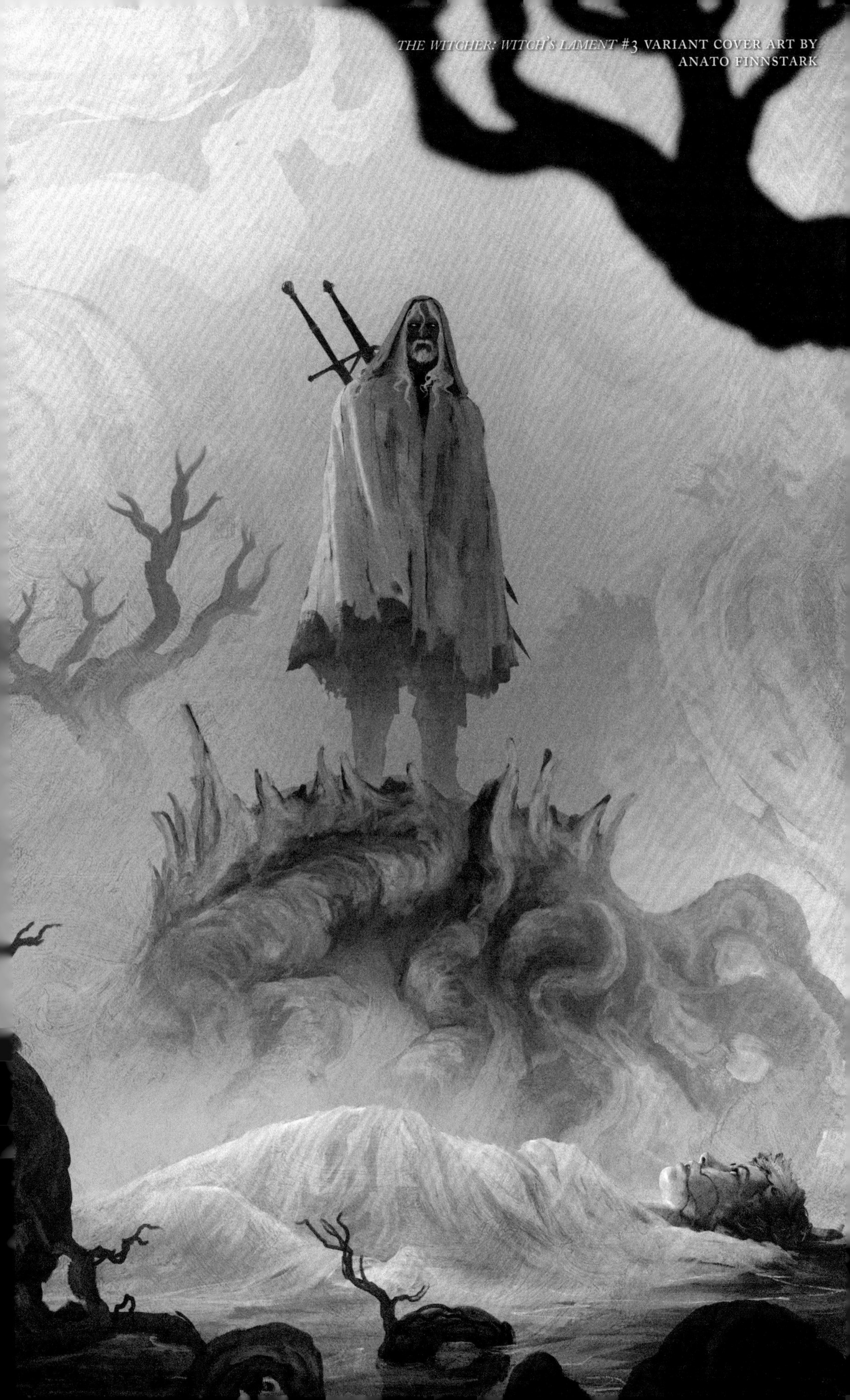

THE WITCHER: WITCH'S LAMENT #3 VARIANT COVER ART BY ANATO FINNSTARK

THE WITCHER: WITCH'S LAMENT #4 VARIANT COVER ART BY
ANATO FINNSTARK

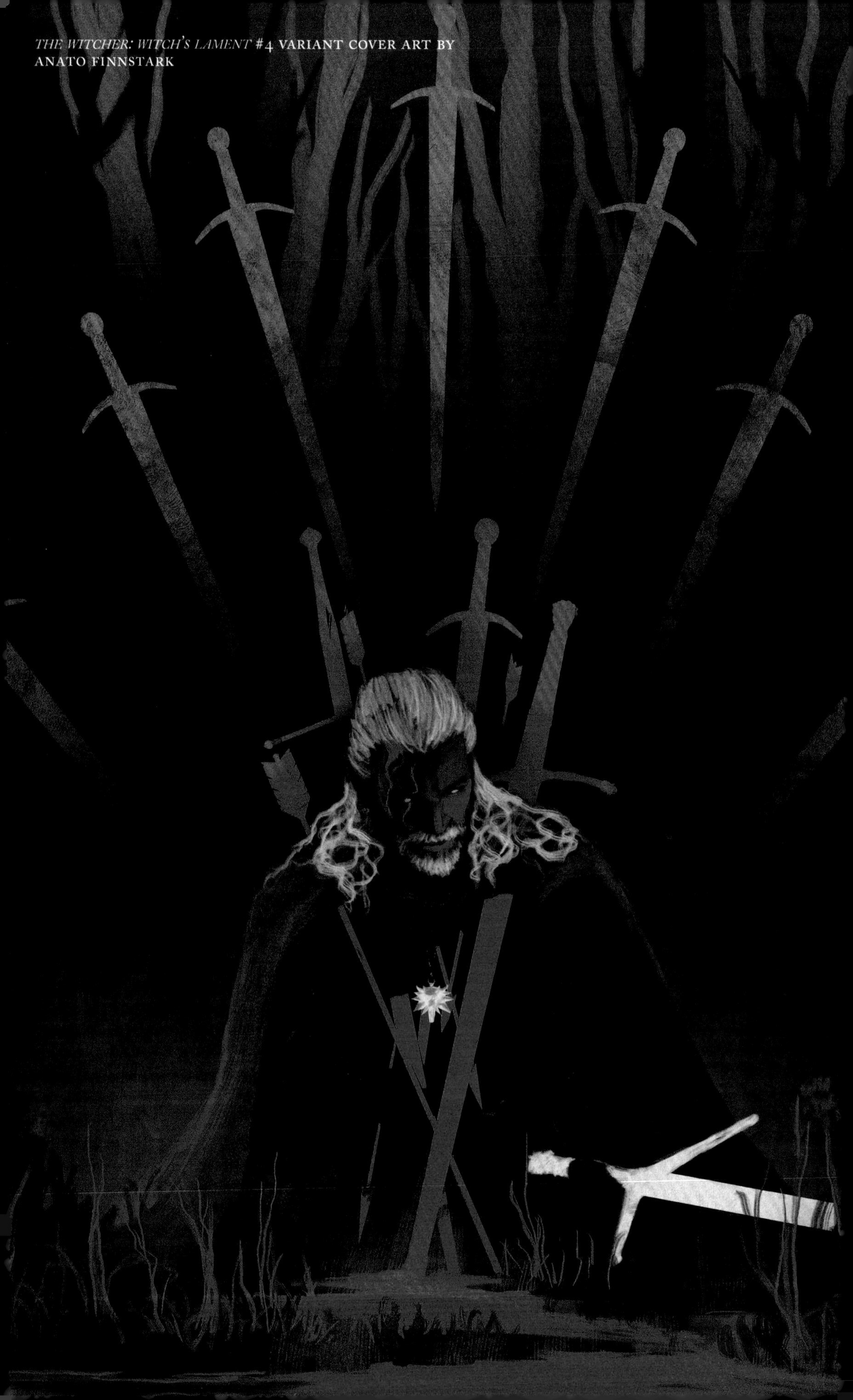

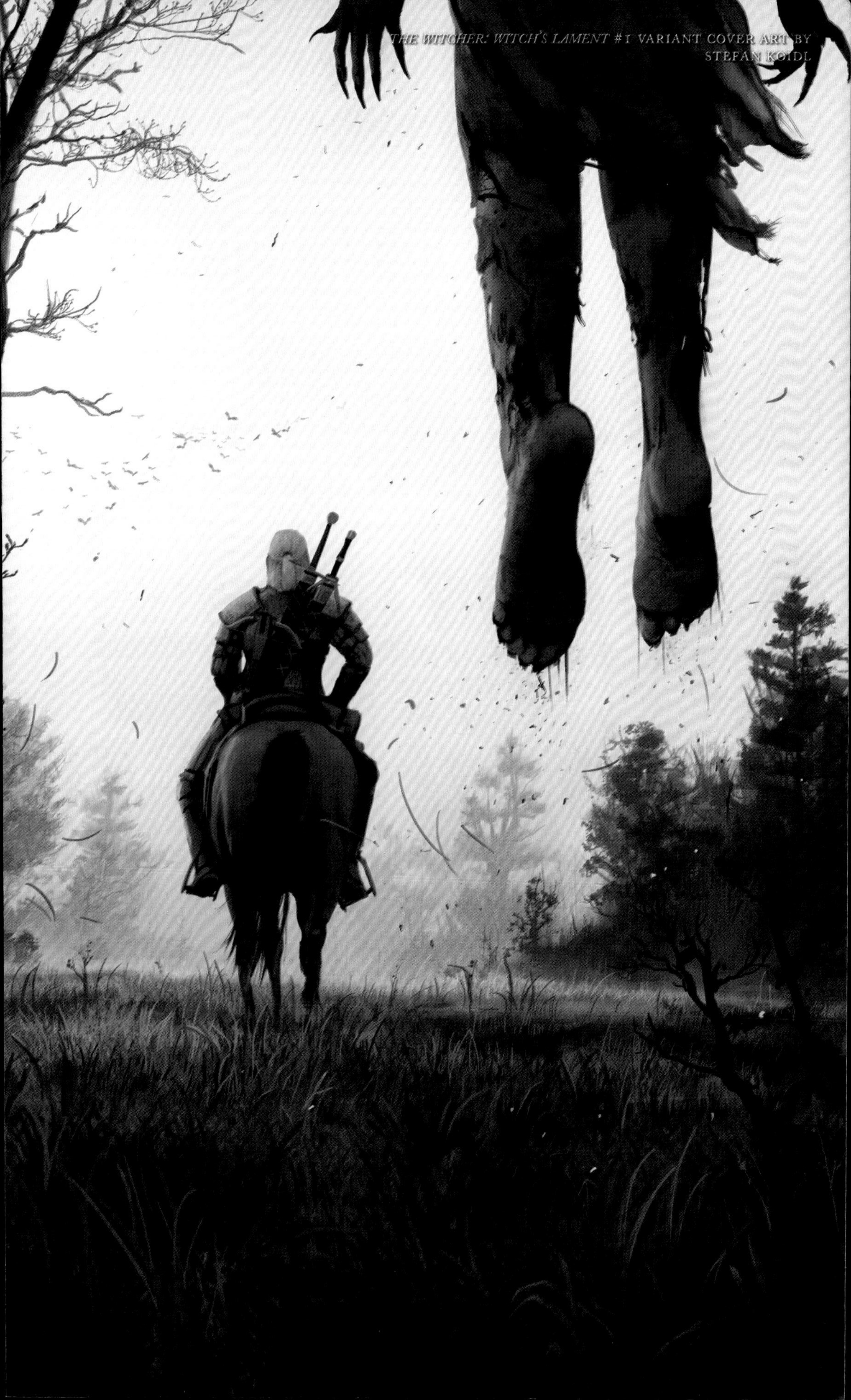

THE WITCHER: WITCH'S LAMENT #1 VARIANT COVER ART BY STEFAN KOIDL

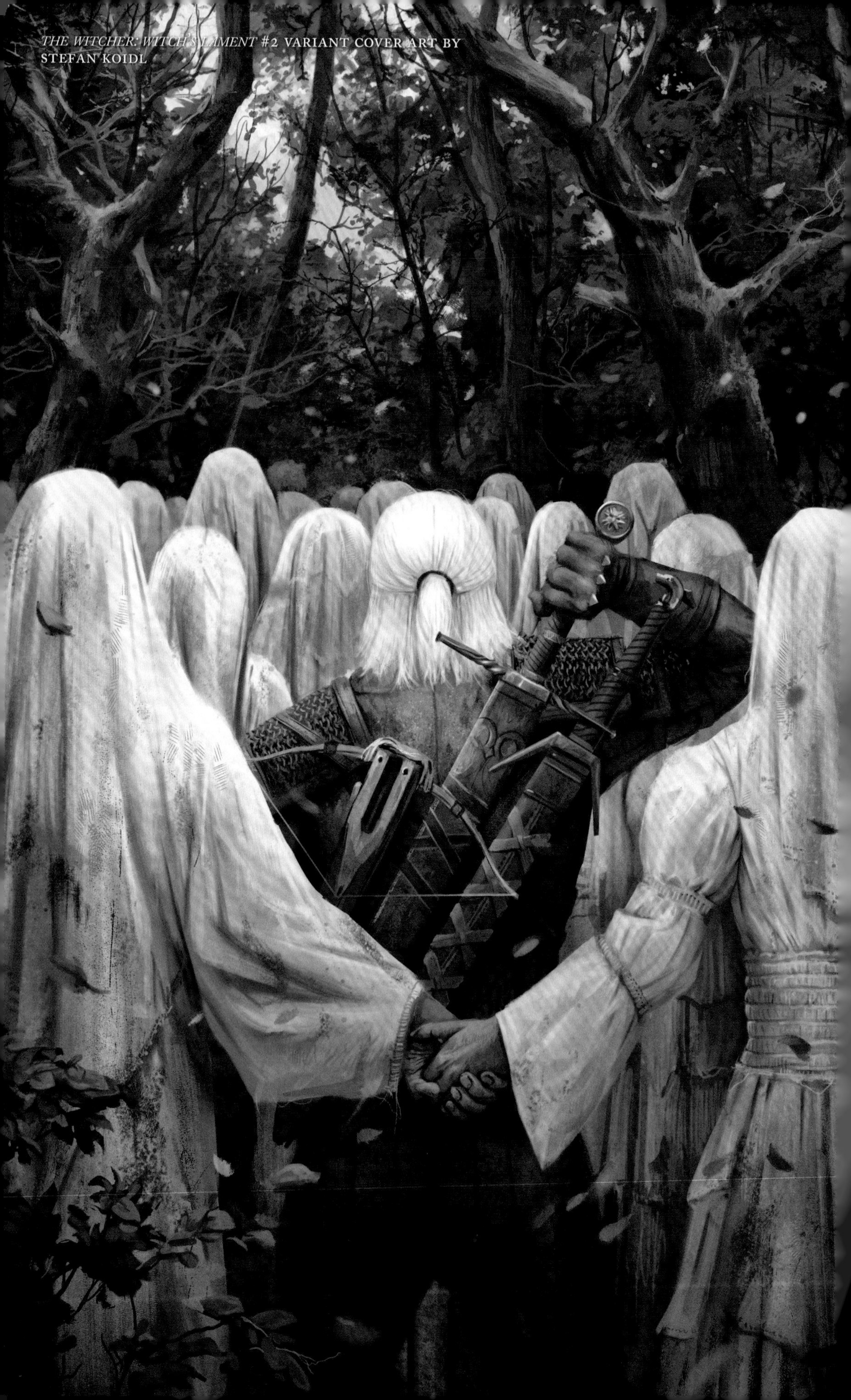

THE WITCHER: WITCH'S LAMENT #2 VARIANT COVER ART BY STEFAN KOIDL

THE WITCHER: WITCH'S LAMENT #3 VARIANT COVER ART BY STEFAN KOIDL

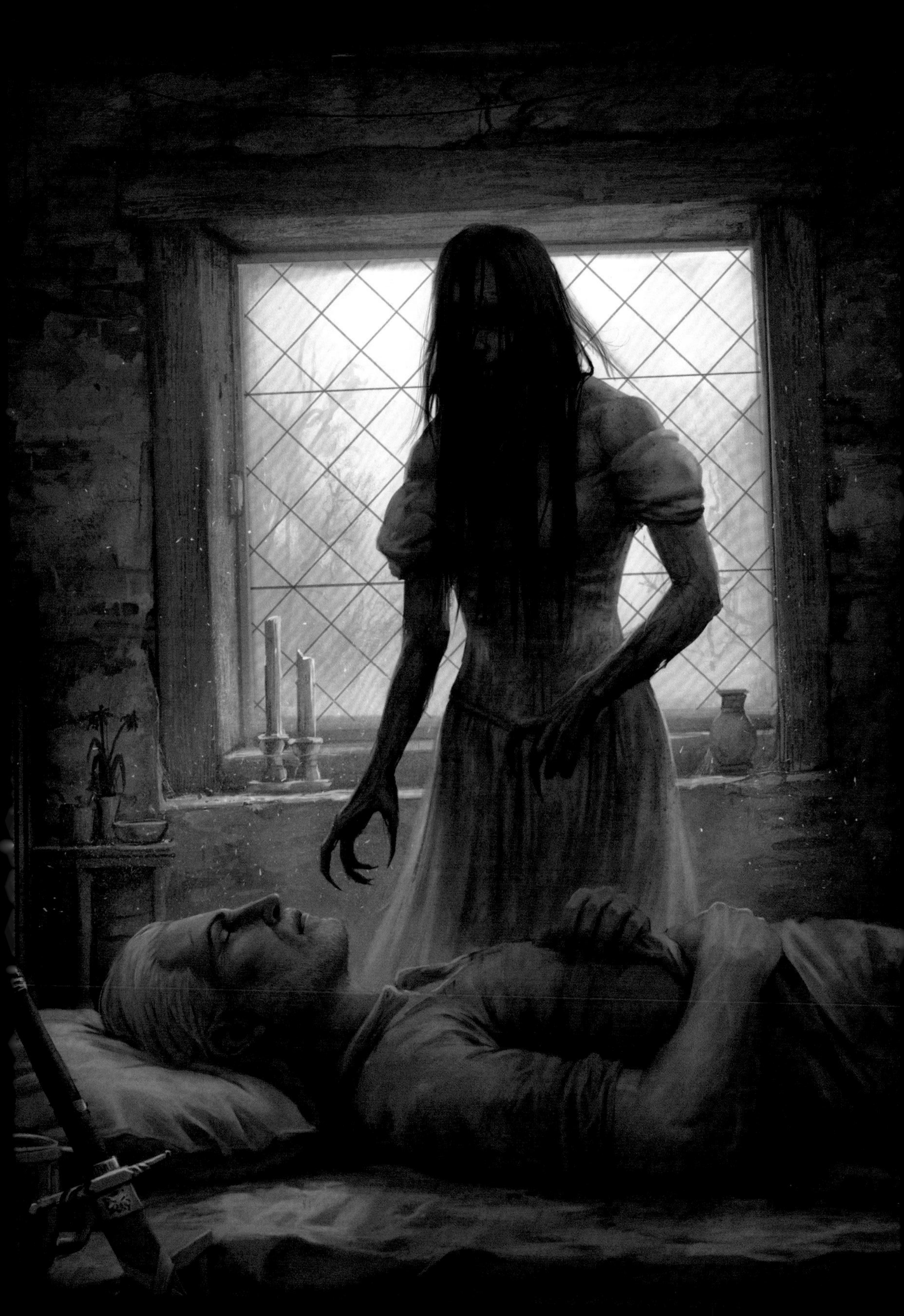

THE WITCHER: WITCH'S LAMENT #4 VARIANT COVER ART BY STEFAN KOIDL

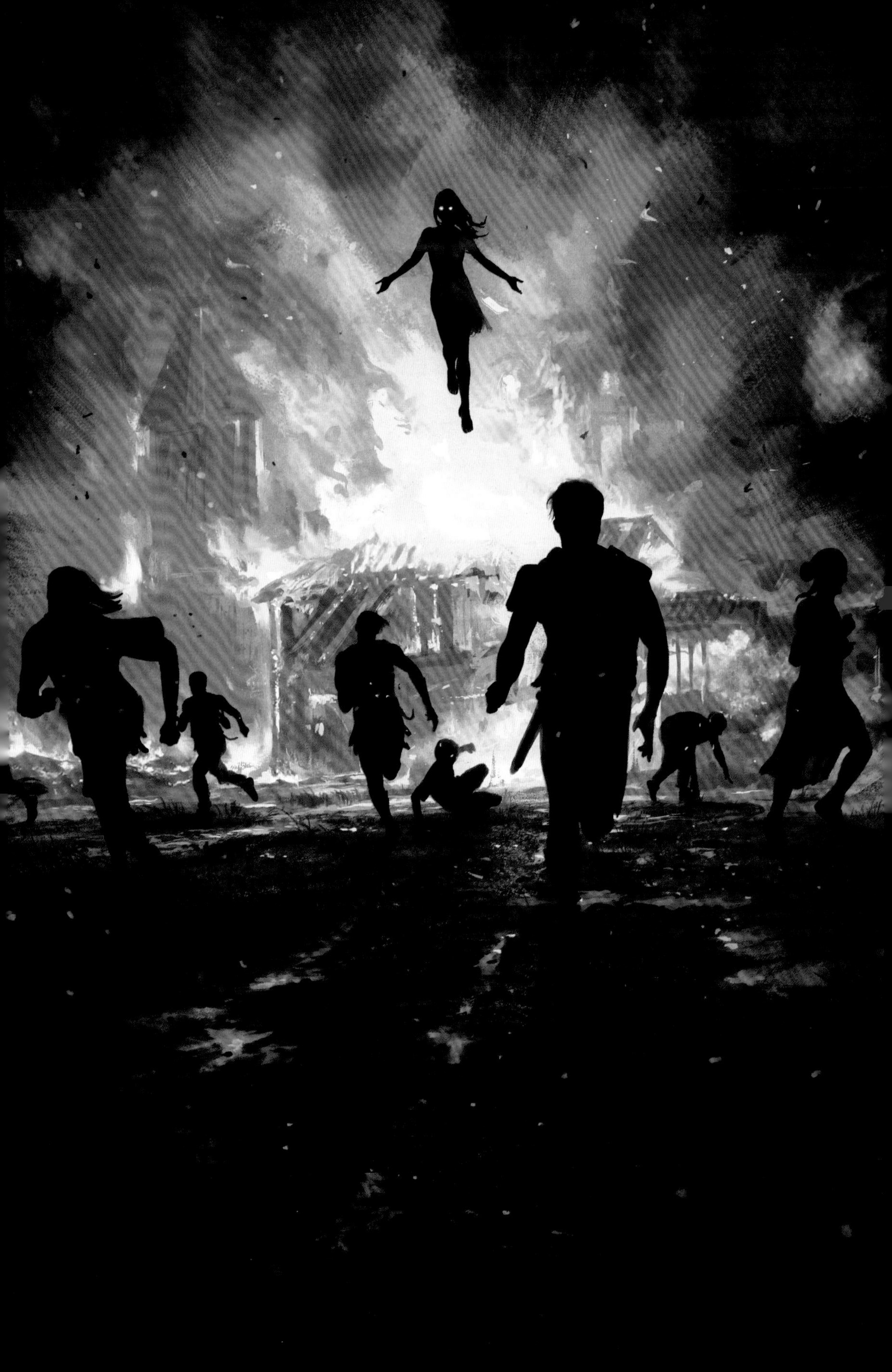

THE WITCHER®

EXPLORE THE WORLD OF *THE WITCHER* BEYOND THE GAMES!

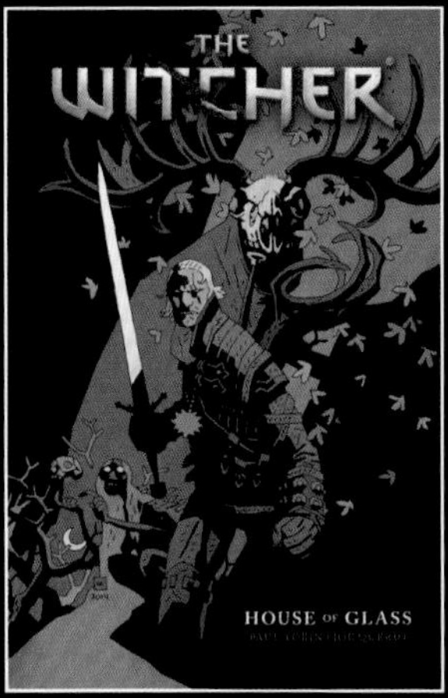
THE WITCHER
HOUSE OF GLASS

THE WITCHER VOLUME 1: HOUSE OF GLASS

Traveling near the edge of the Black Forest, monster hunter Geralt meets a widowed fisherman whose dead and murderous wife resides in an eerie mansion known as the House of Glass.

978-1-61655-474-3 | $17.99

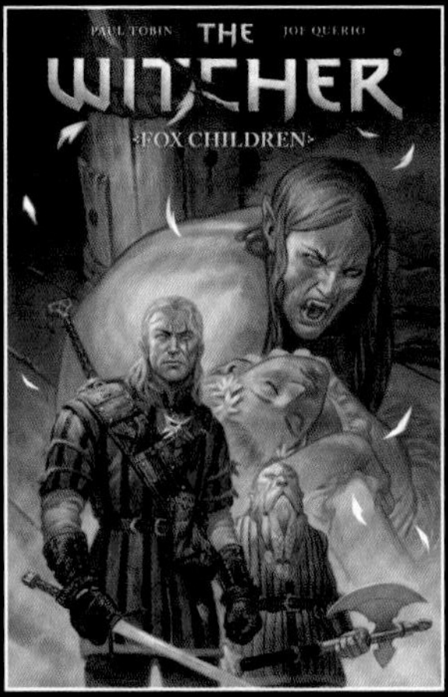
PAUL TOBIN
THE WITCHER
JOE QUERIO
FOX CHILDREN

THE WITCHER VOLUME 2: FOX CHILDREN

Geralt's journey leads him aboard a ship of fools, renegades, and criminals—but some passengers are more dangerous than others.

978-1-61655-793-5 | $17.99

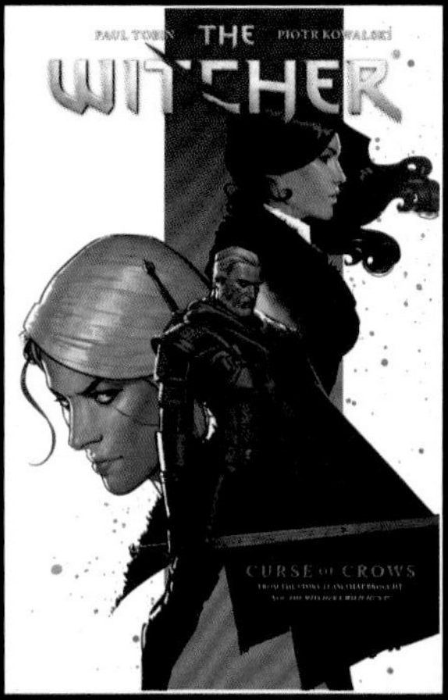
PAUL TOBIN
THE WITCHER
PIOTR KOWALSKI
CURSE OF CROWS

THE WITCHER VOLUME 3: CURSE OF CROWS

Geralt and Ciri become embroiled in a brutal story of revenge—the past always comes back to haunt you, and nothing is as it seems.

978-1-50670-161-5 | $17.99

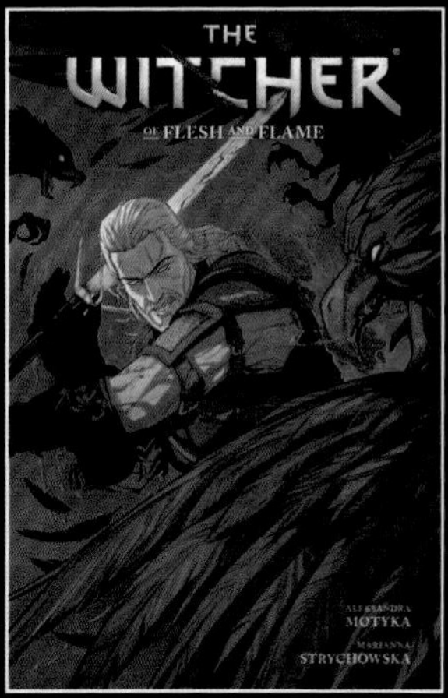
THE WITCHER
OF FLESH AND FLAME
ALEKSANDRA MOTYKA
MARIANNA STRYCHOWSKA

THE WITCHER VOLUME 4: OF FLESH AND FLAME

Geralt is summoned by an old acquaintance to help solve a mystery involving his daughter.

978-1-50671-109-6 | $17.99

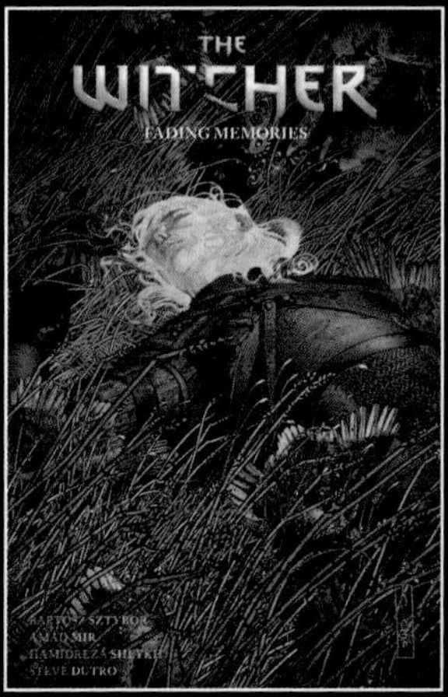
THE WITCHER
FADING MEMORIES

THE WITCHER VOLUME 5: FADING MEMORIES

As Geralt explores new career possibilities, he receives a request from the mayoress of a small town where an unusual pack of foglets attacks children.

978-1-50671-657-2 | $19.99

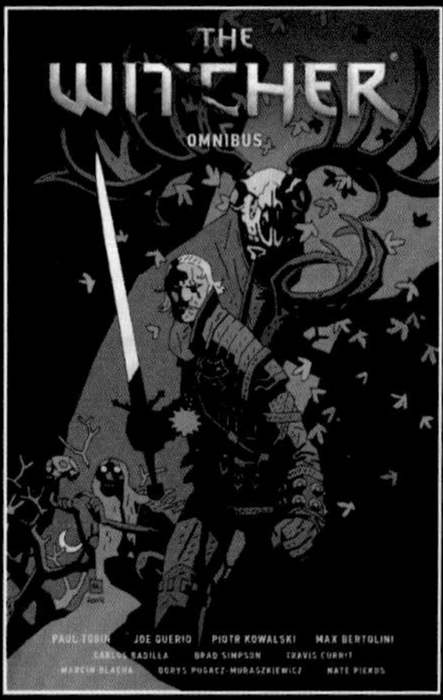
THE WITCHER
OMNIBUS

THE WITCHER OMNIBUS

Collects *The Witcher* comic series *House of Glass*, *Fox Children*, *Curse of Crows*, and the *Killing Monsters* one-shot.

978-1-50671-394-6 | $24.99

AVAILABLE AT YOUR LOCAL COMICS SHOP OR BOOKSTORE!

CD PROJEKT RED®

To find a comics shop in your area, visit comicshoplocator.com | For more information or to order direct, visit DarkHorse.com

DARK HORSE BOOKS

→ DIVE DEEPER INTO ←
THE WORLD OF *CYBERPUNK 2077!*

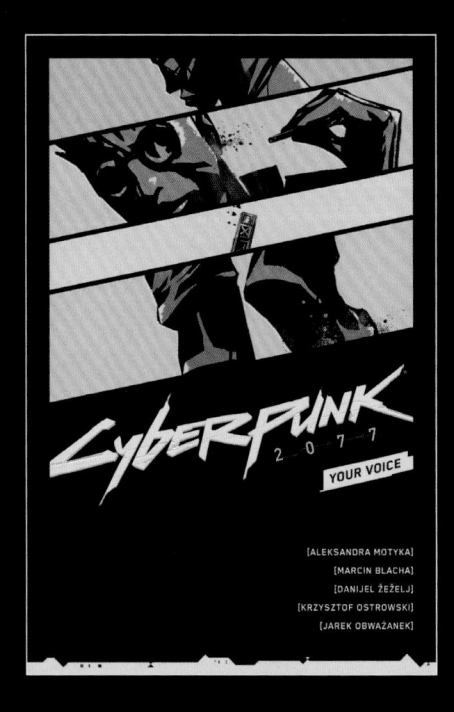

CYBERPUNK 2077: TRAUMA TEAM

A hundred floors high in a skyscraper filled with vicious gang members, an assistant EMT and her team must complete a high-level extraction.

[978-1-50671-601-5]
[$19.99]

CYBERPUNK 2077: YOUR VOICE

During a routine shift, a lonely maintenance worker gets tangled in an anti-corporation operation through the city's seedy mekka and dangerous wastelands.

[978-1-50672-623-6]
[$19.99]

CD PROJEKT RED®

THE WITCHER®
WILD HUNT

BOOKENDS

OFFICIALLY LICENSED FROM THE POPULAR VIDEO GAME FRANCHISE!

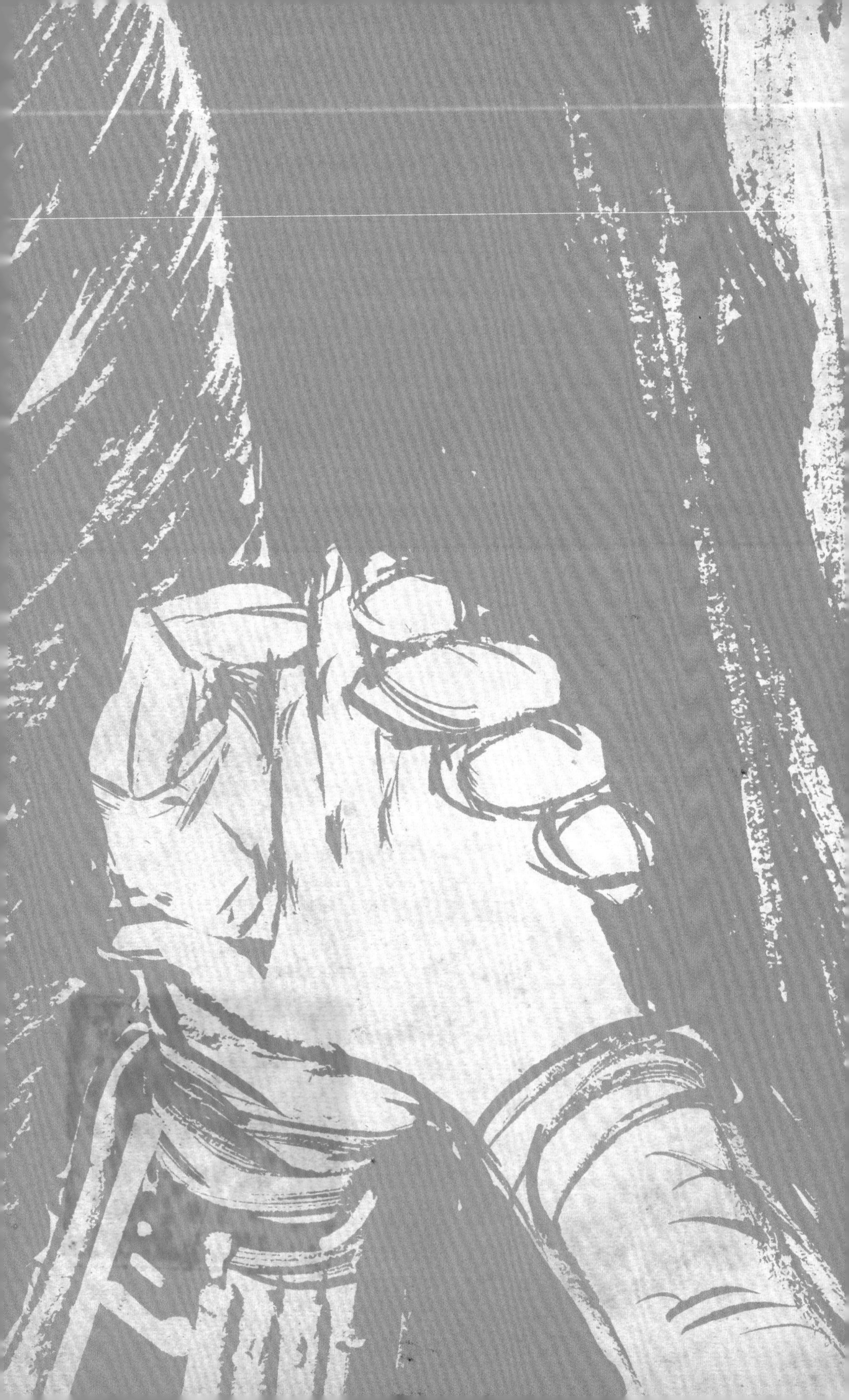